THE LAST EMBRACE

This Large Print Book carries the Seal of Approval of N.A.V.H.

THE LAST EMBRACE

DENISE HAMILTON

THORNDIKE PRESS

A part of Gale, Cengage Learning

GALE
CENGAGE Learning˙

Detroit • New York • San Francisco • New Haven, Conn • Waterville, Maine • London

GALE
CENGAGE Learning·

LIBRARY OF CONGRESS CATALOGING-IN-PUBLICATION DATA

Hamilton, Denise.
    The last embrace / by Denise Hamilton.
        p. cm. — (Thorndike Press large print thriller)
    ISBN-13: 978-1-4104-1048-1 (hardcover : alk. paper)
    ISBN-10: 1-4104-1048-X (hardcover : alk. paper)
    1. Actresses—Crimes against—Fiction. 2.
Murder—Investigation—Fiction. 3. Police—California—Los
Angeles—Fiction. 4. Motion picture industry—Fiction. 5. Los
Angeles (Calif.)—Fiction. 6. Large type books. I. Title.
PS3608.A68L365 2008b
813'.6—dc22   2008028114

Published in 2008 by arrangement with Scriber, an imprint of Simon & Schuster, Inc.

Printed in the United States of America
1 2 3 4 5 6 7 12 11 10 09 08

*This one's for the booksellers
and for
Ray Harryhausen
whose magic enchants us still*

Chapter 1

Hollywood — October 7, 1949

It felt like she'd been running for days. With each step, a searing pain shot through her ankle. Her pace was jagged and she wanted to bend down and shuck off the other shoe, but there was no time, he was closing in, his breathing heavy and excited.

She'd screamed when the man lunged out from between storefronts. The street was well lit, that's why she'd taken this route home. Just a bunch of tidy little shops, the occasional night owl walking a dog.

But the shopkeepers had already locked up and no one was out tonight. He'd grabbed her, and she'd wobbled and twisted her heel. His fingers had slid off her padded shoulder.

Staggering free, she'd balanced on her good foot and kicked. The strap broke as her shoe flew through the air and connected with his groin. The man doubled over with

7

a grunt.

Then time had slowed to one of those black-and-white movie stills she plastered on her bedroom walls. She'd felt herself floating above her body, seeing everything from a great distance. Her attacker staggering, clutching himself while she wobbled on one heel, torn between shrieking and sprinting away. In the way of nightmares, she could only do one.

The man had straightened, an acrid, black-rubber smell rising from him. Then instinct had kicked in and she'd started running.

She had to get back to the Boulevard. It was late, but there might be someone on the sidewalk, cars on the road. Laughter and jazz drifting out of supper clubs. While here there was only the wind roaring in her ears.

A hand reached for her arm. She twisted and her jacket tore, buttons of carved bone popping along her front. She swung her purse, heard a satisfying crack, felt droplets splatter her cheeks.

The Boulevard was closer now, but her ankle throbbed and weakened with every step. A car horn shattered the silence and suddenly she was there, the headlights and neon dancing behind her eyes. If she dashed into the street, a car might hit her. She turned, skittering over the embedded side-walk stars. The man put on a burst of speed and made a last desperate swipe, his fingers sliding through her hair.

"Help!" she screamed, spying two well-dressed men in a twilit doorway.

Startled, they moved apart. The red neon sign above their heads read THE CROW'S NEST.

"Help, oh God, help me."

"Sirs, please!" came a man's voice behind her. "It's my wife. She's been drinking again . . . must get her safely home."

The voice dropped, grew wheedling and reproachful. "Come back, dearest. You know no one's going to hurt you."

"He's not my husband," she screamed. "Oh, someone, please help me!"

The men in front of the Crow's Nest slunk away and disappeared. She ran to the door and yanked, but it was locked. From inside, she heard music and laughter. She pounded, crying "Help!" but took off running as the slap of feet drew near.

Up ahead, a car slowed for a red light.

"Wassamatter, miss?" called a voice from the open window.

It was a black Studebaker, the driver leaning over, holding something aloft that reflected off the streetlight.

A shout went up behind her. "Sir! Grab her, please. She's not well."

The man in the car cruised alongside. He was alone. Without thinking further, she reached for the door handle and hauled herself into the backseat, slamming home the lock.

Ahead, the light turned green. With a screech of tires, the car took off. Braced against the leather upholstery, she tried to catch her breath. The car's backseat was bigger than the Murphy bed in her apartment.

"Oh, thank you."

In the gloom of the car, she saw only the outline of her rescuer's head. The streetlights flickered past, making a jerky magic lantern inside the car. She saw a hat, checked jacket, square-cut jaw. Smelled cigars and leather.

"Well, well," the man said, "Do you always tumble so spontaneously into strangers' cars?"

She gave a wet hiccuping cry. Her ankle was swelling and throbbing in excruciating rhythm with her heart.

"A m-man chased me down the street," she stammered. "He wanted to . . ." — she squirmed at the memory — "to do me harm."

The man's voice cut across the music on

the car radio. "Good thing I came along."

"Who are you?"

He tossed back the thing he'd flashed from the car. She caught it, ran her thumb along the embossed surface. A badge. Was it real, or a studio prop? Its very curves, the cold metal in her hand, unnerved her.

He passed back a silver flask. "Calm your nerves."

His hand was large. A man's ring, set with a stone and a crest, adorned his middle finger.

She took a slug, confused about how close she'd come to being killed. No young woman in Los Angeles could forget Betty Short's murder two years earlier. The one the press had nicknamed the Black Dahlia. For every girl who'd ever walked home to an empty apartment, accepted a date with a man she didn't know well, waited at a bus stop after dark, the fear still lurked, stronger at times, dimmer at others, but always the same refrain: *It could have been me. It could have been so many young women I know. And they never did catch him.*

She had her own reasons to be wary.

"You're some kind of detective," she said, putting together the badge, the unmarked car, the plainclothes. She still hadn't gotten a good look at his face. "You should arrest that animal before he attacks another girl."

The man snorted. "You've just blown my stakeout sky-high. I should blow my cover too?"

"That's what cops do, isn't it?" she said thickly. *If they were honest. If they listened to what a gal told them and did their job.* "That man would have killed me. I could tell."

He appraised her in the rearview, in that clinical way cops did. There was something about his eyes, she wondered where she'd seen him before. On the studio lot? At a nightclub? The Hollywood Police Station?

Self-conscious, she scrubbed at her cheeks. Glancing down, she saw the popped buttons and covered herself. She felt queasy, but she could handle it, only a few more days.

". . . a damsel in distress," the driver was saying. "Aren't I lucky."

There was a gloating, hungry tone to his voice.

The big car turned smoothly to the right. She felt suddenly that she was on a tilt-a-wheel and wanted to get off.

"If you could drop me at the nearest police station, I'd appreciate it," she said. "Hollywood. Is that where you're based?"

"No."

She angled the badge, trying to read it,

but the streetlamps did not cooperate.

"Then what are you doing here? I intend to make a full report, you know."

"Do you really think that's wise?"

Alarmed, she scooted over on the plush leather, snicked up the lock button.

"Oh, all right, police station it is," the driver said, his voice mocking. "I hate to disappoint a pretty girl."

Instead the car turned again, pulled to the curb, and stopped.

The man slung his arm across the seat and turned. For the first time, she saw his fleshy, handsome face. Again, it triggered some memory.

"Why are we stopping?" she asked, her hand sliding to the door handle.

Her senses thrummed with distrust. But after all, he *had* rescued her.

The man held up an empty pack of cigarettes. "I'm all out of smokes," he said, crumpling the paper in his big hand.

She scanned for a newsstand or a liquor store but saw only dark, shuttered buildings, a restaurant at the far end of the block with taxis lined up.

She looked back at the driver, not liking the look that was spreading like a grease stain over his face. Her fingers tightened around the handle, about to fling it wide.

And then she must have done so, because the door swung out. As she steeled her body to flee again, a figure loomed outside and she smelled the acrid odor of black rubber.

The man climbed in, shoving her across the length of the backseat. She hit the far door and began groping blindly for the handle.

"Sorry about that," the newcomer said. "The little minx isn't getting away this time."

There. She'd found it. She pressed with all her weight and the door flew open. She tumbled from the moving car, ready to hit the ground and run again. "Help!" she screamed into the night. "Save me!"

CHAPTER 2

October 11, 1949

Lily Kessler stood at the open window and breathed in the tart green oils riding the breeze. The desert had given way to citrus groves when the train hit Riverside. The glass was warm to the touch, the sky an azure dome with only a few tattered clouds. All of it bathed in a pure intoxicating white light. Lily had forgotten about the quality of the light in Southern California, how it illuminated the landscape. She hadn't seen this kind of brilliance for five years in Europe, except on the Greek islands, where the sun reflected off the glittering Aegean.

But the Santa Fe Super Chief was still two hours inland, miles to go before pulling into Union Station downtown, and Lily knew that the Pacific Ocean tossing in restless slumber off the coast reflected only vast cold depths. Images of her hometown washed over her. Los Angeles. With its sugar-white

15

beaches, pastel bungalows with red tile roofs, hillsides already parched and brown by early autumn. Lily had never intended to return — the place held ghosts and shadows that no amount of sunshine could dispel. And yet here she was.

It was all because of Joseph. She'd met U.S. Army Major Joseph Croggan while working at the OSS London office during the Blitz and they'd started a torrid affair, aware that each night might end in flames, each morning might mean good-bye. Following the German surrender, they'd tracked down Nazi spies and collaborators across the Continent, then stayed on with the new Central Intelligence Agency and made plans to marry. Instead, Joseph was dead, killed eight months ago in a freak car accident in Budapest. Reckless and reeling with grief, Lily had begged for a new mission. Instead, she found herself exiled to a desk job. Lady spies weren't needed anymore, thank you very much. With Hitler vanquished, the Old Boys were reasserting control.

By the summer of 1949, Lily knew she had to go home. She saw Joseph's silhouette on every street corner, envisioned a dreary career filing the reports of less experienced male spies. So she'd quit. Arriving back in

16

the United States only a week ago, her first stop had been the cornfields of Champaign, Illinois, where she'd delivered Joseph's effects to his widowed mother. Lily had planned to stay three days, then take the train to New York City, where a former OSS colleague had offered a couch and a job lead.

Then her plans had crumbled to dust once more.

The train rushed forward, beating a conga line of syncopation in her head. Lily let it envelop her, swaying to its rhythms, hurtling through space while she pondered the mission bringing her back to Los Angeles. She imagined the rails stuttering *Doreen Croggan, Doreen Croggan, Doreen Croggan.* A girl she'd never met who would have become her sister-in-law. A girl who'd come to Hollywood dreaming of stardom in 1944, around the same time Lily had fled in the opposite direction. A girl who'd graduated from walk-on roles to a studio contract, changed her name to Kitty Hayden, and seemed awash with prospects, right up until last week when she'd disappeared into the L.A. air.

After five years of living in bombed-out Europe, the midwestern tranquillity of Illinois had seemed like another planet. Lily found it hard to stop looking over her shoulder as she and Mrs. Croggan walked to the cemetery to lay flowers on Joseph's grave. On the way home, Lily examined people on the street for hidden weapons while Mrs. Croggan pointed out landmarks: the quarry where Joseph and his kid sister, Doreen, swam each summer, the hill where Joseph crashed his bike and chipped his front tooth, the market that sold the coldest pop and creamiest strawberry ice cream.

After dinner, Mrs. Croggan brought out a pitcher of lemonade and they flipped through photo albums. Joseph had been a serious child. Doreen was a leggy, pigtailed tomboy with a mischievous smile who could shimmy up trees like a monkey and outrun all the boys. Here she was with an oriole perched on her shoulder. Lily recognized the photo — Joseph had carried a dog-eared copy in his wallet.

"You're going to love my sister," he'd said, pulling it out one night in a Vienna coffeehouse and giving her that earnest, crooked smile. "I can't wait for you to meet her. You remind me of her, she's absolutely fearless, and she hates like hell to see people get pushed around. This little bird." Joseph stroked the photo, chuckling. "God, I remember him. Orville the Oriole. She found him half-dead in the yard, being stalked by the neighbor's cat, and nursed him back to health. He'd perch on her shoulder and when he finally died, she made us dress up and hold a funeral. I played 'Taps' on my trumpet and Doreen recited a poem by Emily Dickinson. She threw flowers on the grave."

Joseph had already been overseas when Doreen had blossomed into the sloe-eyed beauty who was voted Miss Champaign 1944, and his tomboy stories bore little resemblance to the glossy head shots Mrs. Croggan now brought out, the soft studio lighting accentuating Doreen's cheekbones, her almond-tilted eyes, her glossy waved hair. She'd been in seven movies already, including *The Bandit of Sherwood Forest* with Cornel Wilde, Mrs. Croggan said with pride.

By her third day in Illinois, Lily itched to book her ticket to New York. From the big easy chair in the parlor where she sat flipping through a magazine, she watched a rabbit hop across the lawn. The aroma of pot roast drifted in from the kitchen. Soon dusk would fall and fireflies would appear. Half-asleep, Lily barely noticed the car parking out front, the man getting out.

Later, she'd call up her training and remember he'd worn a uniform and held a letter and rang the bell.

She must have dozed off. She heard Mrs. Croggan talking on the phone in the kitchen, but she didn't fully awaken until the older woman was standing before her, saying something awful had happened.

"The telegram said she's been missing for three days," Mrs. Croggan said with a glassy calm, cooling herself with an ivory fan that Joseph had sent her from Florence.

Lily tried not to sound alarmed. "Did you call the police? What did they say?"

"That it's not unusual for starlets to take trips with gentlemen friends. I didn't like the insinuation in his voice. I told him Doreen was raised to know the difference between right and wrong."

"And what did he say about that?" Lily asked, slipping into the interrogative rhythms of her previous life.

"He made a filthy comment about a long audition. Then I called Doreen's roommate, the one who sent the cable, and she sounded more worried. She wondered whether Doreen had some kind of breakdown and came home without telling anyone."

Mrs. Croggan unfolded the telegram and read the block letters aloud.

KITTY MISSING SINCE OCT 7 STOP CONCERN MOUNTING STOP PLEASE ADVISE BY PHONE TR-75041 STOP SIGNED LOUISE DOBBS STOP WILCOX BOARDING-HOUSE FOR YOUNG LADIES STOP HOLLYWOOD

Joseph's mother looked suddenly fragile, and much older. She placed the telegram on the coffee table and smoothed it with shaking fingers.

"After Joseph, I couldn't bear . . . Dear God, let her be okay. It would be too much . . ." Eyes brimming with pain and bewilderment, she shook her head. "I just don't understand. Doreen told one roommate she had a date that night. She told another girl she had a film shoot."

"A date with whom?"

"Nobody knew."

"What picture was she filming? Where was the shoot?"

"I don't know."

Lily leaned back in her chair and sighed. "What studio was it?"

"I forgot to ask. I wasn't thinking right." Mrs. Croggan shuddered. "Oh, why did I ever let her go? She has no idea what people can be like. She's too trusting. It's not like

21

she's crisscrossed the world and seen the depravities that people are capable of." Mrs. Croggan clasped a dish towel in her hand, twisting until her fingers turned white.

"Not like you, Lily," she said. "You *have* been out in the world."

Lily wanted to point out that Doreen had been out in the world for five years.

"You grew up in Los Angeles and know your way around," Mrs. Croggan said thoughtfully. "You could track her down. Joseph always said how smart you were. How clever at your job."

"Please, Mrs. Croggan. I was a file clerk."

Back in 1944, when she'd joined the Office of Strategic Services, Lily had been warned that her work was classified top secret. She was not to speak of it. Ever. She was to take the stories to her grave. "OSS is an undercover organization authorized by the Joint Chiefs of Staff," a steely-eyed lieutenant in Washington had told her. "We are anonymous. If people ask what you do here, tell 'em you're a file clerk. Nobody's interested enough in file clerks to ask questions."

Mrs. Croggan's lower lip trembled. "You loved my son, Lily, and this is his sister. He'd want you to do this. Besides, Joseph once suggested . . . he gave me the impression . . ." Mrs. Croggan's voice dropped and she glanced nervously behind her. "Joseph said the two of you had ways to find things out. Special training and such."

Lily hid her surprise. She'd taken an oath and intended to keep it. Clearly Joseph hadn't felt the same.

"Maybe he did, but I just filed and typed," Lily said, falling back on her cover story. "Do you really think they'd let girls parachute behind enemy lines? Carry secret messages and do surveillance?"

Mrs. Croggan gave her an odd look and Lily realized she'd said too much.

"Joseph loved you," the older woman said stubbornly, "and that's enough for me."

Lily's heart went out to this widow, who'd already lost one child. She wanted to ask why Mrs. Croggan didn't go herself, but she knew. Joseph's mother was a small-town homemaker wary of big cities — she'd once gotten hopelessly lost in Wichita. She was cowed by authority, suspicious of strangers, and yet ultimately too trusting. In a big chaotic city like Los Angeles, she'd be taken advantage of and lose her bearings and her nerve. And if real trouble had befallen Doreen . . .

"I do worry about you getting sucked into all that intrigue and danger," Mrs. Croggan said. "You'll have to stay away from Errol Flynn. I've read all about his wicked ways in *Confidential* magazine."

Lily laughed. Hollywood was a playground compared to what she'd been through. She'd had so many aliases that sometimes she'd forgotten who the real Lily was. But the thought of going back to L.A. made her uneasy. She hadn't kept in touch with any of her school friends, was estranged from what distant family remained. There was nothing there for her.

"I can handle myself," she said.

"I know you can. And I'd be ever so grateful if you'd check on Doreen."

Joseph's words echoed in her head. *You're going to love my sister. I can't wait for you to meet her.* And in her mind, she saw not glamour-puss grown-up Kitty, but a fierce kid of twelve, nursing a wounded bird.

"I'll go for a couple of days, Mrs. Croggan. But then I really have to get to New York."

"Oh, Lily, thank you," Mrs. Croggan said, clasping her in a hug. "I know you'll find her."

She left the next day.

Lily made her way back to her train cabin and sat down. Brown smog lay like a shroud

24

over the San Gabriel Valley. Signs sprouting from bare fields where farms had recently stood signaled the new westward expansion: MOVE IN WITH NO MONEY DOWN; ALL MOD CONS; PERFECT FOR YOUR GROWING FAMILY.

In Pasadena, a number of people got off and the train entered the final leg. When Lily saw the old East Side neighborhood of Boyle Heights, she thought she was back in Europe. Entire city blocks had been reduced to rubble. Along the alluvial plains east of downtown where vineyards planted by European immigrants had once sprawled, bulldozers were grading highways of dirt. Concrete pillars soared into the sky, steel rods protruding like carrot tops. From them hung Lilliputian figures that hammered, building the new American autobahns. At least the tall white spire of City Hall still stood — L.A.'s fusty dowager, the tallest game in town, surrounded by her constellation of courthouses, movie palaces, and department stores.

With a jerk and a hiss, the train arrived at Union Station. A porter got her luggage and Lily marveled at the cacophony of voices echoing in the huge vaulted rooms — the staccato of Brooklyn, the twang of Oklahoma, the broad vowels of the Upper Midwest, the singsong of Spanish. She noticed the watchful silence of others — gaunt émigrés clad in rough black clothes; an Asian family carrying parcels wrapped in twine, marching single file.

There were babies and toddlers everywhere, sleeping in prams, holding tight to their mothers' hands, riding like General MacArthur astride luggage carts. Lily felt a tightness in her chest. Joseph had wanted a family. She felt his absence most acutely at times like this, alone amid the crush of rejoicing relatives.

"Will it be a taxi for you, miss?" the porter asked. He was old and black, smart in his livery, and spoke with the liquid warmth of the South.

Lily nodded. She had $150 in crumpled bills that Mrs. Croggan had given her plus the $290 she'd cashed from her paychecks. She could afford to splurge.

Another train pulled in and an ash-blond creature in dangly earrings and a satin gown got off, clutching the arm of a man dressed for a night at the Mocambo. People crowded around. Lily saw a flash, heard cameras pop as newsmen shouted. Wincing, she ducked. That was the last thing she needed right now, to show up in a newspaper photo. She wasn't anxious to broadcast her return to prying eyes, had hoped to slip in and out unnoticed. The last five years had taught her that these tiniest unforeseen details could scupper an entire operation.

The couple swept into a limousine. Well, if she was going to track down a missing starlet, she might as well get used to the local fauna. As fans dispersed, Lily asked a schoolgirl who the woman was.

The girl presented her autograph book. *To Betsy,* the scrawled signature read, *with love from Gene Tierney.*

Unfazed, the porter carried her suitcase past the jacarandas and palms to a waiting taxi. Lily tipped him, wondering if fifty cents was too much. She had no idea anymore.

"Where to, miss?" said the driver, a small wiry man.

Lily wanted to find a hotel and freshen up. With any luck, Doreen had come home and Lily could get right back on the train to New York.

But what if Doreen was still missing? Lily imagined tracking Joseph's sister down to some producer's yacht or Beverly Hills hideaway. Maybe she didn't want to be found. Lily thrust away darker possibilities. This was L.A., her childhood home, not some bombed-out European city teeming with war criminals, political intrigue, and refugees.

Suddenly Lily felt a keen desire to see the house where she'd grown up.

"Please take me to Mar Vista," she told the cabbie.

The driver adjusted his hat and they took off.

Los Angeles was clean and prosperous, bristling with brawny energy and determination. Its downtown streets bore no signs of bombs or bullets. The people were tall and well fed, everyone driving big shiny cars. Many wore dark shades like movie stars to ward off sunlight so bright it hurt her eyes.

"Your first visit?" the cabbie asked.

"I grew up here."

The cabbie had his elbow out the window, his arm tanned a chestnut brown.

"It's just that you have a foreign look about you."

Lily gave a rueful smile. "I've been living in Europe for five years."

"We're letting too many of those people in, you ask me. The war's over now, they should all go back home."

Lily wondered if Los Angeles had become more provincial in her absence or if she had grown more cosmopolitan.

The cab passed Echo Park Lake. Lily

knew he was taking her the long way, but she didn't care. The rows of palm trees saluting the sky, the fountains jetting up, the merrymakers in paddleboats making a circuit as the sun reflected off the water — she'd missed this. A tent was pitched on the grass. Lily saw a man carrying a plate of food duck inside the flap. Two more tents sprang into view, then a cluster.

"Is that a Boy Scout campout?"

The cabbie laughed. "You *have* been gone awhile. Those are servicemen. Waiting for housing the government promised."

"They live in the park?" Lily was horrified.

The cabbie gave a dismissive wave. "Just for a coupla days. It's a protest. But there're thousands like 'em in Quonset huts and trailers, even tents on the beach."

"Goodness."

Lily was relieved to see that the Art Deco observatory still nestled into the hills of Griffith Park, a familiar white landmark amid the sun-scorched brush. Then the Hollywood sign came into view. Lily felt a rush of dismay. The *H* had collapsed and the last four letters that used to lean drunkenly were gone altogether, a discarded relic in a city where history was as malleable as movie sets.

The cab turned south, then west onto Wilshire. Above her, a billboard for Sunbeam electric mixers showed a mother serving cookies to her children in a sparkly kitchen. Lily felt she'd emerged from a drab black-and-white world into Technicolor where everything was both familiar and oddly foreign.

Soon they were in Hancock Park, the bastion of old moneyed Los Angeles where her wealthy relatives lived. The Ainsworths. She'd never met them. Her grandfather Clement Ainsworth had disowned his beautiful daughter for marrying an immigrant musician instead of one of the society boys he'd handpicked for her.

A year later, Lily's mother had died giving birth to her and her father's grief had only hardened the estrangement. Lily didn't care; she was devoted to her gentle, cultured father, who spoke five languages and eked out a living with piano lessons and odd studio jobs. When he developed heart disease twelve years later, it might have gone badly for Lily if her mother's sister Sylvia Ainsworth hadn't materialized on their doorstep. After living in Europe most of her life, she'd returned home as Hitler consolidated power and promised Lily's dying father to provide her with a home.

30

Lily clung like a limpet to her sophisticated new aunt, embracing her exuberance, sense of humor, and conviction that anything was possible if one aimed high and wore good shoes. After high school, Lily enrolled at Vassar College because it was Sylvia's alma mater. Then, when she was nineteen, her beloved aunt had died. Desperate to stay in school — the only home she had left — Lily used Aunt Sylvia's inheritance to finish college and keep pace with a clique of privileged new friends. When the money ran out, she learned stenography and worked secretarial jobs, spinning elaborate lies about a hectic social life to mask the true state of her finances. It couldn't have gone on indefinitely, but already Lily was cultivating a gift for dissembling.

By that time, World War II was raging. When a Vassar professor learned she could take dictation at two hundred words a minute and spoke French and German, he recommended her to the new Office of Strategic Services. The OSS recruiter was delighted to learn she had no family and could go anywhere the job required. Soon after graduation in 1944, she made a final trip to Los Angeles to close out accounts, then took the train to Washington and

31

reported for duty.

To her surprise, Lily enjoyed learning how to shadow people, use firearms, steam open letters, and crack safes. She took to the rough-and-tumble of OSS life, the tours of duty in Athens, Berlin, and Berne, even meeting the great spymaster Allen Dulles himself. There was a swashbuckling feel to the work that she thrilled to, a Great Cause to sacrifice for, and she grew used to bivouacking in a crumbling castle outside Cologne one month, a requisitioned apartment in Marburg the next. She was good at getting people to confide in her, knew when to shut up and listen, could ferret out sensitive information with a smile. She thrived on the male attention, swore and told jokes and blew smoke rings with the best of her colleagues, and no one ever suspected that she occasionally locked herself in the women's room and sobbed, overwhelmed by all that she'd seen. In time, Lily learned to anesthetize her fears with booze and calm her night terrors in the arms of Joseph Croggan. In his unassailable midwestern decency, thousands of miles and an ocean from home, she thought she'd found a refuge and a new life. Instead, here she was, alone, adrift, and feeling ancient in her bones at twenty-six, back in L.A., a place she thought she'd left behind forever.

At Centinela, the cab turned and Lily gripped the seat and cried out. Her old block was gone. A bulldozer lumbered, grading the dirt where houses had once stood. At the edge of the lima bean fields where farmers had planted a windbreak of eucalyptus trees fifty years earlier, men with chain saws were hard at work. The denuded trunks lay like piles of bones.

Lily swallowed hard.

"I've changed my mind," she said, pulling out Doreen's address. "Hollywood, please."

CHAPTER 3

The taxi pulled up to a two-story Spanish-style house set back from the street. The architect had supplied whimsical touches — leaded-glass windows, balconies, a high turret. Above the front door, an ornamental iron sign read WILCOX BOARDINGHOUSE FOR YOUNG LADIES.

In the big unkempt garden, Lily saw fruit trees, bougainvilleas, giant birds-of-paradise with prehistoric orange and blue beaks, a pink hibiscus that had grown into a tree. Ivy wound around sycamore trunks like garlands and velvety blue morning glory vines climbed a trellis. Accustomed to the grays of northern Europe, where winter had already taken hold, Lily found the color intoxicating.

"Here we are."

The cabbie turned, revealing a scar from mouth to ear. Lily blanched and he grinned, making the dead purple flesh pucker un-

34

pleasantly. "Okinawa," he said, catching her stare. "But at least I made it home, which is more than some of my buddies."

"Y-yes," Lily stuttered, and tipped him a dollar.

"Bring young ladies here from time to time," he said, depositing her suitcase. "Actresses, every one. But it's an okay joint. Unlike some a them." He tipped his hat. "Good luck in Hollywood," he said, getting back into his car. "I'll look for you on the silver screen."

Don't bother, she wanted to call, annoyed that the cabbie had mistaken her for another starlet in the making. But he was already gone.

Lily walked up the flagstone steps, feeling the grounds stir, rustling and twittering in welcome. The familiar odor of sage hit her, perfumed and almost smoky. The smell of hiking trails and chaparral lashing her bare legs, the hot sun of her childhood.

Lily rapped the iron knocker three times against the heavy oak door. With a creak it swung open, revealing a middle-aged woman with hair pulled into a bun. She was rangy and long-limbed, with an unruly bosom that strained the seams of her pale yellow dress. A smell of perspiration and bleach came from her.

"What can I do for you?" the woman said, the grit of Oklahoma thick on her tongue. Her eyes dropped to Kitty's feet, spied the suitcase. "We don't have any rooms to let right now, though we . . ." Wiping her hands on her apron, the woman tilted her head. "We may have an opening at the end of the month."

"Oh," said Lily. "That's not why . . . I mean . . . I'm a friend of the Croggan family. From Illinois . . . My name's Lily Kessler. I've come to . . ." Lily's eyes darted away. "So does that mean Doreen's still missing?"

The woman stood, silhouetted in the doorway. Lily wondered why she didn't invite her in. Her mind was clogged with cobwebs, sticky and sluggish after her long journey, and it troubled her that she couldn't make out the woman's face in the house's shadows, where dim rooms receded into dusk, though it was high noon outside.

The woman pursed her lips. "You mean Kitty."

Relieved, Lily nodded and launched into how Mrs. Croggan had sent her out to check on Doreen and make sure she was okay.

"Kitty isn't here."

"But has she come back?"

"No, she hasn't." The woman's voice was flat, without inflection.

Lily felt a growing anxiety. The longer Doreen stayed missing, the worse the odds grew.

"In that case, perhaps I might speak with you and the boarders?"

The woman studied her.

"Her mother sent me," Lily repeated. "I've come all the way from Illinois."

The woman shifted, the floorboards creaking beneath her.

"The police . . ." Lily began, and the words appeared to have a magical effect.

"I suppose you might." The woman opened the door wider. "I'm Mrs. Potter, the landlady. Won't you come inside?"

She led Lily into the front parlor. Lily put her suitcase down and sat at the edge of a red sofa. A battered Steinway covered in knickknacks stood against the far wall. The coffee table held a Sears Roebuck catalogue, two well-thumbed *Movie Screen* magazines, and a chipped ceramic ashtray pilfered from Earl Carroll's nightclub.

Mrs. Potter lowered herself into a caned chair. A sleek black cat padded into the room and crouched by her feet, tail twitching.

"Well, Miss Kessler, what would you like

to know?"

Feminine laughter drifted from the back of the house, then a blast of song from a tinny radio. Mrs. Potter's eyes flickered and her lips curved in annoyance. Lily smelled coffee and the tantalizing aroma of angel food cake. In Illinois, she would have been offered a meal by now. Surely something to drink.

"Please, Mrs. Potter. Couldn't I talk to you and the boarders together? I'd like to meet them. I'm sure they've got some ideas of where Dor— er, Kitty might be."

Mrs. Potter stared at her clenched white hands. "Very well. I'll ask them into the parlor."

She left the room, the cat trailing after her. Lily jumped up and followed.

"Maybe you could take me to where they are. I don't want to disturb their coffee klatch."

Lily wanted them to feel comfortable. It wasn't a police interrogation, after all.

Mrs. Potter grabbed her arm. "Miss Kessler," she said, "I run a respectable house."

The cat brushed against her stockings and Lily felt the prickle of static electricity. Something angular jabbed the back of her neck. She turned and saw an iron wall sconce casting a thin watery light into the hallway.

Mrs. Potter's eyes glinted. "We don't have a curfew here, like some of the other places. I know what the studios expect of these girls, and it's the devil's own bargain. So long as they don't bring it home, it's none of my business."

"I see," said Lily, who wasn't sure she did at all.

"If Kitty's off somewhere improving her chances, it's nobody's business but her own."

Mrs. Potter gave Lily's arm an emphatic shake. "She's an ambitious girl, our Miss Kitty. No bad habits. Never any money trouble. Rent's paid up through the thirty-first. She's not one of those as pays by the week."

"Please let go of me," Lily said.

Mrs. Potter's hand fell to her side. She gave a simpering laugh. "Sometimes I get carried away. These girls get to be like daughters to me."

Oh, so you'd prostitute your daughters for a Hollywood role?

There was an awkward silence and Lily feared she'd spoken out loud. Then Mrs. Potter said, "I suppose you'll want to see her room."

She started up the stairs, leaving Lily no choice but to follow. In the winding upstairs hallway, Lily heard a Victrola playing swing jazz. There were closed doors on either side. They walked along a faded carpet runner patterned in cabbage roses.

At the last door, Mrs. Potter paused.

"Kitty had the turret room," she said. "I have a hard time letting it, the girls say it's haunted. That's nonsense, of course."

Mrs. Potter's eyes narrowed. "Now, before I open this door, do you have any proof you're who you say you are? We can't be too careful and there's already been people snooping around, asking questions that are none of their business."

"Who?"

"I don't rightly know. I run them off when they don't explain themselves. The only one I let in besides the police was the man from the studio, and he was polite and showed me ID."

"What was his name?"

"Clarence Fletcher."

"Did he take anything?"

"Not that I saw. And I only left him alone a minute when I went down to pay the dry cleaner's."

Ample time to shove a diary down his shirt, Lily thought.

"So the studio's worried too?" she said.

Mrs. Potter spoke through gritted teeth. "Maybe the studio don't know everything. Maybe she's passing time with someone from *another* studio. So how about it?" She held out a hand.

Lily brought out a letter from Mrs. Croggan and her passport. The landlady examined the letter and flipped through the passport, absorbed in the colorful entry stamps of foreign nations.

"You been in a lot of Communist places." She eyed Lily with sly interest.

"I was a government file clerk in the war."

"Those stamps're more recent than that. You sure you're not a Red spy?"

No, I was a spy for our side.

"They kept me on after the German surrender. The Marshall Plan . . . I just got my discharge papers."

The landlady dug a ring of keys out of her pocket. "I been up here once to make sure she wasn't in bed, too sick to call out. And the police, they was here all of two minutes. Found no sign of foul play and left, not before the young one asked Louise to go out dancing."

She turned the key and pushed. They entered.

The small room had curving walls and a

coved ceiling. The hot still air smelled of newsprint, cigarettes, talc, and stale perfume. Photos of movie stars adorned every wall. The only furniture was a plump armchair, a tall skinny bookcase, and a dressing table on which sat a large bottle of Arpège. Lily wondered if Doreen had a wealthy admirer.

Mrs. Potter pointed out the radiator, where stockings, silk panties, and a lace brassiere had been left to dry. "Does this look like the room of a girl who isn't coming back? Or that?" She indicated the dressing table, where cold creams and potions lay next to a tortoiseshell brush.

"Well, that about covers it." Mrs. Potter began herding Lily out.

"Please," Lily said. "I'd like to stay here until I find Kitty. I'm new to the city and —"

Mrs. Potter crossed her arms. "I don't think that's a good idea."

"But I'm a family friend. And you said the rent's paid through the month."

Mrs. Potter said nothing. *She wants me to offer her money,* Lily realized.

"What did Kitty pay you?" she asked.

"Twe— eh, excuse me, thirty-five dollars a month."

She's just bumped the price up fifteen dol-

lars, Lily fumed. But she reached for her wallet, realizing that Kitty's room was the perfect headquarters for her mission. The landlady counted the bills, then folded and tucked them inside her brassiere.

"Where did she sleep?" Lily said, looking around.

Mrs. Potter gave a short bark. "Ain't you never seen a Murphy bed before?"

She walked to the far wall and threw open a cupboard door, revealing an upright bed. With one tug, it unfolded into the room. The sheets were crisp and bluish white, covered with a clean wool blanket. Mrs. Potter pulled a pillow from the closet and tossed it onto the bed.

"There you go, fit as a fiddle. Maybe you'd like to have a little rest before coming downstairs. Bathroom's at the other end of the hall."

"No, actually I . . ."

But Mrs. Potter was already closing the door behind her.

Lily figured she'd wash her face, then fetch her suitcase and change into fresh clothes before meeting Kitty's roommates. She wanted to make a good first impression.

She walked to the narrow bed and sat down. Up close, the blanket was thin, its satin trim fraying. The box springs groaned in a metallic woe-is-me. The throw rug over the hardwood floor was worn where many hopeful girls had trod a path from the bed to the vanity table.

The room's genteel poverty contrasted sharply with Mrs. Croggan's boasts about her daughter taking Hollywood by storm. Kitty had written home of screen tests, drama workshops, and star-studded premieres. Of dancing at the Cocoanut Grove, wearing designer gowns loaned by Adrian. Of the studio contract that kept her too busy for a visit home. Of how she'd lightened her hair, learned how to shape her brows, saunter across a room, paint her eyes. Of the casting director who'd raised one bored eyebrow at her name and christened her Kitty Hayden.

So this was the reality.

The hum of the radio downstairs, the distant voices, the roof over her head after two days of travel, produced a strange lethargy. Lily knew she should call Mrs. Croggan to tell her Doreen still hadn't turned up. Instead, she kicked off her heels, stretched out, and was asleep before she knew it.

Lily woke up sweaty and hot, drool crusting

the side of her mouth, her suit creased. Pushing herself up on one elbow, she saw that the light outside the window was different now, velvety at the edges. The purple mountains rose in silhouette against the hills like a landscape on a Japanese screen. Something intoxicating bloomed below. Jasmine? Honeysuckle? It made her swoony, like she'd ingested some of Coleridge's opium. She opened the door and almost tripped over her suitcase.

After washing up with a bar of Lifebuoy, Lily hung her clothes on spare hangers. She tossed her heels into the closet, then decided to wear them downstairs. Prodding shoe boxes with a bare foot, she found one right away. Then her toes brushed against something soft and furry. Lily felt it move.

She screamed and jumped back, expecting a rodent to run out. When nothing came, she peered cautiously into the closet and saw a toy ape. She pulled it out. It was about eighteen inches tall, covered with coarse fur, and wearing a remarkably lifelike expression. Lily examined its glassy doll eyes.

"I could have sworn it moved," she murmured.

Gingerly, she touched the ape's arm, recoiling as its elbow bent. So it had moved!

This was no child's toy, it was jointed in all the places a real ape's body would be. Was it a studio prop? A zoological model? Its eyes seemed to follow her as she put on slacks and a blouse.

Lily went downstairs, following the voices to a kitchen where five girls sat around a Formica-topped table, smoking and drinking coffee as a phonograph crooned "Goodnight Irene."

"We heard you scream," said a girl with red curly hair pinned atop her head and a white blouse tucked into slim black pants. "We thought maybe you'd stumbled across Kitty's body."

A nervous titter went around the room.

"That's horrible, Red," scolded a brunette with soft features and little-girl hair who was dismantling a radio.

The girl named Red sauntered over to Lily, hand on hip.

"Mrs. Potter said we should be nice to you because you're Kitty's friend from Illinois and you're tired from your trip. Is everything okay?"

"Yes," Lily muttered, annoyed at herself. "Just banged my foot."

Red gave her a practiced once-over. "Welcome to Hollywood," she said. "You're especially welcome if you steer clear of my auditions. The casting directors are always looking for fresh faces and I don't need any more competition."

"I'm not interested in Hollywood. I'm here to find Kitty. As soon as she turns up, I'll be on the train to New York City."

"Well, la-di-da," said Red.

The brunette put down her screwdriver, got a cup of coffee and a piece of cake, and placed them in front of Lily.

"Don't mind Red," she said, glancing sternly at the brassy girl. "She's not a bad egg. This business makes us forget our manners. I'm Beverly. I'll help you with anything I can."

"Thank you," Lily said.

The other girls introduced themselves. There was Fumiko, a lithe, slender girl with Asian features and glossy black hair that hung down her back. Jinx was tall and sylphlike, with long legs and a swan neck. Jeanne, who was eating a gooey green sandwich, was elfin, with porcelain skin, blue eyes, and curly blond hair. Louise, the one who'd sent Mrs. Croggan the cable, was working late.

"We all came out to Hollywood to get into the movies," Beverly said. "Except for Fumiko. She was born here, though you wouldn't guess by looking at her."

Fumiko's black eyes glittered. "The word is *Nisei,* Beverly. It means a second generation — I was born in America to Japanese immigrants."

"Nigh-say," Beverly said, butchering it. "Fumiko had a hard time of it during the war, didn't you, dear? Whew, aren't we glad that's over."

"Not me. I wish the Hollywood Canteen was still open." Jinx rubbed her calf dreamily. "Dancing with all those gorgeous doomed boys . . ."

Fumiko said nothing. Lily recalled the December day in 1941 when Keiko, the Japanese girl down the street, hadn't shown for the school bus. Their teacher Mrs. Pollard telling the class in hushed tones about the deportations, the internment in remote desert camps. Shifting uncomfortably, Lily asked Jeanne what she was eating.

"Avocado sandwich." Jeanne gestured to a Fiestaware bowl piled high with the bumpy-skinned black fruit. "Tree's out back. Mash 'em with a little salt and pepper, squirt of lemon, and it tides you over between paychecks."

Lily's mouth watered. She'd grown up on the creamy fruit but hadn't eaten one in years.

"What made Louise decide to cable Dor—

48

uh, Kitty's mother?" she asked the room.

"Ever since the Dahlia murder," Jeanne said, eyes darting, "we girls had an agreement. If one of us was spending the night away from home, we'd let the others know."

"And Dor— er, Kitty didn't?"

"No. And she missed an early call the next morning, which wasn't like her, as I'm sure you know."

"Actually, I didn't." Lily proceeded to explain about Joseph and the room fell silent in sympathy.

"My fiancé got blown up by a mine in the Loire," Red said. "Just think. I could have had three squalling brats and a house in Burbank by now."

"We girls may compete for parts and even boyfriends, but we all want Kitty back safe and sound," Beverly said, her eyes lingering on Red, as if daring her to contradict her.

"Mrs. Potter thinks Kitty may be on some romantic rendezvous," Lily said.

Jeanne wiped her mouth on a napkin. "It's possible," she said. "The night she disappeared, Kitty mentioned she had a date but wouldn't give me any details."

"She told *me* she was going on a night shoot," Jinx broke in. "She was wearing her best suit. And new heels. When I complimented her, she said I could borrow them anytime. That's the type of girl she was."

"Mrs. Croggan couldn't remember the name of the picture or where was it filming."

Beverly glanced away. "We checked. The studio didn't have anything that night."

"Maybe she was moonlighting for another studio?"

"She was on contract at RKO. They'd fired her."

Could that be why she was so secretive? Lily wondered.

The colors outside ebbed to a dusky blue. Beverly went around, snipping on the lights. The room filled with a comfy air of a home, even though Lily was sure the girls viewed it as a way station they'd happily trade in for something more permanent.

They told her about a drugstore lunch counter on the Boulevard that offered a five-course meal, with spaghetti, fish, salad, a fruit cup, and coffee, for sixty-five cents. They also explained that the rooms off the kitchen door were Mrs. Potter's domain and boarders were to keep out.

Lily learned that Kitty had been in dozens of movies, including small parts in *They Live by Night, The Farmer's Daughter,* and *Blood on the Moon.* Since landing at RKO, she'd worked on *The Set-Up* and *The Window,* two

B noir films.

Lily wandered to the window, where two giant searchlights swept the sky. Tugging on gloves and pinning hats atop their heads, Fumiko and Jeanne got ready to leave for a premiere of a movie in which Fumiko had a small role.

"I give a very nuanced performance as a Shanghai barmaid," she said.

"But it's great that she got a role, right?" Lily asked after they left.

"I've seen her do Shakespeare in Little Tokyo and bring a drama class to tears with an Ibsen monologue," Red said. "She even started a theater troupe in Manzanar. It makes her crazy that the studios will only cast her as a maid or a prostitute."

"Jinx and Kitty are the only ones with studio contracts," Beverly explained. "The rest of us run around auditioning like crazy for the privilege of busting tail and making scale."

"The camera loves Kitty," said Jinx. "Even if she's only on screen for five minutes, you see the vulnerability, the nakedness. It's like you can gaze through her eyes and see her soul."

"But Hollywood is a monster," Red said. "If you were naked in the last film, they want you skinned in the next one."

51

"That's awful."

Red gave the others a meaningful look. "I'm even thinking of hiking up to the Hollywood sign."

"Why?" asked Lily.

"Kitty used to say that if everything fell through, she'd pull a Peg Entwistle rather than go home in defeat," Red said.

"Who?"

"Peg was a blond bombshell who came out here in '32, dreaming of stardom. Sound familiar, anyone? She landed a contract with RKO, but her picture bombed and the studio didn't renew her contract. She couldn't afford her rent and had to move out of her boardinghouse." Red paused for dramatic effect. "One night soon after that, she hiked up Mount Lee, folded her coat neatly at the base of the Hollywood sign, climbed the maintenance ladder, and jumped off the *H.* Fell three stories."

"Did she die?"

Lily imagined how such a cautionary tale could slip into Hollywood lore, along with which producers had wandering hands and which drugstores offered all-you-can-eat specials.

"She landed in a patch of cactus, and the spines pierced her organs. Took her several days to expire. Two days later, a letter arrived from the Beverly Hills Playhouse, offering Peg the lead in a play. It was about a woman who commits suicide."

Lily was aghast. "That's too horrible. You don't think Kitty . . . ?"

"We all want to hit it big," Red said. "All it takes is one break, so we try to keep our spirits up. We go on auditions until the soles fall off our shoes. But sometimes it's so darn hard."

Lily examined their pretty, wholesome faces. Most of them wouldn't make it. They'd hang around the edges of Hollywood, wasting their youth, losing hope, their beauty receding until their faces took on a wizened simian —

"Tell me," Lily said. "Why did Kitty keep a little ape in the back of her closet?"

"Ape?" Red and Beverly chorused.

"I'll show you."

Lily bounded up the stairs, grabbed the ape, and ran back down brandishing it.

Squeals came from the girls.

"How perfectly hideous!"

"Max must have given it to her."

"No wonder she threw it in the back of her closet."

"Poor fellow, he's got no idea of the way to a gal's heart."

"What *is* this creature?" Lily asked. "And

who's Max?"

"Max Vranizan is a special effects guy for the studios," Red said when they finally stopped tittering. "And that" — she pointed — "is Mighty Joe Young."

"Mighty Joe Young?"

"Didn't they have picture palaces where you were stationed?" Red asked with exasperation.

"Of course they did. Maybe it wasn't out in Europe yet."

"It's been out here since July. It's about a pet gorilla named Joe that's brought from Africa to Hollywood and exploited by a shady promoter." Red fitted a cigarette into a holder and lit it. "I know it's hard to believe." She blew out smoke. "A shady Hollywood promoter."

"Why did Max give her the gorilla from his picture?" Lily asked.

"Because he's sweet on her."

This was the first useful thing Lily had heard. "Was he Kitty's boyfriend?"

"Not hardly," Red said.

"He's not a nice guy?"

"Oh, he's as sweet as a puppy dog," Beverly said. "And just as slobbery."

"I think those special effects guys are weird," Jinx said. "They're like mad scientists, locked up in their workshops, slaving

54

over their dinosaurs and apes and monsters."

"Could he have gotten angry that she spurned his advances?"

"We've wondered about that. She went to premieres with him, but they're just friends. You see him, you'll understand."

"He's no Cary Grant?"

"Not even William Demarest."

"What studio does he work at?"

"Those guys move around. Sometimes the producers put him on a small retainer while they go hunt down the money. He's at RKO now, getting ready for a werewolf picture."

Lily wanted to talk to Max. Glancing at her watch, she saw it was too late to reach him at RKO. Which reminded her . . . she still hadn't called Kitty's mother.

"I'm afraid I don't have any news yet," she said several minutes later when Mrs. Croggan's eager voice came on the line. Then she recapped her day and explained that she'd moved into Kitty's room.

Hanging up, she noticed an evening paper in the hallway nook and was surprised to see a photo in the Society pages of Gene Tierney disembarking at Union Station.

Lily pulled it closer. Off to the side stood a smart-looking girl, simply dressed but elegant. With shock Lily recognized herself.

55

She frowned. After so long in the covert life, it made her uneasy. She didn't want her return broadcast in the evening news for estranged relatives and long-abandoned friends to see. Let the past stay buried.

When the phone rang a moment later, Lily jumped, then told herself to calm down. No one except Mrs. Croggan knew where she was staying.

Red answered, then squealed with excitement.

"I've got some swelligant news," she said, hanging up. "Frank's rehearsing tonight."

The girls burst into excited chatter, prompting Lily to ask who Frank was.

Red said, "You're kidding, right? Frank is only the dreamiest singer and lover boy in the whole universe. Frank Si-na-tra. Ever heard of him, Europe?"

Since when had Angelenos been on a first-name basis with stars they'd never even met?

"Do you want to come with us?" Red asked.

"They're going to let us in?" Lily asked dubiously.

"Of course. That was my friend Lynette. She's the receptionist."

The offer was tantalizing. Lily had danced to "The Voice" in canteens throughout

Europe. But what if they got caught? she asked.

"Don't be silly. We're *invited.* Frank likes an audience." Red pirouetted. "How's that for your first night in Hollywood?"

CHAPTER 4

At eleven-thirty p.m., Lily joined Red, Jinx, and Beverly as they trooped down to Sunset Boulevard. The cobalt sky draped impossibly huge over the desert air. Clouds moved overhead like some great oceanic migration, but the night was mild, gusts of warm wind plucking at their waved hair.

"Ooh, I hate these Santa Anas," Beverly said as they passed an empty lot, the wind sending a beer bottle clanging over gravel. "They make my skin itch and my blood boil."

The hair along Lily's nape stood up and static crackled her dress. She thought the winds made the nightscape dramatic, as if anything might happen. She'd come to L.A. to find Kitty, not to have fun. But as she'd changed into her cornflower-blue dress and her sable-trimmed wool coat, she realized she'd learn more going out with the girls tonight than sitting alone in her room.

When they arrived, Red checked with her friend. Sinatra was running late, so they waited in a huddle on the gusty boulevard, smoking cigarettes and telling jokes, shivering like excited puppies, the winds whipping up dried leaves and the odd, stray cigarette pack. Waiting for Frank.

At one in the morning a black Cadillac pulled up and there he was, hat pulled low over those brilliant blue eyes, emerging from the backseat, surrounded by unsmiling men in dark suits. Red and Beverly called, "Yoo-hoo, we love you, Frank!" and he looked up and his face creased into that million-watt smile and he waved back.

"C'mon in, girls," he said. "I hope you like ice cream."

They shrieked and Lily found herself shrieking too, some indescribable primal release that left her throat and spiraled up to the constellations.

A small, slick-looking man with reddish-brown hair appeared behind Sinatra's entourage. Lily saw him scanning her roommates with feral intensity.

"Where's Kitty tonight?" he asked at last.

Jinx snapped her gum. "We thought *you* might know."

The little man looked like he wanted to

deck her. He would have needed to climb a ladder.

Jinx's bravado crumpled. "She hasn't been home in four days. You think she went back to the desert?"

The man's eyes narrowed. "She should stay away from there."

"Why?" Lily said, stepping up.

The man regarded her like a wolf sizing up a rabbit.

"Who's the looker?" he asked.

"Li—" Beverly began.

"Linda," Lily interjected, not wanting the predatory little man to know her real name. "Linda Desmond. Pleased to meet you. And you are?"

From inside came the excited squeal of female voices, then the tootle of a horn warming up. "Showtime," the man said, hurrying inside.

Lily tried to follow, but two girls in tight sweaters rushed past, blocking her path. Lily turned back to Kitty's roommates. "Who was that creepy man?"

"I don't know his name," Jinx said. "He was here the last time Frank played, flirting madly with Kitty." She lowered her voice. "I think he may be a gangster."

"Did she go out with him?"

Red clucked her tongue. "She could have.

60

Kitty didn't tell us everything."

"If she thought we wouldn't approve," added Jinx.

"Now, now, ladies," said peacemaker Beverly, holding the door. "Let's go inside before we miss the show."

They trooped in. The musicians were yawning and drinking coffee and smoking Chesterfields as they warmed up. They all had day jobs and were beat, but no one turned down an opportunity to work with Sinatra.

Jinx waved at a guitarist she knew named Al Viola, natty in a white suit and mustache. Two college boys uncorked a bottle of champagne they'd smuggled in, sending it fizzing to the floor. The smell reminded Lily of Wiesbaden, Germany, where she'd helped set up files for an OSS office in a champagne factory. The year was 1945, and there weren't many buildings left standing, so they'd made the best of it, working amid pungent winey fumes that left everyone light-headed.

Lily scanned the studio for the unpleasant man and found him on the sidelines, deep in conversation with a larger man who kept mopping his forehead with a handkerchief. Then Sinatra got up and everything went quiet. With his sheet music on the stand, he began to sing, the orchestra backing him all the way.

Lily gave a languid sigh and tried to surrender to the music, vowing to find the little man at the break. It was a waking dream to be here, something she'd tell her grandchildren one day. So what if he'd lost the bobbysoxer crowd and the papers said he was washed up. He'd always have her heart. She swayed with pleasure, losing herself in the melody, mesmerized by the slim, handsome man crooning at the mike, the swoop and dip of his voice, that unique phrasing that made her go all funny inside. Between songs, he joked with them and others who slipped in as the night wore on, solemn as churchgoers, heads bowed before a deity. Lily felt how their presence energized Sinatra, the exhilaration flowing back and forth across the stage. He fed off their adoration, needed it as much as they needed him. He was singing to them, and, if she wanted to fantasize, directly to her, Lily Kessler from the farmlands of Mar Vista.

Lily imagined Kitty coming to Hollywood and getting a taste of this life, the hunger it would awaken in a naïve midwestern girl. Had Joseph's sister met a gangster on a night like tonight and started seeing him? Had something happened? But just as Lily got hold of a theory, it escaped down the maze of her mind, twisting out of reach as Sinatra hit a particularly sweet note.

Finally the spell broke and Sinatra called a break. Lily saw the little man making his way through the crowd. With a murmur about needing the powder room, she slipped after him. She was about to hail him when he turned into a hallway, following the larger fellow, who gripped a third, frightened-looking man by the arm. The big guy stopped, opened a door into what looked like the back alley, and jerked his captive so violently that his hat fell off. With a sharp intake of breath, Lily drew back into the shadows. The little man gave a low chuckle, stooped to pick up the hat, then followed the pair outside. The pneumatic door sighed shut.

Behind her, two men came up, jostling her elbow. Lily jumped, then saw with relief that they were musicians. "Whoa, there, little lady, you all right?" one of them asked, seeing her frozen face.

"Fine," Lily said, nodding. "It's just that . . ." She searched for words.

"Frank has that effect on the ladies," one said, misconstruing her speechlessness. He clapped his pal on the back. Laughing uproariously, they moved down the hall.

Lily got hold of herself. *What would you have done in your old life?* She looked around. Beyond the bathroom was a sign that said STAIRS. Lily ran over, threw open the door, and tiptoed up, making sure her heels didn't clang on the metal steps. On the third landing, she opened the door and stepped into an office, deserted and eerie in the reflected neon light of Sunset Boulevard. She found the emergency exit, opened it soundlessly, and climbed onto the fire escape above the alley. She was three floors up, but sound carried. Crouching, she looked down. The little man was punching the man who'd been dragged outside while the big thug held his arms pinioned back. The little man grunted softly as he landed blows, but the victim made no sound at all, which seemed deeply sinister to Lily. Why didn't he call for help?

Then it was over. The little man took out a handkerchief and wiped his hand clean of blood and mucus.

"When you gonna have it, Jimmy?" the little man said. "The boss is tired of your worthless promises."

Jimmy sagged against the big thug, then fell to the ground and crouched on all fours like an animal.

"I swear, you'll get it next week," he

wheezed.

"By next week you'll owe double."

"No." The man on the asphalt writhed. "I can't . . . It's too . . . Don't," he pleaded, as the big thug aimed a kick at his kidneys. "I'll tell ya . . . I saw . . . something you might . . . About that star . . ."

"I'll make you see stars," the big man vowed.

The little thug tugged on his partner's shoulder. "Ease up, will ya, Monty? Let's hear what he has to say."

The beaten man scrambled to his feet. "It's about that missing actress you been asking about."

"Fer chrissakes, keep it down," the little man said, glancing about the alley in alarm. Lily shrank back into the building's shadows, but the thugs, intent on their business, never looked up.

There followed a whispered conversation that Lily, despite ears sharpened by years of surveillance, could not quite overhear.

Letting the door snick quietly shut behind her, she ran down the stairs and made her way past the audience. She slipped through the lobby, hurrying down the street and around to the alley, where she flattened herself against the brick wall and peered around. Except for two drunks approaching from a block away, singing at the top of their lungs, the alley was empty. They must have scared off her quarry. Lily swore, then walked back inside, scanning the crowd, who were drifting back to their seats. But Jimmy, Monty, and the little thug had disappeared.

"There you are," said Beverly, her big eyes tight with concern. "We thought you'd gone AWOL."

She clasped Lily's arm in a friendly manner and the other girls crowded around, giddy and giggly from flirting with the musicians and eating ice cream. Jinx still clutched a silver dish of orange sherbet. Lily blinked, transported from the brutal world of the alley to one of sugared breath and sweet perfume. Part of her wanted to blurt out what she'd seen. Then her training took over. She needed to learn what the girls knew about Kitty's romantic entanglements.

"I took a walk to clear my head," she said.

Just then Frank strolled back up to the mike and a collective intake of breath rippled through the audience. Uneasy, Lily gave up and surrendered to Sinatra's magic. Wherever Joseph's sister was, there was nothing more she could do tonight.

They tore themselves reluctantly away at

dawn, yawning and stretching, humming snatches of song, their bellies full of vanilla-chocolate-strawberry-pistachio ice cream and sloshing with hot coffee, the bushy fronds of the palm trees along Sunset Boulevard sweeping the ashy night from the sky.

Lily wondered if she'd hallucinated the scene in the alley. In the gray light of dawn, as birds trilled and the first rays of sun rose to illuminate the Hollywood sign, it seemed like a nightmare born of sleep deprivation. Yet the fear that still pulsed in her nerve endings seemed very real.

The buses were filled with commuters, and Lily rejoiced privately that she didn't have a job to go to. All day Red and Beverly and Jinx would slump sleepily at work, trying to catch an hour on their lunch breaks, but they swore that no matter what, it was worth it, because Frank was a dreamboat and he'd joked with them and sung just to them, that's the kind of town it was. Lily wanted to grab a bite of breakfast before the evening's high wore off, then tumble into Kitty's bed and sleep for several hours. She'd start her search right after that.

CHAPTER 5

October 12, 1949

"Hot enough for ya, Mildred?" Harry Jack asked his favorite waitress, settling into a seat at the drugstore counter.

"These Santa Anas get any hotter and the eggs out back are going to hatch into chicks," Mildred said. She sauntered over with her pot, slapped down a doily and a cup, and poured coffee.

Harry was a news photographer. He'd honed his skills during the war, pointing and shooting a camera while others aimed more lethal weapons. Four years after the Allied victory, the world was headed for another showdown, but Harry tried not to think about atomic annihilation; his biggest concern was landing a staff job at one of the big city dailies. For now he was freelance, selling snaps one at a time, which meant cruising the streets with his radio tuned to the KMA367 police frequency, looking for action.

It was only a matter of time, with the turf wars heating up between Mickey Cohen and Jack Dragna as they fought for the spoils left open by Bugsy Siegel's murder two years back. Rumor had it there was a contract out on the dapper Jewish gangster and now even the cops were following Mickey around to protect him. Harry knew one of Cohen's henchmen from Boyle Heights, where they'd grown up together. Maybe he should track him down. If a gang battle erupted and he got it on film, he'd be a cinch for a staff job.

Harry spread out his paper but found his gaze drifting to a pretty gal in a cornflower-blue dress who was eating breakfast and reading her own paper, though she slumped over it like a wilted flower. She had big brown eyes, an upturned nose, a sprinkling of freckles, trim hips, and a nice swell in the bosom department. A gal like that could go far in this town. He pictured her in a grassy backyard, laughing and pushing a toddler on a swing as he came home from work. She'd have lamb chops and mashed potatoes on the table, and later after they put the kid to bed . . .

"You can pop your eyes back in now,"

Mildred said, putting down his breakfast special.

"I can look, can't I?" Harry examined his over-easy eggs. "Glad you found a couple that haven't pecked their way out yet. Least-wise I don't see any beaks."

"Get away with you," she said with a laugh.

Harry ate, sopping up the last of his yolk with a crust of bread. Leaving Mildred her tip, he sauntered over to the cornflower girl.

"Hello, miss," he said. "Didn't I meet you last February at Sammy's wedding?"

The girl tensed. Her eyes danced nervously.

"I'm sure you're mistaken." She played with her napkin. "I just got into Los Angeles yesterday."

"Newcomer, eh?" Harry smiled and rocked on the balls of his feet. "Maybe you'd like someone to show you around. I'm a news photographer. I know all the hot spots."

The girl examined him like he was a stud racehorse she might consider plunking down good money for.

"Do you know any gangster hangouts?" she asked.

"Sure I do. It's part of my job. But why would a nice . . . You think they're glamor-

70

ous? Is that it?" Harry hoped it wasn't a new trend. How could a regular guy compete? "You're one of them gals that likes a little danger, a little roughing up?"

The girl threw her head back and laughed. "Heavens, no! I went through enough danger in the war to last a dozen lifetimes."

Harry wondered if she'd been a WAC or a WAVE. She had that confident, can-do aura.

The gal smiled mysteriously. "I'm . . . doing research for a script, that's all, Mr. . . . ?" She let the word wobble and her voice rose flirtatiously.

"Harry. Harry Jack."

"And I'm . . ." she bit her lip and seemed to decide something. "I'm Lily Kessler. Pleased to meet you."

Harry found his hand caught in a grip that could have cracked Brazil nuts. His gaze fell on Lily Kessler's watch, which said eight-thirty. An involuntary gasp went through him.

"Come on, Mr. Jack, I didn't squeeze that hard."

Harry explained that he had a job interview at the *L.A. Times* at nine a.m. It was a reactionary rag, but a job was a job and he didn't want to be late. He asked for her number and was thrilled when she scribbled it on a napkin.

■ ■ ■ ■

Harry drove downtown in an exalted haze. His luck had changed. Suddenly he had the possibility of a staff job and romance too. By nine-fifteen, *L.A. Times* photo editor Richard Sykes was leafing through his portfolio, praising shots he liked, and Harry got a hopeful feeling.

One of the managing editors walked in, an obstreperous, florid-faced man named Didrickson.

"Who's the kid?" Didrickson asked Sykes, inclining his chin.

"This here is Harry Jack. A fine photographer. He's looking for a job."

Didrickson took a long look at Harry.

"You a kike?" the man asked.

Harry got to his feet in a hurry. "What's it to you?"

"A Jew. That's what you are."

Harry noted the half pint in the back of Didrickson's pants, the smell of spirits on his breath. He felt the blood pounding at his temples as he packed up his portfolio.

" 'Cause the *Times* don't hire Jews. Probably a Red, to boot. Sykes here ought to have saved you the trouble."

"Didrickson, you're an asshole," Sykes

said. "Get the fuck out of my photo lab. Don't you have any copy to mangle?"

Harry tried to look down his nose at Didrickson, which was difficult, since the red-faced editor towered above him and outweighed him twice over. "Never mind, Mr. Sykes. The man's a bigot and a bully. Someone ought to strap him down and read him his own paper's coverage of the Nuremburg Trials. Maybe then he'd understand what this leads to. Didrickson, I wouldn't take a job at your pig-swill paper if you offered it to me on a platter."

Didrickson didn't wait for Harry to finish before he swung. The punch missed wildly. Harry stepped in and hit him in the jaw and the big man fell back and landed on his backside.

There was the sound of breaking glass, then a piercing shriek as Didrickson levitated off the floor, cupping his posterior and screaming, "My ass!"

His shrieks brought the *Times* security goons at a fast clip. By the time they finished roughing up Harry and threw him and his portfolio onto the sidewalk, his left eye was already swelling up and one leg throbbed. But Harry was more worried about his precious photos, which now lay scattered along Second Avenue. Training his good eye to the ground like a cyclops, he ran to collect them while the guards jeered. Down the street, two ladies dressed in black negligees leaned out the third-floor window enjoying a break before the lunch rush of reporters, cops, politicians, and businessmen.

"Yoo-hoo, you missed one over there," one called, pointing down at the street. "By the fire hydrant. Quick, before the car runs it over."

A grubby kid picked a photo out of the gutter and plucked off a dried bit of leaf.

"Hey," Harry called. "That there's private property. Hand it over."

The kid froze and Harry cursed Didrickson, the guards, his sore leg, and his bad eye. The kid gave him the photo.

"Thanks. You can move along now."

Instead, the kid picked up another photo and held it out.

"I don't need your help. So beat it."

Just then Harry saw a city bus bearing down on one of his best photos — Mayor Fletcher Bowron, tie loosened, hat askew, celebrating his latest election win. He lunged for it, but invisible arms yanked him back.

"Why, you . . ." he said, arms flailing. His dander up, the guards' laughter ringing in his ears, the managing editor's insults still smarting his pride, he turned and swung. An absurdly light figure landed with a limp flop on the sidewalk. Too late, Harry realized he'd coldcocked the kid. As he squinted to inspect the damage, a black car whooshed past. He hadn't seen it coming because of his bad eye. Just then the bus arrived, destroying his prize photo.

Harry groaned. "Kid," he said, shaking the inert form. "You okay, kid? Jesus, I'm sorry."

He looked up and beckoned the guards.

A uniformed man stepped out of his box and spat. "What do you think this is, the Union Rescue Mission?"

Cursing, Harry scooped up the kid and stalked back to the twenty-five-cent auto-pay lot where he'd left his car. He removed the kid's knapsack and dumped the unconscious body in the backseat. Light as a puppy, with a musty smell and gray skin. Twelve years old, tops, Harry figured, as he placed a thumb against the inside of the twiglike wrist, feeling for a pulse.

Harry's police radio crackled. The body of a young woman had been found in a ravine below the Hollywood sign. Holy shit, that would bring every news photog in town running. What if the Dahlia's killer had struck again? That sicko had never been caught. If

Harry managed to get off some good shots, he'd have every paper in the country screaming for those photos.

Harry cursed some more. He knew he should take the kid to a hospital. But then he'd miss the shot.

"I'm sorry, junior, but I gotta do this."

Jumping into the driver's seat, Harry hauled ass across town, ear cocked to the radio for more details. When he hit Hollywood, Harry turned north and nosed the car up the narrow windy streets of Whitley Heights that the movie stars liked so much. When he saw an LAPD Crime Lab truck and a coroner's van, he pulled over. The crew was unloading equipment.

In the backseat, Harry saw the kid's narrow chest moving up and down. Grabbing his camera, he ran after the tech men. The fifty-foot letters towered white against the sun-scorched hillside. Harry could see the scaffolding behind the sign, heard the structure creak in the breeze. On the hillside, men were loading something onto a gurney. Damn. She was covered up. A uniformed officer appeared. He flipped his baton sideways and stood, chest thrust out in a belligerent manner.

"You need to wait here."

Harry said okay and snapped a few photos, even though the forensics guys were too far away for him to see much. *Hurry,* he thought, checking over his shoulder for the newshounds he knew would arrive any minute.

The grim procession wound its way up the ravine, past the gnarled grace of manzanita and creosote, the metallic blue of long-tongued century plants, until they reached Harry. After several snaps of the bundled body, he stepped back respectfully. One of the pallbearers was a tech guy Harry knew from the police bars he patronized.

"Hey, Mack, wouldja mind . . . ?" Harry pantomimed pulling the sheet back.

"Not gonna happen right now. Sorry," Mack said. Harry dropped to his knees and took a few more shots, then followed the cortege along the fire road to the coroner's vehicle, back doors open to receive the body.

By this time, reporters had arrived.

"We got a jumper or a homicide?" one called out.

"If she took a dive," said a KNX reporter, "then my money's on the *D.* Nice and roomy up there. Who'll give me twenty-five dollars on the *D?*"

"The *Y,*" another voice said. "Thirty on the *Y.*"

The techs began loading the body and a

cry went up, all bets momentarily forgotten.

"No fair. C'mon, fellas, give us a peek."

The techs stopped and turned to the commanding officer.

"All right," the LAPD sergeant said. "Let's hold it right there a minute."

The techs put the stretcher down and lit up cigarettes. The sergeant counted the waiting journalists.

"Ten dollars apiece and she's yours," he announced. "Smithy will bring around the collection plate."

A patrol officer upended his police hat and circulated among the flacks, who grumbled but stuffed in bills. Then the unveiling took place, with so many cameras going off at once that Harry got a prickly, panicky feeling in his scalp that he was back in the war.

The vic's face and neck were grotesquely swollen, bloodied, and scraped, her head crooked at an unnatural angle. The chestnut hair was matted with dirt and leaves, her clothes torn, bits of brush embedded in the fabric. Decomposition was well under way, and the body gave off a sickening odor. Even so, Harry could see this had been a pretty girl, with a smart figure and a lush mouth that even now was faintly outlined in red lipstick.

"Got an ID for us, Sarge?" he called out.

"She's Jane Doe Number Fifteen for now, boys," the sergeant said, covering the dead girl to provide a semblance of dignity. But he yanked the shroud too high over her head, exposing her legs.

"Wait a minute. Would you look at that shoe," someone yelled.

Harry followed the long coltlike legs down — the girl's skirt was hiked above the knee — and saw a dirt-streaked, high-heeled red patent leather shoe still strapped to one foot, which swelled over the ankle strap like a loaf of rising bread. The other foot was bare.

"Where's the other shoe, Sarge?" came a voice from the crowd.

"Your guess is as good as mine, boys."

"Not already bagged and tagged?"

"Negative."

"You've canvassed the area?"

"Affirmative."

There was a hum of excitement as the full import hit them — here was the detail that would send papers flying off the newsstands.

"So it's Cinderella's Slipper, then," a man called out.

"The Princess and the Missing Slipper," said another.

"Red Cinderella," came a third, the call and response heating up as the reporters tried out, then discarded various names. Because every journo worth his salt knew that a lurid death required an equally lurid moniker.

"Not Red Cinderella," someone said, "or everyone'll think it's a HUAC thing."

"This look like the Dahlia killer's handiwork?" asked a female voice from the back. Harry recognized Florabel Muir, a spitfire for the *Mirror.*

An excited murmur rose from the crowd. "Good thinking, Florabel. Is our boy back in action?"

"We don't know that it's a murder yet, gentlemen. And let me point out that she's in one piece."

"Was she raped?" someone asked.

"We'll leave that to the coroner."

The journalistic hive brain began to hum with purpose again.

"We need a name," one said. "Something like Dahlia."

"Smithy, be a good fellow and pick us a flower off that bush, tuck it behind her ear, and she'll be the Red Bougainvillea," said another.

"Red. Crimson. Scarlet. How about Scarlet Sandal?" a third voice said.

A roar of approval went up for the Scarlet Sandal and everybody wrote it down.

"So come on, someone did her, right, Sarge?" a man called out.

The sergeant scratched his chin. "There's severe bruising, possible ligature marks on her neck."

There was momentary quiet. Then a buzz of excitement.

"Strangled?" a man said, whistling. "We got ourselves a Hollywood Strangler?"

"Let's leave pronouncements to the coroner."

"Which letter was she found under, Sarge?"

The sergeant stared for a long moment. "The *D*," he said finally.

"What'd I tell ya?" a voice crowed. "You owe me twenty-five dollars."

"Banyan, you disgust me," Florabel Muir said. She turned to the sergeant. "So the vic wasn't killed elsewhere and dumped in the ravine?"

"We'll have more in a few days, folks," the sergeant said. He signaled the techs, who threw down their cigarettes, ground them out with their heels — it was fire season, after all — and walked back to the gurney.

The photogs took a final set of snaps as the body was loaded into the van. Harry snapped away too, wondering who he could sell the photos to. He didn't see the *Daily*

Mirror photographer, a roustabout named Larry Bostone. Inquiring, Harry learned the man was sleeping off a drunk in a whorehouse in the sticks of Ventura Boulevard. *Ka-ching.* Harry heard the sound of a cash register.

The kid was sitting in Harry's backseat, eating an apple. When he saw Harry, he froze.

"I'm not gonna hurt you, son. I owe you an apology. You saved me from getting run over back there at the *Times.*"

Harry got in the car, the film itching a hole in his pocket. "You really better?"

The kid nodded.

"Good, because we've got a little errand to run. Hold on, we need to fly."

Fifteen minutes and an inch of tire rubber later, Harry pulled into the *Mirror*'s parking lot.

"Back in a flash," he told the kid, who watched beadily from the rear seat but said nothing. Harry hoped he'd be gone when he returned.

Taking the stairs three a time, Harry burst into the *Mirror*'s photo lab. Photo editor Steve Chawkins was screaming into the phone.

"What the hell do you mean, he's on assignment on Ventura Boulevard and you can't reach him? Excuse my French, Mrs. Bostone, but this is the last straw. Tell him not to bother to come in to work tomorrow. He's fired."

The photo editor threw down the phone and Harry popped the film out of his camera and held it up.

"It's okay, Mr. Chawkins. I got it. Here it is."

Chawkins was cross-eyed with rage.

"Here's what, you simpleton?"

"Film of the dead girl in Hollywood. It's all here." Harry was so excited he could barely get the words out.

Chawkins snatched the film out of Harry's hands, ran to the darkroom, and tossed it to a technician. Stepping back out, he said, "How much do you want for it?"

"Um, a hundred dollars?" Harry closed his eyes in terror at the unmitigated gall of asking for so much money.

"Fifty," Chawkins snapped.

"Seventy-five."

"It better be good."

CHAPTER 6

Lily opened one eye, saw buttery light filtering through the bedroom window, and knew it was past noon. She rolled over and promptly fell onto the floor. She'd forgotten the strange bed, the rickety frame. For a moment, she lay there, stunned. Then a sense of urgency seized her. She had a lot to do today.

Grabbing her toiletries, she headed for the bathroom, then squealed as her bare foot landed on something furry and wet just outside her door. It was the small, bloody haunch of a mouse. Ugh. Who'd left this nasty calling card outside her door? Mrs. Potter's cat?

Once she was dressed and groomed, she went down to the kitchen, which was deserted. The icebox held Carnation cottage cheese, fried chicken, and a bottle of milk. Peeling off the foil top, she chugged in a most unladylike fashion.

"Would you like to contribute to the dairy fund?" Mrs. Potter stood in the doorway.

Lily blushed and reached for her purse. Then she mentioned the mouse remains.

"Caligro's a good ratter," Mrs. Potter said, spooning chunks of meat and congealed fat into the animal's dish. "Come get your reward, my pet."

A queasy feeling settled over Lily and she hurried from the house. The day was half gone. She'd grab a quick bite at the drugstore, then call Max Vranizan at RKO. And she'd ask the police about the odd little gangster from last night.

"Extra, extra," a newsboy shouted as she reached the corner. People crowded around, pushing and shoving, eyes darting and eager. "Here ya go, folks. Read all about it. Strangled girl found in Hollywood Hills. Read all about it."

With a sense of foreboding, Lily tapped the shoulder of a gray-haired lady who'd managed to get a paper.

"May I see?"

Obligingly, the woman held it up.

"Body of Strangled Young Woman Found Below Hollywood Sign," the enormous headline read. "Search Continues for Scarlet Sandal's Identity and Her Killer."

A girl's face stared from the front page,

puffy and waxy and rigid, with the closed lids and blurry impersonality of death, her hair askew, makeup smudged, cheeks scraped. Add in the blotchy ink and rough newsprint, and it looked very little like the artfully lit glamour shots of Kitty Hayden that Mrs. Croggan had shown Lily. Still, there were undeniable similarities to Joseph. The large generous mouth, high forehead, and wide-spaced eyes.

"Oh god," Lily said, as the world tilted and spun. She staggered backward. At that moment, a truck screeched up to the newspaper stand and burly arms tossed out two stacks of papers so fresh they still reeked of newsprint. Lily grabbed blindly to brace herself, the stack wobbled, and she tumbled off the curb, the papers falling on top of her.

The truck, which was already pulling out, swerved to avoid hitting her. Someone lay on the horn and a man leaned out the window.

"Jesus, lady, do you want to get killed?"

The newsstand employee helped her up, then stared dolefully at his scattered goods. Lily helped him pick up the mess, then bought every paper the guy had — the *Mirror,* the *Herald,* the *World,* the *Hollywood Citizen News,* the *Times,* the *Examiner.*

"They're going like hotcakes," the man intoned. He had an Eastern European accent, Romanian, she thought. Unwilling to accept that the dead girl might be Kitty, Lily instead recalled the night at Bucharest's Athénée Palace when Joseph had clipped amber teardrop earrings to her lobes and asked her to marry him. Lily had rejoiced, then, to think of the family she'd be joining. Now she could only hope the blurry newsprint had played a cruel trick.

"You should maybe sit down, miss," the Romanian man said.

He wore a woolen vest over a threadbare white shirt with long sleeves, and through the cloth Lily saw the outline of ghostly blue numbers on his forearm. You never really left the past behind, she thought. It lurked under a fraying shirt, in the guttural inflection of a voice, the face of a dead girl on cheap newsprint.

"I think I know her," Lily said.

The man regarded her impassively. "Then you must go to police."

"How do I get there?"

Forty minutes later, Lily sat in a bare room downtown, explaining what she knew to two detectives from the Central Homicide Bureau.

Magruder was built like a pickle barrel, with red braces and a tough glint in his eye, tapping cigar ash into a cupped hand as he talked. Pico was younger and loose-limbed, with a long classic nose, hazel eyes framed by long black lashes, and hair so stiff with Brylcreem you could see the toothmarks where he'd dragged the comb.

"I already told you I never met her," Lily said patiently. She knew from experience that they needed to verify her story, but she didn't like the way their eyes roved up and down her body, especially the older cop's. They'd insist they were watching for signs that she was lying or nervous, guilty in some way, but she knew better.

"Kind of beats all, don't it? You strolling in here, offering to identify the body of a girl you never even met, convinced it's this missing" — Pico checked his notes — "Kitty Hayden."

His skin was tawny, sun-kissed by the climate, and he moved with the easy grace of an athlete. Lily was used to the pallor of northern Europe, the bundling greatcoats and endless drizzle. The only thing these detectives shared with the agency men she'd known in Europe was their lazy arrogance. Some kind of yearning must have suffused her face, because Pico stepped back, eyes suddenly flat and wary.

"How do we know you're not a nutcase?" he asked. "Or one of those Looky Lous."

Lily felt exasperated. "I'm here because I promised Mrs. Croggan I'd track down her daughter."

Lily opened her purse and pulled a small photo out of her wallet. "She gave me a recent picture, so here, check it yourself." She placed the head shot of the smiling starlet next to the newspaper photo. The air around her tightened and the men grew still and watchful. Finally, she had their attention.

"And one more thing. Mrs. Croggan told me Doreen had a brown mole in the shape of a teardrop under her left breast. That should allow you to make a positive identification. There are always fingerprints, of course, but unless she's been convicted of a crime, it's unlikely her prints would be on record anywhere."

The detectives' eyes spiraled in surprise. Pico cleared his throat. "Miss Kessler, do you have a background in law enforcement? You seem to know somewhat more than the average —"

"Civilian dame," Magruder interjected.

Who'd believe it anyway? Lily thought. Turning down the corners of her mouth, she stared at the floor as if trying not to cry. To her surprise, real tears welled.

"My fiancé was in military intelligence," she said, "so I picked up a few things here and there. He died serving his country. Kitty was his sister."

The detectives shot each other a look and murmured their condolences. Lily knew they had pegged her as just another uppity ex-WAVE or WAC who'd picked up a hot-shot boyfriend during the war and some fancy lingo to go along with it.

It is entirely in my interest for you to under-estimate me, she thought.

Five minutes later, they escorted her through the warrens of the LAPD headquarters and to the county morgue, where Magruder asked to see Jane Doe #15.

Outside the door, he turned to her.

"Brace yourself, Miss Kessler. It's not all nice and pretty like at a funeral parlor."

Lily had seen bodies blown apart by bombs and emaciated corpses in striped uniforms piled like firewood. In a Dresden alley, she'd seen a rat nibble a dead man's toes that protruded from boots held together by twine.

"I'm ready," she said.

A blast of refrigerator air hit them. The stench of ammonia mingled with decaying meat. The medical examiner was prepping for the autopsy, a cigarette clasped between his lips to ward off the worst of the smell. When he pulled the sheet back, Lily took an involuntary breath.

Seeing her in the flesh, she was struck by the desecration of such beauty and the undeniable similarity to Joseph. The detectives took turns comparing the photo with the body before them. Then Magruder explained about the birthmark and the coroner nodded and sliced down the front of the girl's suit, pulling the fabric apart with his hands. Another slice and the brassiere gave way, releasing two creamy white breasts that flopped to either side. Lily saw the mole right away. From the corner of her eye, she saw Magruder ogling. She turned away, hand covering her mouth, and the men gave her a wide berth, sure that she was about to get sick. Instead, a sob welled up in Lily's throat as she said, "It's her, all right."

Lily declined the detectives' offers to call a cab, insisting she was fine, and could take the streetcar. The morgue smell clung to her nostrils, refusing to dissipate even after she was back at the boardinghouse. No one was around. She set her stack of newspapers on the kitchen table and slumped into a chair. This wasn't some anonymous cadaver, but Joseph's baby sister. Slowly, Lily's horror darkened to outrage. Who had done this? What possible motive could there be? She thought about Mrs. Croggan sitting on her couch as the police broke the news to her, the handkerchief bunched and twisting in her hand. It was too much for any mother to bear. First Joseph, now Kitty. Both her children gone in less than one year. She had to call Illinois, but first she needed to calm down and get all the facts.

After checking that all the doors were locked, Lily put the kettle on for tea and forced herself to read the newspapers, struck with distaste by the nickname Scarlet Sandal, as if Kitty weren't a human being anymore, but a piece of titillating footwear. The body, which showed significant decomposition, had been found below the Hollywood sign by a man walking his dog. Kitty had been wearing a suit and one red high-heeled sandal. The other shoe and her purse were missing. There was no obvious sign of sexual violation.

Lily found herself distracted by a blue-bottle fly that kept kamikazeing into the window. A foreign word, strange and harsh on the tongue, that had become part of a new lexicon of horror during the war. Lily imagined Kitty flinging herself against her attacker. Praying that someone would hear her screams and come to her aid. When the kettle whistled, she jumped.

She'd been lulled because Los Angeles was prosperous and peaceful and didn't *look* dangerous. It was like a brash, self-absorbed adolescent, tripping over its own ungainly feet. Yet evil lurked here too. It wore a mask to disguise its appetites and walked in shadow. Do not be deceived by the glittery surfaces of things, Lily reminded herself.

A half hour later, Lily said into the receiver, "Mrs. Croggan, I . . . it's about Doreen . . . I know the police —"

"We know," Mrs. Croggan said in a faraway voice. Lily heard muted voices in the background and was relieved that the woman wasn't alone.

"I'm so sorry."

"Is it being carried on the radio, then?" Mrs. Croggan asked with glassy calm.

"And in the newspapers. That's how I found out. I went down to the police station and —"

"A famous actress like her. Of course it would be." And then Mrs. Croggan began to weep. "My poor baby. I should have never let her go."

"You couldn't have stopped her, Mrs.

Croggan. It was what she wanted."

"Thank you for helping to identify her," Mrs. Croggan said politely. "It must have been horrible for you . . ."

"It was the least I could —"

"Will you arrange to have Doreen shipped home for a proper funeral?"

"I don't know if I can. It's been several days. The body . . ."

"They have refrigerated cargo." Mrs. Croggan's voice was barely audible. "Mr. and Mrs. Pettit are here, from across the street, and our minister, and he says —"

"The coroner has to finish the autopsy. And I don't know if —"

"You'll try, though, won't you, Lily?"

"Yes, ma'am." Lily grew distracted as Red walked in, wearing a look of shocked disbelief.

"Are you at the house now?" Mrs. Croggan asked. "Is it a nice place, where my Doreen lived?"

Lily thought of the tiny room with its peeling paint, Mrs. Potter with her strange eyes, and Kitty's roommates meting out friendship and casual cruelty, silky and competitive as cats.

"It's homey and cheerful, and in a good part of town." Lily stared at Red. "And all the other girls at the boardinghouse loved her like a sister."

A strange look flashed across Red's face. She turned and fled.

"You tell those detectives she was a good girl, hear?"

"Yes, Mrs. Croggan."

"She didn't run with bad company. She worked hard. She wanted to make a name for herself, on talent."

"She had plenty of it."

"If only the police had done more when I first called, Doreen might still be alive."

"She's with the angels in heaven now." Lily didn't know if she believed this, but it felt like the right thing to say.

"That's what my minister says. Oh, why did I ever let her go?"

"I swear to you, Mrs. Croggan, I'm going to track down the animal who did this."

"Will you work with the police?"

"I'll try," Lily said diplomatically, but she knew they'd laugh her out the door if she suggested it.

"Please don't do anything rash . . . or illegal," Mrs. Croggan said. "If Joseph were alive, he'd be out there, asking questions. It's no job for a young girl."

Lily realized she was shaking. "But Joseph's not here," she told the woman who would have been her mother-in-law. "There's only me."

CHAPTER 7

"Yoo-hoo," Mrs. Potter called as she knocked. "I'm so sorry to disturb you, but we've had terrible news."

"I know," Lily said through the closed bedroom door, drying her hair. Even though it was four in the afternoon, she'd taken a bath. It was the only way to get rid of the morgue smell.

"Well, hon, my heart goes out to you, but there's some detectives here to see you and search the room. I took the liberty of bringing them upstairs."

Lily dashed on makeup, molded her damp hair into waves, donned a skirt and blouse. Put on earrings, her watch. Finally, she flung open the door. Pico and Magruder walked in, their eyes already scanning the room.

"I'd ask you to sit down," Lily said, "but as you can see . . ." She spread her hands.

Magruder merely grunted and asked if

she'd tidied up or thrown anything away.

Lily said she hadn't, but added pointedly that five days had already elapsed since Kitty's roommates first reported her missing. "I don't think the police took it seriously. They poked around and left."

Pico's lip curled, his eyes pensive in the moment before he looked away. Magruder's small, humorless eyes drilled into her and he said, "Do you have any idea how many young women come here from all over the world and disappear into the wilds of Hollywood?"

Without waiting for an answer, he launched into a speech so canned he couldn't even feign earnestness anymore. "The vast majority turn up alive, and each one's got her own reasons for not being found. They're running from parents. Husbands. Boyfriends. Brats and bad reputations. They come to reinvent themselves, start new lives. And contrary to what the public may think, the LAPD is not a human fetch-and-retrieve service. Unless there's evidence of foul play or reason to suspect a crime's occurred, we don't get involved. Which is why Mrs. Croggan's calls to the Hollywood station got the response they did. But we're Homicide. This is a whole different ball game."

"Now that it's too late," Lily pointed out.

"Why don't you go downstairs and have some coffee, calm your nerves," Pico said. "The Crime Lab boys'll be here any minute and they'll turn the place upside down, dusting for prints, looking for blood residue."

Lily felt her heart flip over. "You think it happened here?"

Pico crossed his arms and made a disparaging noise.

"It's all part of our investigation," Magruder said. "Maybe the killer knew her. Maybe he left a pack of matches we can trace back to a bar he frequents. Maybe his dog shed on his sports jacket and we'll match those to hairs found on the deceased. You'd be surprised at what we can do these days."

"Mrs. Croggan would like the body shipped home to Champaign for burial," Lily said. "Do you know when the autopsy might be complete?"

Magruder checked his notes. "She gave us permission to release the body to you," he said. "But the coroner'll need to run tests. With an open investigation, we'll want to keep the body on hand."

Lily cleared her throat. "What tests?"

"That's police business."

"Did the medical examiner confirm how she died?"

"Death by ligature," Pico said. "She was strangled."

"Dear God." Lily closed her eyes and prayed they'd catch Kitty's killer soon so Mrs. Croggan could bury her daughter. "I'll let the mother know."

"She knows," Magruder said.

Lily noticed Pico bending over the ashtray on the vanity table.

"Did Miss Hayden smoke?" He held it up.

"I keep telling you we never met," Lily said. "Her roommates will know."

"You can bet we're going to talk to them," Magruder boomed. "Boarders, neighbors, boyfriends, studio people. Everyone she ever batted an eyelash at. We'll research her life, her troubles, her finances. We'll reconstruct what she did and who she saw the day she disappeared. Maybe she was careless about the company she kept."

Pico was behind her, just out of range of the vanity mirror. The skin along Lily's back rippled. He was watching her. She moved to catch his reflection, but he glided back out of sight.

". . . and if you think of anything after we're gone," Magruder was saying, "pick up the phone." He scribbled the number. "Day or night, someone's there. Now. Do you know if she kept an appointment book? A diary? An address book?"

Lily waved her hand. "You're welcome to check. Did Mrs. Potter tell you that a man from RKO came by a few days ago, asking questions and looking through her room?"

"Clarence Fletcher," Pico said. "We intend to talk to him."

Magruder gave a sudden belch. "Excuse me." He swabbed at his mouth with a handkerchief. "Big lunch today with the Culver City chief of police."

"Culver City," Lily said. "Isn't that where RKO is?"

Where Kitty had worked?

A foxy expression lit up Pico's eyes.

"Yes," Magruder said with a hearty laugh. "And also Metro and Monogram and Vanguard. It's quite a movie town and they've got their hands full with those unruly stars."

He shifted, and she felt suddenly how big and out of scale he looked in Kitty's turret room.

"Especially the ones who date gangsters," Lily said offhandedly.

Magruder was at her side in an instant.

"What have you heard?" he asked in a menacing tone.

She gave him an innocent look. "Weren't

all the actresses crazy for Bugsy Siegel?"

"Bugsy Siegel was shot to death in his Beverly Hills living room two years ago. His killer was never caught. What's that got to do with Kitty Hayden?"

"Maybe she liked the fast life too, and it caught up with her. I'm sure Kitty's roommates can tell you whether she knew any gangsters."

"Thanks for the job tip," Magruder said sourly.

He scowled and flipped open Kitty's portfolio, scrutinizing each photo — modeling jobs and studio stills — the sultry poses in evening gowns, then shorts and a straw hat, bathing-suit cheesecake.

"I hope you interview Mrs. Potter too," Lily said, flashing to the landlady's odd demeanor when they'd met, her suggestion that a room might come available. *As if she knew.*

Magruder guffawed. "Mrs. Potter and the department go way back, Miss Kessler," he said. "As for the girls, I'm gonna sic Pico on 'em. He's got a way with the ladies. They call us Beauty and the Beast, don't they, Pico?"

Detective Pico leaned against the windowsill and crossed his lanky legs in a slow and deliberate fashion. A red flush stained his throat, crept up his jawbone. Something told her it was anger, not embarrassment. She felt a strange desire to goad him, to see the two cops come to blows. She smelled spilled beer, peanuts, rubber mats, blood-lust, the roar of the crowd. She blinked and was back in the room.

"Miss Kessler is too smart to be seduced by the surface of things," Pico said.

Car tires squealed out front. Magruder walked to the window.

"Here come the boys now." He turned to Pico. "Let's meet up at the Boulevard substation. And now, if you'll excuse me, we've got a murderer to catch."

He tipped his hat and slipped out.

With Magruder's departure, the room seemed to expand. Lily hadn't liked the bull-necked detective, found him conde-scending and full of false heartiness. She disliked Pico for different reasons. His ar-rogance, cynicism. But mostly, the unnerv-ing sense she'd gotten, back at the station, that he'd instantly disliked her. Still, she was used to law enforcement types and their games. The jaded older one who didn't take anything seriously and his intense young partner who never lightened up.

"What did your partner mean by that

crack about Mrs. Potter?" Lily asked.

"I'm afraid I can't tell you."

Again that tone that suggested he was throwing down a gauntlet. She walked to the window, watched the LAPD men unload metal boxes out of a van. Pico followed her, shadowing her, mimicking her movements. She wished he wouldn't stand so close.

"I'm sure Kitty's roommates will have some names for you to pursue," Lily said. She wondered how to bring up what she'd overheard in the alley. "Did they mention any boyfriends? Any trouble Kitty might have been in?"

"We already spoke to the redhead." Pico checked his notepad. "Roseanne 'Red' Viertel. She gave us a coupla leads."

"Like what?" Lily was surprised; Red hadn't told her much of anything.

With a tight smile, Pico tucked his notepad away. "What's this, Miss Kessler? Are we playing Twenty Questions?"

Lily's cheeks grew hot. She'd slipped unconsciously into the rhythm. You asking questions, them parrying, you rephrasing, the pressure building until finally they broke and something useful emerged.

But he unsettled her, this long, tall drink of water. And now he was following her around the room, trying to spook her. They learned it in detective school. Well, she knew a few tactics too.

"Just one question, then."

She gave him a tomboy smile that hid more subtle wiles and leaned her ass against the sill. Examined him from downcast lashes.

Use what you've got.

"Have you talked to Max Vranizan?"

Behind Pico's eyes, something clicking into focus. "I thought you only got here yesterday, Miss Kessler. Yet you seem to know an awful lot. What can you tell us about Mr. Vranizan?" he asked, his voice cool and businesslike.

Lily shrugged. "Just that he was a special effects guy who also worked at RKO. He was sweet on Kitty, but she had her sights set higher than a toy maker."

"When did he tell you that?"

"He didn't. The roomies did last night."

Pico's eyes grew razor sharp even as his voice grew more measured. "Red said this Max fellow was obsessed with Kitty."

"That doesn't mean he killed her. He's probably a harmless freak," Lily said, fishing for information. "A grown-up guy who lives in a fantasy world of dinosaurs and apes and monsters. A little kid."

"Little kids can be cunning. I'd stay away

from him. And stay away from RKO too. You're unlikely to get discovered."

So that's what he thought she was after!

She regarded him coolly. "I have no desire to be an actress."

"Then again, if you play your cards right, you might even be able to take over Miss Hayden's contract."

"I would never —"

His eyes crinkled. "Of course not. That's why you showed up here as soon as you heard, then moved right into Kitty Hayden's room and into her life."

Lily uncoiled herself, stretched to her full height, but still barely saw over his shoulder.

"You know nothing about me. I'm hardly some starstruck ingénue. I grew up in L.A. And I'm staying here because Kitty's mother asked me to find her daughter."

Pico rolled his eyes. "Then you're free to go. The professionals will take over."

"Don't tell me what to do."

She was irked that he'd riled her so easily. "I hope you display a better bedside manner when you talk to Kitty's roommates or you won't get very far."

A wicked light danced in his eyes. "I've never had any complaints about my bedside manner. In fact . . ."

"Then let me be the first," she said, ignoring the innuendo.

He shook his head. "You don't give up, do you? Anybody ever tell you that you have a masculine brain?"

"Now you're insulting me?"

"Far from it." The idea seemed to entertain him.

"Maybe I just have a criminal brain," Lily said.

"Oh?"

"You want to catch a murderer, you have to think like one. That's all."

The amusement faded from his eyes. "That's exactly why they'll never let women on the force," he said.

"What's why?" she asked.

"Because if you want to catch rats, you've got to swim in the sewer, and that's no job for a girl. You'd lose your sense of wonder and goodness about the world, and we can't have that."

Lily's mouth twitched. "Save it, Detective. We're not helpless simpering creatures that have to be protected. We've held down jobs, traveled the world. Seen people die. Nobody's innocent anymore."

"The war's been over four years. Things are going back to how they were."

Lily thought of the CIA, reassigning its women agents to desk jobs. Her bosses had claimed their Soviet contacts felt more comfortable handing over secrets to men. That the female temperament was unsuited to surveillance, interrogation, high-stakes dissembling. That women were ruled by their emotions, while espionage required cool, hard reason. No matter what successful female spy Lily brought up, they had an answer: Virginia Hill was an exception; Christine Granville had gotten lucky; Amy Thorpe traded intelligence for sex. Lily's gorge rose at being lectured by yet another man in authority.

"Not everyone wants to go back to how things were."

"Sure they do. People are settling down, having families. It's the American way."

The taunting tone was back. *You want it too,* his voice seemed to say. *Just admit it.*

"I guess I'm un-American, then."

Pico clicked his tongue. "I'd watch where you say that. You said you've been gone since 1944. Well, things have changed at home."

"I didn't mean I was a Red," Lily said frostily. "I mean I want to be able to work and live on my own and walk home from the trolley stop at night without looking over my shoulder. That's why Kitty's murder terrifies me and every woman in L.A. It could have been any of us."

Pico looked ready to argue. But just then the LAPD Crime Lab squad arrived at the door — four men who carried metal tool-boxes and cameras.

"I'll be in the kitchen if you need to ask me any more questions," she said, slipping past them into the doorway.

"I think we're through, Miss Kessler."

And good riddance.

But they weren't through. An hour later, Pico appeared downstairs. Jinx, who'd been recounting a story about how Kitty had once loaned her an expensive dress for an audition, trailed off. A crackling tension and flirtatiousness seeped into the kitchen, chasing away the worst of the gloom.

"Coffee, Detective?" Red swished over with the pot, her hips approaching a rolling boil.

"Just what I needed, thank you." Pico sat down.

"Sugar and cream?" She bent over the table, cleavage popping.

"This is wonderful." Pico beamed at the young women arrayed around him like petals of a flower. Lily wondered if he meant to pluck them, one by one.

A new girl walked into the kitchen. She

was about Lily's height and weight, with brown hair in a similar cut, but her features were more angular, her posture straighter, her demeanor brisk, reminding Lily of a female pilot she'd known during the war.

"You must be Louise Dobbs," Lily said, going up to her.

"Yes," the girl said. Her eyes were bloodshot and swollen. "And I'm so sorry. When I sent the cable, I never imagined . . . maybe if I'd done it sooner . . . ?"

Lily squeezed her hand and was about to respond when Pico broke in.

"It wouldn't have made a difference, Miss Dobbs. She'd been dead several days by the time . . . Hey, now, hey, now," he said with embarrassment as the girls launched into wordless snuffles and tears.

Jinx was the first to recover. She propped her trembling chin in one hand. "Tell us, Detective, do you have any idea who killed her?"

Pico leaned back. "Well, now, the LAPD always has leads."

God, he was too much, Lily thought. And Kitty's roommates, veering from coy flirtation to tragic swooning and back in the blink of a mascaraed eye, as if this were some kind of audition. But maybe it was at that. A *husband* audition.

110

Fumiko, busy at the stove, was the only one who didn't join in.

Red pulled her hair back with one hand, cupping her temple Greta Garbo–style. Lily could have sworn her voice had dropped an octave. "Detective Pico," she asked in a sultry voice, "do you always get your man?"

"I always get my woman too," Pico said. "We can't assume anything at this stage."

Pico took a sip of coffee, sighed with appreciation. "You make a fine cup of joe, Miss Viertel," he told Red.

"Do you want to brief us on what you've got so far?" Jinx asked, eager to reclaim center stage.

"Since you asked so politely," he said with an arch look at Lily, "all right. But first, I'd like to know. Did Kitty keep a journal? Or a calendar? How about a phone book?"

Jeanne, hands fluttering with her hair, said she'd walked into Kitty's room to borrow a sweater once and seen her writing in a white leather journal.

Pico frowned. "We didn't find anything like that."

"Wouldn't she keep her calendar and phone book in her purse?" Beverly asked haltingly.

"There was no purse found with the, ah, Miss Hayden," Pico said.

Lily cleared her throat. "What about the RKO man? Could he have taken it?"

Annoyed, Pico jotted in his notebook. "I certainly hope not."

The detective now told them that Kitty had been seen dancing in Palm Springs nightspots two weeks earlier with known associates of gangster Mickey Cohen. Lily flashed immediately to the small man who'd administered the brutal beating. Was he one of them? No wonder Magruder had lit up when she'd mentioned gangsters.

At Cohen's name, Beverly gave a small moan. The detective turned to her.

"What can you tell us about that?" he asked sharply.

"I don't know anything about gangsters," Beverly said. "She told us she went there with a girlfriend."

"Ah," Pico said. "What was her name?"

Lily watched the girls ripple uneasily under the detective's gaze. She felt the swirl and eddy of conflicted allegiances. The OSS had taught her to listen and observe, to be patient. Kitty's roommates were afraid of something. They hadn't told the detective everything they knew. From the way Pico's thumb and forefinger tightened almost imperceptibly against his pen, Lily knew he sensed it too.

"Kitty never told us her name," Red said, looking around the room, as if defying anyone to contradict her.

Pico raised one eyebrow.

"Do you think there's any connection to Mimi Boomhower?" asked Louise, practical once more.

"Who?" said Lily.

"Mimi was a Bel Air socialite and widow who disappeared several months ago," Pico explained. "Left her front door open and her lights burning. No one's seen her since. And no body's turned up." He grimaced. "Unlike your roommate.

"Now," he said, surveying the solemn faces, "I'd like to question each of you separately. And I want you to answer me as thoroughly as you can, thinking hard to dredge up every tiny detail you can remember, because it might be that one insignificant thing that helps us catch her killer."

"She was such a dear," said Beverly with a sniffle. "If she caught a fly she'd release it outside. Some of the memories I've got, they're almost too painful to recount."

Pico's smile grew wider, his voice more expansive. "Well, take a couple aspirin for the pain and try, or I might think you're withholding evidence."

At his words, Fumiko, who was peeling

and chopping a gnarled brown root on a cutting board, cursed under her breath and popped a finger in her mouth.

"Sorry," she said. "I cut myself."

While Pico interviewed Kitty's roommates, Lily went for a brisk walk to clear her head. As she slipped out, several men clutching notepads and cameras scurried toward her.

"Miss, were you a roommate of Kitty Hayden? Can you tell us about her boyfriends? What was she like?"

The questions came fast and furious, a barrage of words, the cameras exploding in front of her. Holding up her purse to block her face, Lily made her way down the street, but they followed her like a moving organism. Most persistent of all was a young blonde with coral lipstick and a matching jacket. At least she didn't have a camera, just a notepad. The woman's heels clicked conspiratorially as she whispered questions to Lily just out of reach of the men, appealing to their shared bond as young women. Lily put her head down and kept walking.

Undeterred, the reporter trailed after her.

"I'm with *Confidential* magazine, miss, and I've been authorized to offer you a onetime payment in exchange for an interview. Perhaps we could go somewhere private" —

114

a meaningful look back to the men five paces behind them — "where we can —"

"Please stop," Lily said. "I don't want to talk to the press."

Lily saw face powder dusting faint hairs on the reporter's upper lip. The woman smiled, exposing small milky teeth. Reaching into a pocket, she pulled out a bill, snapping it crisply.

Despite herself, Lily looked. It was a hundred-dollar bill.

"I thought so," the woman said with a laugh.

Lily slapped the bill from the woman's hand. "*That's* what I think of your foul offer."

As she ran off, the woman called out, "Violet McCree at *Confidential.* Call anytime, twenty-four hours a day, the service will find me."

CHAPTER 8

Detective Pico left the boardinghouse with only a pounding headache to show for two hours of questioning. Make that thirty minutes of questions and an hour and a half of leg-crossing, eyelash-batting, and moist actressy snuffling into tissues. He shook his head. And that annoying Kessler girl. She was sharp, and not afraid to show it. Pico knew a lot of men didn't like brainy gals. He didn't mind, especially when it came in a package like that.

The girls and Mrs. Potter swore Kitty had no enemies or vices. She worked long hours and dated a lot but had no one steady. There were no jilted lovers either, but Pico was keen to interview that special effects whiz Max Vranizan. The girls had also mentioned a thuggish fellow at Sinatra's rehearsal who'd flirted with Kitty and claimed the starlet had stood up his friend, but they didn't know his name. He'd have to bring over some mug shots for them to look at.

Pico resented Magruder for leaving him to conduct the interviews alone, especially on his first homicide case. Maybe the veteran cop didn't realize it, but Pico had paid his dues, first with five years as a beat cop attached to the Seventy-seventh Street Division, then two as a detective in Central Robbery. Now he itched to find Kitty's killer quickly and establish a reputation as a straight shooter. But he'd already learned that any serious police work he and Magruder did would be shoehorned between restaurant meals, drinking sessions, and visits to stores with small back rooms where his new partner placed bets several times a day.

Magruder was a perfect example of why Angelenos didn't trust the police. Drinking on duty, leering at everything in skirts, the never-ending vicecapades. Just like the brass. The papers had been full of stories all summer, how the grand jury had indicted LAPD Chief C. B. Horrall and Deputy Chief Joseph Reed and charged a slew of others with perjury. Then there was Hollywood Vice, a gravy train with half the squad on the take and openings so rare that twenty-six officers had vied for the job when his father retired in September after thirty-five years. The thought of his father made his head throb more painfully. Pico had fantasized about how he'd come home from vanquishing Nazis in Ardennes, France, with the Forty-fifth Infantry Division and tackle evils closer to home. He hadn't realized how entrenched things were and how easy it was to slip into it. A few drinks here. A meal there when you were short. The sense, conveyed with hand gestures, winks, and offers everywhere a cop went in Los Angeles, that the spoils were there for the taking.

At the Boulevard, Pico turned right and soon came to a bar called the Firefly. Boulevard substation! Ha, that was a good one. Inside the swampy light of the room, Pico spied Magruder sipping something blond and creamy from a highball glass. The older cop waved him over and Pico slid onto the adjoining stool. Magruder's drink had yellow flecks in it. Some kind of fruit. All those GIs coming home from the South Pacific and decorating their houses with tikis and mixing up tropical drinks. Just went to show you how selective memory could be.

Magruder stubbed out his cigarette, pushed aside his racing form. "What'll you have?"

"What have you got?"

"Buttermilk." Magruder rubbed his belly. "Coats the stomach. Always my first drink of the day."

Pico made a face. "Brew 102," he told the barman.

As they drank, he recounted what he had learned at the rooming house and described his suspicions about the animator. Magruder agreed that Pico should talk to him.

"Reckon I'll head out to Palm Springs," the older cop said. "Work my gang sources."

Pico could imagine the debauch as Magruder toured the nightspots.

"I want you to work the L.A. angle," Magruder continued. "Find Mickey's people, see what they say. And pay a visit to that wop Dragna, who everyone says is trying to kill Mickey. Nighttimes he's at his club, Largo. Daytime try his restaurant on Westwood Boulevard. Vernichello's."

Pico nodded, glad for the marching orders. If he broke the case on his own, he'd make sure everybody knew it. He ran one last thing past Magruder.

"The body boys said they found some unusual hairs on the vic's clothing and possibly under her fingernails."

Magruder looked thoughtful. "Dog hair.

Cat. Could tell us something."

"They don't think it's dog or cat. I told 'em to send it to the lab."

Magruder raised an eyebrow. "Coyote, then. That happens when a body stays in the hills too long."

"It wasn't coyote either. Or mountain lion. It was black."

"We'll wait and see, then. Maybe it's nothing."

Pico wondered why his partner was so quick to dismiss this potential evidence. Magruder smoked and contemplated the wall.

"You're a good-looking fellow," the older cop said after a pause. "A man doesn't usually comment on another man's looks unless he's a fruit, but I saw those dames making cow eyes at you. You can use that. Someone in that henhouse knows more than they're saying and I'll bet it's that stuck-up one who ID'd the body. Work things right, she'll be eating out of your hand."

"What if I don't want her eating out of my hand?"

The older detective gave a worldly laugh. "That too. Little on-duty action never hurt anyone. Some of us get all our action at work."

Magruder gave his pants a hitch. "Why don't you tail her when you get a chance? See what she's up to."

He winked, avuncular now. *This is how it's done, old son. Watch and learn.* Pico wondered if the older cop saw him as the son he'd never had. He recalled something about a child, but as far as he knew, Magruder lived alone, full of coppish swagger and rough lessons, glorying in the camaraderie of the badge, the closed clubhouse air of it, no girls allowed, forever rumbling with lewd innuendo and hoary wisdom. He wrapped himself in the fug of cracked leather, oiled weapons, Cuban cigars, distilled liquors, and strong cologne. A man's man.

"It's a hard town," Magruder was saying, "and I'd hate for that li'l gal to get hurt. In fact, I'd rather . . ." He chuckled. "Stuck-up dames like that need a good pounding. Under all the priss, they're just asking for it. Every damn one of them."

"She didn't strike me as particularly prissy," Pico said.

"It's all a front. Believe you me. When you've been around as long as I have . . ."

And Magruder proceeded to lecture Pico on what women really wanted. Then he asked how Pico's father was enjoying his retirement. "I hear he was flush there for a while," Magruder said.

Pico had heard the same thing. There had been elaborate dinners, trips to Catalina, visits to Big Bear. But the lucky streaks never lasted.

"I wish they'd stop taking him to the track."

"There are those who like to have him beholden," Magruder said. "And you as well."

"You know I don't play the ponies."

"There are many ways to be beholden, Stephen. You'll find that one hand washes the other. It's about loyalty. Respect. Your pa understood that."

"They knew he couldn't say no, and they took advantage of it."

"Your father's a grown man, Stephen. No one forced him to do anything."

"He has a sickness."

"And now he must pay." Magruder's voice had gone quiet and whispery. "And if the father cannot pay, they turn to the son to make them whole. They are reasonable people, Stephen. They don't want money. There are things more valuable."

"Like what?"

"When the time comes, you will know it."

Magruder slid his bulk off his stool. "All

this talk has got my blood up. Let's go roust Olga," he said.

"Who's Olga?"

"Surprised your old man never took you around. You're gonna love Olga."

The alcohol glow made Pico feel he was sliding through glass as he drove, the colors bright and electric. Beside him, Magruder stirred.

"Those actresses probably had you pegged as a Latin lover, that olive skin of yours," he said. "You're part Mex, ain't you, Pico? Name like that?"

Pico felt the alcohol warmth ebbing away. He'd noticed he was "Stephen" when Magruder felt friendly and "Pico" when he didn't.

"You know my family's been here a long time."

"A breed, even. Your white great-grandpappy found him a squaw?"

"We were already on the *rancho* when your ancestors were grubbing for rotten potatoes in Ireland."

Magruder shot him a dirty look. "Maybe so, but we were God-fearing people. We didn't go in for fornicating with the natives."

"I hear you fornicate with them plenty today."

Magruder guffawed. "I'm partial to the native *blonde*."

They drove in silence. Then Magruder said, "Pico Boulevard. That named after your people?"

Pico stared out the window. His mouth twitched. "Naw," he said "I don't think so."

Following Magruder's directions, he turned south on Vine and parked in front of one of the fancy buildings with several floors.

As they walked up the front steps, Pico heard a jazzy piano tune inside. A man stepped onto the landing.

"How ya doing, Detectives?" he said in a nasal twang, coins jingling in his pocket.

Pico wondered if he had purposely lingered on the last word.

"Haven't I warned you, Henry, about addressing us in that manner?" Magruder's voice was so low that Pico strained to catch it. "We don't need to advertise it."

Henry's upper lip curled. "Sorry, Detective. Just remember, you want rough stuff, go over to Hattie's. We don't do that here."

Magruder caught the bouncer by his bow tie, shoving him against the wall so hard that Pico heard his head crack. Grabbing the man's neck, Magruder squeezed.

Henry made spluttering, choking sounds,

124

his face turning purple as he tried to pry Magruder's meaty hands from his windpipe. The cop's eyes were wide, his jaw working.

Pico tried to pull him off, but it was like trying to move a mountain.

"Magruder," he yelled. "Let the fuck go."

Slowly, the older cop's fingers loosened. The bouncer fell to his knees, gasping for air. Magruder stared down dispassionately.

The door was opened by a uniformed maid with café au lait skin and a welcoming smile. They stepped over the still-writhing body and went inside.

CHAPTER 9

Lily gaped at her bedroom in dismay. Every drawer had been pulled out, its contents dumped. The trash can was missing. A residue of powder coated many surfaces. The contents of the closet lay strewn across the bed.

Red, who'd offered to help, was busily placing hats and shoes back into their proper boxes. Lily saw piles of clothes — formal gowns, suits, frocks gauzy and light as a summer breeze, dungarees, and checkered shirts. There were also homespun dresses of modest cut and a heavy overcoat made for Midwest winters, clothes from a former life that Kitty had shed upon arrival as casually as her name.

There was no sign of Mighty Joe Young; the officers must have taken it.

They heard a rap at the door.

"Come in," Red said absentmindedly.

In walked Jeanne. Behind her stood a man

in a brown suit, clutching a hat. He was about forty, with a receding hairline, a large toffee-colored nose, and a bobbing Adam's apple. He craned his neck like a large, cautious bird. His pale, watery gaze slid across the room's wreckage as if memorizing each detail.

"Who are you?" Lily blurted out.

"This is Freddy Taunton," Red said, introducing them. "For goodness' sakes, Freddy, don't just stand there like a startled goose, come in."

The man obliged, his eyes still moving like minesweepers.

"Freddy's originally from England," Jeanne explained. "He came here to write scripts for the studios. Kitty was his muse, so he's quite shaken up."

"His muse?" Lily's eyebrows arched.

"An exquisite young woman," Freddy said in a cockney accent. "We are all devastated."

"Poor Freddy, how will you be able to finish your script now?" Jeanne asked mournfully.

"We must soldier on," Freddy said. His gaze lingered at Lily's sable-trimmed coat, now slung across a chair. "I don't suppose you've seen a black and gold silk scarf? I, ah, loaned it to Kitty last time I saw her. She'd complained of a draft, so I did the gallant thing."

How could this man bring up his stupid scarf right now? Lily wondered. Especially when Kitty had been strangled. An image came to her of a silk noose tightening around a pale neck and Lily took an immediate and violent dislike to Freddy. She'd long counted on these intuitive feelings to guide her. In Rome, she'd once handpicked German POW volunteers to infiltrate back across Nazi lines to spread rumors and scatter propaganda pamphlets. All sixteen had returned, some with coordinates of camouflaged tanks for the Allies to bomb. Now without being obvious, she began to study Freddy more closely.

"Have a look," Red said. "We're not sure what the detectives took."

"Ah, yes, I saw one of them leaving," Freddy said. "An unmarked car, was it? Did they take her journal?"

"How do you know she kept a journal?" Lily asked.

Freddy gave her a patronizing look. "Don't all young ladies confide their most fervent hopes and dreams in journals?"

"Freddy's got a scene in his new script," Jeanne interjected, "where a man reads the diary of a girl he's secretly in love with and believes she's writing about her passion for

128

him. When he finds out she loves someone else, he's so devastated that —"

"Save it," Red said. "Lily's not interested."

"Sure I am." Lily gazed earnestly at Freddy Taunton. "What does he do?"

"Well, I . . ."

"It's soooo tragic," Jeanne said. "He lures his rival to a meeting to kill him, but the girl intercepts the letter and goes in his place because she suspects her lover's cheating on her. The lovesick guy ends up killing the girl by mistake."

"Fascinating," Lily said, watching Freddy Taunton turn five shades of red. A vein near his temple began to pulse.

"Isn't he a genius?" said Jeanne, her large green eyes glowing. "He's also minor nobility." Freddy began to object. "It's okay, Lily won't tell anyone. Freddy's family has estates all over, but he doesn't want any part of that world. He wants to succeed in Hollywood on his talent, not his title."

Lily had met plenty of upper-crust Brits. *If he's a titled English gent, I'm a Rockefeller,* she thought.

"When's the last time you saw Kitty Hayden, Mr. Taunton?" she asked.

"Hrrm, it was . . ." Freddy scratched his chin vigorously, "last week. We had cocktails at the Formosa."

"Do you know anyone who might have had any reason to kill her?" Lily asked.

"Why, no, young lady. I certainly didn't."

"Didn't what?"

"Kill her."

Lily was silent. Why had he jumped to the defensive so quickly? "I'm sure the police will be around soon to interview you."

"Yes," murmured Freddy. "Do they have any leads yet? Suspects?" He licked his lips.

"They're looking at gangsters," Jeanne said.

"Might be something to that," Freddy said, nodding too emphatically. "Our Kitty liked flash and a bit of danger, found it glamorous. Told me as much."

Red came over, crossed her arms. "What else did she tell you, Freddy?"

"Oh, that's about it. We were just talking hypothetically." His pale cold fish eyes swam over them. "Or at least I was."

He fingered the brim of his hat. "I hope they catch him. A real pity. Lovely girl, just lovely. Everything to live for."

He clucked a few more platitudes, then wandered to the window and looked both ways.

"I really must be going. A friend's invited me to go deep-sea fishing, and we leave San Pedro at midnight."

Lily waited until she heard the front door shut. "How well do you know that fellow?" she asked.

"Jeanne and Kitty met him last year," Red said. "He took quite a shine to Kitty. He based several of his heroines on her. I think she was flattered."

"I would have been flattered," said Jeanne fervently.

"What pictures did he write?"

"He hasn't actually *sold* any of them yet."

"Ah."

"He says true genius is rarely rewarded," Jeanne continued. "But he's absolutely devoted to his art. Once he tied me to a chair and gagged me and took notes while I tried to break free."

"Good God, Jeanne," said Red, "you never told me he's a pervert!"

"You have a filthy mind, Red. It wasn't any kink. I gave him permission. He was writing a scene about an abducted girl and wanted to make it as realistic as possible."

"You poor sap, and you believed him?"

"Kitty did too." Jeanne pouted. "He gave us money for 'modeling' when he had any. His family is very stingy with him. It was fun, like method acting. And when he read us the scenes, well, they were magnificent."

"What a load of hogwash," said Red.

131

"Lily, I had no idea what they'd been up to with him. Jeanne, did you tell Detective Pico about this?"

Jeanne blinked. "I didn't think it was relevant."

"You didn't think . . ." Red threw up her hands.

"Kitty and I both posed for those pictures, and I'm still alive, so it can't be Freddy," Jeanne said. "Besides, he's an aristocrat, he wouldn't be capable of —"

"I hate to break it to you, girls," Lily said, "but I've lived in England and Freddy Taunton is no more a British aristocrat than I am."

She explained about posh accents and added, "So if he's lied about that, what else is he concealing?"

Had Freddy gotten carried away while doing "research" on Kitty, then panicked and dumped the body?

Lily asked where Freddy lived.

"The Radcliffe Arms, near Santa Monica and Western. Sixteen fifty-seven Radcliffe. He's in Apartment E."

As Red marched Jeanne downstairs to inform the police about Freddy's "photo shoots," Lily decided she wanted to look through his apartment. If he was really leaving on a fishing trip, that wouldn't prove

132

too difficult. She'd wait a few hours, then set off. But if he was lying . . .

Lily picked the last of Kitty's sundresses off the floor and noticed a strained seam. Just then Red returned, saying they'd left a message for the detectives.

"Didn't Kitty have nice clothes?" Red asked. "Here, let me help you with that."

She tugged the dress out of Lily's hands. "Why don't you take a rest, I'll finish up."

Lily walked to the upholstered chair by the window and sat down. Across the street, the mottled trunk of a western sycamore glowed silver in the moonlight.

"Red, you've told me about Max, and now there's this Freddy, but did Kitty have any serious boyfriends? Someone she might have kept secret? A gangster, maybe?"

"Kitty, serious?" Red tittered and put a hand to her mouth, not very convincingly. "Kitty was a gal who liked to keep her options open."

"Red," Lily persisted, "was Kitty seeing anyone regularly?"

Red inhaled sharply. "Sometimes she acted as if she was suffering through a bad love affair . . ."

"Do you know his name?"

Red pouted. "No. But as I told that Detective Pico, whatever was troubling her seemed to fall away a few weeks ago. Like she'd made up her mind about something. 'I've had a hard time of it lately, Reddy,' she said one morning, just the two of us in the kitchen, 'but everything's going to be okay.' Then she squeezed my hand. Some of the girls here, they resented her, they thought she put on airs, but not me. I was probably her best friend, though Beverly thinks she was."

"She never told you any details?"

Red reared back, insulted. "I didn't ask. She was very private. So am I. And now I've really got to —" She opened the door and took a quick breath. Fumiko stood in the hallway, her ear to the door, a guilty look on her face.

"You were eavesdropping," Red accused.

"I didn't mean to. I was walking to my room when I heard you. You shouldn't repeat what Kitty confided in you," she told Red. Regaining her poise, she turned to Lily. "Why are you stirring up trouble? It's none of your business."

Lily was taken aback. "I'm just trying to —"

"Why don't you just go back where you came from?" Fumiko said angrily. "Stop asking questions or the same thing might happen to you."

Fumiko stalked off, her gauzy red robe flapping behind her, and Lily saw her in a new light. Of all the aspiring actresses here, she might be the most ambitious, and the most thwarted. Lily wondered if there was bad blood between Kitty and Fumiko. Her description to Mrs. Croggan of the rooming house as one big happy theatrical family with Mrs. Potter presiding over everything like a plump motherly hen was unraveling into Hollywood fantasy.

Red drifted to the vanity table, picked up an emery board, and began buffing her nails. The scratchy sound made Lily's skin crawl.

"Did she just threaten me?" Lily asked.

Red gave her a guarded look. "She's upset, that's all."

"Did Fumiko and Kitty have a falling out? Over a boyfriend, or an acting job?"

"She did lose a minor role to Kitty a few months back, but I told her she wouldn't have been cast anyway. They were looking for a white girl."

"Maybe that just made her resent Kitty all the more?"

Lily's mind began to consider new possibilities. Fumiko wasn't physically capable of strangling her roommate, but what if she'd had an accomplice? Jealousy was a

135

perfectly viable motive for murder.

"Oh, pshaw," said Red, reading her mind. "Fumiko's just being dramatic. She wouldn't hurt a flea."

"Then why did she warn me off?"

"She was probably just humiliated that we caught her listening."

"Then why didn't she get mad at you?"

"Because, darling" — Red preened — "I am her friend."

Lily sighed. Red could be so aggravating. "So back to Kitty. What did you tell Detective Pico about that gangster who supposedly flirted with her? Could she have been dating one of Mickey Cohen's men?"

A frightened look crossed the girl's face. The nail file ripped across her nail and she gave a cry of pain. "Ooh, I just can't bear it. Poor Kitty," Red said, and ran out the door.

Lily bent down and picked up Kitty's emery board. She laid it on a lace doily atop the vanity table. A drop of crimson blood seeped into the white linen, leaving a ragged stain.

CHAPTER 10

Several miles away, Florence Kwitney waited for the Wilshire bus after a night with her girlfriends. She looked forward to these monthly outings. She and the gals treated themselves to a restaurant, had a few drinks, and reminisced about the war. They'd met on the assembly line at Hughes Aircraft in Playa del Rey, but aviation and shipbuilding had foundered after V-Day and they'd lost their jobs like thousands of others and scattered to the four winds. Before Florence knew it, the evening had gone. And now it was near midnight and the bus wasn't coming. Florence was a little tipsy. No. She should be honest with herself. She was drunk. She'd been drinking too much lately. She meant to stop, but the days just slid into one another, and each sunset her resolve slipped away with the light and she unscrewed the cap on the bottle of rye. She'd had a few nips before leaving home, then drinks with dinner. Florence decided she'd better duck inside the coffee shop by the bus stop and have some coffee. She wanted to keep her wits about her. She'd keep a look out the window, and if the bus came, she'd drop her coin on the counter and run for it.

The coffee shop was full of large groups and Florence felt a stab of resentment at the happy couples. She and Tom would have been married by now, except that Tom hadn't made it back from the South Pacific. After that, her life had never quite caught fire the way she'd expected. Florence sat at the counter. It was dark outside, fog creeping in, and she strained to see the big lights that would signal the bus's approach. The waitress brought the bill with the coffee, which was weak and tasteless, like the grounds had been run through twice. Halfway through it, she saw lights, tossed down a coin, and ran out, only to find a truck heading toward her instead of the bus. Her shoulders sagged. Florence looked inside and saw a busboy sweep her cup into a bin. So much for a refill.

"Waiting for someone, miss?" a pleasant voice said.

Florence turned and saw a man. He reminded her so much of Tom she almost cried out. And then she must have done so, because the man gave a queer smile.

"How did you guess my name is Tom?"

"You remind me of someone," Florence said, embarrassed.

"Were you going in?" he said, inclining his head toward the coffee shop.

"Why, yes. No." A beam of yellow light washed over them and she realized the man didn't look like Tom after all. "I — I don't know," she stuttered. A bus was coming. She ran to the bench, but it drove past and she saw a NOT IN SERVICE sign in the front windshield.

"Are you all right, miss?" the man asked. "May I be of assistance?"

She gripped her purse. She had to get home. Everything was spinning around her. She missed Tom so much, even four years on, that it was like a physical ache inside of her. She wanted to sink to her knees, bang her head against the cool tiles of her bathroom floor. She knew she couldn't go back inside the bright lights now. Everyone would see her tear-stained face.

"I'm fine," she struggled to say. "I'm just waiting for the bus home." She plopped down on the bench, tucking in her skirts.

"And I remind you of someone?" he probed.

"My fiancé. He died at Subic Bay."

The man hiked up his trousers and sat down. She thought she heard the jingle of keys. He offered her a cigarette and, when she declined, lit one for himself. She noticed that he had an interesting signet ring on his left middle finger, but no gold band. A girl noticed things like that.

"I'm an actor," he said with nonchalance, as tattered wisps of fog crept east along the Boulevard and enveloped them. She saw the red cherry of his cigarette rise and fall. "People often say I look like their uncle, their cousin, their neighbor, a guy they knew in the service. I guess I have one of those rubbery actor faces." He gave a little laugh. "Looks like we're waiting for the same bus. Why don't you tell me all about him, and it'll be here before we know it."

At twelve-thirty a.m., Lily stood at Santa Monica Boulevard and Radcliffe, dressed in a black shirt, black pants, and the woven canvas shoes worn by Italian peasants. She'd found the Radcliffe Arms without much trouble. It was a fancy name for a shabby building. Three stories of faded red brick, no doorman, only an overflowing brass spittoon.

She guessed that Apartment E was on the

ground floor, in the back. Doing a reconnaissance, she saw that one of the rear units was dark. A thin woman carrying a baby moved past the window of the other unit. Lily entered the lobby and found the mailboxes. Located Freddy's name next to APT E. Cautiously she tiptoed down the hallway to make sure that she had the right apartment. Yup, it was the dark one in back. She'd gotten his number from Jeanne and called from the corner liquor store, ready to hang up if he answered. But the phone rang and rang. And the Rambler Jeanne said he drove was nowhere in sight. Lily tried the doorknob, careful to make no sound. It was locked.

Lily slipped out of the Radcliffe Arms and walked down the driveway to the rear apartment, glad that the baby's cries drowned out a dog barking next door. She tried Freddy's windows, but they were locked too.

Back on the sidewalk, Lily sprayed on Je Reviens and freshened her makeup. Then she reentered the lobby and knocked on the manager's door.

"I'm sorry to bother you," she told the heavyset man who answered, wearing an undershirt and smelling of beer. "Mr. Taunton was expecting me at ten to go over a script, and I got held up. He must have stepped out. Do you think you might let me in to wait? A girl doesn't like to walk around by herself in the dark, men could get the wrong idea."

Lily gave the man her most innocent, persuasive smile and held out a bottle of gin she'd picked up. "For your troubles, sir," she added.

The man looked at her, his hand closed around the bottle.

"Who is it, Mel?" came a harsh female voice.

"Just another actress for Taunton, but he ain't here." Mel scratched his belly and leered. "Jeez, I must be in the wrong business."

"Tell the little tart to go away," came the woman's voice.

"She brought us something for our troubles, Mother," Mel said.

There was a shuffling and a florid-faced woman peered out from behind the man's meaty shoulder.

She saw the gin and shrugged. "Go ahead and let her in. This dump don't pay us enough to be the morality police."

The manager pulled a large ring of keys out of his pocket and lumbered down the hall, the woman standing watch, hands on her hips, for which Lily was grateful. He unlocked Apartment E, calling out, "Mr. Taunton, are you there?" Lily thought she could always make some excuse if Freddy appeared, but the apartment was still, dark, and silent.

The manager flicked on the light and made his way back to his own apartment. Lily slipped inside, locked the door, and sighed in relief. Freddy Taunton lived in a one-bedroom apartment and took his meals in a brown-paneled kitchenette, the sink piled high with dirty dishes. The place smelled of pipe smoke and old grease. Somewhere nearby, a fly buzzed.

First things first: Lily hastened to the living room window, threw up the sash window, and opened the screen. *Always leave yourself an escape hatch.* Even as her heart pounded, she felt her brain click into sharper focus, sensed dormant skills stirring.

Even if he came back unexpectedly, Taunton would have to unlock the door. Right, Lily thought, grabbing a chair from the kitchenette and propping it under the knob.

Lily moved through the apartment quickly. In the bedroom closet, she found a length of rope and, wrapped in a sheepskin, an ugly bowie knife. Lily held the knife to the light, looking for bloodstains, but it was clean as a marine latrine awaiting inspection. Kitty had been strangled, not stabbed. Still, why did a guy need a knife like that? A knife made to eviscerate a deer in the wilderness.

Lily worked her way methodically through the apartment, finding little of interest. She stopped at the kitchen table where the Remington portable sat, a half-typed page in the carriage. Lily leaned over the typewriter and read:

He stands, the knife clutched and suspended in midair. On the cold ground, the girl squirms and begs. Her dress is torn. "No, please, no. I'll do whatever you say."

(It is winter in California, the trees are bare of leaves. Only the light of the moon illuminates her terrified face. Her attacker wears a mask. His voice is muffled.)

So darling Freddy fantasized about hurting women. Shuddering, Lily glanced around. The wastebasket was filled with balled sheets of paper. Lily uncrumpled a page. It said virtually the same thing. She tried several more and gave a harsh laugh.

Freddy Taunton was blocked. He didn't know what happened next. Or maybe he did, but couldn't bring himself to write the murder itself.

Lily straightened. The rope and knife had been stashed in the bedroom closet. Lily decided to make one more sweep through there. At the door, she squatted, then lay completely flat, one cheek on the carpet. It stank of sweaty socks. Seeing a slight rise in the material, she ran her hand along it. Sure enough. Grasping the farthest corner between her nails, Lily tugged. A triangle of carpet peeled back in her hand. She tugged some more. It was loose, not nailed down. Underneath lay an envelope. She removed it and slid out some photos. And stared.

There was Kitty, tied to a chair and gagged just as Jeanne had described. Except Kitty's clothes were in disarray, her brassiere exposed, her dress pushed up. And she was bleeding. There were six photos, each slightly different, of Kitty writhing, her mouth contorted in a scream, as she stared at a large knife on the floor beside her.

Feeling nauseous, Lily ran to the living room lamp, desperate to know if they were real. Blood ran down Kitty's clothes and legs, but she didn't see any wounds. It

145

looked like someone had splattered Kitty with red paint. Lily examined the girl's pupils, brows, the muscles around her mouth. Her lips were parted in an O. But her eyes were fixed, watchful. As if she weren't really scared. *As if she were acting.*

Calm down, Lily told herself. Kitty had been found in a suit, not a dress, and she hadn't been drenched in blood. This wasn't documentation of Kitty's murder. But why would she subject herself to this? Lily decided to bring the photos to that smug Detective Pico, let him figure it out. But Taunton couldn't learn that she'd been here, or he might bolt before they could arrest him.

Lily's skin itched. Every instinct she had screamed at her to get the hell out right now. She really, really didn't want to go back into that bedroom. But she knew she should take only one photo and leave the others, so Taunton would see the envelope safe and sound if he checked.

She was crouched in the closet, sliding the envelope back under the carpet, when she heard the noise she'd been dreading — a key entering a metal lock. Jumping up, clutching her one photo, she ran out of the bedroom, making for the window. The lock had given way and Taunton was

146

rattling the door, trying to dislodge the chair. Lily heard swearing, then a thump as he threw his shoulder against the door. The chair moved.

Lily sprinted. *Please just let me get out the window before he gets inside,* she thought.

The chair screeched, then splintered as the back came off. The door flew open. A large figure stumbled inside, the stink of beer and gin wafting in with him.

In her fear, Lily's hands grew moist and the photo slipped from her hand. She hesitated, torn between picking it up and making for her escape hatch. It was enough.

"What do you think you're doing?" a voice said. Not Taunton. The manager.

Lily reached the window. With a great roar, the manager was across the room. "You lying little whore, I'm going to give you what you deserve, then you'll know what a real man —"

His fingers grabbed her blouse as she dove, arms extended, legs kicking, through the window. Lily heard material tear, felt her heel slam into something as she flew through the air. Then the bellow, as if of an elephant. She landed on a bush, then fell to the ground with a thump that knocked the wind out of her. Lily scrambled to her feet, taking ragged painful breaths as she sprinted up the driveway and down Radcliffe, running until she hit the safety of Santa Monica Boulevard.

It wasn't until she was panting in an alley a half mile away that she considered what she'd done: illegally entered into a man's apartment and attempted to steal his property. The manager would say he'd grown suspicious after Taunton failed to arrive, gone to check, and caught her stealing. He'd deny he'd threatened her, but she'd seen the lechery on his face, knew he'd only been waiting for his chance.

Still, the photos suggested something sinister. She'd broken the law, but she'd also discovered something that might link Freddy Taunton to Kitty's murder.

Lily breathed slowly, willing her panic to subside. Then she found a pay phone and called Detective Pico. He wasn't there, but she explained about the photos of the murdered girl, gave the operator the address, and urged her to hurry. When asked for her name, she hung up.

Lily caught the last streetcar home, ignoring the appalled looks from the other passengers — luckily there weren't many this late — and then ran all the way back to the rooming house. Tiptoeing upstairs, she knocked on Jeanne's door, calling her name softly, anxious to find out what the girl knew about the more extreme photos.

But Jeanne's room stayed silent as a tomb. Biting her lip, Lily thought about waking Red, then decided to wait until morning, by which time the police would have confiscated the photos and, she hoped taken Taunton into custody as he returned from his fishing trip.

Lily woke up at three-thirty a.m., slick with sweat. She threw back the covers, her limbs rigid from a nightmare. The glow from a faraway streetlight cast the room into unfamiliar shadows. The bed was lumpy, the furniture all wrong. It took a moment to remember she was in Kitty's room. In the boardinghouse. In Hollywood, California. In her dream Lily had been trapped inside Freddy's apartment by the manager who held the bowie knife, sharpening it against a whetstone.

In the room's dimness, she saw the doorknob turn and heard the metal *snick, snick* of her dream. She'd locked the door last night before climbing into bed, unnerved by her close call. But she'd left the key in the lock.

Now she heard the wood strain as someone on the other end put weight against the door, pushing to see if it would give. The metal key rattled in its hole. The noises stopped. Lily shrank back, trying to make herself invisible. She was sure whoever stood in the hallway could hear the blood pounding in her temples. She had to keep perfectly still. The doorknob eased back into its original position, its cut-glass facets catching the dim light.

After an eternity, she heard quiet steps moving away. Lily strained her ears to make out where they went. Perhaps it was one of the girls, plagued with a headache and wanting to borrow an aspirin. Soon she'd hear a knock at another door, a muffled conversation down the hall. But her visitor hadn't knocked. Was one of her fellow boarders a thief? But then why wouldn't she just wait until Lily left the house? Lily slid out of bed. Silently, she tiptoed to the vanity and poured some water from a pitcher, her teeth chattering against the glass when she drank. Then she went to the window and stood at one side, careful not to show herself. She pulled the lacy curtains open a crack. The sidewalk was empty. She stood there for a long time, but nothing moved. She wondered if it was possible to conjure up evil by thinking about it too much.

Shivering and stiff, Lily moved through the milky gray light and got back into bed.

CHAPTER 11

October 13, 1949
Walking downstairs for breakfast, Lily heard the exasperated voice of Detective Magruder in the parlor, interrogating Jeanne. The girl was weeping.

"I'm not lying," she said. "I was sound asleep at twelve-thirty a.m. I haven't left the house since you were here yesterday. I swear it."

Lily froze in the hallway.

"The female who called our hotline said it was an emergency. She gave the operator the name and address of Freddy Taunton, the same man you called Detective Pico about last night. She mentioned the existence of pornographic photos involving the deceased. I'd like to know what's going on."

"I've got no idea," Jeanne wailed.

Lily stepped into the parlor.

"Good morning, Detective Magruder. Has there been a break?"

Magruder gave her an annoyed look. His eyes were bloodshot and his clothes rumpled, like he hadn't slept all night. The cologne he'd applied didn't quite dispel the reek of a brewery.

"You girls and your mass hysteria have us running around like chickens with our heads cut off," Magruder said.

"Did you find pornographic photos of Kitty Hayden at Freddy Taunton's apartment?" Lily asked.

"No, we did not," Magruder roared.

Lily blinked. "You didn't?"

"We found nothing except a foiled burglary. The manager let some girl into Taunton's apartment last night after she fed him a sob story. When he got suspicious and checked on her, he caught her going out the back window."

"What was she trying to steal?" Lily asked shakily.

"Maybe your friend here can enlighten us all," Magruder said, jabbing a thumb at Jeanne, who buried her face in her hands. "Because of her, I drove back from Palm Springs in the middle of the night and tore apart an apartment with nothing to show for it. Because of her, my partner's spent five hours down at the harbor, tracking down every passenger manifest for the deep-sea charters. None of them have a Taunton on their lists."

Lily looked Magruder in the eyes. "Maybe the trip was a red herring. To give Taunton time to get away. Jeanne said he used to tie her and Kitty up, gag them, then watch them try to escape. Maybe he got a little rough with Kitty and things got out of control." Lily turned to Jeanne. "Did he ever splash red paint on you to make it look like blood?"

"He suggested it once." Jeanne blushed furiously and stared at the floor. "I told him it made me uncomfortable, so he dropped it."

Lily raised an eyebrow in Magruder's direction. "Maybe there are pictures of Kitty too."

She couldn't believe the police had missed the photo she'd dropped in the living room, the pulled-up carpet in the bedroom closet, the envelope beneath.

And then it hit her with the force of a thunderclap. The sleazy manager! He would have picked up the first photo, gotten interested, then found the others she'd left half stuffed in the bedroom closet. To a guy like him, those photos were a gold mine. He could sell them to a porno outfit or use them to blackmail his tenant. And if he

154

recognized the girl in the photos as the infamous "Scarlet Sandal," he might stash them safely away until the heat died down.

If Lily confessed to lying and sneaking into Freddy Taunton's place, it would be her word against the manager's, and who would believe her, especially if the photos had disappeared? From the look in Magruder's eyes, she had little doubt that he'd toss her in jail for breaking the law and interfering with the murder investigation.

No, Lily needed proof before she said anything about the photos.

After Magruder left, Lily plotted her day over coffee and toast. By eight a.m., she was riding the bus on her way to RKO Studios in Culver City to find Max Vranizan. The horizontal city was bathed in golden light, making everything shimmer — glitzy department stores, nightclubs, restaurants, record company headquarters, and swank apartments. Farther off, a beige shroud of smog blanketed the horizon, the legacy of the factories and refineries that had sprung up during the war. Amid the morning traffic Lily saw a new phenomenon: white government coupes that said "air quality control."

Lily got off a block from the studio, found

a taxi, tipped the driver $5, and asked him to take her through the studio gate.

"Tell the guard it's Miss Kessler, just in from New York, to see Mr. Max Vranizan in Special Effects about the model-making job," she told the driver.

Lily had grown up on the fringes of the movie industry, which had proved handy once in a newly liberated part of France when they'd captured a little Nazi who'd refused to speak, even after being roughed up by the Maquis. When it was the Americans' turn, Lily made small talk and learned he greatly admired Charlie Chaplin and hoped to move to Hollywood after the war and become a comedian. Lily explained that she'd gone to school with Chaplin's daughter. If he cooperated, she'd use her contacts to get him a screen test. Soon he was dictating names and locations — it turned out he was the paymaster for more than a hundred Nazi agents left behind liberated lines. After the man told all he knew, Lily's bosses handed him back to the French, who promptly shot him.

The RKO guard waved them through gates that rose like castle walls. Inside, the studio resembled a factory more than a fairy tale, a series of nondescript hangars and bungalows. The taxi cruised past a glass and muslin building stenciled with the words SOUND STAGE 1. Then a western town appeared, complete with Main Street, saloons, hitching posts, and townspeople in homespun cloth. Men bent over movie equipment. A camera on a dolly. Someone yelled, "Action," and a passel of cowboys on horses came galloping up, scattering pedestrians.

Lily memorized the landmarks so she could retrace her steps. In the rearview mirror, the driver grinned.

"I was a soundman here before the war. But the studios have cut back and I needed a steady job when I got out of the service." He slapped the dash. "Got a mortgage and a kid on the way."

They pulled up to a warehouse and the cabbie gestured with his cigarette. "That's where they do the special effects."

Lily studied her driver. "Any chance you know this Max Vranizan?"

"Nope, but you won't have any trouble. They don't get too many pretty girls on those monster movie sets."

As her eyes adjusted to the artificial light of the warehouse, she realized the cabbie had brought her to the wrong place. A row of seamstresses sat bent over sewing machines, working pedals. Off to the side, two women sewed appliqué onto high heels.

"Is this Special Effects?"

"You ask over there." A man with a heavy accent gestured into the next room, where a team of women ironed Renaissance gowns while a supervisor urged them to hurry, everyone on the set was waiting. Steam hissed from the irons, mingling with the acrid smell of perspiration that rose from garments previously worn under hot stage lights.

Lily kept walking.

In the next room, a beautiful woman was being fitted in an evening dress, three ladies kneeling, pins in mouths, hemming her gown. She looked familiar. With a shock, Lily realized it was Ingrid Bergman.

"Excuse me," she asked again. "Could you please direct me to Special Effects?"

A seamstress rocked back on her knees. "You're in the wrong building, dearie," she said. "Step outside, go left one block, turn right and it's the first building on the left."

Lily followed her instructions and saw actors hurrying by in costumes from the last two thousand years. Props rolling along on wheeled carts, a man leading a white Lipizzaner stallion. Lily came to a white two-story building with grand columns that reminded her of George Washington's home in Mount Vernon. This couldn't be it. Was she lost again? Seeing a group of modest buildings to the right, she walked in to ask, but before she could say anything, a horse-faced woman wearing a severe suit appeared.

"It's about time." She threw up her arms, striding toward Lily. "I called the agency at seven a.m. He's been holed up since yesterday afternoon and we've already gone through three —"

"But —"

"And I'll be gone most of the day."

The woman clasped Lily's wrist and tugged her like a determined shepherd dog into a large office with two secretarial desks facing each other.

"No excuses. I'm sure they told you *he* doesn't like to hear them."

Lily knew her ruse was about to be discovered. "I think there's been a —"

"That's quite enough," the woman said. "And you'd better not try that with *him.*" She stepped back, appraising Lily. "Now. Where's your steno pad?"

"Excuse me?"

"Honestly, these agencies today, I don't know what's —"

"I'm not a secretary," Lily said, but at that moment a door opened and a tall husky man in gray flannels stepped out from an inner office. From behind round spectacles beamed a brisk intelligence.

"Here she is, sir, I'm so sorry. I —"

"Thank you, Myra. Come along, then," the big man said in a hoarse voice, holding the door. "We've got a lot to get through."

Myra shoved a steno pad and two pencils in Lily's hands and pushed her into the man's office.

"You can go now," she told a girl slumped with exhaustion inside, steno pads stacked beside her. The girl left.

The man in the suit exuded an aura of power. Lily hesitated. She could either confess the truth now and get thrown off the lot or try to turn this case of mistaken identity to her advantage. Perhaps she could learn something about Kitty's murder if she kept her eyes and ears open.

Lily walked to the just-vacated chair and sat down, knees pressed together demurely, steno pad on her lap. From downcast lids, she examined her new boss and saw a brash, ungainly, and yet somehow charismatic man with wavy salt-and-pepper hair. Leaning back in his leather chair, he tapped a pencil against his palm, eyes focused on the far wall, where a framed and signed poster of *Gone With the Wind* hung.

"The first item of correspondence is a letter to LB," the man announced, propping his feet on the enormous desk stacked high with papers.

Lily waited for the rest of the name, but the man launched into the memo, approving the loan of an actress to MGM for a picture.

He concluded, "Sign it, 'dictated but not read by David O. Selznick.' "

Lily blinked and looked up. She'd spent the last five years abroad, but even she knew *that* name. She stared at her first Hollywood mogul.

"Ready?" Selznick drummed his fingers on the desk.

"Excuse me, Mr. Selznick." Lily recovered herself. "I didn't catch LB's last name."

Selznick looked disgruntled. "Mayer. Louis B. My, you are green. But if you caught everything else, you're everything the agency promised. Now. The next letter is to . . ."

Lily flipped the page.

"Miss Betty Goldsmith, New York, New York." Selznick's eyes twinkled. "Would you like to know who she is?"

"Why, no, Mr. Selznick, I —"

"She's my foreign rights coordinator. Now, if we might begin . . ."

"Of course, sir." Lily bent her head.

Selznick dictated in a brilliant but meandering style that reminded her of a Dickens novel, and he stopped often to take calls. When he began a long phone discussion with someone about Howard Hughes, Lily slipped out to use the powder room.

As she returned, a woman ran into Selznick's outer office, clutching a steno pad.

"I'm sorry I'm late," the woman said. "My son threw up blood on the way to the babysitter's and I had to rush him to the hospital."

Lily saw the notepad and realized who the woman was. Luckily Selznick was still on the phone, arguing good-naturedly with someone named Leland. She hurried to the young woman and led her back to the lobby.

"Don't you worry about it, honey," Lily said, "the studio sent me over on loan from, uh . . . Special Effects. Why don't you go back to the hospital and stay with your son? We're fine for today."

"Do you really mean it?" the woman cried.

"Here." Lily slipped her a $20 bill. "Buy him some toys, and tell the agency you worked all day. Same if they call tomorrow. And let's keep it between us, shall we?"

In any other city, the woman would have wondered what was going on. But this was

Hollywood, where people did crazy things to get discovered. The girl thanked Lily and hurried away.

Harry Jack woke up wondering why he was on the couch. Then he saw the kid in the kitchen, cramming a piece of bread into his mouth. He also smelled him.

"It's shower-time for you, kid — Gadge," he added, remembering the odd name the kid had given him yesterday. He'd said that was the name pinned to his shirt when the people at the orphanage had found him.

Harry lit a cigarette, took a hit, and exhaled thoughtfully. After his windfall at the *Mirror,* he'd taken the kid to lunch at Taylor's Steakhouse and then offered to drive him back to the orphanage, but Gadge wouldn't tell him the name and where it was located. The kid had stuck to him all day and had ended up falling asleep at a craps game, so Harry had no choice but to bring him home. But the kid couldn't stay here.

"I'm sorry kid, but you're going to have to go back."

"I'll help you take pictures. You can teach me how to use that camera."

Harry examined the lit cherry of his cigarette. "You want I should train my competition?"

"I'll help you set up shots. Be your assistant."

"I don't need an assistant. And you're not supposed to set up shots in the news business," Harry said, even as he considered the beat-up tricycle in his trunk that he tossed into intersections whenever a car accident needed a more tragic touch. Other photogs kept battered strollers, squashed shoes, mangled lady's purses.

Harry went to get a towel and some old clothes out of his dresser. When he came out, the kid was shoving something into his knapsack. Harry scrambled eggs, toasted bread, and made coffee while Gadge showered. He ate half the breakfast, drank his coffee, and read the paper. The water kept running. Harry tapped another cigarette out of his pack and looked for his silver lighter. He loved that lighter. It reminded him of a girl. She was a cigarette girl at the Trocadero, and a big wheel had left it on the table one night and she'd given it to him. Harry recalled Gadge shoving something into his knapsack. He knew where his lighter was.

Stomping to the bathroom, he flung the door open. Steam filled the room. Behind the curtain, the kid sang a nursery rhyme, his voice high and pure. Harry grabbed the knapsack and tiptoed out.

Poking through Gadge's belongings, Harry found his lighter shoved inside a ratty wool sock. He also saw a red strap sticking out of a sweater. Curious, he tugged and it came free.

It was a lady's fancy high-heeled sandal. Harry knew where he'd seen the shoe before. Or rather, its mate. Yesterday, in the canyon. It had been strapped to the ankle of the dead girl.

Just then, something hit Harry in the back.

"Put that back," Gadge shrieked. "It's mine. Who said you could go through my stuff?"

Harry dropped the shoe and the lighter. He grabbed the kid and held him, fists pumping, at arm's length.

"You tricked me into taking a shower so you could steal my stuff," Gadge cried.

"Calm down, kid. Nobody wants your crappy stuff. I went into your backpack because you stole my lighter and I wanted it back."

"I just wanted to look at it because it's beautiful. I would have given it back."

"You collect beautiful things, do you? Where'd you get that shoe?"

"What's it to you, mister?"

"It belong to someone you know?" Har-

165

ry's low voice invited confidence.

The kid shook his head. "I found it."

"Where?"

The kid looked up anxiously. "In a street."

Harry wondered what Gadge knew about the shoe's owner.

"That shoe belonged to a woman who was found strangled yesterday in Hollywood. You know, under the Hollywood sign. You were in the car when I drove out there to take photos."

The kid blanched. "I don't know anything about that."

"That shoe is evidence in a murder."

"I didn't kill anyone. Honest."

"For Pete's sake, I know that. You're just a kid. But the cops will want to talk to you."

The boy got a hunted look in his eyes. "No," he said. "I'm a runaway, they'll just lock me up or put me in another lousy home. You don't know, mister. The staff treat us worse than prisoners. Some of them like to hurt kids."

Gadge stuffed clothing back into his rucksack. "It's been nice knowing you, but I've got to get moving."

An image came to Harry of Gadge smiling into the camera and holding up the red high-heeled shoe. A photo like that could break the Scarlet Sandal murder investiga-

166

tion wide open. And Harry could sell versions to every paper in town. It would be his ticket to a cushy staff job anywhere he wanted. Harry placed an arm on either side of the hallway to block the kid's escape.

Gadge looked like he was about to cry. He tossed the red leather sandal at Harry's feet. "Take it," he said. "That old shoe is nothing but bad luck." He shouldered his knapsack.

"Hold on a minute," Harry said. "Why don't you eat breakfast, then you can show me where you found it?"

"Why? You going to take a photo and sell it to the papers? Will you give me half, on account of I'm your assistant?"

What an operator this kid was! "I'll give you a quarter," Harry said.

"Deal. But only if you don't take me to the police."

Harry knew it would be out of his hands once the pics hit the paper.

"I promise." Harry chose his words carefully. "But if they come looking for you, that's another story."

"Can I tell them you're my uncle? Say, what's your name, anyway? You know mine."

"I'm Harry Jack."

"Well, hey howdy, Harry Jack. And don't worry about the competition. I don't want to work for any cruddy old newspaper. I'm figuring on a job with the studios."

The nerve of this kid, Harry thought. "Those are a different kind of camera, son. Moving cameras. So how long have you had that shoe?"

The kid counted on his fingers. "About a week. Found it early in the morning, on my way down from the old estate to get breakfast after the Van de Kamps deliveryman makes his rounds."

"What estate?"

"Above Franklin. It's abandoned. I come down around six a.m. to swipe a bottle of milk and some cottage cheese. And I saw it there and it was pretty so I took it."

"What street?"

"Off the Boulevard. It's near a nightclub."

"There are nightclubs all along the Boulevard," Harry said, exasperated.

"Between Hollywood and Sunset. I remember that. A few blocks east of Vine."

"That narrows it down."

"I'll show you."

"Was there anything else nearby? Clothing? Jewelry?"

"If there was, I would have taken it. You can sell nice things like that."

"What about a purse? Papers?"

The kid paused. "Nope."

"Did you see any signs of a struggle?"

"Like bloodstains or a knife? Nope."

At that moment, they heard men yelling and feet pounding the sidewalk below. Harry went to the window and saw a man getting beat up. Grabbing his camera, he ran out the door, his shirttails fluttering behind him.

"You wanna be a shutterbug?" Harry told Gadge. "Your first lesson starts now."

The beating that Harry saw from his window was taking place in front of an appliance repair shop that occupied the ground floor of an apartment building across the street.

As Harry and Gadge raced downstairs, people were already gathering. Some were cheering wildly. A lone Samaritan loped off to flag down help. Into the fray ran Harry Jack, snapping away, Gadge behind him, screaming gibberish and covering his eyes.

And then Harry stopped. He removed the camera from his face. He looked stunned.

"Shorty Lagonzola, is that you?" he called.

The man had his fist back, ready to slam into the victim's face. He turned, and his mouth gaped.

"Harry? Harry Jack?"

Just then they heard a police siren.

"Son of a bitch," Shorty said. "The watch

commander promised to have the station zipped up tight. Something's queered it. I'd like to stay and catch up, Harry, but we've got to go. C'mon, boys, fun's over."

Shorty and his cronies jumped into the waiting car and tore off.

Harry watched the crowd mill around the police car, everyone talking at once. Someone pointed to Harry and his camera.

Shorty Lagonzola, Harry thought, gripping his camera tighter. A face he hadn't seen in years. A face that brought back childhood memories of Boyle Heights, a place where neighborhood loyalty was bred in the bone and maintained each week with your fists.

Harry was ten and newly arrived to the Heights when he was befriended by a kid whose skinny frame and reddish hair gave him the look of a raggedy lit match. Shorty didn't have a father and he pretty much did what he wanted. By fifth grade, he was already skipping school, hanging out at the pool hall, and mixing up juniper juice and raw alcohol in the back rooms of pharmacies with his brothers, only teenagers themselves but already deep in the rackets with local gangster Mickey Cohen.

Harry would have jumped at the chance to join them, but Shorty steered his friend

170

clear of that world, telling him he couldn't disappoint his law-abiding mom and pops.

Now the policeman was walking toward him. Harry's hand went to his Leica.

"Damn it all to hell," he said, as the copper reached him. "There's something wrong with my camera. Sorry, Officer, I accidentally exposed the film."

Harry trudged back to his apartment with Gadge.

"What a lousy break," the kid said. "The papers would've paid good money for those pics."

Harry wasn't much of a drinking man, but now he poured himself two fingers of rye, sat at the table, and downed it in one gulp. His hand was still curled around the empty glass when there was a knock at the door.

"Harry?" a man's voice rasped. Something familiar about it. The second time in seven years.

Harry opened the door and saw a figure in a coat and hat, the brim pulled low. Pulling him inside, he said, "You're taking a big chance coming back here."

When Shorty was settled in an armchair with his own glass, Harry asked him how the heck he'd found out where he lived and why he'd come back.

"I owe you for what you did back there,"

Shorty said.

"How the hell do you know what I did?"

Shorty waved a hand like he was brushing off flies. "One of my boys saw."

"I've owed you for a long time," Harry said, unable to forget how Shorty's older brothers had stopped local hoodlums from killing his grocer father after his pop refused to pay protection money.

"We're even, then. What happened to your eye? Do I need to beat up somebody else?"

"Naw, I'm okay."

Shorty glanced at Gadge. "Got a kid, I see. Nice little place. Where's the wife?"

"No wife. Not my kid either."

Harry saw Shorty's look of alarm. "Don't worry, he knows how to keep his mouth shut."

"I don't know, Harry, maybe you better . . ." Shorty made a shooing motion.

"Kid's got his own reasons for not talking to coppers."

Shorty nodded. "If the badge boys had gotten hold of those pics, they would have indicted the lot of us. But hell, Harry, ain't you gonna ask me what we was doing?"

Harry shrugged. "Figured you'd tell me when you were ready."

"I'm ready. We was beating up the pervert that owns the building and runs that repair shop. Uses his key to walk in on tenants, especially ones of the female persuasion that . . ." Shorty's hands carved a voluptuous form in the air. "Mayor Bowron's daughter lives there and that schmuck let himself in, got a good look at her in brassiere and panties. He needed to be taught a lesson."

Harry snorted. "When did you start wearing a cape and avenging the honor of maidens?"

"Mickey sent us out after receiving a personal request from Hizzoner."

"But you beat that man within an inch of his life," Harry said.

"Wanted to make sure he got the point."

Shorty grinned. He'd taken off his coat, and underneath he wore an expensive suit, the effect somewhat ruined by sleeves that hit the first knuckle of each hand. The pants had been taken up. A homburg perched on his head. Harry's practiced eye saw a bump at Shorty's right ankle and the straps of a shoulder holster.

"You're looking good," Harry said. "Life treating you well?"

" 'S okay."

"Fancy threads. Never figured you for a clotheshorse."

"Mickey's a generous man. Never wears a suit more than a few times before he hands it down. So you pursued that photography stuff?"

"It bit me hard. And when I got drafted, Uncle Sam put me to work taking pictures on battlefields all over Europe. How about you? Were you over there?"

Shorty squinted at the wall and looked embarrassed. "I've got problems with my feet. It kept me out."

Harry remembered Shorty running away from the neighborhood beat cop just fine. But he probably had a record, which would have disqualified him. Or else money had changed hands.

"I'm trying my damndest right now to get on with one of the daily papers."

"Maybe Mickey can help."

Harry considered. But he needed to get there on his own merits, not as a favor to a mob boss. And he knew the invisible skeins that Mickey wove around everyone he helped.

"Shorty, you've helped me out more than a guy has a right to. I'll never forget what you did for the old man. Never thanked you properly for that. Guess I was embarrassed."

"No need. We all admired your pops for sticking to his guns. Even if it was stupid. Maybe I wished I had a dad."

"He was a good man. I thank the Lord he

didn't live to see what Hitler done. Died in 1939 and my moms sold the store to the Takahashis. Remember them? Fumiko Takahashi, cute little thing with bangs and dimples, was in our class?"

"You know I was never much for school."

"After the war, they come back long enough to sell the store. We lost track when I moved to Larchmont."

Harry still went back to Boyle Heights to take pictures of the neighborhood. Most of the Japanese were gone. The Jews were leaving too, moving west. He'd heard one of the Canter brothers had opened a deli on Fairfax Avenue and the other two might follow. What a sacrilege. Harry couldn't imagine Brooklyn Avenue without its landmark deli. The war had shaken people loose, busted up the old ways. Whole cities were rising on the outskirts, with cleaner air and backyards. Who could blame folks for leaving? Even Hollenbeck Park had been sliced up to build a freeway.

"So," Shorty said at last. "What you been taking pictures of lately? Besides our brawl?"

"I guess you don't read the papers. The *Mirror* bannered my shot of that murdered girl they found below the Hollywood sign yesterday."

Shorty's antenna went up.

175

"The Scarlet Sandal?"

"Yeah. And Gadge here has got something that's going to make me the hottest news photographer in town come tomorrow."

Shorty's small eyes flickered over Gadge.

"The kid has her other shoe. Found it in a Hollywood side street."

A fountain of rye sprayed out of Shorty's mouth. He grabbed a napkin and dabbed his mouth.

"What's it to you, Shorty?" Harry said.

"It's a dirty business. The bulls won't hear it from me, but the boss knew her."

Harry shook his head in disbelief. "You're mixed up in this!"

"We didn't do her," Shorty said. "But Mickey wants to know who did. She was supposed to be at Slapsie Maxie's on Tuesday but she didn't show."

"Why does Mickey care about a dead starlet?"

"On account of she was hanging around with him and some of the boys. Little Davey Ogul and Frank Niccoli. Mickey's a gentleman and he feels a responsibility."

"Like hell," said Harry.

Shorty screwed up his face. "Well, here's the thing. Li'l Dave and Frank have disappeared off the face of the earth. At first Mickey thought the three of them might have gone down to Mexico. Then the girl turns up dead. So he figures once we find the girl's killer, we can put the screws to him, see what he knows about the boys. You know Dragna's been trying to get Mickey ever since Benny Siegel was killed. He could be picking off our people one by one."

Shorty said nothing about the other angle he was investigating. What Jimmy had told him in the alley the night they'd watched Sinatra rehearse. It was too sensitive, and he didn't know enough yet.

"Wouldn't it be easier for Dragna just to kill Mickey?" Harry asked.

The gangster shook his head. "Mickey's got the coppers guarding him now, the wolf guarding the fox and to hell with the henhouse." Shorty snickered. "But he's sweating. Dave and Frankie were fighting a rap, see, and Mickey bailed 'em out of jail, which means he forfeits the bond if they don't show for the trial. But if he can prove they're dead, he's off the hook."

"How much is it?"

"Seventy-five thousand dollars."

"Piece of cake."

Shorty shook his head. "It's cash. Even for Mickey, that would hurt."

"Dragna wouldn't kill an innocent girl, would he?" Harry asked, trying to remember what he'd heard last night at the craps game.

He'd run into a gossipy RKO operator named Edith Blyton who told him the dead starlet ran with a rough crowd and got a lot of calls from someone at Warner's. Detectives had spent several hours at RKO interviewing a special effects wizard who'd been in unrequited love with the girl. Max Vranizan had a volatile temper due to some shrapnel he'd taken in his head during the war, but Edith said he was brilliant, he'd been Ray Harryhausen's right-hand man on several films and the studio hoped to groom him into a hit-making machine.

"Maybe the three of them disappearing is just a coincidence," Harry told Shorty now.

"How so?"

"I heard the cops are looking at one of them whiz-bangs at RKO. Special effects. He worked on *Mighty Joe Young* and had the hots for her. Maybe she led him on one too many times and he snapped."

"Yeah?" Shorty asked casually. "What's his name?"

Harry got a flush of nervous sweat under his arms.

"I don't know," he lied.

That's okay, thought Shorty. *I can find out.*

CHAPTER 12

After taking dictation for nearly five hours, Lily staggered out. Everything had to be typed up by four p.m. The producer hadn't mentioned Kitty's murder, but that didn't surprise Lily. She hoped to have a quick snoop through the files before she left. Then she'd go find Max Vranizan. Lily fed a carbon and two pages of stationery into the typewriter and started to transcribe.

She was halfway through when a man appeared at her desk so silently that she jumped. He wore a good suit that draped to hide his girth. He had sloped shoulders and sallow skin. His eyes were set deep in their sockets and filled with a probing animal curiosity.

"Where's Myra?" he said.

"Pardon me, sir, but I don't know," Lily said. "I'm filling in from the agency."

"Myra's always here."

"Well, sir, she's not here now." Lily put on

her most formal voice. "Do you have an appointment with Mr. Selznick?"

"Myra never goes anywhere," the man said mournfully. "She's like Cerberus, guarding the entrance to the Underworld. Not," he added quickly, "that I am implying in any way, shape, or form that Mr. Selznick's domain is remotely like Hades. You can quote me on that." He snapped his fingers and winked unpleasantly. "Tell him Frank is here."

"Frank who?"

"He'll know."

When Lily knocked and announced Selznick's visitor, a shadow fell over the producer's big fleshy face and he said he'd be free in a minute.

Frank waited, jiggled one foot, whistling a show tune and reading a newspaper clipping. When Lily saw it was about Kitty's murder, she tried to hide her interest, but he noticed immediately.

"Is something wrong, Miss . . ." He stretched it out, angling for her name.

"Lily Kessler," she said automatically. "And it's just that . . . I noticed . . ."

"You sound flustered, Miss Kessler."

"Not at all, I . . ."

"Maybe you knew this unfortunate young woman? From around the studio?"

The words were offered up casually, but his foot had stopped jiggling and his eyes were watchful.

"Sir," Lily said firmly. "I am not employed by this studio on a regular basis. But a murder like that frightens all women. It might have been any of us."

The man looked pensive. "Perhaps. But we're all born with choice. Some people make bad choices."

In that moment, Lily realized there were people in Hollywood whom Kitty hadn't charmed and placed under her spell. Maybe her efforts had only made these people resent her all the more. She imagined such resentment gathering like a cold oceanic wave to crash down on all the starlets and factory girls who'd grown cocky and independent during the war.

"I'm sure Kitty Hayden was an upstanding young woman. You've no right, sir, to speak that way of the dead."

The man got up, walked around the desk, hands clasped behind him.

"Don't speak of things you know nothing about," he said.

A moment later Selznick rang and asked Lily to bring in his visitor. Frank approached the mogul's desk, already hunching into a servile posture as the door closed.

Lily went back to her desk, waited, then walked over and stood by the door, trying to listen.

"Frank," Selznick's voice boomed, "you've done a fine job so far, but I need an update."

Frank's response was too low for her to hear. Could they be talking about Kitty? Was that why he'd clipped out the story? Oh, to be a fly on the wall!

"What do you think you're doing?"

Lily jumped as Myra marched up. She looked like an angry dog now, not a horse. In fact, with her jowls quivering, she looked just like Cerberus.

"Admiring the wood grain on this door," Lily said, stroking it. "Is it cherrywood?"

"I have no idea. And you're not paid to admire wood grain. Now hurry and finish those letters or you'll never work on this lot again."

"Glad to see you back on the job, Myra," Frank said when he emerged five minutes later.

"Work, work, work," the secretary simpered.

Lily was dying to know who this man was. As soon as he left, she asked.

"And what business is that of yours?" Myra snapped.

"If he's important, I shouldn't keep him

waiting. If he's not, then I shouldn't interrupt Mr. Selznick."

Myra looked as though she smelled a rat but couldn't put a finger on where the rat was.

"Like what?" Lily offered her most innocuous smile.

"Never you mind. But make sure to let Mr. Selznick know immediately if he calls."

Lily typed for a few moments, then said, "Myra, I'm dying to ask, did you know that RKO actress they found yesterday under the Hollywood sign?"

The secretary shot her a suspicious look. "No. Why?"

"Just wondering." Lily rolled a pencil. "You never saw her at the commissary?"

"I eat lunch at my desk," Myra sniffed.

"Of course, how silly of me. By the way, where do they do special effects for movies like *Mighty Joe Young*?"

"She wasn't in that one," Myra said immediately.

"I thought you didn't know her."

"I don't." Myra grabbed a manila file and walked briskly to the cabinet. "And unlike some people, I've got a lot to do before quitting time."

Like sharpening your tongue, Lily thought.

"You want to be an actress, Ms. Kessler, I

recommend the usual route. Get an agent, head shots, that kind of thing."

"An actress?" Lily snorted. "That's the last thing I want."

Myra regarded her. "I see you've already got a head start. Your outrage sounds almost sincere."

Lily bit her tongue and bent her head. As soon as Myra took the letters in for Selznick's signature, she dialed the operator and asked to be put through to Max Vranizan. When a voice answered, "Special Effects," she asked where they were located, saying she had a delivery. The man gave her directions.

At five p.m., Myra said she'd need her again tomorrow. Lily said good-bye and smiled as she hurried off to the Special Effects building.

Ten minutes later, Lily was looking around a cavernous space. Industrial lights hung from the ceiling. Lathes, drills, worktables, painting easels, and sawhorses filled the room. A man with tools dangling from a work belt walked by and gave her a huge wink. A set painter observed her curiously from behind a desert landscape he was finishing. Sprawled on a beat-up couch, an unshaven man snored.

The hangar smelled of glue and machine

oil, turpentine and wood shavings. The wood floor was splattered with paint of every color. Lily walked to a table and inspected models of spaceships, dinosaurs, and monsters. Some were fashioned of clay. Others were skeletons assembled from bits of metal.

In a corner, two men were inspecting what looked like a miniature stuffed wolf. One was about sixty, with a kind, sad face. The other was tall and skinny, about thirty, with the stooped shoulders of someone who spends his days tinkering over a worktable. His tie was tucked inside his collared shirt and his chestnut hair was an unruly mass that rose up from his forehead like a cresting wave.

As Lily drew closer, she noticed the wolf's ragged fur, humped back, fangs, and blood-shot eyes. A werewolf.

"I know how it gets ahold of you," the older man said. "Used to stay up all night myself. Now I need my beauty sleep. See you in the morning."

"G'night, Obie," the young man said with affection.

When the older man had gone, Lily said, "I'm looking for Max Vranizan."

The man stroked the werewolf. "That's me."

"My name is Lily Kessler and I'm a friend of the Hayden family in Illinois. Kitty's mother asked me to find out what I could. She's desperate for information and the police aren't saying much. So I'd like to talk to you, if I might."

Something in Max Vranizan's face withdrew to a great distance, then peered out.

Most of the other workmen had drifted away. But several drew closer at hearing the name of the missing actress. The set painter hauled buckets of paint into a cart and rolled it to a new backdrop.

Max Vranizan picked a daub of cadmium paint from his wrist. "If you're a friend of Kitty's, why haven't I met you?"

"Because I've been living abroad. Just got back to the good old U.S. of A."

"The police were here yesterday." Max frowned. "I haven't seen her for a month, if that's what you want to know."

Lily found it interesting that he'd jumped the gun.

"It was Labor Day," he said. "We drove to Santa Monica Beach and she brought a picnic lunch. We swam in the ocean. At dusk, I drove her home."

"Did you know she'd gone missing?"

"One of the gals from the rooming house called to ask if I'd seen her." Vranizan strode

186

to the wooden table and adjusted the wing of a pterodactyl. He lifted it up and swooshed it through the air like a kid.

Lily followed him. "Had you?"

"I told her I hadn't. We had words out on the beach, that last time," he said mournfully. "I didn't like some of the people she spent time with. She said it was none of my business."

Max Vranizan reached out a hand and touched the fur collar of Lily's coat.

"Sable," he said absentmindedly.

"How did you know?" Lily asked, surprised.

He shrugged. "You get a feel for the fur after a while."

"Interesting. So, who was Kitty spending time with?"

"People she thought could help her get places. People she'd met at nightclubs."

"Like Mickey Cohen? The gangster?"

Max smirked. "Hollywood considers him more of a *businessman* these days. Lots of respectable people go to Slapsie Maxie's. Movie people. Businesspeople. Politicians. Judges. Out here, we like to mix it up."

The gaiety in his voice didn't reach his eyes. The only thing this guy mixes up, thought Lily, is paint.

Max Vranizan slipped his fingers under

his glasses and rubbed his eyes. "Sometimes I thought she just kept me around like a sad clown to prop up her ego."

"How long have you been friends?"

Max told her they'd met late last year when he was at RKO making a movie about giant bats. He often had to wait to screen the daily rushes until David O. Selznick finished watching footage that had been flown in from Havana, where the producer's inamorata, Jennifer Jones, was filming *We Were Strangers* with John Garfield. As Max hung around, he noticed a girl, a brunette with long filly legs and full lips, kibitzing with the projectionist. Max coveted her from afar the way a starving man stares through the window at a feast he'll never be invited to. There was always someone at Kitty's elbow, young men with money and pizzazz who wore two-tone shoes and cashmere sweaters and silk scarves and roared off the lot with her in convertible roadsters.

Max probably wouldn't have spoken to her that December night at the Pig 'n Whistle either, he told Lily, but he'd pulled off a particularly tricky action shot that day and emerged from the studio exhilarated and filled with uncharacteristic bravado.

She'd walked into the Pig 'n Whistle just ahead of him, ignoring the hunched row of backs at the lunch counter and couples in the wooden booths up front. Her destination was the back room, where a large and boisterous crowd gathered each night to be serenaded by the best pipes in Hollywood — studio musicians and singers who could play what they wanted once they punched off the industry clock.

Located across from Grauman's Chinese and next door to the Egyptian, the Pig 'n Whistle was a popular watering hole with a majestic organ. The farther you walked into the Pig, the more elegant it felt thanks to the beamed ceilings, stained-glass windows, and hand-carved wood. Max watched Kitty sit down at the bar, turn to the bartender, and announce more loudly than necessary, "Somebody ought to buy me a drink, don't you think?"

"Why is that, Kitty?" the bartender asked, playing the straight guy.

Kitty looked around and gave a tight nod as Max made his way toward her, wallet in hand.

"Because I deserve it. Because I'm a poor girl in a hard town. Because all my money goes to acting classes."

The bartender snorted. "You're already the best actress in town, Kitty."

Then Max was at her side.

"Why, hello." Kitty gave him a demure smile.

"Could I buy you a drink, miss?"

"That would be lovely. I'll have a glass of champagne."

Max leaned against the polished wood bar. "Would you like white or pink?"

Kitty's smile grew pained and she fiddled with the brooch at her lapel.

"She always has white," the bartender said, already pouring the pale effervescing liquid into a long-stemmed flute.

"It's going to be quite a night," Max said. "Mr. DeMille's coming in."

"Here?" Kitty squeaked.

"I have it on good word from his secretary. He loves to play the organ, and he's quite talented."

Kitty gave Max her full attention.

"You know him?"

"You think I'm blowing smoke. But I've done pictures for him."

"Have you? What's your name?"

"Max Vranizan."

"Kitty Hayden. I'm an actress." She gave him the full-on face now, lips pouting into a red rosebud.

I know, he wanted to say. *I've seen you at RKO.*

He felt a flicker of sadness that she hadn't

190

noticed him, the long hours he'd mooned over her as he glued fur onto his creations, caressing the glossy pelt and imagining it was her. She was so close that he could smell her violet scent. Still flying high from the day's shoot, Max didn't see the usual intimidating creature in a dress, but rather a girl with whom he had a natural affinity, a girl who toiled in the same world of illusion as he.

"You're awfully good-looking," he said, giving her a loopy grin.

Kitty got out a cigarette and Max pulled out a pack of matches and lit it.

Kitty sipped her champagne. "And what do you do for the studios, Mr. Vranizan?"

He rolled onto the balls of his feet, grinning. "I'm in Special Effects."

"Does that mean you hold the hose when the script calls for rain?"

"Nope, I'm an animator. The man I work for, Willis O'Brien, he's a genius. Why, the movie we're working on now, it's going to rev —"

"Is that like puppets?"

Max winced. "Not exactly. See, a movie camera, it shoots twenty-four frames per —"

But Kitty had only heard one word.

"Cameras? You take photos?"

"I suppose I could."

"Would you take photos of me? The head shots I have are ancient."

It would give him an excuse to see her again. They could do the shots at night, after everyone left. He'd be alone with her. He'd show her some of his creations, play her the animated sequences he and Obie had devised. She'd be so impressed that she'd throw her arms around him. *Oh, Max,* she'd whisper. *You're incredible.* She'd bring her face close, parting those amazing full lips. And then . . . No. He couldn't allow himself to think that way about such a nice young lady.

"It would be an honor," Max said.

"Max. Hey, Max," his friends called from across the crowded room. "Stop being so selfish. Bring her back so we can all see."

Kitty looked over. One had jug ears and a bow tie. Another's pants were too short. A third had a cowlick and thick glasses.

"Let me guess. They work in Special Effects too."

Max gave her a big grin. "How'd you know?"

"Just a lucky guess."

Max's heart swelled with rapture. He couldn't believe his luck. He was talking to a pretty girl with wavy chestnut hair and golden skin. For a moment he saw himself as that noble grotesque King Kong, Kitty as Fay Wray. With a whoop he grabbed the girl and swung her off the stool.

"Now, wait a minute, there, fella."

"You looked like you were waiting to be swept off your feet," Max said. Vivid fantasies flooded his mind of another misunderstood hero, Mighty Joe Young, climbing up a burning building to rescue an orphaned girl. How the giant ape would bellow as the flames singed his fur. Yes! He'd storyboard it tonight.

"You think you're man enough?" Kitty teased.

The magic flared and spluttered. The gorilla fled back into the jungle, leaving him paralyzed with awkwardness, just a tall stooped young man with an obsessive hobby that only those similarly afflicted could understand.

"Are you under contract?" she asked coyly.

Max gulped and his Adam's apple bobbed up and down. He tried to explain how the special effects boys moved from studio to studio like gypsies but choked on his saliva and doubled over, red-faced with shame at the disgusting spectacle he was making. Any second now, she'd walk away.

Instead, a small hand patted his back.

"Hey," Kitty said. "Take it easy, big boy. It isn't a trick question. Why don't we go meet your friends?"

And so their teasing dance had begun. Kitty liked him like a kid brother, while he burned with hidden lusts that made him blush and whinny with loud equine laughter whenever she was around. At night he bucked against his pillow and caressed the imaginary shape of her, dreaming of their future. She'd have dinner ready when he came home. When he crawled into bed, sore from stooping over a model, high from the glue fumes, he'd bury his long face in her bosom and they'd make love until dawn.

He had to be patient, win her over slowly, seduce her with his art. Max had never known a starlet before. They'd always been inaccessible ice goddesses. He felt like an insect in their world, bulbous and alien, sharpening his mandibles in confusion. He wanted to devour Kitty, build an altar to her. He didn't know where to begin.

Now he stood amid the tricks of his trade, reminiscing about Kitty to another pretty young woman.

"You loved her, didn't you?" Lily said.

"We had fun together. She was my date for the *Mighty Joe Young* premiere and we

194

had dinner at Ciro's afterwards. It was the most wonderful night of my life."

His hand slid into his pocket, his fingers closing around something. His eyes grew thoughtful and far away. Then, plucking a pencil from behind his ear, he began to sketch. Within thirty seconds the lines had nuance and movement. Thirty more and they had personality. It was Kitty as a barely clad cavewoman, astride a soaring pterodactyl. Below them stood a T. Rex, toothy jaw gaping open, ready to devour both bird and girl.

Max crumpled the paper and tossed it into a wastebasket.

"Don't! You're really . . . talented," Lily said, disturbed by the symbolism but seeing a way to keep him talking. "Will you show me more of your work?"

Nodding brusquely, he led her past props draped with white cloth. The set painter who'd gazed at Lily earlier stood at a sink, cleaning his brushes. Now he turned and watched them stroll off, unaware of how their voices carried in the acoustics of the big hangar. The set painter waited until they entered Max's office. Then he put away his last brush and hurried out of the building.

Max's office was lined with comic books, zoology texts, taxidermy manuals, and fantastic fiction by Lord Dunsany, Mervyn Peake, H. G. Wells, Jules Verne, and Hope Mirrlees. He pulled out a volume called *Dark Carnival.*

"It's a collection of short stories by a friend of mine. He's got a novel about Mars coming out next year."

Lily checked the spine. "Ray Bradbury. He any good?"

"I sure think so. He and I and another of our pals, Forrie Ackerman, are in a science club that meets at Clifton's Cafeteria downtown every Thursday at six p.m., you ever want to drop by. We talk about dinosaurs, moon rockets, time travel. It would be nice if a girl joined."

"Thanks for the invitation," Lily said politely.

She walked over to the wall, where a series of sketches showed Vikings astride giant prehistoric eagles fighting air battles with dinosaurs.

Max gave a rueful laugh. "Obie worked on *War Eagles* for two years, made the models, did two hundred sketches and oil paintings, shot a test reel. Then the director killed the film."

Lily moved on to sketches of a giant gorilla.

"Those are preproduction sketches we do

to block out the action. They're like a story-board for how the director'll shoot each scene."

"I know that gorilla," Lily said. "Mighty Joe Young. You gave him to Kitty, and I found it in her . . ." She stopped.

"That's right. We made five models because they get banged up, the fur wears down in filming, so one's always in the repair shop. Kitty's got one, I've got three, and one's lost. My favorite one was named Jennifer."

"A girl's name?"

Max Vranizan smiled. "You work with these models every day, you get a sense of their personalities, what they're thinking and feeling."

"And you're feeling like Gepetto?"

She saw the intelligence that burned behind his eyes, a mind honeycombed with strange pathways. *If only we all got to build the world we want to live in,* she thought.

"I'm just doing everyday magic," Max said. "Sleight of hand. We don't broadcast what we do, because the mystique is part of the illusion itself."

"But you'll tell me, won't you?"

He studied the floor. "Most girls find it boring. What Obie and Ray and I do takes a tremendous amount of dedication. Obsession, even."

Lily shifted uneasily. She imagined him fixating on Kitty. Wanting to play God, control her every movement, like he did his creations. But Kitty wasn't a doll.

"After sketches, we move to clay models. Then we build an articulated skeleton out of metal, using custom-made parts we stamp out on lathes. That's called the armature."

He fetched a metal dinosaur skeleton from the cupboard.

"Pretty nifty," she said, moving the long neck.

"That's first-generation. Primitive," Max said dismissively. "Nothing like Jennifer."

He snapped on thin white gloves — skin oils from his fingers would turn the fur greasy, he explained — and removed a gorilla model from his desk. It was the twin of the one in Kitty's room. Carefully, Max manipulated its limbs.

"We even build sponge rubber muscles onto the armature, so the skin'll ripple. See? And there's an inflatable bladder inside the chest to make Joe breathe. Each finger has movable joints so he can pick things up. He's got ball-and-socket joints at the elbow. Marcel, he's our model builder, he ran wires through the eyelids so they'd open and close. The lips are rubber, modified with clay. Sometimes we use plasticine. Each of these babies costs twelve hundred dollars."

"What goes over the armature?" Lily asked.

"Cotton batting. Then foam rubber, then latex over that. We've even got a taxidermist working for us, George Lofgren, a very talented man, who embeds the fur into the rubber."

Lily ran her hand along the fur. It didn't feel like mink. Or rabbit. Or lamb or sable or any coat she knew. She raised one eyebrow quizzically.

"Fur of unborn calf," Max said. "We went down to the Vernon slaughterhouse to buy it. Farmer John thought we were nut jobs."

"Ugh." Lily pulled her hand away. "That's disgusting."

Max hadn't noticed her distaste. In his element, he was relaxed and confident, his earlier awkwardness gone.

"Joe moves like a gorilla but emotes like a human. His mouth turns down when he's sad, his eyes squint up when he's angry. When Joe throws a rock, we move it with nylon wires — monofilaments — that are almost invisible. We build him with sponge rubber, cotton batting, metal hinges, and fur. Then I wave my magic wand and bring him to life."

"How?" They were getting far afield of Kitty, but she had to know.

"It's a process we call stop-motion animation. The cinematic art of moving models meticulously, frame by frame, to create the illusion of motion."

"You'll have to explain in English."

"Well, a thirty-five-millimeter movie camera shoots twenty-four frames per second. So I position Joe, then shoot a frame of film. Then I move him a tiny bit, shoot another frame. Then repeat. All day long. Any more than one frame and it looks jerky instead of fluid and natural."

Lily pictured bored cameramen smoking cigarettes while the special effects wizard set up shot after shot.

"It can take twelve hours of shooting to do a few seconds of screen time. More if it's really tricky."

"You must go stir crazy."

Max looked insulted. "I'm never bored. I play each scene in my head, figuring out what I need for the next frame. At night I can't wait for the rushes, to see if I've caught it on film. It's thrilling when that happens. You could say I have a Zeus complex. I want to control all the little creatures in my world."

There it was again, Lily thought. Had Max Vranizan tried to control Kitty, then killed her when that proved impossible?

She looked down so he wouldn't guess her thoughts and her gaze fell on a movie still of Mighty Joe Young, looking morose as he accepted a bottle of booze through the bars of a jail cell from three jeering men in suits.

"That jail cell is twenty-four-inches tall," Max said, mistaking her interest. "All Joe's sets are miniature, built to scale. The African scenes? We had matte artists paint the jungle landscape on glass, to give it depth. We've got one painter, he's a Chouinard Art Institute dropout, and he's fantastic, when he stays off the dope and bothers to come in. But his dad's a mucky-muck here so no one can force him to do anything."

Lily noticed a publicity photo of Joe and some lions running amok inside a nightclub as people ran away shrieking.

"How do you insert actors?"

"In layers. We shot the big cats out at the RKO ranch in Tarzana. Then we projected that footage behind the actors and shot the human scenes. Then we projected the new footage one frame at a time onto a rear projection screen on a miniature set while we animated Joe's scenes. You have to synchronize the movements for all three to give the illusion it's happening on the same plane."

Lily whistled. "Is that how they shot *King Kong*?"

"Exactly." Max looked pleased. "That was Willis O'Brien too — the older guy who just left. He invented all this. Bloody genius. People had no idea how he made that movie. They guessed it was a man in an ape suit, or a bunch of people inside a giant ape costume, moving different parts. Obie's a true Renaissance man. What Michelangelo is to sculpting the human form, Obie is to animation. But few artists are appreciated in their lifetime."

Lily said she'd sensed a sadness clinging to Willis O'Brien, the feeling of something lost or broken.

"His family was killed in a tragic accident," Max said. "And his pictures often get scrapped because producers decide they don't want to spend the money. All they care is whether they can get it in one shot, fast and cheap. The world got lucky with *Kong,* it was a masterpiece."

"I'm sorry about Obie, I think his work . . . your work . . . is marvelous. It's too bad Kitty never appreciated the artistry behind it. You mentioned she was hanging out with nightclub people when she disappeared?

Ever hear her mention any names? Louie or Monty or a skinny little guy with reddish-brown hair and a mean face?"

But Max had shut down. "I don't want to talk about it," he said. "Look, can I give you a ride home?"

"I thought you had work to do."

"I can work at home."

Lily explained she was living at Kitty's rooming house.

"I could drive that route blindfolded. Come on."

They were traveling north on La Cienega when the radio interrupted the music program to report that the body of a strangled woman had been found in the Hollywood Hills. Lily felt the car lag as Max took his foot off the gas. In that moment, she realized she was alone with a man the police had interviewed about Kitty's murder. A man Kitty's roommates had warned her was eccentric and prone to obsessions. It was nighttime and no one knew where she was. When Max's large hand reached out, she flinched, then realized he was just turning up the volume.

Florence Kwitney, twenty-eight, had last been seen waiting for the bus to her midtown apartment after a night out with girlfriends. Her body had been discovered below the Hollywood sign late this afternoon by two boys hunting for arrowheads. The announcer said Kwitney was the second girl within a week to be found strangled and dumped in the hills with only one shoe. But unlike Kitty Hayden, a Hollywood starlet, Florence Kwitney was a secretary at an electronics store and had no connection to the movies. The newscaster said speculation was building that a new killer was on the loose in the streets of Los Angeles, preying upon its most vulnerable citizens.

"Should we drive over and see what we can see?" Max asked eagerly.

Lily thought of the dark hills, the isolated streets.

"Are you crazy?" she said. "Take me home."

CHAPTER 13

Shorty drove to Palisades Park, cut his lights, and watched the breakers roll in. He'd spent the afternoon on the phone. Mickey had eyes and ears all over town, found it useful to tip extravagantly and often. It sharpened the memory. Waiters and valets, whores and servants, suddenly remembered things, were happy to pass on information. The boss had friends in Hollywood too, but he kept it on the q.t., the way the movie people liked it. Oh yeah. They'd drink his liquor and borrow money and gamble at his clubs, but they wouldn't be seen in public with him. Shorty knew that hurt the boss's feelings, though Mickey would never admit it. Still, the studios and the rackets had always worked together behind the scenes; Shorty had helped break up a few strikes himself.

But today the well was dry and nobody seemed to know anything about the Hayden murder. After exhausting all other possibilities, Shorty had dialed a number he tried not to use too often.

A little after ten p.m., a Cadillac pulled up and Shorty got in. The car took off, nosing its way down the California Incline and onto Pacific Coast Highway.

"So," said the driver, cloaked in darkness. "What can I do for you?"

"It's about that actress," Shorty said. "The one they found in the hills."

"Yes?" The man's voice was wary.

"I need to find out what happened."

There was a small cough. "I'm afraid I can't help you."

"Oh really?" Shorty chuckled nastily. "Then let me jog your memory. Tell me about her and . . ." He repeated the name Jimmy had whispered in the alley the night of the Sinatra rehearsal.

The prickly silence that followed told Shorty a lot.

"That's ridiculous," the man finally sputtered.

"Why is it ridiculous?" Shorty said with singsong sarcasm.

"He didn't have anything to do with it," the man behind the wheel said.

"They were seen together."

"Impossible."

"Bellhop at the Chateau Marmont who I ran into in an alley the other night saw her slipping into one of the VIP bungalows where he was delivering champagne."

"So?"

"A couple hours later he brought breakfast for two, and the place was registered to one. Caught a glimpse of them when he knocked, wrapped around each other like snakes. Says this fellow always checks in under a false name when he's on the prowl."

"Ah," the driver said, groaning. "This is not good."

"Everyone knows he can't keep his trousers zipped."

The man sighed. "It is highly indiscreet of both parties. But I can assure you —"

"The fuck you can assure me. Go pound the truth outta that cocksucker or my people will."

The man passed a hand over his brow.

"We've already talked to him about it," he said. "It was an affair, and it's over. He feels terrible, but he doesn't know anything about what happened."

"You and the boss," said Shorty, "have always helped each other out in the past. He would be hurt to learn you wasn't telling the truth."

"I swear it on my mother's grave," the

man said.

There was silence in the car after that, just the purring of the big motor.

"Shall we head back?" the driver asked after a while.

"No," snapped Shorty. "I need to think."

Several more miles passed. The houses were more sparse now, moonlight reflecting along the empty beach and the bare rolling hills.

"Say," said Shorty, his voice genial. "I saw one of your flicks the other day. *Mighty Joe Young.* That ape was amazing."

"We've got one of the best trick men in the business working for us," the driver boasted.

"Oh yeah, who's that?"

"Guy by the name of Max Vranizan. He can animate anything. Give him a pile of dog shit and he'd have it tap dancing and blowing kisses in five minutes."

"No kidding," Shorty said. "So he did the whatchamacallit on the ape?"

"Yeah." The driver grew suspicious. "Why?"

"My nephew," said Shorty. "He's nuts for that stuff. I told him I'd find out."

"I'll put a couple movie passes in the mail," the driver said, relieved. "If we don't get more kids going to the pictures, this industry is sunk."

Shorty grunted out a thanks. The driver, his courage restored, said, "Your interest in this girl still puzzles me. If there is anything that I can do to —"

"You can keep your eyes open," Shorty said. "The boss wonders if this is connected to the disappearance of two of our guys he holds close to his heart."

"Ah," said the man. "All three were acquainted, then?"

"She was a gal who made friends easily."

"These are dangerous times," the man behind the wheel said. "Young women should not be so free with their affections."

"You use what you got."

"She had it. In spades."

"Spades," Shorty said. "Spades of dirt, falling on her head. That's all she's got now."

"I'll ask around," the man said. He cleared his throat. "But I can't say I'm sorry about the way things have turned out. It's certainly solved my problem."

The Caddy dropped Shorty at his car. Marine air had fogged up the windows and he had to wipe them down to see. He turned the car around and headed for Slapsie Maxie's.

Once inside, he made for Mickey's table.

The gangster was holding court, as usual. Shorty saw Dean Martin walk by with an entourage and salute Mickey from across the room. Mickey extended two fingers, pointed them toward his eyes, and stabbed the air in Martin's direction. Then he disentangled himself from a young lady wearing pasties and harem pants and patted the seat next to him. Shorty sat down.

"Our friend at the studio don't know nothing about it," he said without preamble.

"He's a lying sonovabitch," Mickey responded. "Look into it some more. And what about Dragna?"

Shorty winced. Mickey had asked him to track down rumors that the Sicilian was behind it, but he hadn't gotten anywhere yet. "I've put out feelers," he said.

"We are going to whack this killer, even if it's not Dragna. And now, with a second girl? The city will thank me."

Shorty saw his opening. "Maybe, for once, our movie friend speaks the truth."

"It is a language with which they are unacquainted."

"Because there is also this special effects fuck."

"What special effects fuck?"

"Guy by the name of Max Vranizan. Turns out he was in love with her."

Mickey didn't say anything. You could almost hear his brain whirring. Mickey had a phenomenal memory and never forgot a name. He was so smart he could have headed up a Fortune 500 company, become president, if he'd grown up different.

"She was boning him too? Jeez, that gal got around."

"She just went with him to premieres. Maybe he finally snapped."

"Special effects, huh?"

"Yeah." Shorty screwed up his face and flapped his fingers. "He builds flying saucers and dinosaurs and apes and shit for the pictures. He worked on *Mighty Joe Young*."

"*Mighty Joe Young*? I *loved* that movie," Mickey interrupted excitedly. "How'd they do that, anyway? Was it a man in a gorilla suit?"

"I don't know, boss."

"Find out, will ya?" Mickey said.

"I'll try."

"The scene at the nightclub, with Joe swinging on the vines and all a them lions, that was amazing."

"I'll say. So, boss, you want us to take care of this special effects fuck?"

Mickey's caterpillar eyebrows drew together. "Don't be an idiot. I still think Dragna did it. But you need to nail it down."

211

"Got it, boss."

"And be discreet, will ya, Shorty? I can't have any more heat coming down on me."

CHAPTER 14

October 14, 1949

Lily wondered when Pico and Magruder slept. They looked bleary and unshaven, arriving this morning at six-thirty to quiz the boarders about Florence Kwitney. But none of the girls had known her. Other than the fact that she'd been strangled and dumped in the Hollywood Hills with one shoe, there appeared to be no connection.

"Maybe whoever murdered Florence Kwitney wanted police to *think* that Kitty's killer had struck again," Louise suggested.

"Or maybe Kitty's murderer killed a second girl as a decoy, to throw everyone off the track," Lily said.

Pico and Magruder refused to speculate. After reminding the girls to lock all doors and windows and avoid walking home alone at night, they left and Lily hurried upstairs to get properly dressed. She arrived at RKO at 9:20 and breathed a sigh of relief that

Selznick and Myra weren't in yet. The phone was ringing.

"Hello," she said, trying not to sound out of breath.

"Where's Myra? I've been calling for twenty minutes." It was a peevish Selznick, phoning from home. "Don't you know the rules? It's nine a.m. around here, no exceptions. Who is this, anyway?"

"It's Lily the temp, from yesterday. I don't know where Myra is."

"Well, Lily the temp," said David O. Selznick, "is your steno pad at hand?"

Lily's neck and shoulder were throbbing from holding the phone while taking dictation when Myra walked in two hours later. At noon, Selznick finally finished and said he'd be in soon. Lily hung up and massaged her neck.

Just then a woman walked in holding some papers.

"I'm here from the agency," she announced brightly.

Lily's heart galumphed. This wasn't the same temp she'd bribed away yesterday. Something had gone haywire. She braced herself. Myra looked at the woman, then at Lily, who was suddenly busy with her stenography. She asked to see the newcomer's papers.

Lily jumped up. "I think I'll go to lunch."

"Hold it right there, both of you. Lily, where's your paperwork?" Myra asked in a quiet but deadly voice. "I was so distracted yesterday I forgot to get it from you."

"I, uh . . ." Lily began.

The temp sat down and lit a cigarette. Myra's gaze grew flinty. "We'll soon get to the bottom of this," she said. She called the agency and began asking questions.

"As I suspected." Myra slammed down the phone. "Miss Kes—"

Just then Selznick blew in.

"Look at you three, just sitting around when there's so much work to be done," the producer said.

"Mr. Selznick." Myra pointed accusingly at Lily. "This young woman has been masquerading as a secretary from the temp agency. She's an imposter."

Selznick's intelligent brown eyes looked Lily over. "Takes pretty good dictation for an imposter."

"Thank you, Mr. Selznick," Lily said. "The truth of the matter is —"

"Not to worry, I can use all three of you. Even imposters." The producer winked at Lily. "I'll work you in shifts."

"You don't understand, sir. She's some

kind of spy, from the questions she's asking."

"Really?" Selznick rumpled his hair. "Did Joe Schenk send you? That dirty bastard. What he knows about making movies, you could stuff up a cat's ass. Tell you what. I'll pay you double to report a pack of lies back to him. Ha-ha. That'll fix him."

"Nobody sent me, Mr. Selznick. I'm . . . I'm . . ." Lily glanced at Myra. "The truth is that I've come here to RKO in the hopes of being discovered. I'm a wonderful actress, really I am. My drama teacher at Sioux City High School said I could do anything. Oh, please, won't you give me a screen test? I'll do anything."

"I knew it," Myra said triumphantly. "Mr. Selznick, if you'll pardon my saying so, I think we should get Security to throw her off the lot."

"I suppose you're right. Pity to lose such a good stenographer, though."

He disappeared into his office with the real temp and a few minutes later a uniformed guard arrived to escort Lily out.

The guard was surprisingly chatty. Lily tried not to gape as he pointed out the Atlanta train depot from *Gone With the Wind* in the distance.

They were passing Max Vranizan's workshop when a familiar figure shambled out and headed down the street, bent in thought.

"Max," Lily called.

The guard protested, but Lily explained that he was an old friend and hurried over, the guard trailing behind.

Lily hoped the animator would understand the pleading expression in her eyes. When she explained the "mistake" in Selznick's office, Max seemed to get it. He nodded and told the guard Lily was visiting the studio at his invitation and must have gotten lost. The guard studied the animator, trying to determine whether he was important enough to cross.

"If anyone asks, tell them I insisted," Max said. "I'll take full responsibility."

"Suit yourself." The guard shrugged, then left.

Max turned to her, frowning. "What are you up to now, Lily?" He began walking. "And make it snappy, because I'm on my way to a meeting."

"Who with?" She fell into step.

"Maynard Wylie." Seeing her blank look, he added, "The legendary producer. He's flush with cash from several war films and wants to do a special effects picture about a monster octopus."

"Max, I need your help. Would you introduce me to the makeup and wardrobe people and say I'm your friend so they'll talk to me?"

"When I get back," Max said. "This is like getting an audience with God."

They turned a corner and Lily saw Myra gesticulating to another security guard.

"Oh no," Lily said. "I can't let them see me."

"Lily, if you scupper this meeting, I swear I'll never talk to you again. I already wasted several hours trying to convince those damn detectives I'd never met Florence Kwitney."

Lily stopped. "Did you go out there last night?"

"Naw. That was a stupid idea. They showed up at the studio this morning. Now, really, I've got to go."

"Just tell me where Makeup is."

He gave her directions and strode away.

Lily hurried across the lot, scanning nervously for Myra. Several little kids sat on a pile of gravel in the sun, flicking pebbles at one another and looking miserable. A girl with a pink ribbon in her blond ringlets curled in her mother's lap, sucking her thumb.

Seeing a soundstage, Lily popped in to see if there was anyone to talk to. It smelled of fresh paint. High on the catwalks, technicians stood, adjusting equipment. Onstage, a man with a clipboard was blocking out shots. The only action seemed to be around a small circle on the soundstage floor, where grips, gaffers, and crew members were on their knees, faces tight with concentration, shooting craps. Lily moved on.

When she reached Makeup, Lily found a row of actors sitting in chairs, having their greasepaint applied and their hair done. Some of them looked familiar, like faces Lily had seen in the movies, but she couldn't place them. They weren't headliners, though — all the really big stars had private trailers. Lily scanned the makeup girls, looking for a friendly, open face. She spied a likely candidate swabbing a damp cotton ball across the forehead of a fortyish man in a toga who was reading a folded-over sports page.

"Hello," she said, walking up. The girl put down a bottle of witch hazel and began applying whitestick under the man's puffy eyes. "I'm a friend of Kitty Hayden's family," Lily went on. "I wonder if I might speak to you."

The girl popped a bubble of chewing gum. She moistened an eyebrow pencil between her lips and began to thicken the man's brows. Busy with his paper, the man didn't look up.

Lily thought maybe the girl hadn't heard.

"Excuse me," she said. "I was wondering —"

The girl stepped back to examine her handiwork. Her eyes flickered over Lily. She carefully placed the pencil back and picked up a grease stick.

"Sure, I knew Kitty," she said at last. "Great gal. We're all in shock."

"Thank you. What's your name, by the way?"

"Marion Szabo." The girl wiped her hand on her smock, extended it. They shook hands. "Pleased to meet you. I'm Lily Kessler. Did you ever do Kitty's makeup?"

The girl put down the grease stick. The man unfolded his paper and made a notation in the margin.

"She usually did her own," Marion said. "But sometimes she'd borrow a lipstick."

"Did she ever talk about boyfriends? Any problems?"

"Not that I recall. I hope they find the sicko who did this to her," Marion said.

"Me too. What about this other girl, Florence Kwitney?"

"Never heard of her. You know what I think?" Marion leaned in. "They should take another look at that special effects guy. I heard he's a little cuckoo."

"Was she afraid of him?"

"Honey, I don't know. I'm just saying."

Just then, another makeup artist rushed past with the metal box that held the tools of their trade. "Soundstage Five," she told Marion. "They need us on the double."

Lily said good-bye and moved on. Some girls were eager to chat. Others scurried away when they heard Kitty's name. Lily didn't hear anything new. Walking through Wardrobe an hour later, she stopped before a girl who was picking apart the seam on a satin bodice stitched with tiny seed pearls.

Lily leaned against the table. "That's absolutely gorgeous," she said. "A girl could get married in a gown like that."

The seamstress gave a faint snicker. "First comes love, then comes marriage . . ."

"Then comes the mama with a baby carriage," Lily said, supplying the last line.

"Seems one of our leading ladies forgot the middle part," the seamstress said, giving the thread a savage tug. "I have to let her dress out."

Lily grew very still. Trying to remember. Dresses, seams. She was in Kitty's bedroom, holding a sundress after the police had searched the room. The seam was strained.

Darts had been let out. Then Red had snatched it out of her hand.

"Pregnant," Lily said out loud.

"Not for long," the seamstress said in a sly voice.

Lily studied her. "Where would you . . . ? I mean, if you had a problem that . . ." Lily's hand made a curving motion over her belly.

The girl's eyes narrowed. "I'm sure I don't know," she said, suddenly prim. "Who are you anyway, and what's your business here, asking all these questions?"

"I'm a friend of . . ." Lily bit her tongue, realizing that the other seamstresses had begun to listen. She felt the temperature plummet. "I was just wondering if —"

"I have work to do," the seamstress said, ducking her head as a woman with dyed red hair and a brisk manner strode into the room. The other girls bent their heads too. As the woman approached with an inquisitory look, Lily hurried through Wardrobe and back outside.

"Hey," she heard a woman call behind her. "Wait a minute."

Lily hunched her shoulders and kept going.

"I'd like to talk to you," the voice said, closer now. A hand grabbed her. Lily whirled around, desperate to think up a new lie. And saw Marion Szabo.

"I was hoping to run into you," the makeup girl said. "I remembered something. A few months back I ran into Kitty in the commissary and she was giggling like she'd had too much champagne. Floating on air. She asked if I could keep a secret, then told me she had a new beau. Someone she called 'the Big K.' "

Relieved excitement flooded through Lily. "Have you spoken to the police?"

Marion shrank back. "No one's come to ask me about Kitty."

"Did she tell you his name?"

"No."

"Was it serious?"

"I asked her. She said, 'No, it's not serious, Marion, but it sure is a lot of fun.' "

Lily took a deep breath. "Did Kitty ever hint that she might be pregnant?"

An alarmed look crossed Marion's face. "We weren't that close, just to say hi and —"

"But let's say a girl did get into trouble, where would she go?"

Through the grapevine, every girl at the studio probably knew exactly where to find the abortionist, how much he charged, even how to get the cash in a hurry. There were things a desperate girl could do. What did it matter, one last time?

"I've really got to go," Marion said, inching away.

"Please," Lily said. "I'm trying to find Kitty's killer."

"I don't see how . . ."

The girl was frightened. But she knew, Lily could almost see the address floating there behind her eyes. She had to make it okay for her to tell.

"Look, I know you're not the kind of girl who'd ever get herself into a bind like that. But what if this guy who did the operation is a butcher? What if he had something to do with Kitty's murder? A guy like that ought to be put away so he can't hurt other girls, don't you think?"

Marion Szabo bit her lip and looked away. Lily got out a pencil and a piece of paper.

"You don't need to say anything, just write it down. I won't reveal where I got it. Promise."

A moment later, Lily hugged her and said good-bye, a scrawled address tucked securely into her pocketbook.

Lily picked her way back to the Special Effects hangar. Just outside Max's office, she heard a man say, "Show some imagination, for god's sake."

"It's because of my imagination that I can't do it, Mr. Sullivan."

Walking in, Lily saw Max and another man examining a terrarium. Amid the rocks and dirt were two lizards, the kind that sun themselves on every L.A. hillside. Someone had painted blue and red stripes down one lizard and green and purple spots on the other. Lizard One also had an Elizabethan collar around his neck and a spiky club at the end of his tail. Lizard Two sported metallic spikes down his back and horns. Lily could see the white dots of dried Elmer's glue where the reptiles had been modified.

The man in the suit turned to Lily.

"Don't you think they look like dinosaurs? All he has to do is rile them up a little so they'll fight. Shave eighty thousand dollars off production costs, just like that."

Red blotches were visible on Max's high, pale forehead. He compressed his lips. "I can't do it, Mr. Sullivan."

"Why not?" The man was apoplectic. "I've done all the prep work already, you lazy sonovabitch."

A vein began to throb at Max's temple. Lily remembered him explaining the weeks of painstaking sketches, the building of the armature, the search for the perfect fur or skin, the obsessive detail and love lavished on his creatures. She wondered how much of Max's soul got whittled away with each of these battles, how long before hunger won out over creative pride. Or did these high-strung artists just crack?

"Because they're *lizards*," Max said.

The man couldn't believe his ears. "Of course they're lizards. Dinosaurs were lizards too."

Max gazed at the terrarium. One hand went out. Lily saw his long delicate fingers twitch. He had the hands of an artist. She imagined those hands holding a length of fine wire, stretching it taut. The deft way he'd wrap each end around those ink-stained fingers, the look of intense concentration on his face, much like the one he wore now.

"But lizards can't move the way I want them to," Max said, his voice low. "They can't show anger, fear, hunger, greed, malice. They've got no personality."

"Personality?" screamed the producer. "We're talking about a fucking dinosaur movie."

Max didn't say anything. He heaved up the terrarium and brought it down on the producer's head.

Dirt, rocks, reptiles, and shattered glass

rained down. The producer let out a cry —
half gasp, half scream — as blood flowed
from his forehead. He backed away slowly,
raw fear in his eyes.

"You belong in a cage, you know that,
buddy?" He spit out bits of glass. "They
told me you were temperamental, but you're
off-your-rocker dangerous."

Max dusted his hands, squatted, and
picked up a shard of the terrarium glass. It
glinted in the light. He straightened, pointed
it at the producer, and said, "Get out of my
office, you fat prick."

"Jesus Christ," the producer yelped, running away.

The door slammed. Lily heard a clink as
the shard of glass hit the floor. The animator sagged into a chair. He gave a low moan
and passed one hand across his forehead as
if he couldn't believe what he'd just done.

"You could have killed him," Lily said,
recalling the red haze in Max's eyes right
before he exploded. Now she saw only a
spent, bewildered man. It was like he was
two different people.

"They'll fire you," she said.

He laughed, a queer light suffusing his
face. "They can't afford to."

"Why not?"

The animator pushed himself out of the

chair and walked over to the closet, where he got out a broom and dustpan and began sweeping up the mess.

"Because I make them a lot of money," Max said, his voice a curious mix of boasting and loathing. "Haven't you heard? After Willis O'Brien and Ray Harryhausen, I'm the best trick man in the business."

Lily wondered if Max had killed Kitty and the studio had covered it up. The phone rang, startling them both.

"This is Doris. Mr. Rhodes would like to see you in his office right away," a female voice announced.

Max turned, making it difficult for Lily to hear the rest of their conversation.

"Who was that?" Lily asked when he hung up.

"She works for the director of Studio Security."

Lily wondered why Max didn't look worried. "I *told* you. That producer ran right over there and complained."

Max waved away her protests with a languid hand. "It's only a few scrapes. Let him take his piece-of-shit idea to one of the B outfits, I don't need him. Besides" — Max examined Lily — "that's not why they called. Doris said I'm supposed to bring the girl who's been roaming around asking questions."

Lily's stomach plummeted. They must have spies on the lot. Or had Myra reported her?

"The studios are paranoid," Max explained as they walked over. "Anytime anyone gets killed, it's bad publicity. The almighty Hays Code."

"Wasn't he some congressman?"

"Will Hays founded the Production Code, which lays out what can be shown on screen." He ticked it off. "No immorality, adultery, homosexuality, drug use. The villain must pay. Good must triumph."

"What does that have to do with a murdered starlet?"

"The 'morals' clause. Actors sign contracts promising not to do anything immoral."

"How ridiculous. Hollywood is rife with sex, drugs, and excess."

"It's hypocritical, I know. But the studios are terrified the government will step in and say, *okay, you obviously can't police yourselves, so we're going to decide what movies you can make.*"

"So the studio would go to great lengths to cover up a scandal?"

"Absolutely. I've heard that the dossiers Rhodes keeps on people would put Stalin's secret police to shame."

"What does he use them for?"

Max gave a sick grin. "He doesn't. They're his insurance that the stars behave."

The security chief was behind closed doors on a telephone conference when they arrived. Twenty minutes passed. The secretary apologized for the delay. After a half hour, Max grew annoyed. "I've got a picture coming out in January," he fumed, "and I can't waste time like this."

When the door finally opened, Lily was surprised to see the man who had sidled around the desk in David O. Selznick's office asking questions. She could tell he recognized her too. Lily recalled an old OSS saying: if caught, stick as close to the truth as possible.

"Haven't I seen you before, Miss . . . ?"

"Kessler," Lily said.

"That's right." Frank Rhodes smiled. "In David's office. And now you've popped up again like a bad penny. Why are you nosing around asking questions and churning the gossip mill?"

"I'm a friend of Kitty's family in Illinois," Lily said. "We're just trying to get some basic information . . ."

"Max, how did this woman get on the lot?"

"She's visiting me."

"I wasn't trying to cause trouble."

"I won't have you dragging this dead actress through the mud. We at RKO stand for decency and good clean entertainment. The last thing we need is a scandal."

"Has there been any suggestion of a scandal?" Lily asked.

"Of course not. But you can't just come here and harangue people. You're not with the police. You're not a family member. You're nothing but a troublemaker. Max, I'm banning her from the lot."

"I'm sorry for the disturbance," Lily said, "but perhaps you could tell me what your security man found when he searched Kitty's room."

Rhodes's eyes were flat and distant. "I don't know what you're talking about."

"His name was Clarence Fletcher. He showed the landlady an RKO card."

"The police already asked me about that. We don't have anyone here by that name."

"So someone impersonated an RKO employee to gain access to Kitty's room?"

Rhodes checked his watch. He looked impatient to have them gone. "I don't know."

The secretary popped her head in. "Mr. Rhodes, your stepson called to cancel lunch."

A look of aggravation crossed the security chief's face. Lily imagined an insouciant young man with a peeling nose and white flannel pants, holding a tennis racket. Hollywood's Golden Youth.

"Call him back and tell him he's got twenty minutes to get here or he won't see his allowance this month."

The secretary withdrew.

"What if this fake RKO fellow was the murderer?" Lily continued stubbornly.

"Then the police will catch him and the landlady will identify him," Rhodes said. "One hates to speak ill of the dead, but Miss Hayden wasn't too choosy about the company she kept."

So much for not dragging his actress through the mud.

"What do you mean?" Lily feigned innocence.

"She consorted with gangsters, Miss Kessler. And there's a gang war under way in this town right now. Max, tell her what I'm talking about, will ya?"

He pressed a button and the secretary appeared to herd them out. As the door closed behind them, they heard Rhodes get on the phone, but his voice was too muffled to make out.

They picked their way through a group of

vestal virgins marching toward a Roman temple. At the studio gates, Max waved to the guard.

"How's it going, Charlie?"

"That's a hell of a 'special effect' you got there, Max. Good day, miss." The guard doffed his hat. "Say, my son's a nut for those movies of yours. Spends all his spare time sketching dinosaurs and giant apes. Any chance I could bring him around one afternoon?"

"Sure thing, Charlie. Be delighted."

Max turned to Lily. "Where are you going now?"

"An errand," she said, thinking of the address the makeup girl had given her.

CHAPTER 15

"This is the street," Gadge said as they turned onto Morton Street. "I'm sure."

Harry's voice rose in exasperation. "You were sure last time too. And the time before that."

"I remember that dry cleaner's. There was a cat in the window."

Shaking his head and muttering about snipe hunts, Harry parked and they set off along the sycamore-lined street.

He'd spent most of the previous day chasing photos for the Florence Kwitney murder investigation and they'd run out of light before Gadge could show him where he'd found the shoe. Today he swore not to rest until he had some answers.

They'd started at home this morning, trying to pin down exactly which day Gadge had made his discovery. The kid didn't know, but he produced a copy of *Treasure Island* that he'd checked out of the library the same day.

"Jesus Christ, kid." Harry chuckled. "You don't have a roof over your head, but you've got a library card. If that don't beat all. How long they let you take books out for these days?"

"Two weeks."

"God bless Andrew Carnegie and his libraries. So we count back from the due date."

The card was stamped OCT. 22, so they subtracted fourteen days, which meant Gadge had found the shoe early on the morning of October 8. The papers said no one had seen Kitty Hayden since the evening of October 7. Harry had a hunch she'd been abducted and killed that night. Possibly from this very street.

Now they scanned the sidewalks, gutters, and vacant lots for any evidence to support their theory. The Santa Anas had shaken loose the season's first leaves, making a brown carpet that crunched underfoot. How the heck were you supposed to find anything under all that? Harry thought, kicking the leaves and feeling melancholy at this annual reminder that all things die.

A hundred yards below Hollywood Boulevard, they came to a row of tidy shops.

"Here," Gadge said, stopping. Harry

examined the sidewalk but saw nothing —
no thread, hair, dried blood, earrings, scraps
of cloth. It was a long block. He imagined
Kitty hurrying home late at night. Then a
sudden assault, in a lonely place with shuttered shops and no witnesses.

Harry questioned each shopkeeper, but as
he expected, they all closed by ten p.m. and
didn't recall anything unusual that evening.
Walking back to the sidewalk, he hiked up
his pants and got on his hands and knees
for a beetle's-eye view.

"You sure the shoe was here?" he asked
finally.

"Yup, and it wasn't there at eleven the
night before."

"How're you so sure?"

"The owner of that deli" — Gadge pointed
to a store that Harry had just canvassed —
"sometimes throws away perfectly good
sandwiches. I waited until he went home at
eleven to go through the trash."

Harry pushed himself off his knees and
dusted off leaf crumbs. He'd narrowed it to
a seven-hour window — Kitty Hayden had
run into trouble between eleven p.m. and
six a.m. the next morning when Gadge
found her shoe. Something bad had happened here, he could almost feel it.

He decided to give it one more try. Head

bent, eyes scanning, hands clasped behind his back, he walked slowly to Hollywood Boulevard, then crossed the street and came down the other side. This time, he spied something wedged into a crack where the sidewalk had buckled from the tree roots. It looked like a big dirty pebble. He picked it up, saw that it was a button. Stylish. Carved of bone. A woman's button. With a bit of dirt-encrusted red thread still in the hole. To match the red suit? Kitty Hayden's body had been found a mile away. But the shoe suggested she'd tussled with her attacker right here. And now a button. Was it even hers? Harry scraped off grime with his fingernail. He needed to look at photos of the suit again. But first . . .

Harry slipped the button into his pocket and called Gadge. They hiked back up to Hollywood Boulevard and Harry studied the businesses on either side of the intersection. A greengrocer, a leather shop, a florist. Lots of offices. They all would have been closed by eleven p.m. Half a block down, Harry saw a nightclub called the Crow's Nest. Bars stayed open late. Maybe a patron had heard something.

The sign on the nightclub door said CLOSED, but the front door was unlocked. They walked in.

The place smelled of last night's sweat, spilled alcohol, and a miasma of stale perfume and smoke. In the dirty aquarium light, couples danced. A man sat at an upright piano, picking out tunes with one hand while holding a drink. Seeing Harry, he put down his drink and launched into "God Save the Queen." He played atrociously and Harry thought he might be drunk.

There was a sudden shuffling on the floor. A wary watchfulness descended. The bartender, a handsome guy with a ruffled white shirt, plunged glasses into hot sudsy water. Harry made his way to the bar.

"I'd like to ask your customers something. It's about a woman who's mur . . . disappeared. I wanted to know if anyone heard anything unusual the night of October seventh out on the street. Like screaming or the sounds of a fight."

"You a copper?"

"No. Just a . . . friend of hers."

"And I'm Joan Crawford," the bartender said. "Sorry, bud. I don't know anything about your lady friend. And we're closed."

"No, you're not."

"It's a private party. Didn't you see the CLOSED sign out front? I suggest you leave."

"Now, wait a —"

The bartender put down the glass he was washing and began walking around the bar. He was bigger and burlier than he had looked from behind the counter.

Harry said thank you, grabbed Gadge by the collar, and left.

Back at the car, he found his newspaper photos of the dead girl. Most of the buttons on the girl's jacket had popped, revealing the blouse beneath. But one was intact. Harry held his button next to the glossy black-and-white image, feeling a strange tingling at the base of his neck. It matched.

The sign on the stucco building said DOCTOR S. R. LAFFERTY & ASSOCIATES, DERMATOLOGY, but the door was locked. Maybe Dr. S. R. Lafferty no longer helped girls in trouble. Lily was about to leave when the venetian blinds in the window parted and a pale doughy face looked out. Then the door opened.

"Yes?" said a man who wore stained hospital scrubs.

"A friend of mine sent me . . . I'm looking for Dr. Lafferty . . ."

Lily wasn't sure how to go on.

"We're closed for lunch," the man said, staring at her lower belly as if she'd drawn a crimson bull's-eye in lipstick.

"I can come back."

"If you're here for a skin care consultation, please call us for an appointment."

"That's not what —" Lily began.

The man craned his neck around her to see if she was alone.

"What do you want?" he asked, his words fast and insinuating.

The man leaned over and coughed so violently that his body convulsed. Pulling a wadded handkerchief out of his pocket, he hacked and hacked. There was dirt under his fingernails. She prayed this wasn't Dr. Lafferty. Lily wanted to flee, but she pushed on.

"I was hoping to talk to the doctor about some trouble I've been having."

He licked his lips. "How long has this been bothering you?"

"Nine weeks," she said, feeling that they were talking in code.

A flicker passed over his eyes.

"The doctor can help you, miss. Come back after two."

Lily was back at two-fifteen after eating an egg salad sandwich and drinking a cup of coffee at a lunch counter. This time there was nothing sinister — she walked into a clean and pleasant reception area appointed with magazines and ashtrays. Nurses in crisp white uniforms called patients. One woman had a pimply teenage girl with her. Several older women with bejeweled, liver-spotted hands hid their faces behind hats and oversized dark glasses. The man with the begrimed fingernails was nowhere in sight.

Lily signed the patient roster and waited for her name to be called. After an hour, she checked with the receptionist and was told the doctor would see her last because she didn't have an appointment.

Finally, the nurse led her into an examination room filled with glass cabinets and advertisements for face-care products. Twenty minutes later the doctor came in.

He was in his sixties, but his hair and eyebrows were dyed the color of shoe-black. His cheeks were ruddy, the skin clean-shaven, and he smelled faintly of antiseptic. The skin around his eyes was stretched taut, giving him the look of an aged doll. When he picked up a clipboard, Lily noticed a tremor in his hand.

"Welcome. I'm Dr. Lafferty. What can I do for you, Miss . . . Corcoran?" he said, using the name she'd given.

Lafferty peered at Lily's skin. "Your complexion looks fine to me. Bit pale, maybe."

"A friend told me about you," Lily said. "I have a problem."

He looked up. "Ah, yes. I believe my associate mentioned a girl. Lie down on that table and let's have a look at you."

Lily froze. "But —"

"Do you want to take care of this or don't you?" he said sternly. "It's all the same to me."

Lily felt trapped. She didn't like being alone in an examination room with this strange doctor, couldn't bear the thought of him touching her.

"This isn't a pelvic exam, Miss Corcoran. No need to take your clothes off. I'm just going to palpate your belly, see how far along you are."

Reluctantly, Lily lay down on the stainless steel table, holding her legs tightly together and smoothing her skirt down as far as it would go. She tried not to shudder as she felt his hand slide under her girdle, her fist cocked for the moment when his hand would stray lower and she'd punch him in the mouth.

He probed the contours of her stomach, face furrowed in thought. The hand withdrew.

"All right, you can sit up now."

Lily feared Dr. Lafferty had caught her out, and started preparing a lie in her head.

"You're ten weeks pregnant," the doctor announced with authority.

Lily couldn't believe that he'd take her money and scrape up her insides when she wasn't even pregnant.

"We can help you," he continued. "It'll be a hundred fifty dollars. Cash. What do you say?"

Lily was so stunned she couldn't say anything.

"Don't look shocked. You girls think it's fun and games. Now you've got to pay the piper."

Lily wanted to slap his face. Instead, she smiled.

"Do you see a lot of girls like me?"

He gave a sandpaper laugh. "More and more." He shook his head. "I reckon it's the war that did it. All you gals getting jobs and running around on your own."

Seeing something in her face, he added, "Mind you, I'll do anything I can to help a girl in trouble. And it's not for the money, because there isn't any. Not after the precautions I take."

"I bet the studios send you business." Lily inclined her head west and smiled enigmatically, letting him decide whether she meant facials, nose jobs, or abortions.

"They've got accounts here," he said, adding with sudden suspicion, "Who'd you say sent you?"

"A friend from Hollywood." Lily felt her way through the conversation. "She might have gone by the name of Doreen."

A strange light flashed, then banked, behind his eyes.

"Don't recall anyone by that name."

"Kitty, then," said Lily, watching him.

"Nope," he said.

Dr. Lafferty pressed an intercom and said, "Reginald, Room Three, please."

Again, she noticed the tremor in his hand, shuddering to think of him performing surgery.

Lily had sensed the air in the room shift as soon as she mentioned the name Doreen. She felt pretty sure that Kitty had been here, using her real name.

"Miss Corcoran, I'm afraid there's been a misunderstanding. I don't think I'll be able to help you after all. And I'm a very busy man. Good day to you. My associate will see you out."

He left and Lily, her heart galloping in her chest, made to follow him. She took a step and ran smack into the man in the orderly's outfit. A hand with dirty fingernails gripped her wrist, tightening until her flesh burned.

The walls echoed with silence. It was late afternoon, no one left in the building. Reginald hauled her to a back door and shoved her out. She stumbled and fell to her knees, found herself in an alley. The man stood in the doorway, arms crossed.

"You don't want to get on the doctor's bad side," Reginald said. "He's got friends who could make life difficult for you. Now get lost and don't come back."

Lily retreated to a safe distance. She'd blown her cover by uttering Doreen's name. This was her last chance to goad Reginald into revealing anything useful. In daytime, here in suburban Culver City, Lily felt perfectly safe.

"Or what?" she taunted. "You think you can take care of me the way you did Kitty Hayden? Did she die on Dr. Lafferty's operating table? You don't care about the girls you butcher, do you? So long as you get paid."

"Miss, are you okay?" came a quavering voice from across the alley. An elderly woman in a flowery print dress stood on her porch.

"I'm fine," Lily said, pushing her hair off her face. "But did you know that you're living next to an abortionist?"

"There's no call for that kind of language, young lady." The woman shook her head and Lily heard the screen door slam as she went back inside.

Lily calmed down as she dusted herself off. She'd call Magruder and Pico, tell them her suspicions. Suggest that they investigate. As if on cue, a police car pulled up to the mouth of the alley. A uniformed policeman got out, baton in hand.

"We got a report of a disturbance in the alley, miss. What seems to be the problem?"

"I'm glad you're here, Officer. I'd like to file a report. I was just manhandled in that doctor's office," she said, pointing to the red brick building. "The doctor in there performs abortions on young women in trouble and I think he may know something about —"

"Dr. Lafferty?" the policeman interrupted.

"Yes sir, that's —"

"Dr. Lafferty is a dermatologist in good standing in this city, miss. Are you impugning his reputation?"

"He just told me I was ten weeks pregnant when I wasn't and offered to take care of my 'problem' and —"

"Why are you telling a dermatologist that you're pregnant?"

"Because he's using dermatology as a

246

cover to perform —"

"Why did you lie? Are you on some kind of medication, miss?"

"No," she cried, "I'm trying to tell you that —"

"Because I'm inclined to take you down to the station and arrest you for disturbing the peace."

"There's no need to do that, Officer Tranow," said a man behind her.

It was Dr. Lafferty, wearing a suit and carrying a briefcase.

"Doctor," the policeman said with a warm smile. "Maybe you could tell me what in heaven's name —"

"This young woman is clearly disturbed," the doctor said. "She came into my office several hours ago, demanding to be seen. She is suffering under the delusion that she's pregnant. I called you because I was afraid she was a danger to herself."

"*You* called the police?" Lily said in disbelief.

Lafferty smiled. "Officer Tranow's our neighborhood beat cop. He makes sure everything's running smoothly."

"That's right." Tranow's eyes flickered distastefully over Lily. "So how about it, Doctor? You want to swear out an affidavit for Camarillo?"

Lily blanched. Camarillo was the state mental hospital in Ventura County. Seeing the cozy way the doctor and the cop spoke, so casual and friendly, filled Lily with unease. It was simple enough for doctors to get people locked up. She saw herself screaming endlessly, the sound ricocheting silently in a fun house hall of mirrors.

She began to back away.

"Why don't we step inside my office?" Lafferty suggested.

Officer Tranow's hand tightened on his baton and he walked toward her. They flanked her.

At that moment, a car appeared at the end of the alley, speeding toward them. As they scattered to get out of the way, it stopped with a shriek of brakes. Detective Pico vaulted out. Then he was standing beside her.

"This little gal giving you trouble?" Pico said.

Tranow regarded him with annoyance. "This is a police matter, sir," he said. "We'll thank you to step aside and be on your way."

Pico flipped open his LAPD detective badge and grinned.

But Tranow was not so easily dissuaded. "You're out of bounds, Detective," he said with a nasty smirk. "This is Culver City, which falls under the jurisdiction of the Culver City Police Department, not LAPD."

Pico's smile grew broader. "I know that, Officer. But this young lady and I are friends, if you take my meaning."

He turned to Lily, talking low and fast. "How ya doing, sweetheart? I haven't seen you in a blue moon. Why'dja run out on me like that?"

Lily was speechless.

"So if you two don't mind," Pico said, "I'm going to escort my little friend back across the city line."

"Get her out of here," Lafferty said. "Miss Corcoran, I recommend that you go home and lie down. You have suffered a hysterical episode. If this condition reoccurs, you'll need to go for a full evaluation. I can recommend a specialist."

But Officer Tranow wouldn't give up without a fight.

"If I see you in Culver City again, I will arrest you for disturbing the peace."

"Okay, Miss *Corcoran,* off we go now," Pico said, maneuvering and pushing Lily to his car. Hands on her shoulders, he shoved her into the passenger seat, whispering "Shut up," as his lips grazed her cheek. Then he slammed her door and went around to the driver's side.

"Thank you kindly," Pico called out in parting. "Be happy to return the favor someday."

He yanked the car into reverse and quickly backed out of the alley. When they'd gone around the block and were back on Venice Boulevard, he spoke.

"You want to tell me what you were doing, using a fake name and riling up a studio abortionist? You almost got yourself in all kinds of trouble."

But all Lily could think of was the burning sensation on her cheek where his lips had been, the shock that had run down her spine at his casual touch. No one had touched her like that in eight months, not since Joseph. Then an overwhelming, knee-quaking relief hit her. Underneath the civil conversation in the parking lot, she'd sensed menace, a powerful net drawing tight.

Still, it wouldn't do to let her emotions show. Turning to Pico, she asked with numb calmness she didn't feel, "Why are you following me, Detective?"

CHAPTER 16

"Following you?" Pico said, in a perfectly modulated voice. "I was just on my way to pick up some Danish at Helm's Bakery down the road. Boys at headquarters love their crullers."

Lily laughed. "Danish? At five in the afternoon? You expect me to believe that?"

"Why wouldn't you?"

His even tone told her that not all good actors work for the studios. He was staring straight ahead, concentrating on driving. Under his breath, he hummed a song.

"Will you please tell me what that was all about?" she said.

He stopped humming and gave her an earnest look. "You looked like you needed rescuing."

Pico chuckled, shook his head. "And you actually listened to me back there. Amazing."

"Did I have a choice?"

His eyes crinkled. "No."

"I can take care of myself."

"I'll bet that's what Kitty Hayden thought too."

Lily frowned. He'd dodged her question deftly, turned the conversation back to Kitty. Of course he was following her, nothing else would explain his sudden appearance. But maybe, just for once, it wasn't a bad thing.

"Did Kitty go see Dr. Lafferty too?" Lily asked.

"I don't know. But you sure seem to think she did."

"Was she pregnant?"

Pico's hands tightened on the steering wheel, but he said nothing.

"Is that why someone killed her? What did the autopsy show?"

"We're not releasing those results."

"Why not?"

"No comment."

"Isn't the family entitled to see the autopsy?" Lily probed, figuring that Mrs. Croggan would tell her what it said.

Pico pressed his lips together. "When we conclude the investigation. Until then, it's evidence."

Lily felt the truth wash over her, telling her what Pico wouldn't. Kitty *had* been pregnant.

"Kitty went to Dr. Lafferty to get an abortion, I know it. He's as phony as a three-dollar bill."

Pico turned somber eyes on her. They were the gray-green of the sea before a storm, shadows moving in their depths. "Unfortunately, he's all too real. One of these days, we'll have enough evidence to put him away. But the studios protect him."

Lily leaned back. She wasn't going to get a direct answer on the autopsy results, but she could infer plenty. It was time to move on to other questions.

"Have you learned anything more about Florence Kwitney?"

Pico shot her a sideways glance. She felt him hesitate.

Then he said, "The head of detectives assigned it to another team, at least for now. Figures we've got our hands full."

"Indeed. Speaking of which, what happened with Freddy Taunton?"

Pico rubbed his chin. Again, there was a moment's lag. He shot her a look, then said, "Turns out he really did go fishing. Arrived at the San Pedro dock five minutes before the boat left, gave a false name, and tipped the captain fifty dollars to take him on. Boat just got back from Baja."

"Is he in custody? What did he say?"

"He didn't come back. Had an attack on board of what appeared to be appendicitis. They dropped him off in Ensenada yesterday, told a taxi to take him to the hospital. Medical staff say he never arrived."

"Of course not," Lily groaned.

Pico regarded her with amusement. "We've wired Scotland Yard to see if he's got a record and alerted the Mexican police and our Border Patrol. Whether or not he's our man, we'd like to talk to him."

"I can't believe those girls bought his 'landed gentry' story and let him tie them up and take photos. Like lambs to the slaughter."

Pico gave her a sideways look. "Unlike you, who waltzed into his apartment after sweet-talking the manager. And after you found the dirty pictures, you called to tip us off. Don't look at me like that. I've figured it out. Did you take them? Because Magruder already warned you —"

"I had one photo," Lily admitted. "But I dropped it trying to escape. They're horrible photos, Detective Pico. Posed images of Kitty being tortured. I can't believe anyone would buy such filth. And then the manager . . . he nearly caught me. He was drunk. He wanted to rape me; I barely made it out of there. He must have found the photos."

"Jesus," said Pico. "Why didn't you tell me? I'll get a warrant, we'll search his place."

Lily shook her head. "He will have sold them, or moved them somewhere safe."

"We'll see about that," Pico said grimly. "Meanwhile, if Taunton tries to slip back into the country, we'll nab him."

"The border's long and mostly un-guarded."

Lily shivered. Pico glanced over.

"You cold?" His voice softened. "I'll turn on the heater."

"No, I'm . . ." She paused, touched by how responsive he was, how attuned to her. But that was only a cop thing. They were trained to be keenly observant. She knew because she was that way too. It was noth-ing personal.

A blast of warm air hit her, caressing her, enveloping her. On the car radio, Les Brown & His Orchestra were playing "I've Got My Love to Keep Me Warm."

His eyes locked on hers. "Better?"

She nodded.

Slowly the tightness left her limbs. But suddenly she missed Joseph so much. Her body ached for him, the press of his flesh against hers.

"What's the matter, Miss Kessler?" Pico's voice was gentle. "Does it give you the heebie-jeebies? First Kitty, then this Florence Kwitney?"

"No. Well, maybe a little. But that's not it."

He stayed silent, letting her work it out.

"It's just so weird . . ." She struggled to put it into words. They were at a red light, the ruby glow casting warm shadows inside of the car. She glanced up. The detective's face was patient, his eyes steady.

"Take your time," he said.

Lily sniffed. "I mean, it's strange to be back in L.A. after so long." She shook her head. "And under these circumstances. I thought everything would be safe here. And it isn't."

"I know how you feel. That's why I became a cop. Does that make me hopelessly old-fashioned?"

A replay of their conversation the other day. But from a different angle, without the gamesmanship and swagger. Had she been wrong about him?

"Not at all," she said.

They drove through the darkling city.

"Where are you taking me?" she asked, sensing he was just marking time.

"Where do you want to go?" His voice was more soft and melodious than she could have imagined.

Lily felt something lurch inside of her. She braced herself against the seat.

"You can take me ho—" She gave a rueful laugh. "The boardinghouse, please. Funny, I almost called it home. But it's not home. Not by a long shot. Problem is, I don't know where home is anymore, or if I'd even recognize it." She paused. "Sorry, I'm not making much sense."

He was watching the road, a serious expression on his beautiful face.

"Maybe home's not a physical place," he said at last, "but something we make in our heart and carry around with us."

His words conjured up two birds building a nest, weaving rushes, twigs, and fluff with great care. She caught her breath at the delicacy of its construction, felt its rough weave prick her cupped hands.

"And if we're lucky," he went on, "one day we meet the right person to share that home with."

His eyes searched hers. The intensity she saw there made her glance away.

"Yes." She felt raw and vulnerable, afraid of her own voice. "Maybe that's the way it is."

Twilight deepened as they drove, the buildings receding into shadow, the hills turning a luminous shade of purple. Pico pulled in front of the rooming house and they sat there, talking about Kitty, cocooned in their own world as one by one the lights went on in the houses around them, casting an amber glow. The heater blasted out warm air. She wanted to stay there forever, suspended in time and place.

"Detective Pico?" Lily said at last.

"Yes?"

His voice sent her blood racing. She felt the thud of her pulse against her temple.

"Thank you," she said.

"You're welcome, Miss Kessler."

She felt something gather in the air and thicken around them, grow clotted and expectant. The thought of it terrified her.

"G'night," she said, and slipped from the car.

Behind her, she felt it rush out, a silent roar of disappointment.

He waited for her to run up the stairs, and then he drove away.

The spell broke as she walked into the rooming house. Then the nagging uncertainty descended again. What if Pico had swooped down, not to protect her from Lafferty, but to prevent her from learning something about Kitty?

Lily walked into the kitchen, got a glass of water. Standing at the sink, looking out onto the backyard, she heard a faint scuffling on the back porch, claws against wood. She went to the screen door, saw Mrs. Potter's cat under the light, playing with a mouse. The little dun thing scurried away and the cat let it reach the top step before batting it back. Then it pounced once more, holding it down with one paw while the mouse quivered in fear and exhaustion.

Lily flung open the screen door and ran out. "Shoo!" she said, waving her arms and stamping her foot.

The cat shot her a baleful look and slunk away. The mouse huddled on the wooden boards, too stunned or injured to move.

"Go on." Lily nudged it with her shoe. "Now's your chance."

Blood oozed from a slash on its back. Slowly, creakily, the mouse crept down the steps and disappeared.

"You're dreadfully cruel," she scolded the cat, which she knew waited nearby.

Something shifted on the porch behind her. She turned and saw Mrs. Potter's bulk in a wicker chair, shrouded in shadow.

"It's the natural order," the landlady's

voice drifted out, calm and disembodied. "And now you've gone and spoiled his fun."

"Hello, is anybody home?" came a voice from the front of the house.

Grateful to escape, Lily ran inside and saw the Carnation milkman, snappy in his brown uniform, standing on the porch.

"Is Mrs. Potter in?" he asked. "Got a bill here for twenty-two-fifty that's three months old. Boss says we'll have to stop service next week if she doesn't settle up."

"I'll see if I can get her," Lily said.

She found the landlady standing behind the kitchen door.

"Please tell him I'm not in," she whispered.

"Howdy, Mrs. Potter," the milkman called. "Are you there?"

The landlady retreated to the sink. She grabbed a towel and ran it along the tile counter. A high flush rose in her cheeks, a granite coldness filled her eyes.

"Why doesn't he just go away?" she said.

"I know you're in there, Mrs. Potter," the milkman sang out.

"Tell him now," Mrs. Potter said, whirling on Lily.

Lily went back and explained that the landlady was indisposed but she'd deliver the message. She shut the door, wondering how many other tradespeople Mrs. Potter owed.

Lily had dropped her purse when she came in and it gaped open, exposing her wallet. As if drawn by a magnet, Mrs. Potter glided over, eyes riveted by the bills.

"You carry quite a bit of money around," she said.

"Not usually," Lily answered. "But this trip . . . I wasn't sure . . ."

"It's dangerous to carry so much money," Mrs. Potter said. "You shouldn't let anyone know you have it."

Lily agreed. Mrs. Potter paced the parlor, as if agitated. "Money causes a lot of trouble," she said, apropos of nothing. "There are a lot of murders committed for money."

"You think Kitty was murdered over money?" Lily asked.

Mrs. Potter nodded slowly. "I wouldn't be at all surprised."

"But I thought she didn't have any."

"Other things have value too." Mrs. Potter regarded Lily with cold, clinical eyes. "Information, for example. There are people who pay well for that."

"Or kill for it?" Lily asked.

"Killing isn't what upsets people. It's getting caught." Seeing Lily's face, the landlady tried to explain.

"I interviewed a lot of murderers when I was a matron at the county jail. It gave me insight into their minds."

"You worked at the jail?" Lily said, surprised. "And you quit to run a boarding-house?"

"Yes." Mrs. Potter's eyes flickered. She sat down beside Lily.

"You don't think I could commit murder, do you?" Mrs. Potter placed a hand on Lily's shoulder and it took all her willpower not to flinch. It came to her now that Mrs. Potter saw the world quite differently than she did. Than most people. For the briefest moment, Lily walked in the shadows of Mrs. Potter's world, traversed a dead land-scape of ash.

"Well, I'm going to find some food, I'm starving," Lily said, standing up with a show of great casualness.

"Would you like me to scramble you some eggs, hon? I can go out to the garden and snip some herbs?"

Lily thought of the more sinister plants that dwelled in Los Angeles gardens. Pretty flowering shrubs like oleander and castor bean, with its bristling red-green leaves. She imagined a folded omelet, nicely browned with butter and topped with these diced plants, fishy chicken embryos tucked inside, tiny beaks and wings crunching between her teeth. She thought of the knob on her bedroom door in the middle of the night, the measured tread. The blood sport with the cat. Two strangled girls.

"That's okay," she said, trying not to shudder. "I'm craving chicken potpie. They have them at the lunch counter up the street."

CHAPTER 17

Detective Stephen Pico walked into Verni-chello's in West L.A. and looked around. Damn, but it smelled good. The tables were filling up, platters of food sailing out from the kitchen, a waiter presenting a bottle of something called *limoncello* to men with vulpine faces who sat at a corner table, a wall mural of an Italian hill town soaring up behind them.

The maître d' came up and Pico identi-fied himself and asked to speak to Jack Dragna. The man disappeared into the back. Pico hoped he'd get further with Dragna than he had at Mickey Cohen's haber-dashery.

Cohen had set up his clothing shop along an unincorporated stretch of Santa Monica Boulevard, just over the county line. Not that he didn't have friends at LAPD, but everyone knew he and Sheriff Biscailuz had grown up together on the East Side and were practically brothers. Mickey could be assured of peace and quiet, the LAPD left to cool its heels just across the border. Like Pico had been the other day, stonewalled by a small, ferrety guy named Shorty Lagonzola.

Soon the mâitre d' returned and led Pico into an office where a thickset man with hair combed straight back was eating dinner on a folding table, a napkin tucked into his shirt, his eyes riveted to the television. Dragna grunted and waved an arm to indicate for the detective to sit down. He had a droopy face like a basset hound, sallow skin, a large nose, and rough, thick-fingered hands, as if he wrenched giant turnips out of the ground for a living. So this was the mastermind behind half of L.A.'s prostitution and gambling rings.

"Mr. Dragna, I —"

Dragna held up a finger. "Quiet, please," he said with a reproachful look, then turned back to the black-and-white screen.

Pico considered turning it off, but was drawn in despite himself. The show was slapstick, funny. He wished he could afford a television. It was a helluva way to spend time. With a surge of music, the program broke for a commercial. Dragna gave a strange and melancholy sigh and turned his attention to the detective.

"You're not one of the usual faces they send," the gangster said. He opened a beer and called out something in Italian.

A thin young woman with black hair popped her head through the door, wiping her hands on an apron. She had the biggest shiner that Pico had seen outside the ring, blooming all yellow and purple.

Dragna snapped his fingers and said to bring Pico a beer and the woman returned a moment later with a bottle and a glass, which she placed on the TV tray. Dragna said something in Italian and the woman flinched, then reached into her apron pocket for a bottle opener. She opened Pico's beer, then left.

"I gotta be the only wop in town who don't drink red wine," Dragna said. "Gives me headache."

Pico was still staring at the door. "What happened to her eye?"

"My wife, she's very clumsy. Walked into the cupboard door. Again."

Pico allowed himself a moment to feel sorry for Mrs. Dragna. Then he said, "I'm here about the Kitty Hayden murder."

Dragna's face tightened, reminding Pico of an intelligent, aging bird of prey. On the TV, a man was extolling Chevrolet cars.

"What makes the LAPD think I know any more than what I read in the paper?"

"C'mon, Mr. Dragna, the whole city knows you and Mickey Cohen are at war. Kitty Hayden partied with two of Cohen's men in Palm Springs last week. They've disappeared and she's dead."

Dragna turned back to the screen, where the commercial was winding down.

"We are gonna be quiet and watch Lucille Ball now. I'll tell you whatever you want when it's over."

"Mr. Dragna —"

"She's got a thing for Latin men," Dragna said. "She married that greaser Desi, but he's running around on her."

The commercial ended. Dragna put down his beer and rubbed his hands together. "Here we go."

The program resumed. It was a variety show. Miss Ball and some other actresses Pico didn't recognize were arguing while making pies. Next thing he knew, Miss Ball got a pie in the kisser. She opened her mouth in outrage, but her expression changed as she began to taste the delicious pie.

"Mangia, mangia," Dragna urged the screen. "You'll be sexy with a few more curves, Lucy. Your ass is flat as a board.

Nothing to hold on to."

Then Desi Arnaz made a surprise cameo. Dragna scowled.

"Look at that Cuban faggot," Dragna jeered. "He doesn't deserve a woman like you, Lucy. He doesn't appreciate you. Drinking his rum daiquiris and playing them congas and disrespecting you. Maybe he oughta have an accident. Would you like that, Lucy?"

The skit ended with everyone sitting down happily to pie and coffee. The orchestra music surged and the credits rolled.

"I give that prick Desi six months," Dragna told Pico. "She serves him with divorce papers, that's when I make my move. She'll need a shoulder to cry on."

Pico couldn't believe the gangster was mooning over Lucille Ball. And what? Threatening to kill Desi Arnaz in front of a detective? It had to be an act.

Pico cleared his throat. "What about your wife?"

"Annulment," Dragna said. "The Pope is a fellow Italian and will do the right thing, once he is presented with all the facts and a donation."

Pico hadn't cracked the *Baltimore Catechism* in years, but he didn't think it worked that way.

"Ever hear that redheads are the most passionate?" Dragna mused.

"It's a dye job," Pico said. "Now can we please get back to Kitty Hayden?"

Dragna's eyes bugged out in disbelief. "Naw, it's natural. Cuz she's got the spitfire personality to go with it." He swigged his beer. "There's only one way to find out if it's a dye job."

"What do you hear about Kitty Hayden's murder?" Pico asked.

With great effort, Dragna wrenched his attention away from hair color.

"I hear exactly nothing," he said. "If Mickey's men want to kill girls and each other, that's not my problem."

His eyes lingered over a framed publicity still on the wall: *To Jack, with fond regards, Lucille Ball.*

Pico wanted to snatch it and snap it over his knee. Instead, he said, "Some British nutcase named Taunton took dirty photos of the victim. Tied up. Probably fake blood."

"Really?" Dragna sounded intrigued.

"Have you heard anything about that?"

"No, Detective, I have not."

"But you'll let us know if you do? They may come up for sale."

"Of course, Detective."

"Who else might have wanted her dead?"

"I hear nothing. But the way that Meyer Cohen conducts his business, I am not surprised."

"Where were you the night of October seventh?"

Dragna gave him a shrewd, appraising look and Pico realized that even if he'd ordered the hit, he hadn't carried it out.

"I attended the *Inside U.S.A. with Chevrolet* taping at KTTV in the afternoon. Then I was here, having dinner with my wife. Then I was at Largo until three a.m., all facts to which dozens of people can attest."

"And then?"

"And then I visited the apartment of a young lady, a very talented dancer. Would you like her name?"

When Pico nodded, Dragna scrawled a name and number on paper, folded it, and gave it to the detective.

"She's a redhead too," Dragna said. "Natural."

"What does your wife think of that?"

"She thinks what I tell her to think." Dragna grew contemplative. "I'm hoping it won't be too long until Miss Ball is free. I told her at the taping that I'm her number one fan."

Harry and Gadge were eating dinner at the

drugstore when Lily Kessler walked in. She sat down and began reading the paper.

With all the excitement, Harry had forgotten to call her. After finishing his meal, he ambled over to renew their acquaintance.

"I remember you," Lily said. "What happened to your eye?"

"Walked into a pole," Harry mumbled. He glanced at her paper and saw she was reading about the Scarlet Sandal. "It's a damn shame when something like that happens."

Lily blinked and looked away. "I knew her. Actually, I knew her mother and her brother. He was my —"

Harry's mouth dropped. "You knew Kitty Hayden?"

Lily drew back. "I forgot that you're with the press."

She crumpled her napkin and threw it onto her half-eaten chicken potpie.

"You've got the wrong idea about me, miss. I'm a photographer, not a reporter. Why, I took the snap that ran on the front of the *Daily Mirror* when they found the body. I was there when they brought the stretcher up."

Lily breathed fast. "Really? Was there anything that hasn't been reported? Markings on the body? A note?"

271

Harry wanted to give her an honest answer, but he figured the longer he talked, the better chance he had.

"My cop source says they're working every possible angle."

"Well," said Lily, seeing through his bluster, "I'd better go."

"Could Gadge and I walk you out?" Harry motioned to the boy. "A young woman can't be too careful after what's happened." Harry paused. "Especially if she's on her own."

"I'm not scared," Lily said. "There are six girls at the rooming house, plus Mrs. Potter. Safety in numbers."

"Mrs. Potter? Kitty's landlady? You're living *there?*"

A vision came to him suddenly, of the dead girl's room, the clothes slung over a chair, the knickknacks. The photo layout it might make.

"Kitty's mother asked me to stay and take care of the arrangements. So thanks, but you and your little brother don't have to accompany me."

Harry and Gadge followed her out. "He's not my brother, he's my friend," Gadge piped up. "Even if he did steal my red sandal."

Lily froze. "What?"

Harry lowered his voice as they walked. "Gadge found Kitty Hayden's missing shoe on Morton Street in Hollywood."

Harry explained how he'd met Gadge, taken him in, and found the sandal in his knapsack. By now they'd stopped in front of a two-story house with an overgrown lawn. The door opened and a tall leggy girl walked out.

"Yoo-hoo, Lily, see you later." She waved, striding off. "Red just made a fresh pot of coffee."

Lily sighed. "So now you know. This is where Kitty lived."

"Every reporter in town worth his salt has had Kitty's address for two days now," Harry said, pointing to several parked cars whose dashboard placards said PRESS.

"Too bad you have to go so soon," he added. "We're off to Gadge's hideout now to get the rest of his belongings."

Lily wondered whether Harry had turned Kitty's shoe over to the police. Pico hadn't mentioned it. But then, he probably wouldn't.

"Mr. Jack? Maybe I've been hasty. I'd like to hear more about the red shoe your little friend found."

"Be happy to, if we could go somewhere private." He inclined his head to the newshounds.

"I can hardly invite you up to my room."

"Why don't you come with us and we'll talk in the car."

"Didn't you just warn me about being careful?" Lily huffed. "Now you want me to get in a car with two strangers? At night?"

Harry laughed. "Gadge is a kid, and I'm a harmless shutterbug. Dozens of people will vouch for me."

"In seamy bars throughout Los Angeles, I'm sure."

He shrugged. "It's your loss."

Lily hesitated. It was dark. It could be dangerous. There were two of them. She'd be at their mercy. They seemed like regular Joes, but so had some of the most genocidal Nazis she'd interrogated after the war. Was she being too trusting?

Lily took a deep breath. "I'll go."

They followed Gadge's instructions into the hills above Sunset, and Harry told her about the button.

"You've got to call the police," Lily said when he finished.

Harry gave a nervous laugh. "First I'm going to photograph everything. Then I'll sit down with a reporter I trust and tell him the whole story so the cops can't pin it on me."

Lily considered Detectives Magruder and Pico. She could easily imagine Magruder being dirty, but she had a harder time with Pico. She thought of that car ride home, and a fizzy anticipation gripped her at seeing him again. And yet the two men were partners.

The night was pitch-black, the moon not yet up as they parked and hiked up into the hills with only a flashlight to illuminate the way. Lily's fears bloomed anew. Where were they taking her? Could she trust them? By the flickering beam, Gadge led them to an abandoned stable where the ancient warm smell of animals lingered.

Harry said he'd be right back, and from the purposeful way he hiked off, Lily hoped it was nature calling, not a prelude to an ambush.

"You're going to have to come in here with me and hold the flashlight so I can see," Gadge said.

With a quick glance over her shoulder, Lily took one hesitant step.

"Over here," Gadge called from inside.

Lily bit the inside of her mouth. She didn't want to get trapped.

"Hurry up, I can't see anything," the boy

complained.

Lily played the flashlight along the barn and saw nothing ominous, though the light didn't penetrate the deepest shadows. Slowly, she advanced, keeping the beam focused on Gadge, who pulled a U.S. Army duffel bag from a horse stall piled with moth-eaten blankets. The barn smelled of fermenting hay.

Gadge seemed twitchy, and she wondered why. A shaft of moonlight appeared, slanting in from a high window. Finally, it was up! She'd take every scrap of light she could get tonight. Lily heard a rustling and froze, ready to run. She turned the light in the direction of the noise.

"Hey!" Gadge shouted. "Bring back the light."

An orange tomcat padded into the flashlight's beam, trilling and rubbing his back against the boy's legs. Lily's knees almost buckled with relief. Gadge squatted down to scratch the cat under the chin. Lily noticed two chipped bowls against the wall, one empty, one with water.

"What's his name?" she asked, still keeping an eye on the barn door.

"Trouble." Gadge gathered the cat in his arms and his pinched face softened.

The ragged-earred cat began to purr like

a jet engine. Lily moved toward him and tripped, putting out her arms to brace her fall. The flashlight fell, going out, and she cursed as she landed against a stack of hay bales. She groped frantically. Nothing.

"Gadge?"

Silence greeted her.

A shriek of fear rose in Lily's chest and she tamped it down and pushed herself upright. She pressed her back to the hay, scanning the dark. Instead of soft straw, something hard poked into her back. Lily flinched, then felt behind her. She wondered if Gadge kept a knife at the ready for trouble. Her fingers closed around a sharp corner. She dug out more straw, saw a darker shadow amid the bale. She pulled. One last tug and it gave, Lily stumbled. Just then the flashlight went back on and Lily saw Gadge close by, training it on the thing she held in her hands. His face was awash in fear.

"No," he said, and yanked it from her hands. The cat stood to one side, tail twitching.

Gadge darted toward the door, only to collide with Harry.

"Whoa." Harry grabbed the boy. They stood in the shaft of moonlight, staring at the red leather purse in the kid's hands. It had a broken strap.

"What have you got there?" Harry asked.

"It's mine," said the kid. "I found it." He crouched, guarding it like a dog with a bone.

Lily's brain was buzzing. The purse was red. The shoes had been red. Women liked matching accessories. "Where did you find it?"

"Just . . . on the street."

"The same street where you found the shoe?" Lily asked in even tones.

"A half block up."

"What was inside?"

"I spent the money," the kid said. "How did I know?"

"How much was there?"

"Twelve dollars and forty-three cents."

"And what else?" Harry asked.

"Makeup. A mirror. A change purse. I traded everything to a girl for a bag of pears."

Was it really Kitty's purse? The leather was stained in one corner. Blood?

"How about identification?" Lily asked.

Gadge shook his head.

"So that was it?"

"There was a note."

"Let's see."

Reluctantly, Gadge surrendered the purse. Harry unclasped it and looked inside. He took out a folded piece of paper, opened it, and read it aloud:

Dear Kirk,
I'm going to see the doctor next week. I think it's for the best.

Love,
Kitty.

Bits of straw clinging to their clothes, they reread the letter once, twice, ten times by the weakening beam of the flashlight, the questions roiling in their brains.

"Kirk," Harry said. "The only Kirk I know in Hollywood is . . . this letter couldn't be meant for Kirk Armstrong, could it?"

"The movie star?" Lily said, thinking about the virile young actor with the leonine mane of hair, the patrician good looks. The vast gulf that separated such a famous Hollywood player from a struggling fifty-dollar-contract starlet. "I wonder if she knew him?"

Lily slid the note out of Harry's hand and into her own purse.

Gadge had gathered up the cat again. He knew they were angry. "What does it mean?" he asked.

"That's the question, isn't it?" Lily said.

"When we find out, maybe we'll know

who killed Kitty Hayden," Harry said. "All right, Gadge, you got everything?"

The boy nodded.

"Put the cat down and let's go."

Gadge gripped the animal tighter. "I can't leave Trouble. He's my friend."

Harry's eyes narrowed into slits. "I'll say trouble's your friend."

"Please, Harry. He won't bother anyone."

"The cat'll be fine. Plenty of mice here."

Gadge sat down. His lower lip thrust out. "I'm not going without him. He needs me."

Lily considered that Gadge needed the cat even more.

"To hell with all of you." Harry made a dismissive motion and clomped off.

Gadge buried his nose in Trouble's fur and sniffled.

"C'mon," Lily said, pulling Gadge up. "Let's just go. We'll work it out later."

The cat didn't flinch when Harry started the car, just hunched into a bread-loaf position on the boy's lap, the two of them watching warily. No one spoke as they drove down to the stretch of Morton Street where Gadge had found the purse. Harry had already canvassed the block. Now he and Lily walked it once more, but didn't find anything new.

"Maybe the murderer tossed Kitty's purse out of a moving car," Harry said.

"Wouldn't he have removed anything incriminating first?" Lily asked. "What if she threw it out herself, in hopes that someone would find it?"

The street held no answers.

Back in the car, Harry said, "Why did you hide the purse, Gadge?"

The boy shrank back in his seat. "If you don't hide beautiful things, somebody comes along and steals them."

On the radio, a sultry female voice was singing "Diamonds Are a Girl's Best Friend."

"Did you see it happen?" Lily made her voice soothing. "Maybe you were scared and you hid, but you watched. Please don't be afraid to tell us."

"I didn't see anything. Honest."

Harry took some photos out of the glove compartment and handed them to the kid. "Look closely. This is the girl whose shoe and purse you found. Ever see her before?"

"No." The boy pushed them away.

"Did somebody give you the purse, maybe?"

"I told you, I found it."

Lily looked at Harry. "We need to call those detectives."

"No," Gadge said, his voice muffled. "They'll send me back. And they'll take Trouble. He'll die without me."

Harry sucked his teeth. "How about a milkshake down in Beverly?" He made his voice jovial. "And a burger for your feline friend?"

Gadge stirred. "Okay."

They drove to a Beverly Hills drive-in, where a waitress in a red cap and tight slacks attached metal plates to the car doors and took their orders, smiling as she caught sight of the cat. When the burger came, Gadge fed morsels of meat to Trouble, drank his shake, and fell asleep in the back, arms curled around the cat.

Lily took the note out of her purse and they read it again:

Dear Kirk,
   I'm going to see the doctor next week. I think it's for the best.

Love,
Kitty.

The RKO makeup artist had said Kitty was dating someone she called the Big K. Finally Lily had a name. Kitty's roommates hadn't mentioned anyone named Kirk. Maybe the romance was clandestine because

Kirk was married. Kirk Armstrong certainly was married.

Beside her in the car, Harry shifted, and Lily considered how odd it was to be sitting here with this practical stranger. Neither of them had known Kitty in life, but her murder had created a strange bond. Lily sensed from the gruff but kind way Harry dealt with Gadge that there was no bad in him. And she needed a confidant. Under the bright glare of the drive-in's sodium lights, Lily recounted everything she'd learned at RKO, her unsettling visit to Dr. Lafferty, Freddy Taunton's dirty pictures.

"You think this Kirk got her knocked up and she had to get an abortion?" Harry said.

"Maybe she tried to blackmail him into marriage and it didn't work."

"She signed her letter *love*," Harry pointed out. "That doesn't sound like a blackmail letter."

"The two aren't mutually exclusive," Lily said dryly. "She must have been terrified. Pregnant and unmarried? That would have ended her career. She'd have to go home in shame."

"The letter's awfully cryptic. Maybe it's a red herring to throw us off the scent. Is this even her writing?"

"I can check at the rooming house."

"But what if someone forced her to write it at gunpoint?"

"Kirk is the key," Lily said. "If we can find out who he is."

"You've got the note. Take it to the cops. You didn't make the kid any promises, I did."

Lily glanced into the backseat.

"All of a sudden you're worried about him?" Harry said. "You want to adopt him?"

"Me?" Lily said. "They don't let single people adopt children."

The photographer examined her steadily. "They don't, do they? We'd have to get married."

Lily felt a flush rise up her throat.

"I'm just kidding," Harry said. "But I'm serious about the cops, Lily. This is some very sensitive stuff we've uncovered. Dangerous, even. I'd hate for you to get hurt."

Lily shrugged off a twinge of fear. "I promise to be careful. So. Have you canvassed the shopkeepers along Morton?"

"There's one place I need to go back to, they were closed for a private party today. The Crow's Nest. It's a strange joint. Piano player — god, he was horrible — started playing "God Save the Queen" as soon as I walked in. Maybe he thought I was British."

Harry photographed the note and gave it

to Lily. He kept the purse so he could shoot Gadge later, holding it with the red sandal. "The *Mirror's* going to be on its knees," he said.

"So you're going to take the kid home with you after all? And the cat?"

"I suppose another day won't hurt."

"Bless you," said Lily.

CHAPTER 18

"What's new, Miss Kessler?" a grating voice called as Lily walked up to the rooming house.

"Nothing," Lily said, as the reporter named Violet McCree fell into step beside her, gliding along like a perfumed shark.

"Did you have a productive day?" Violet asked with an insinuating smile.

Lily felt the devil playing the xylophone along the knobs of her spine. Had this gal followed them?

"Please go away," she said. "I don't want to talk to you."

"Well, I had a very productive day, Miss Kessler. I thought you'd like to know . . . I'm working on a story about you."

"Me?"

The reporter smirked. "It's called 'Who's the Mystery Girl at the Heart of the Scarlet Sandal Investigation and What Isn't She Revealing About the Starlet's Murder?' "

Lily swallowed. The headline was more apt than Violet McCree could imagine.

"That's horrible," Lily said. "You're not even a real journalist, all you do is print lurid gossip and innuendo. You're like a vampire, feeding off people's misery. Leave me alone."

The reporter cocked her head. "Perhaps you've been gone from America too long, Miss Kessler."

Lily's head jerked up. How the hell did she know that?

"Surprised that I've done my *research?* That I know you've spent the last five years in Europe, long after most loyal, God-fearing Americans have come home? Makes me wonder whether you've fallen prey to foreign influences. I'm as real as Eric Sevareid and Edward R. Murrow and I'll bet more people read *Confidential* than listen to those blowhards. Americans are tired of wars. They want glamour. Entertainment. We take them inside Hollywood, show them what the stars are really like. People have a right to know."

"You disgust me."

"And you make me wonder, Miss Kessler, what strange people you've befriended on your travels. Those who might loathe the American way of life, be bent on destroying it. Hollywood is full of such people, working deep undercover. It's our job to root them out. Do you get my drift?"

Lily shut the front door on Violet McCree.

"How's tricks?" said Red, who was drinking coffee and reading a typed manuscript with a blue cover. A script.

"You got a part!" Lily said. "Congrats."

Red looked especially pretty tonight, almost glowing. Her wool sweater clung to her bosom. Her lips and nails were painted luscious red.

"I went down to RKO today and met with the casting director."

"About what?"

"I made him a proposition and, well, he wants me to finish out Kitty's contract."

"Oh, Red, he doesn't!"

Red looked squarely at Lily and pouted. "Why shouldn't I? A girl's got to eat."

"It just seems so prema . . . as if . . ."

"Premature? She's dead, Lily. She's not coming back."

"I know but . . ." Lily remembered Pico accusing her, the day they'd met, of wanting to take advantage of Kitty's disappearance.

"You should try it sometime, lining up at auditions, praying for two minutes of a

288

director's time. Waiting for a callback that never comes. When you're under contract, you don't go out on cattle calls, you get a screen test. Understand the difference? And I deserve it. I'm every bit as talented as Kitty and I'm sick to death of modeling clothes for J. C. Penney."

Once again Lily felt how opportunistic this business was, the envy that churned just below the surface, how one actor's tragedy meant another's big break. She wondered, then, how big a step it would be from wishing for your rival's demise to orchestrating it.

Lily studied Red in her furry slippers, legs propped up, memorizing her lines. No, it was ridiculous. She was just being paranoid.

"I learned some things today about Kitty's murder," Lily said, "that I'd like to discuss with you and the other girls."

Behind Red's eyes, something flared, then banked. "Fine," she said. "I'll make a fresh pot of coffee."

Lily ran upstairs to see who else was home and found Mrs. Potter emerging from Beverly's room, looking like she'd been caught red-handed at something. The landlady hurried down the hall. Beverly was at her vanity table, sniffling.

"What's wrong?" Lily wondered what

Mrs. Potter had done to upset the girl.

"Nothing." Beverly composed herself. "I'm just being silly." Her apple cheeks quivered as she tried not to cry. Lily could smell the Jean Naté perfume she wore. "Oh, Lily. I found out today I got passed over for a role I really wanted."

Lily considered Beverly's high forehead, her barrettes and little-girl hair, her matronly bosom. She exuded common sense and favored conservative clothes — blouses never too tight, skirts never too short. Jinx said she'd done well in the war years, when the studios wanted girl-next-door types that homesick soldiers could pine for. But as the decade inched to a close, it was glamour girls like Red and Kitty, all sexual allure, curves, and cleavage, that excited the public's imagination.

"Did you hear about Red?" Beverly asked.

Lily nodded.

"I'm so happy for her," Beverly said, and her eyes shifted sullenly.

"Don't worry, another casting director will snap you up in no time," Lily said.

But in her heart, she wondered.

Soon everyone was in the kitchen except Louise, who was at a photography studio, having new, glammed-up head shots taken so she'd stop getting typecast in girl Friday roles.

Lily recounted for them how she'd met Harry Jack and Gadge and what they'd found, leaving out the note for now.

Fumiko put her hand to her mouth. "Kitty bought that purse last month."

Just then Mrs. Potter walked in with a basket of tea towels and aprons. She began to fold them and put them away and Lily wondered if she wanted an excuse to listen in.

"Oh God," Jinx said. "I bet Kitty was on her way home when it happened. She probably screamed and screamed, and nobody heard her."

"We don't know that," Beverly chided.

"Did Kitty ever talk about someone named Kirk?" Lily asked.

"Why?" they chorused.

"Just wondering," Lily said. She noticed that Mrs. Potter had stopped folding towels. She stood at the sink, slowly washing a glass.

"Did Lily know anyone named Kirk, Mrs. Potter?" Lily asked.

Mrs. Potter turned, regarding Lily with blank eyes.

Lily repeated the question.

"The girls don't confide their affairs in me," she said at last.

"What have you learned, Lily?" Jinx said. "Out with it."

"There was something in the purse?" Red said, going pale.

Lily explained how Gadge had bartered away everything except a note. Screwing up her eyes, she recited it from memory.

The girls sat in stunned silence. Finally, Beverly asked Lily if she'd turned the note over to the police.

"Not yet," Lily said. "I wanted to talk to you all first."

She didn't point out the obvious — that Magruder and Pico would shut her out of the investigation as soon as she surrendered it.

"Kirk," said Red thoughtfully. "Well, I have no idea if this is significant, and I don't want to jump to any conclusions, but Kitty had a small part in a Kirk Armstrong movie called *Young Man with a Horn* over at Warner's just before RKO signed her. She said he's just dreamy."

Lily pondered the enormity of this. What if Harry Jack had been right?

"Could they have been" — Lily cleared her throat — "seeing each other?"

"Kitty never mentioned it," Beverly said stoutly.

"Kirk Armstrong is married. Lovely wife

and three girls," Fumiko said.

"That never means anything," Red said in a tone that made Lily think she'd dallied with married actors herself.

"So Kitty never even hinted she was dating a star?"

"No," Beverly said. The rest shook their heads.

"I always wondered if she might have caught the eye of Howard Hughes," Jinx said. "He's notorious at RKO. Treats the place as his own private harem. And someone sure was showering her with silk lingerie and perfume."

"Naw," said Red. "He would have moved her into fancy digs."

"Not if she turned him down," Jeanne said.

"I think Howard Hughes is as farfetched as Kirk Armstrong," said ever-practical Beverly.

Fumiko looked at her watch and left, saying she was late for a date.

Lily recalled a movie magazine she'd flipped through in a Berlin canteen, how she'd stopped at a photo layout of the handsome star, his beautiful wife, their children. They'd been posed with the family dog by a swimming pool, a white mansion in the background, the living embodiment of the

Hollywood dream.

"Maybe he swore her to secrecy," Lily said. "It would have ruined his career. And imagine if she was pregnant on top of it . . ."

"I can't believe it," Beverly said.

"Say, let's see that note." Red licked her lips.

Reluctantly, Lily brought it out, admonishing the girls not to touch it.

Five heads bent over the kitchen table.

"Sure looks like her writing."

"Who's got a sample?"

Jinx got a thank-you card Kitty had written her and they laid them side by side. The Kirk note had been dashed off in a hurry, the letters sloppy and running together, but it looked like the same hand.

"The police will analyze it," Red said, sliding it over to Lily. "You'd better call them now."

"I suppose I should."

In the hallway, Mrs. Potter was on the phone. When she heard Lily's tread, she hung up and moved past Lily in the narrow hallway.

Lily dialed. An LAPD operator answered and said she would take a message. Lily left word for Magruder or Pico to call her as soon as possible.

■ ■ ■ ■

Back in the kitchen, the girls were disappointed to learn that the detectives weren't on their way. Soon they drifted upstairs. At midnight, after eating an avocado sandwich and drinking a glass of milk, Lily joined them.

Lying in bed, she tried to recall her fiancé's face, but the image that came to mind was blurry and indistinct. When she focused harder, what materialized was a tawny face with wavy hair, a long straight nose, and hazel eyes flecked with gold. She saw a full, sensuous mouth, lips parted, asking in a hushed voice if she was cold.

CHAPTER 19

October 15, 1949

"How dare you withhold evidence from the LAPD!" Magruder screamed.

Mrs. Potter had roused Lily before dawn to tell her the police were on the phone.

"Pardon me?" she asked, still half asleep.

"Don't play coy. It's splashed all over today's *Confidential.* The note. The purse. The missing shoe. You're tampering with evidence in a murder case, you stupid girl, and your fingerprints are probably all over everything. It'll be a miracle if we can lift anything useful —"

"Detective Magruder —" Lily began.

"And this base speculation about Kirk Armstrong? A fine actor and devoted family man. How could you have mouthed off to the press like that?"

"I didn't," Lily said, wondering how Violet McCree had found out.

"The hell you didn't. I'd like to put you

both in lockup until you come clean."

The idea of being thrown in a cell with Violet McCree filled her with alarm.

"Please, Detective Magruder —"

He gave a blubbery sigh. "But that would just create an even bigger scandal than we've already got. I'm warning you, though. Stay put. Detective Pico is on his way to collect the evidence and take your statement. Meanwhile, give me the address of that freelance photographer and the orphan's last name."

When Lily said she didn't know, Magruder exploded again, threatening her with bodily harm.

"I have his phone number," Lily said.

"Then speak, woman. What is it?"

"I have to get it."

"Run."

Lily ran back upstairs and got the number Harry had jotted down the night before, realizing she'd have to warn him.

"We told you to call immediately if you learned something," Magruder said in a whispery voice that frightened her even more than his tirades.

"I did. Last night."

His early morning phone call had caught her off guard. Now her confidence began to return.

"Perhaps you should check with your operator," Lily said testily.

"I suppose the message could be on my desk somewhere," the detective backpedaled. She heard papers rustling. "But you're still in hot water for talking to that reporter."

"I keep telling you I didn't."

"Then who did?"

"I don't know."

"Who knew about it?"

"Me. Harry Jack. The kid. Kitty's roommates and the landlady." As she ticked off their names, Lily recalled how Violet McCree had accosted her outside. Had she been listening at the window? Did she have an informant inside the boardinghouse? Lily flashed to Mrs. Potter on the phone, Fumiko dashing out for a date.

"Someone's got loose lips," Magruder said. "And I intend to find them and sink their ship. This is not information we would have chosen to release to the public, with the killer still at large."

Then maybe it's for the best that it leaked, Lily thought. *At least now nobody can cover it up.* She wondered what other evidence had been suppressed.

"Well, now that it has," Lily said, "I hope you plan to interview Kirk Armstrong."

"That's department business, and not

298

some snot-nosed gal's who's already caused enough trouble for one lifetime," Magruder roared. "Now sit tight on that bottom of yours until Pico gets there."

He hung up.

Hands shaking, Lily replaced the receiver. It scared her, the way he bounced between glassy calm and unhinged mania. She wondered if he was dangerous. At least he wasn't coming with Pico. She suppressed a sudden twinge of anticipation. Pico would just yell at her too.

Lily cleared the line then dialed Harry Jack.

"I just saw *Confidential*," he said. "Who the hell leaked?"

"It must have been someone here," Lily whispered, realizing whoever it was could be in the kitchen. The smell of coffee and cinnamon toast wafted out to the hallway. "And I had to give your phone number to a detective this morning. He's furious."

"Christ Almighty."

"You better get those pictures to the paper before they confiscate everything."

"Thanks for the heads-up."

"Will you let me know how it goes?"

"You bet."

"You're in big trouble," Detective Pico said,

sitting down at the kitchen table.

Lily had managed to shower and throw on her blue serge suit before he arrived. She brought him a cup of coffee with cream and two packets of restaurant sugar the girls smuggled home in their pockets.

"I left a message for you last night," Lily said, joining him.

His hair was still damp from the shower. There was a crimson pearl on one side of his throat, where he'd nicked himself shaving. She wanted to grab his jaw, rub it off with her thumb. She could almost feel the rasp of his skin.

"You also blabbed to that reporter," Pico said.

"I never said a word to Vile Violet. But I'm afraid someone did."

"We're going to find out."

Lily slid down in her chair. "At least you've got some new leads now."

Magruder was right, Pico thought. She was a bossy, nosy, full-of-herself little bitch. But he couldn't take his eyes off her. The blotches of color staining her cheeks. Those porcelain nostrils, flaring with annoyance. The way her auburn hair fell softly, framing her oval face.

"I haven't threatened you," he said. "Don't be so high-strung."

She averted her eyes. "Better than low-strung."

"Okay Miss High-Strung." He sounded amused. "Let's take it from the beginning."

He proceeded to question her in depth about the previous day's events. When she explained she'd met Harry Jack at a lunch counter, Pico's brow furrowed.

"You shouldn't go off with strangers you meet on the Boulevard," he said. "L.A.'s not the safe place you knew before the war. And not everyone is as honorable as this fellow apparently was."

"I know," she said wearily. "He told me the same thing. It was the kid who swayed me."

The detective tried to poke holes in her story. He made her repeat exactly where Gadge had found the shoe, then consulted his notebook.

"Hmm, that's four blocks from where our special effects fellow lives. Max Vranizan."

Lily stopped in surprise. They looked at each other, both of them wondering the same thing

"Where's the note?" Pico said at last.

"Upstairs. I'll go get it."

"I'll accompany you." *Just in case there's something else you're hiding,* he thought.

He followed her up, forcing himself to

look at the flocked red velvet wallpaper instead of her swaying ripe peach of an ass.

At the door, she paused, hand on the glass knob.

"It's a bit of a mess," she said. "I wasn't expecting visitors."

"There's nothing in that room that could possibly surprise me."

She shrugged and unlocked the door and he admired her foresight in having locked it.

In her room, Pico's eyes fell on a silk robe crumpled in a heap. He imagined sliding it off her shoulders, pressing his lips to the warm hollow below her neck. He looked away, his glance falling on the closet that hid the Murphy bed. He scowled. Thinking of beds was no better.

Lily brought over a manila envelope. She slid out a piece of paper, handling the edges with her palms.

"Why are you holding it like that?" he asked.

"Force of habit."

"What habit might that be?"

She swayed a little, but didn't answer.

"You've handled a lot of evidence, have you?"

A shadow crossed her face, in the moment before she turned away. "A bit," she said, her voice muted and distant.

"What aren't you telling me?"

She glanced back at him over her shoulder. A small, demure smile.

"I was a file clerk during the war. And after. You pick up things."

He sensed a universe opening in the spaces between her words. He found himself reassessing what he knew about her. This trim figure in the blue suit. Feminine. And yet so hard. Like a steel blade wrapped in crushed velvet.

"You worked for military intelligence too," he said triumphantly. "Not just your fiancé."

Lily flinched at the mention of her lost love but said nothing.

Of course! he thought. She would have been sworn to secrecy. He felt a flare of jealousy.

"I suppose you saw a lot of action. What was it like?"

She picked her words carefully. "It was a long trip through hell. It was also the most alive I've ever felt."

He felt embarrassed, remembering how he'd strutted and lectured her when they'd first met.

"So you know all about hunting people down and espionage?"

She threw her head back and gave a

tinkling laugh. She had a long, swanlike throat, and it arched, lovely and white.

"Sorry to disappoint you, Detective, but it really was mainly stenography and filing. I'm hardly Mata Hari."

But the color rose in her cheeks at the fib. He could see that she was made for the chase, a thoroughbred, every fiber in her body yearning for it. He felt the air charging, like ions before a storm. Almost unconsciously, he leaned toward her.

She ran a hand through her hair. "Besides, *Detective,* you're the one who said we have to be protected from evil."

He felt a hot flush of embarrassment. "That was back when you were just a girl."

"And what am I now, Detective? A boy?"

She seemed to be enjoying his discomfort, that every word out of his mouth was coming out wrong this morning.

"You'll have to forgive me," she said. "I came back to America to get a new start. But it seems I've forgotten how normal life works. Have you ever noticed that people who shine in times of crisis don't always adapt well once peace returns? That frightens me.

"Ah well." She made a dismissive motion. "I want this killer caught as much as you do. So tell me, what did the manager of the

Radcliffe Arms say about the photos?"

Pico snorted. "Denied all knowledge. Offered to let us search his place."

"Did you?"

"Clean as a whistle."

"He got rid of them already."

"Then they'll turn up. We've got eyes on the street, watching."

"Unless they go directly into private hands. Photos like that, it's a specialized taste."

"I wouldn't know." He held out the note. "Please. I'd like you to read this again and tell me what you think. From a girl's perspective."

Lily came and stood behind him, reading over his shoulder, so close he could smell the lilac soap she'd used that morning, hear the rustle of her skirt, the soft rhythmic puffs of her breath.

"This her writing?" Pico asked gruffly.

Lily went and got another manila folder labeled *Kitty Hayden handwriting sample.* She handed it to Pico. "See for yourself."

The girl was just full of surprises, Pico thought admiringly. Whip-smart. No nerves that he could see, totally bloodless. Plus she could charm the stripes off a skunk.

"If they didn't use you in military intelligence, they certainly should have," Pico said.

Lily looked up with surprise. "Women are natural spies," she said. "We're taught from childhood to be quiet and listen. We're patient, and we're good plotters. It's bred into us. For centuries we've had to use subterfuge to get our way."

She gave him an enigmatic smile that both annoyed and aroused him. He forced himself to concentrate on the notes, holding them side by side, comparing the handwriting. "We'll run it by the experts. But it looks the same to me."

After a moment, he went on. "The big question is, did she write this to Kirk Armstrong, or another Kirk?"

Lily grew pensive. "If it was the actor, she didn't kiss and tell. Her roommates knew nothing about it."

Pico rocked in the chair, debating with himself. He shouldn't tell her. It broke all kinds of protocol. But there was something about her . . .

"Kirk Armstrong called us this morning after he read the paper," he said.

Lily's eyebrow went up. "And?"

Pico knew she was pumping him, her face oozing sympathy and encouragement. But suddenly, he wanted to tell her everything.

"He remembers her from *Young Man with a Horn.* She had a bit part and he'd seen her around the set. But that's all."

"Then why didn't he contact you earlier?" Lily asked immediately.

"There was nothing to say."

"They weren't having an affair?"

"He'd barely spoken two words to her."

"And you believe him?"

"I'll let you know after we meet with him. We're doing a formal sit-down at Warner's at noon."

"Take me with you."

"Impossible," he said with exasperation. "The studio would scream holy hell and so would Magruder."

Lily paced the room. It had been a long shot, she knew. But she enjoyed batting ideas around with this handsome detective. Running through the possible scenarios. There was an appealing purity to it, this game of building a narrative step by step, using inference, deduction, and logic. She'd been good at it once.

"Why are you questioning him at the studio?" she asked. "Wouldn't an interrogation room at headquarters be more appropriate?" She waved her arm. "Exposed lightbulb. Bare table. Glass of water and strategically doled-out smokes."

Pico rubbed his jaw. "Because he's in the middle of shooting a picture, and he is not a suspect in Kitty Hayden's murder. He volunteered to meet with us. As a courtesy. The LAPD wants to make it as painless for him as possible."

"Oh, I'll bet they do."

"Don't be cynical."

"It's my nature. I thought it was yours too."

"It used to be. I grow less cynical with each passing year. And more skeptical."

"Okay. Let's be skeptical, then. It's very clever of him, don't you think, to make the first move?"

"Maybe you've forgotten our code of justice. In America you're innocent until proven guilty. Mr. Armstrong isn't being accused of a crime."

"Not yet."

"Maybe not ever."

"You cops have too much respect for Hollywood."

"Maybe you don't have enough."

"It just bugs me how stars get special treatment. Even in a murder investigation. You're going there, hat in hand."

"They invited us."

"They?"

"Jack Warner will be there. Plus the head

308

of security and a studio PR man."

"See? The fix is in. They're probably off right now getting their stories straight."

"I'm not saying all the stars are angels. But maybe he's telling the truth."

Lily paced the room. "Movie stars are like gods who can do anything they want," she said. "Imagine having the money and power to satisfy every desire. Life gets boring and empty after a while. So you chase the next thrill. Look for that rush. Knowing you'll get away with it. Who's going to stop you? Because, after all, you're a god."

She strode to the far wall and Pico followed her, drawn to her, liking her. The swagger, the slim hips, the abrupt gestures. When she suddenly reached out and pulled down the Murphy bed, he had trouble staying focused. What was that about? He imagined throwing her onto it. He'd pin those slender wrists against the sheets. *I have an urgent police matter to discuss with you,* he'd whisper, just before he placed his mouth over hers. And she'd squirm against him, but only to get into a better position. And behind that combative exterior, she'd burn with a white-hot flame.

But no, she was off again, into the closet this time. She emerged bearing a handful of

Kitty's outfits and hurled them onto the bed.

"What do you notice about these dresses?"

He leaned forward. "They're pretty."

During the war, OSS spies infiltrating behind enemy lines had been outfitted with battered suitcases and clothes bought from refugees and secondhand stores. The OSS even removed U.S. dry-cleaning marks. Money would be shuffled and crumpled, smudged with dirt, since sequenced banknotes were a dead giveaway. Outside Nice Lily had a close call once when a fellow agent tossed down a half-smoked cigarette, something a real Frenchman would never do. Lily had snatched it and relit it and her colleague had realized his error and feigned a coughing fit.

"Look at the seams," Lily said now. "This one is strained. And she took out the darts on that one. She'd gained weight. Kitty Hayden was pregnant, Pico. Probably with Kirk Armstrong's child. That's what the note was about. She'd decided on an abortion."

Pico stared at her with an unfathomable expression. Then he stuck his hands in his pockets and walked over to the window.

"The coroner's final report came back yesterday evening," he said. "She was eleven

310

weeks along. But she died of strangulation, not a botched abortion."

Lily sat down on the bed.

"But the pregnancy might have been a motive. We need to find the baby's father."

"The father's not necessarily the murderer. If she was planning to abort, that would have solved everybody's problem."

"The letter's very troublesome," Lily agreed.

She leaned back on the narrow bed, thinking. Suddenly Pico saw her grow flustered as she realized they were alone. She jumped up, pressing down her skirt, muttering something he didn't catch.

A strange energy filled the room, drawing him toward her. She seemed impossibly alluring. He wanted to kick aside the pile of dresses and sink with her onto the thin mattress, could almost feel his hands and lips and body on hers. You could never fully own a girl like that, he thought. Part of her would always remain mysterious, tantalizing, and out of reach. She'd want to be treated like one of the boys, and she'd match you drink for drink and swear like a stevedore and drive recklessly down empty highways late at night, just another one of the boys, until you took her to bed, and then she'd press against you and make little noises and you'd be glad she wasn't a boy, and clutch her tight, but in the morning she'd be gone.

The room was silent, the air still, as he took a step closer. She stared, wide-eyed and solemn, barely breathing.

"Well!" came a nasal voice outside the open door.

They sprang apart like two electrons that collide and ricochet to opposite ends of a force field. Mrs. Potter stood in the doorway, holding a lamp. Lily gazed out the window, her cheeks burning. Pico stood by the vanity table, examining the bottle of Arpège.

"I thought you might want a better light to read by. But if I'm interrupting police business, I can just set it in the hallway."

They both spoke at once.

"Not at all," said Lily. "Come in."

"If you could give us a few minutes, ma'am."

"I see."

Mrs. Potter placed the lamp just inside Lily's room, then retreated. "Sorry I interrupted." She pulled the door closed.

"Perhaps . . ." Lily began.

"I might as . . ." Pico said.

They subsided, flustered. "Ladies first," Pico said.

"No, really, you go."

Pico certainly hadn't planned what came out of his mouth next. Maybe he was desperate to change the subject. Maybe he felt some bond, or desire to protect her, that he couldn't yet articulate.

"I want you to be careful around Magruder," he said. "I'm not sure I trust him."

Lily was uncharacteristically subdued as she showed Pico out of the rooming house ten minutes later. Pico had refused to elaborate, leaving her simmering with vague anxiety. Dreading what she had to do next, she picked up the phone and asked the operator to connect her with Champaign, Illinois.

"Mrs. Croggan? It's Lily."

"My dear girl. I was wondering when you'd call. The police have been so close-mouthed. How are you holding up out there?"

She's lost both her children and her first thought is for my *welfare,* thought Lily, pushing her fist against her mouth. *I am not worthy to even know her.*

"I'm okay," Lily said, wondering how to tell Mrs. Croggan what she'd learned. "The police say they can't release the body yet, until —"

"Yes, I told them that was fine."

"But they've found Doreen's purse, and her missing shoe, and a note that seems to indicate —" Lily began.

"I heard that on the radio this morning," Mrs. Croggan said briskly. "But I don't believe that talk about gangsters and Kirk Armstrong. My minister explained how the studios make up outrageous stories about the stars to generate headlines."

"I guess the police are still sorting it out," Lily said. "But Mrs. Croggan, have they talked to you at all about the autopsy? The coroner's report?"

"What about it?" she said after a pause.

Lily bit her lip, then plunged in. "One of the detectives told me that Doreen was eleven weeks pregnant when she was killed."

A small strangled sound came from Mrs. Croggan.

"Detective Pico called me last night. But Doreen never even mentioned a boyfriend." Mrs. Croggan's voice rose. "How could this have happened?"

"I don't know," Lily said numbly.

"It's too late now," Mrs. Croggan said, beginning to cry, "but how I wish she would have confided in me. She could have come home. We could have concocted a marriage to a GI who'd died. I am her mother. I'd never turn her away. We could have named the child Joseph. Josephine if it was a girl."

Lily was glad that Mrs. Croggan couldn't see the tears running down her face.

"I'm so sorry," Lily said. There was no sense in telling her about the dirty pictures. Her daughter's memory had been sullied enough.

"It's gone, all gone now," Mrs. Croggan said, her voice muffled. "At times I think I can't go on. But I must go on. I want to live to see Kitty's killer found and put away. You're working with the police on that, aren't you, Lily? Getting closer every day?"

"I hope so."

"Good. I want you to hold your head high when you talk to those people. Don't let them drag you down to the gutter."

"I'll try," Lily said, before she hung up.

She almost collided with Fumiko in the hallway. As she grabbed the girl to steady herself, Lily's fingers touched soft crepe. She stepped back for a better look and whistled appreciatively. "Nice frock."

Fumiko looked away. "Thank you," she said. Lily's gaze followed the dress down. "And new shoes too?"

She remembered Beverly saying that Fumiko struggled to make ends meet.

"Yes. I have a boyfriend. He gives me

many presents."

"Oh," said Lily, her suspicions aroused. "Does he work for *Confidential* magazine?"

"Pardon me?" Fumiko gave a confused smile.

"You told Violet McCree about our talk in the kitchen, didn't you? You sold her information."

"Why would I do that?" Fumiko looked bewildered. Lily had to remember that she was an actress — a damn good one, according to the other girls.

"Because you never liked Kitty, did you? She got the parts you wanted."

"That's not true."

"Maybe you wished she'd disappear. Maybe you had something to do with it."

Fumiko's face froze in disbelief. "You . . ." she said, then swallowed, "are a horrible person. Kitty was my friend."

She gave a sob and ran out the front door.

Lily walked huffily into the kitchen. Then her better instincts kicked in and she turned back, eager to apologize. Outside, a woman screamed.

Heart pounding, she threw open the door.

Fumiko stood on the stoop, her face glazed with fear. Below her in the garden, crawling on all fours, looking delirious, was Max Vranizan.

Fumiko ran in and locked the door, then went to the parlor window and looked down.

"We have to call the police," she said. "He's gone crazy."

"Did he hurt you? What happened?"

Between jagged breaths, Fumiko said, "I walked into the garden and he rushed out of nowhere and grabbed me. He was muttering and he smelled of drink and I . . . I thought he wanted to hurt me, and I didn't recognize him, it all happened so suddenly. I kicked him between the legs. He doubled over, writhing and cursing, then he said, 'I'm sorry, Fumiko. I deserve it. It's all my fault. Nothing's turned out the way I planned.' "

They watched Max get to his feet, swaying. His hat had fallen onto the gravel path and his hair was plastered wetly to his skull. His pants hung loosely, like he hadn't eaten in several days.

"I don't think he's dangerous," Lily said. "I want to ask him what turned out so wrong."

Lily figured she could keep her distance and run back inside if she had to. She spotted several large rocks in case she needed a weapon in a hurry.

She opened the door and descended the

317

stairs, Fumiko behind her. "Hullo, Max. Shouldn't you be at work?" Lily said.

"I've called in sick," he mumbled.

"You grabbed Fumiko. That wasn't very nice. And you've been skulking around."

"I wanted to see the house again. Kitty and I had nice times here. Then a girl walked by and from the back . . . she looked like . . . I was afraid she'd disappear again . . ."

Lily crossed her arms. "Fumiko and Kitty don't look anything alike, Max."

"But she reminds me of Kitty. All you girls do."

Max's wistful tone and his erratic behavior scared her. She didn't want him fixating on one of them now.

"Why is Kitty's death your fault, Max?" Lily asked.

"Because I wasn't able to make her fall in love with me. If she loved me, she wouldn't have run around with all those other fellows. She'd be alive today."

He fell to his knees and beat his head against the earth.

"You need to go home and sober up," Lily said. "Take a shower, drink coffee, get some food in your belly. Then go to work. It'll take your mind off Kitty."

"Work," Max groaned. "Do you know

what I did last night in my studio? One of my headaches was coming on, the lights pulsing and dancing like some electrified Milky Way. When I came to, I'd destroyed two thousand dollars' worth of models with a hammer, just pounded them to pieces. Fur and glass and thread and batting and screws everywhere."

"What are you saying?" Lily asked. "Did you kill Kitty?"

Max's eyes darted wildly. "I wouldn't kill Kitty. I loved her. I miss her so much."

"We all miss her," Fumiko said softly. "But she's gone. You have to go on living."

Max Vranizan collected his hat and rose to his feet. "Yes. I'll go now."

As he walked down the street, Lily apologized to Fumiko. "I'm sorry about what I said earlier. It was uncalled for."

Fumiko nodded. "We're all on edge. Poor Max. His brain is like a fragile eggshell. He feels life so deeply, and he can't filter things the way we can. It's his genius and his downfall."

"That's very generous of you," Lily said. "But the bottom line is he's unstable. We need to tell the detectives about this. What if he killed Kitty and he's starting to crack?"

CHAPTER 20

Pico pulled up in front of an American Legion Hall in Atwater. The place looked closed. But it was the right address. Magruder had wanted to meet here, then head off together to their appointment at Warner's.

He found a side door and walked in, wrinkling his nose at the smell of spilled beer. It wasn't yet eleven a.m., but the American Legion Hall bar was already doing a brisk business with the World War I vets. Faded pennants and bunting from long-ago Fourth of July parties draped the bar. Photos of Little League teams the chapter had sponsored over the years covered the walls. Magruder was perched on a stool, quaffing a steaming drink. Beside him was a briefcase.

"Have a seat." The older cop waved him over, all liquored-up bonhomie, and roared at the bartender to bring another Irish coffee.

"I thought we had to go meet Kirk Armstrong."

"Got a little errand to run first," he said thickly. "Just working up to it."

The combination of booze and caffeine gave Magruder a dangerous edge. His voice grew louder, his movements more broad and exaggerated, but also tightly wound. After the two men finished their drinks, he placed his briefcase on the bar. He pressed the metal levers and the top flew open, revealing unmarked envelopes, a manila file, a brown bag, and a bundle of cash tied with a rubber band. Disgusted, Pico looked away. He didn't want to be complicit in Magruder's black business. It was one thing to eat a meal or have a few drinks on the house, but this was graft of a whole different magnitude. They were supposed to be in Burbank at noon, for chrissakes, and here was Magruder, trying to squeeze one last payoff out of a sunny autumn morning.

Magruder closed the case and they walked out into the blazing sunlight and across the street to a yellow building with a sign that said NORMANDY MANOR.

The smell of piss and disinfectant hit them at the door. Magruder seemed to know his way around — he tipped his hat with a florid and expansive greeting to the receptionist and sailed along the linoleum corridor. The strong odors seemed to have sobered him up, he wasn't slurring his words anymore.

They turned the corner and entered a small white room. A uniformed nurse with a starched tricorn hat sat at the edge of the bed, spooning Cream of Wheat into the mouth of a young man whose limbs and muscles were twisted into unnatural angles. The youth had brilliant green eyes and bluish white skin and wore Coke-bottle glasses and some kind of helmet strapped to his head.

"How's he doing, Martha?" Magruder said.

"Up bright and early this morning, sir," the nurse replied. "I brought him some autumn leaves so he could watch the seasons change and he seemed to enjoy that a great deal." She inclined her head to a table where maple leaves lay in gnarled splendor — yellow, orange, red, magenta, and brown.

Magruder stood impassively at the young man's bedside, then opened his briefcase and pulled out a black-and-white photo of Clark Gable. Pico noticed that it was signed, *To Bruce Magruder, a brave cowboy. From your friend Clark.*

Magruder held it up to the boy and Pico thought the sea-green eyes grew more alert. The young man's mouth moved as if to form words, and the nurse swooped down with a napkin to mop a string of saliva.

"You'll put it up on the wall with the others, won't you, Martha?" Magruder handed it to her.

Pico looked around and saw what he'd missed because he'd been focused on the broken boy in the bed — the wall plastered with movie stills, all the most masculine, outdoorsy male stars, every last one autographed to Bruce Magruder. There was Gary Cooper. The Duke. Mitchum. Rhett Taylor. Rory Calhoun. Bogie. Burt Lancaster. Errol Flynn. Gene Autry. Tom Mix.

Now Magruder fished something out of the paper bag in his briefcase. It was a Brooklyn Dodgers cap. The boy's clawlike fingers reached out to caress the fabric. The cap slipped to the floor. Magruder picked it up without a word. Frowning with concentration, he perched it atop the boy's helmet.

"There you go, champ." He leaned in. "One day, we'll have a team of our own in this town."

Then he chucked the boy under the chin, kissed him on the cheek, and turned to

Martha.

"I want to thank you for taking such good care of him," Magruder said, handing her one of the unmarked envelopes from his case. "I know I can count on you."

"Oh really, Mr. Magruder," the nurse said. "He's one of God's angels, fallen to earth." She dropped the envelope into the pocket of her uniform.

They said good-bye, then retraced their steps down the corridor. At the reception desk, Magruder paused, pulled out three more envelopes.

"For you, Sadie," he said. "And one for the doctor and the night nurse. Be sure they get it, ah?"

"You're a kind and generous man, Mr. Magruder."

The older cop tipped his hat and left, Pico following.

Magruder plodded down the sidewalk, his head bent. At the car, he squinted against the sunlight. There was a weary look about him that Pico hadn't seen before. "We'll take one car to Burbank. You can drive while I sober up," Magruder said, "I want to hear all about your talk with Lily Kessler."

"Kirk Armstrong?" screamed Mickey Co-

324

hen, rattling his *Confidential.* "Did he kill her?"

"Boss," Shorty said, his pretense of calm undermined by the wet stain creeping down his shirt. They were at Mickey's house in Brentwood, could hear his wife moving around in another room. "I told you about that. The studio says it was just an affair."

For a moment, Shorty thought he was going to go off.

"They lie like they breathe over there. No honor at all." Mickey got himself under control, shook his head. "It's pretty obvious, isn't it? She was blackmailing him on account of she was pregnant."

"Boss, the note indicates she was gonna abort. And it's signed, *love, Kitty.* That don't sound like blackmail to me."

"We don't know what it means. I told you to get to the bottom of this," Cohen snapped.

"I'm trying, boss. But the girl got around and it's taking time. I got her and Armstrong at the Chateau Marmont and a makeup girl who saw them in his trailer. But that don't mean he killed her."

"They were doing it in his trailer?" Mickey's eyes glittered.

"That's the trouble. Girl says she walked in at six-thirty one morning to make him up and found them in a clench. Everybody had their clothes on. They broke apart and claimed he was coaching her on her lines, but the makeup girl didn't see any scripts."

"Where was Armstrong the night of October seventh?"

Shorty closed his eyes in relief that he'd gotten this piece of information.

"Mâitre d' at Romanoff's said he was there with a large party on October fifth and presented his wife with a large diamond necklace." He paused. "A guilt offering, the way I see it. The harbormaster says they took off on a producer's yacht for Catalina for a long weekend. They got back October ninth."

Mickey shot him a suspicious look. "I thought he was filming *Young Man with a Horn.*"

"They'd been filming twelve days straight. Kirk and the wife needed a little break."

"What about that prick Dragna? And that animator."

Shorty winced. "I'm working on it."

"I'm giving you a couple more days. Then I want answers."

Pico pulled up to the gate at Warner Brothers Studio, showed his badge, and was waved through. They were ten minutes late already, but Magruder didn't seem concerned as they parked and walked to the office of Bennie Jones, the head of Warner security and an old friend of Magruder's.

The security bungalow was on the far side of the lot and Pico resisted the urge to stop and watch as senoritas in colorful rickrack-trimmed dresses and scoop-necked embroidered white tops flounced past.

Jones had his feet propped on the desk, smoking a Cuban cigar, when they walked in. He offered them one. Pico declined, but Magruder accepted, and they went about the fussy rituals that precede the smoking of fine cigars. "You're late," Jones said when they settled in.

Pico glanced at his watch. "Only by fifteen minutes, sir. The traffic —"

"Kirk sends his apologies. He couldn't wait. The director was screaming bloody murder, they're shooting today. So I took his statement for you."

Pico looked with alarm at Magruder, who was puffing his stogie and grinning idiotically. Things were shaping up exactly as Lily Kessler had predicted. He felt let down. His one opportunity to talk to Kirk Armstrong up close, gaze upon that famous face, searching for signs of sincerity, and it had been snatched from him.

Pico licked his lips. "What did Mr. Armstrong have to say, sir?" he said hoarsely.

Magruder and Jones looked at each other and burst into laughter.

"Just pulling your leg, son," Jones said. "Kirk's shooting and they're running late. We're going to walk over to Jack Warner's office soon."

Pico looked around and suddenly realized what was missing. "We should have brought a police stenographer," he said.

The older cop waved his arm in dismissal, his cigar etching an S in the air.

S for slimeball, sordid, sleazy.

"It's an informal chat."

"Before we go," Jones said, handing Magruder a manila envelope. "Got a few more photos. Autographed, like you wanted. Coupla nice ones of Kirk in there." Jones winked and Magruder looked embarrassed and slid them into his briefcase.

They chatted a little longer, then Jones said, "Let's go," and they walked across the lot to Jack Warner's lair.

The mogul kept them waiting a half hour. Finally they followed the secretary into Warner's inner sanctum, bunched up behind her like ducklings. Warner sat behind a large desk, with three men around him. One was small and plump, the second slender and nattily dressed. The third was Kirk Armstrong. The actor was shorter than he appeared on screen, and his head was bigger. A thick mane of hair so glossy it could have been a wig sat upon his head, and he wore thick beige makeup.

"Gentlemen, sit down, please," Warner said. "Let's get started."

Jones made introductions. The sharply dressed man was a studio publicist and the plump one was a Warner attorney.

"And I'm sure everyone recognizes the man to our left." Jones made a small bow in Armstrong's direction.

Magruder nodded, then launched into fawning praise of Kirk Armstrong and vowed to make the interview go as quickly and smoothly as possible.

Kirk Armstrong gave a regal nod. It was hard to read him, but Pico thought he seemed eager to get on with it.

"Please tell us how you met Kitty Hayden," Magruder said.

"As I mentioned on the phone, I'd seen her around the set. She had a small part in *Young Man with a Horn.* She'd say hello each morning and we'd chitchat. She told me how much she liked my movies. She'd seen *The Summit* three times, it was one of her favorites."

Pico had heard that stars were narcissists. Here was proof. He'd already turned a murder investigation into a discussion about himself.

"She was a pretty girl, wasn't she?" Pico interjected. The rest of the room looked shocked at his impertinence, but Armstrong only chuckled.

"Right you are. And I appreciate a pretty girl, same as the next man. But it never went beyond hello, how are you, how was your weekend, when's the weather gonna cool down. That sort of thing."

"Ever call her at home? Share a meal with her? Go for a stroll? Anything along those lines?" Pico persisted.

Armstrong's face assumed the earnest expression of a Boy Scout. "No, sir. Our relationship was strictly work."

"Your relationship?" Pico pounced.

"An unfortunate figure of speech."

"We're sorry to put this so bluntly," Magruder said, "but we have to ask. Were you and the deceased sexually involved?"

Armstrong's face grew extremely serious and troubled. "No, sir."

"Were you aware that the decedent was eleven weeks pregnant?"

A stricken expression crossed the actor's face. "That's terrible."

He's an actor, thought Pico. *And this is the role of his life.*

Kirk Armstrong's voice was modulated. Filled with respect and concern, just the right tinge of sorrow and outrage. He held Magruder's eyes, didn't look away or blink. His hands rested on the arms of the chair. His feet didn't twitch. In fact, Kirk Armstrong seemed to be holding himself perfectly still. What did that mean? Wouldn't it be more normal for him to be somewhat agitated and nervous, fearful of negative publicity that could damn his career, scandalize his marriage? Shouldn't he be more upset?

"All right," said the attorney. "If that's all you gentlemen need, we can get back to making this picture." He stood up.

"Wait a second," Pico blurted out, surprising himself. "Mr. Armstrong, you said you never left the set with Kitty Hayden or saw her outside the studio. Is that right?"

"Now, look here, he's already told you that. I thought we were through," Jones said.

"That's quite all right," Armstrong said. "Yes, Detective, that is correct."

"Mr. Armstrong, do you have a trailer on the set?"

"Of course."

"You're out of line, Detective," Jones said.

Pico threw up his hands. "I just want to determine if Kitty Hayden ever went inside his trailer."

Kirk Armstrong turned his expressive eyes onto Pico. There was something in them now that hadn't been there earlier.

"I'm sorry, gentlemen. I've told you all that I know. I was not personally acquainted with the deceased. My heart goes out to her and her family. She was a promising young actress who showed great talent, and her death is a tragedy."

"Brilliant, Mr. Armstrong," the publicist said, jotting his words down on a legal pad. "I'll make sure the trades get a copy of your comments, especially how you volunteered to speak to the police. Make it clear we have nothing to hide."

"Nothing at all," Armstrong said, beaming at the room. "I'm a family man. Happily married. Three little girls."

"Well put, Mr. Armstrong," Jones said. "We have nothing to hide."

Magruder waited until they were in the parking lot to lay into him.

"What the hell was all that about? You were supposed to keep your trap shut and let me do the talking."

Pico shrugged. The slick way things had been handled made him uneasy. "I didn't think the kid-gloves treatment was appropriate."

"Kid gloves? He's a movie star. And he came to us. Remember that, Pico."

"Only because he knew the crapola had hit the fan. They were desperate to put the studio spin on it. Make themselves look good."

"And they did. This afternoon, every paper in the city will praise Kirk Armstrong for coming forth to clear his name."

"So he's cleared his name? That's it?"

"You heard the man. I'm satisfied he had nothing to do with the Hayden murder. Aren't you?"

"I don't know," Pico said moodily. "Aren't we going to interview everyone on the set? See if they saw anything different?"

"I don't think there's any need. And it would cost the studio money if they had to stop filming. Bad for business."

"Who cares? We have a murder to solve."

"Listen, Pico. All those little grips and makeup artists and extras are going to read the paper today and if he's lying, someone will call us. But I'm betting they won't. Armstrong has a reputation to keep up. He wouldn't lie about a thing like this."

"He would if the alternative was the San Quentin hot seat," Pico said.

CHAPTER 21

The *Confidential* story had brought the reporters back in droves. They milled just over the hedge, lounging against their cars, and Lily was relieved that they hadn't been around earlier to witness Max's drunken performance.

From the backyard, Lily heard the scrape of a metal rake, smelled the incinerator burning leaves. Reducing autumn to ash. A giant swallowtail butterfly fluttered among the bougainvillea outside the window. Shouldn't it be migrating by now? She'd seen flocks of small black birds triangulating south, squirrels burying acorns, apples ripening on trees, the only signs by which Angelenos knew winter was gathering over the Tehachapi Range, preparing to pounce.

"Ooh, there's a nip in the air today," Jinx said, looking flushed and happy. "I should have gotten my winter coat out of storage. Now I'm going to freeze down in La Jolla."

"Borrow mine." Lily tossed it to her.

"Gosh, thanks. We've all been admiring it."

A honk came from out front.

"Oops, gotta run. Thanks, Lily of the Valley. Wish me luck."

She winked and ran out. Lily went to the window and saw two heads leaning together for a smooch as a little convertible roared off. Jinxie had a date!

The mailman strode up the street, and Lily couldn't help staring. He was six feet tall and sun-bronzed, with chiseled features and muscles that moved under his uniform. He might have been an actor playing a mailman. Soon he was hiking up the rooming house stairs, pulling out letters and a brown package that would never fit inside the mailbox.

Lily cracked the door and offered to bring it inside.

"Sure, miss." The mailman beamed a thousand-watt smile. "Say hello to Jeanne for me."

The package was for Mrs. Potter. Lily shuffled through the letters. An envelope addressed to Doreen Croggan on official L.A. County stationery caught her eye. It had been stamped and rerouted because it bore the wrong address. Lily checked the postmark, saw it went back ten days.

She was still staring when Mrs. Potter came in from the yard. Her hair was gathered up in a kerchief. A smoky fire smell clung to her clothes.

"I'll take the mail."

Lily slid the letter into her skirt pocket. Then she handed over the package and the rest of the mail. "Is that all?" Mrs. Potter glanced suspiciously at Lily.

"Yes. I gave a friend this address and she's already written, bless her heart."

"Awfully fast for the mail," Mrs. Potter said skeptically, but her attention wandered as she shook her package. "It's from my sister. Wonder what could it be." She walked out.

Lily waited until Mrs. Potter's footsteps receded. Then she ran upstairs, sat at her vanity table, and examined the envelope more closely.

District attorney's office, read the return address. With the name *B. Keck* above.

Lily slid a nail under the flap of the envelope and slit it open. She pulled out the watermarked sheet, unfolded it, and read:

Dear Miss Croggan:
Pursuant to our conversation of October 5, I have made discreet inquiries

regarding the matter we discussed and learned enough to satisfy myself as to the veracity of your statements and to open a file. I have tried unsuccessfully to reach you by phone to discuss my findings. Please call my office at your earliest convenience so that we may proceed.

Sincerely,
Bernard Keck, Investigator
Office of the District Attorney for Los Angeles County
BK/ph

Lily read the letter twice. It was dated only days before Kitty disappeared. She knew that the district attorney's office prosecuted crimes in L.A. County. What had Kitty discussed with Bernard Keck? Could it have triggered her murder?

She closed her eyes and considered her next step. Rummaging through her suitcase, she found a notepad and copied the letter. Then she tore out the page, folded it, and stuck it inside a Bible on Kitty's bookshelf, placing the original in her purse. Going downstairs, she picked up the phone, then thought better of it. Someone in this house had almost certainly blabbed to *Confidential*. Had that person also kept the DA investigator's messages from reaching Kitty? Lily flashed again to Mrs. Potter, hand out-stretched for the mail.

When she stepped outside, the pack of journalists moved like a primitive ectoplasm toward her. She ignored them and hurried to the drugstore where she ate most of her meals, heading for the wooden phone booth in the back. When she found the directory listing for the district attorney, she thumbed in a nickel and asked to speak to Bernard Keck.

"He's out sick," a secretary said.

"Has he been ill long?"

"Who's calling?"

"This is Li— this is a friend of his. I've been trying to reach him."

"He's been out since October twelfth with a respiratory bug."

The day Kitty's body was discovered.

Lily swallowed. "Can I reach him at home?"

"He sure ain't in Reno."

"All right. Well. Thank you." Lily pursed her lips, nodded. "Ah, miss, would you by chance happen to have his home —"

"No, I don't." Lily heard the phone being replaced in its cradle.

She looked around, saw a man just outside the booth, watching her. He had a shifty look to him. Was he following her? Had he been listening in?

The man stuck his face against the glass. He tapped his foot. "Lady, you gonna spend all day in there?"

Flustered, she walked out. The man went in, muttering about crazy dames who think life is a coffee klatch.

Lily retreated to the powder room. When she came out, the booth was empty. With relief, she hurried back in. She flipped to the residential section of the phone book this time and found an address and phone number for Bernard Keck. She jotted it down, then inserted another nickel and dialed.

"Hello?" said a gruff male voice.

"Mr. Keck?"

"Who's this?"

"Is this Mr. Keck?"

The line went dead. Lily frowned and called again. This time it rang and rang.

Lily hung up. A new thread had emerged in the pattern, was growing more discernible with each step she took.

She didn't want to go to Bernard Keck's house alone, but a glance at her watch told her Pico would still be at Warner Brothers. She reread what she'd jotted down: 817 Park Place. The telephone prefix indicated MacArthur Park. It was the middle of the day. What could happen in broad daylight?

There were children feeding stale bread to the ducks at MacArthur Park and men playing chess at the tables. A vet in a wheelchair, some kind of medal pinned to his chest, pushed himself along. Several pensioners with canes sat on benches overlooking the lake. Flanking the park on all sides were apartment buildings. Some were elegant and well kept, with awnings and liveried doormen, and others looked like they needed a new coat of paint and masonry repairs.

Lily hopped off the trolley and found Keck's building. It was one of the nicer ones, flowers growing in coffee cans, lace curtains billowing in the afternoon breeze. She looked up the tenant roster, found a listing for B. Keck. Apartment 706. She entered. The elevator was decorated with Art Deco tulips etched in brass. She closed the metal accordion door and pushed the button for the seventh floor. The old elevator lurched up.

She emerged into a hallway and followed the numbers to Keck's apartment. The door was ajar. She stood there nervously, then knocked. A uniformed policeman came out.

"Who are you?" the man said. "What are

you doing here?"

"Pardon me." Lily didn't like the look of things. "I must have the wrong apartment."

She turned to leave, but the policeman asked her to step inside, where a second policeman was going through the pockets of a man's coat.

"What's the matter, Officer?" Lily asked.

"I'll tell you what's the matter." He turned to the other cop. "Sarge, this girl was snooping outside Keck's door."

The sergeant turned. He had a narrow face and deep-set eyes that crinkled suspiciously.

"I was not snooping," Lily said with indignation.

"You live in this building?"

"I'm apartment-hunting. I must have the wrong place, though. So I'll just be going."

"Wait just a minute."

"Why can't I go? Who's Keck, anyway, and what are you doing in his apartment?"

"He's dead," the sergeant said shortly. "Took a walk out his living room window an hour ago."

"What?" Kitty pressed her hands to her cheeks.

"You a friend of his?"

"No. I told you —"

The sergeant put his hands on his hips.

"Yeah, you told me. The detectives will want a word with you. Meeks, escort the lady downstairs."

Lily went back down in the elevator with Officer Meeks. From the lobby, they cut through a courtyard and out into an alley where a queasy-looking cop stood guard over a bulky tarp. Lily saw concentric rings of splattered blood and something more solid where the body had landed. The warm unpleasant smell of viscera filled the air. Lily turned, her gorge rising.

Meeks led Lily to two detectives named Topper and Chubb who were taking statements from neighbors. There were also several reporters and a news photographer. Lily was disappointed not to see Harry Jack. She would have appreciated a friendly face.

Meeks described her sudden appearance and Topper asked what the hell she'd been doing in the building.

"I told the other officer, I'm apartment-hunting and I must have lost my bearings and ended up at the wrong one. The numbers are so poorly marked around —"

"Did you know Bernard Keck?" Topper interrupted.

"No," Lily said truthfully.

"ID, please," Topper said in a bored tone. She pulled out her passport. His eyes flicked over it, then up at her. "What brings you to Los Angeles, Miss Kessler?"

"I grew up here. Came back to see if I wanted to stay."

"Well, you sure don't want to settle in this building. Fellow named Bernard Keck just jumped off the seventh floor. Or was pushed, we're not sure yet."

"Good heavens."

"Where you staying, Miss Kessler, in case we need to ask you further questions?"

Lily bit her lip. "Hollywood."

"Address, please."

In a low voice, she rattled it off.

The muscles around Topper's mouth twitched. "That address sounds mighty familiar. Now, why would that be?"

She looked levelly at him. "I don't know."

Topper snapped his fingers. "Chubb," he called, "I need you here a minute."

When the other detective arrived, Topper rattled off the Wilcox Street address. "Isn't that where the Scarlet Sandal lived?"

"That a boardinghouse?" Chubb asked, sticking his little finger in his ear and twisting vigorously. Lily wondered if it stimulated his memory.

"Yes," she admitted with reluctance.

The two detectives drew closer. *They're about to put two and two together,* Lily thought. *They'll go back to the bullpen and tell Magruder and Pico and they'll grill me and I'll end up having to tell them everything.* Lily clutched her purse where the letter nestled.

"Did you know that dead broad?" Topper asked.

"Was she as good-looking as her va-va-voom publicity photos?" Chubb added.

Breathing a sigh of relief, Lily saw her escape hatch. She made her face guileless.

"I never met her," she said. "I just moved in the other day."

"Must've met our buddy Magruder, then." Topper grinned. "And his wet-behind-the-ears partner."

"That Sam Pico's kid?" Chubb said.

Topper nodded. "The fix was in on that one."

They chortled, then turned back to her. "They talk to you yet?"

"Briefly," Lily said, her cheeks scarlet. "But since I didn't know Kitty Hayden, I didn't have anything to tell them."

They gave her the cold stares of seasoned pros who smell a liar. It was her unexplained presence here, her halting answers, the sick look plastered across her face. They must not have been aware of Keck's connection to Kitty or they would already have bundled her off to headquarters for questioning.

What had the DA investigator learned? Something explosive enough to get him killed? All of a sudden Lily was afraid. She'd planned to tell Pico about the letter, but these detectives had just hinted that he was dirty too.

The fix was in on that one.

And Pico himself had warned her not to trust Magruder. So who *could* she trust? Until she figured that out, she'd better keep quiet or risk the fate of poor departed Bernard Keck.

"If you've got a place in Hollywood, why you looking to move?" Topper asked, sniffing out her lies.

Lily tried to look pious. "Not being an actress, I don't have much in common with those girls."

" 'S quite a coincidence, still," he said, closing in. "You crossing paths with two suspicious deaths in less than one week." He stared, trying to flush her untruths into the open.

Lily shrugged. "I can only hope it's the last," she said with utmost sincerity. "Now, if that's all the questions you've got, Detective" — Lily looked at her watch — "I've got an appointment to look at a bungalow court in South Pasadena."

"You can go," Chubb said. "Magruder wants you, he knows where to find you."

CHAPTER 22

Lily took the bus back to the rooming house and ran the press gauntlet. One photographer stared with predatory intensity. He was a new face, she hadn't seen him before, and he aimed his camera right for her and snapped away like she was Kitty Hayden come back to life.

Inside, her anxiety spiked again when Mrs. Potter handed her a message to call Pico at once. Lily tucked the note inside her purse.

"Aren't you going to see what he wants?" Mrs. Potter hovered by the hallway phone.

An icy wave of paranoia washed over Lily. "As soon as I freshen up," she said.

And you're gone, she thought.

An unmarked cop car was parked outside her window when Lily came out of the shower. Magruder and Pico hadn't wasted much time. Just this morning, she'd been eager to tell them about Max's erratic behavior. Now she wanted to avoid them, but they were waiting downstairs.

Still, she dressed with care in the waning light, clipping on garnet earrings, even a splash of Kitty's Arpège. Detective Pico was in the parlor, flipping through a movie magazine. Magruder wasn't in sight. A fizzy warmth flooded through her. She knew she shouldn't trust Pico any more than his partner after what she'd overheard today, but she couldn't help it.

"Ah. Miss Kessler." He rose, tossing aside the magazine. "Mrs. Potter said you didn't answer your door when she knocked. Have you been hiding from me?" Hands clasped, gaze steady and impersonal.

"I was in the shower. And I . . . didn't get the me —"

One eyebrow went up. "Mrs. Potter insists she relayed the message."

"I mean, I was going to call you when —"

"Fine. Let's go." He gave her an inscrutable look, already heading for the door.

"Where are we going?"

To jail? she wondered. Would he arrest her for withholding evidence? Should she show him Keck's letter now, get it over with?

She followed him, a million questions blooming, then dying, on her lips. When he

348

stopped, they almost collided. He smelled like a canyon after thunderstorms have pummeled the wild thyme and rosemary. For a moment they regarded each other.

Then his mouth twitched. "You hungry?"

They were driving in his car again, and it was dark, the city lights sparkling like a pirate's chest, and without even asking, he'd flipped on the heater, placing his large hand over the vent to test the air temperature. She had no coat tonight because she'd loaned it to Jinx. KNX was on low, the newscaster reporting that housewives from the Pasadena Women's Club had marched through downtown wearing heels, pearls, and gas masks, demanding that the city clean up the smog.

"Where are you taking me?"

"I'm supposed to be following you, so I figured I'd make it easy on myself."

So she'd been right the other day in Culver City.

Her nerves twanged like a plucked string. "Why?"

"Magruder thinks you're going to lead us to the killer."

"I thought you didn't trust Magruder."

Pico gave her a rueful look, like he regretted his earlier words. "I was wrong. Magruder's an okay guy."

"I see. So how am I going to lead you to the killer?"

One side of his mouth curled up. "Just keep nosing around and asking questions. He'll find you."

"I'm the bait?"

"Sure. But don't worry, we'll swoop down right before he strikes."

Seeing her alarm, he added, "I wouldn't let anything happen to you."

Had she imagined a husky tone creeping into his voice?

"Fumiko told us you found Max Vranizan crawling around in your shrubbery this morning," Pico said after they'd driven awhile.

"It was worse than that. He was drunk as a skunk and tried to grab her."

"I asked if she wanted to file charges, but she declined. We had a little talk with him anyway, told him it better not happen again. He knows we're watching him."

"What happened with Kirk Armstrong?" Lily asked.

"Nothing," he said glumly. "He's either a very good actor or he's telling the truth."

"Any word on Freddy Taunton?" Lily asked, thrilled at this rush of information.

"No, but his apartment manager, Mel

Booker, was found shot to death this morning outside the Radcliffe Arms."

Lily gasped. "I bet he tried to sell those photos to the wrong person. I'm telling you, it's all connected. We just don't know how yet."

"You be sure to let us know when you figure it out," Pico said.

He headed downtown and turned right onto Commercial Street. The tantalizing smell of baking bread filled the air. TAIX FRENCH BAKERY, the sign said. He pulled up to a yellow loading zone, not even making a pretense at parking legally. One more *droit de cop.*

"Bakery?" she asked, making a pretense at gaiety. "Does that mean it's bread and water and I'm your prisoner?"

"The restaurant's next door." Pico gave her an enigmatic look. "French. Figured you'd like a classy joint." He fumbled for the door, held it open.

His awkward gestures, his thoughtfulness, touched her. Despite everything, she gave in to the voluptuous danger of trusting him. Not the uniform but the decency she sensed at the core of him.

The tables were set with red-and-white-checked cloths, an oil lamp, fresh carnations in a vase. The owner bustled over,

351

bowing and inquiring about Pico's family. He served them himself, and they ate crusty loaves of warm bread, coquilles St. Jacques in real scallop shells, gratinéed potatoes, a salad and cheese plate at the end of the meal. A bottle of red wine with no label, filled from a cask in back. Two tumblers.

"This is lovely," she said, refusing to believe it was *The Last Supper.*

He looked at her hungrily, buttered one last piece of bread, and chewed it solemnly.

"Topper and Chubb said they ran into you today," he said.

Lily's stomach turned over. How stupid she'd been, with her flights of fancy. She should have known the detectives would tell Pico and Magruder immediately.

"Oh my goodness, that was such a co-incidence, I was —"

He looked almost sad that she would lie to him. "Detective Magruder and I would like to know why you showed up at Bernard Keck's apartment shortly after he jumped to his death."

He'd been clever, she saw now. Softening her up with food and drink. Playing on her insecurities.

"Do you really think he jumped?" Lily said.

"Do you?" Pico asked, after a moment's

hesitation.

"No," Lily said.

"Why'd you go there?"

She had her story ready. "I found his name scrawled in the margin of an old newspaper in Kitty's room, along with a phone number."

Pico smacked his fist on the table. "Why didn't you tell us right away?"

Lily turned large, frank eyes on him. "I didn't know it was important, so I threw it in the incinerator. Then, last night when I was in bed, it hit me. Thank goodness I have a good memory."

"How did you know where he lived?" Pico asked, convinced he'd caught her in a lie.

"It was a brilliant investigative feat: I looked him up in the phone book."

"And you just happened to arrive right after he jumps? You're lying," he said, his voice rising with every word. "Now tell me the truth. How did you learn about Keck?"

Lily tried to look hurt and upset. "I *did* tell you the truth."

Pico leaned over the table. "You had a narrow escape today. An hour earlier and you would have met Keck's killer in his apartment. Do you realize that?"

"I thought you weren't sure he'd been murdered."

"I'm assuming the worst, for the sake of argument. Jeez." He shook his head. "My first homicide, and it's exploded into the most sensational murder case of the year."

"They must really trust your detection skills," Lily said, delighted to change the subject.

"Maybe they don't want someone with a lot of experience digging into it."

"Magruder's got years of experience."

"Yeah, well, there you go. He worked the Dahlia case. Great job they did with that one."

"You just told me Magruder was okay. And lots of people tried to find Betty Short's killer. It's not his fault." She paused. "You think Kitty's murder could be related to the Dahlia?"

"Nobody in Homicide is saying that."

"What are they saying?"

Pico's eyes tightened almost imperceptibly. Then he shrugged and Lily realized the confidence was over. They got up to go. Mr. Taix came up, bowing and murmuring thanks in Franglais.

"You didn't pay," Lily said when they were on the sidewalk.

He looked at her lazily, clicked his teeth. "You just didn't see me. Contrary to what people may think, we're not all racketeering crooks."

Lily remembered the insinuations of Topper and Chubb.

"Old Alfonse likes to have us in his restaurant. Makes him feel safe. He and the boys in blue have a long tradition. During Prohibition, even the Feds left this place alone."

"They get paid off with coq au vin?"

"It was all out in the open. Alfonse sold plenty of wine. 'For medicinal purposes only.' "

Flushed and warm from the food and drink, Lily laughed. "How do you know?"

His face darkened, and Lily felt the temperature plunge. "My father used to drink here."

"Where'd you grow up?" she asked, eager to draw him out.

"You shouldn't be here," he said abruptly.

Lily was confused. "What are you talking about? This was your idea."

"You don't want to get mixed up in this. Any of it. Me included."

"Why shouldn't I trust you?"

His face loomed in, angry and distorted in the yellow glare of the streetlight. "You don't even know me. I could drive you to the railroad tracks right now, slit your throat, and throw your body on the slag heap, and no one would be the wiser."

"You wouldn't do that."

"Because I'm a cop?"

"Because you're decent. I can tell."

"People can't tell anything. They delude themselves. Criminals, the ones who are sick inside, they know how to bury it so deep that even they don't remember it, most of the time."

"What are you telling me?"

"Nothing good will come of this."

"Of what?"

A struggle played out across his face. He seemed to be deciding whether to tell her something. Then he kicked the car tire.

"I don't always do the right thing. Like not paying for that dinner tonight. Like turning away when I see another cop do something wrong."

"But that's small stuff. Things you can fix."

"Just because you put a uniform on a monster doesn't make him any less of a monster."

The vehemence with which he spoke made Lily afraid.

"Detective Pico," she asked, "do you know who killed Kitty Hayden?"

"No, but I bet she was just like you. Thought she knew better. Now you're running around town, doing the same thing, lying about —"

"I'm not going to get killed," Lily interjected quickly.

"How do you know?" he said hoarsely.

"Because if I get into any trouble, you'll bail me out," Lily said, wondering if she was right.

He wouldn't meet her gaze. For a long moment there was turbulent silence.

Then Lily said, "So are you going to tell me where you grew up?"

Her words seemed to break the black spell. Slowly his face lost its stormy expression.

"Whittier," he said, staring at the sidewalk. "How about you?"

"Mar Vista. There were lima bean fields all around. One of our neighbors had a goat farm. The fog crept in at night. You'd see ghostly shapes moving and hear the tinkle of bells." She sighed, recalling the changes. "What about Whittier?"

"It's always had a pretty good-sized downtown. They used to call it Picoville."

"Cuz so many Picos lived there?"

It was the wrong question again. She felt like she was walking on eggshells.

"No," he finally said. "Just one."

"Who was that?"

He stared at her, not seeing her, focused

357

on something far away. His eyes were smoky pools. "My great-grandfather."

"Your people have been here a long time, then?" Lily probed.

He flung open her car door and it creaked in protest. "It's all dust in the wind now."

She got in. Why was he so touchy? "I doubt that," Lily said.

He leaned against the open car door, a sardonic look in his eyes. "Want to see for yourself?"

He expected her to decline. Fine, she'd call his bluff. She was curious about him.

"Sure," she said.

Pico drove roughly, jerking the car, staring straight ahead, not saying anything. The car shot over an old Egyptianate bridge with curved serpent lampposts that spanned the L.A. River. Lily looked down and saw that the earthen banks where she'd once caught frogs, chased great blue herons, and marveled at hawks riding the thermals had disappeared. So had the willows, the wild roses, the biblical rushes. Mile by mile, the untamed river of her youth was being encased in a concrete channel. She recalled the floods of '38, how they'd ravaged the city and killed dozens. This was necessary, she told herself. It was progress. And she was hardly sentimental. So why, she wondered with vague annoyance, did she feel a sense of loss?

Soon the road grew dark, fields stretching on either side. It felt peaceful to leave the city. She could see so many stars. She smelled the pungent whiff of nearby dairies, heard the lowing of cattle. They passed crops of corn and lettuce and strawberries. Then slowly the farmscape gave way, first an occasional house, then clusters of them, streetlights, the stars dimming overhead, the buildings growing more dense. A main street, shops.

"Welcome to downtown Whittier," Pico said, pulling up to a three-story white-washed adobe that had once been grand. She felt they'd crossed an invisible border back to the nineteenth century.

PICO HOUSE HOTEL, the faded sign read. Two bandit-faced fellows lounged on a wooden bench on the front porch. Dead plants trailed from upstairs balconies. A wooden shutter banged in the night breeze. Under the streetlight, Lily saw the adobe was grimy with years of accumulated dirt. There was a wooden hitching post along its side where horses had once been tied up. In the back somewhere, there would be a stable.

They got out of the car, coughing from

dust the tires had kicked up. Pico held the front door open for her. It was framed in wood, etched in gorgeous smoky glass. At the bottom, someone had patched a crack with tape.

"After you, mademoiselle."

Lily held back, wondering why he'd brought her here. "What is this place?"

"You said you wanted to see."

He coaxed her inside, and she stepped into the lobby, marveling at the glory and decrepitude. In the middle of the room, a double staircase made of marble curved up to the second floor. You didn't climb such a staircase, you *ascended.* Preferably with a page trotting behind you, holding your velvet train. But the carpet, once colorfully woven wool, was unraveling and faded. Above her hung an enormous gas chandelier. Painted wood beams held up the high ceiling. Carved rosewood furniture lay scattered around. Five men sat in the bar, smoking cigarettes and playing cards. They stared at Lily and Pico, then, with the instinctive cunning of ne'er-do-wells who smell John Law, packed up and slunk outside.

Lily looked around. Tarnished brass spittoons were stacked in a corner. Gigantic birdcages of filigreed iron gaped empty, the paper on the bottom littered with petrified bird droppings. The lace curtains were yellowed from generations of tobacco smoke. The once-fancy wallpaper peeled off the walls. Dead flies decayed on the windowsill. Lily's nose wrinkled.

Far away on a tinny radio, Esther Williams and Ricardo Montalbán were singing "Baby It's Cold Outside." At the reception desk, a man's head suddenly popped out from behind the counter. He yawned and said sleepily, "Will you be wanting a room, sir?"

Lily's breath caught. She was suddenly hyperaware, felt the same stillness as earlier in her room. The loaded words of the song, Montalbán's sly seduction, had never resonated so strongly.

"I'm just showing a friend around," Pico said.

"Very well, sir."

They continued their stroll. Lily felt the excess energy drain away. The song was just a song again, not a suggestion.

"Years ago, this was the best hotel in all Los Angeles," Pico said. "Out there" — he pointed past French doors at the rear of the lobby — "was a courtyard planted with exotic flowers and trees. The most expensive rooms overlooked the fountain. The restaurant was known as far away as Seattle and Denver for its French chef. Guy by the name of Sharles Laugier."

"How do you know all this?"

He gave her a sad, melancholy look. "My great-grandfather built it."

A little shock of pleasure and curiosity coursed through her at his revelation. "Who was your great-grandfather?"

Pico shoved his hands in his pockets. "His name was Pío Pico."

The name rang a bell with Lily. A fourth-grade field trip to the San Gabriel Mission. California history. "Wasn't he . . ." Lily's voice trailed away. He wasn't a bandit revolutionary like Pancho Villa or a Franciscan missionary like Father Junípero Serra, or an explorer like Gaspar de Portolà. Queer, it was on the tip of her tongue.

Pico waited, a glazed, expectant look on his face. When she finally gave up, he said, "Pío Pico was the last Mexican governor of California. He died in 1870."

"Mexican?" she said, shocked. "But you've got light skin and brown hair and, what, hazel eyes?"

Now that she examined them, they were more tawny than hazel, flecked with gold as they caught the light.

"Never fear, the blood's been quite diluted since then."

She blushed. "I didn't mean . . ."

"That's okay, don't worry about it."

"So how did . . . ?"

"My great-grandfather believed in sowing his seed. Had three kids with his 'official' mistress. Then, toward the end of his life, a Scottish maid at the Pico mansion caught his eye. He was in his seventies and she was eighteen when she gave birth to my grandfather. The family never acknowledged the kid. Not that there was any money left by then."

Her history came flooding back. "Didn't Pío Pico get one of the original Spanish land grants?"

Pico scuffed his shoe and looked wistful. "At one time he owned twenty-two thousand acres in San Diego County. Where Camp Pendleton is today. Plus his *ranchita* here in Whittier. All gone. To con men, gambling debts, bad luck, and worse investments. He died penniless."

"So how'd your great-grandmother raise an illegitimate child?"

"She sold the jewels he bought her with the last of his money. My grandfather grew up rough, though. Betwixt and between. Married a pretty waiter girl from France he met at the San Antonio Winery and they had four children before he split for good." He gave a tight smile. "I come from a long line of wastrels."

"What about your father?"

"Oh, he turned things around, all right," Pico said. "He became a cop."

That Sam Pico's kid?

The fix was in on that one.

"Well, there you go," Lily said stoutly, pushing the memory away. "Each generation makes its own destiny."

Pico's mouth twitched. She sensed his mingled pride, shame, and melancholy that his once-heralded bloodline had passed into history. Alta California was gone, its rulers and lineage dispersed, its families and vast ranchos broken up. New gods of commerce and celluloid strode the arid land. Even the language had changed.

"You're, like, original California royalty," Lily said in a low voice.

"Are you not seeing this place? It's a dump."

"Just think what that land grant would be worth today. Millions." A shiver ran through her. "If Pío Pico hadn't been swindled. If he hadn't been greedy and impulsive."

"I need a drink," Pico said.

They walked into the dingy bar. Pico slid into a booth. Lily made for the other side, then saw that flaking plaster from the ceiling had rained chalky dust across her seat.

She wiped it off but only smeared it further. With an exasperated sigh, she scooted in next to him.

The detective's arm draped along the top of the wooden booth. Immediately he removed it, careful not to touch her shoulder. He ordered them brandy, then seemed to retreat deep inside himself.

"Sometimes I come here to think," he said after a waiter brought the drinks. "I know it sounds strange, because he's been dead almost eighty years, but I can feel my great-grandfather here in this place he built. When I get a day off, I come and poke through stuff in the basement and the attic, hunting for traces of him. I've salvaged a few paintings, some furniture, a handful of letters. Odds and ends. They keep a room for me upstairs, and I store everything there and pay a lady to keep it clean. Don't know why, really. Can't think who'd ever want it. It's more because I can't stand the thought of his stuff moldering into dust or getting tossed out with the trash. So I polish and fix it up. And I talk to him about what I'm doing, tell him about my cases. I guess it's my way of praying."

"Does he answer you?"

Pico laughed. "I'm not that crazy. But when I leave, my head's more clear, and I'm at peace. Even sitting here tonight, watching it crumble all around me, it feels all right. Reminds me of my mortality. That's not a bad thing for a homicide detective to keep in mind."

His voice was slow and hypnotic, his eyes deep wells that receded further away with each sentence he spoke. Lily felt she was disappearing into them, tilting, spinning, falling, head over heels.

"I'm glad you brought me here," she whispered.

"Never shown anybody this place, leastways a girl." He took a long drink. "My pops thinks I'm nuts for caring about some old Mexican the rest of the world has forgotten. He said it's not something you go around telling people when you're a cop. Especially not after Sleepy Lagoon and the Zoot Suit Riots."

He shifted restlessly beside her. With a sudden motion, he tossed back the rest of his drink. Soon he'd take her home. A sense of impending loss swept over her. She wanted to prolong their time together, couldn't bear the moment when they'd say good night.

"Would you show me the unofficial Pío Pico Museum?"

He looked at her in surprise. "You actually want to see more of this raggedy-ass place?"

"Consider it an impromptu history lesson."

He pulled back, blinking. "Well, all right."

He paid and they walked back to the lobby and made their way up the staircase. On the second floor, the stairs grew more modest. They passed a group of men in crew cuts walking down.

Lily turned to watch. "And here I thought this place was almost abandoned."

"They're vets. Living in temporary housing on the third floor. They'll be gone soon."

Holding the carved railing, Pico led them to the top floor and down a hallway. The walls were freshly whitewashed here, the carpet threadbare but clean. Behind a closed door, Lily heard an ad for Adolph's meat tenderizer. At the end of the hallway, Pico fished out a ring of keys. He selected an ornamental black key that looked like it belonged in an antique store, inserted it, and turned the lock.

The room had eighteen-foot ceilings and most of the space was given over to boxes and carved wood furniture stacked taller than a man. It smelled of ancient dust, rosin, cracked leather, and wood oil. Lily saw a hand-tooled leather saddle worked in silver perched atop one of the stacks. A large oil painting of a fierce, hawkeyed man on horseback hung over the fireplace. He wore nineteenth-century finery and had long wavy black hair, olive skin, and a familiar nose that started high on his face and came straight down. Other paintings, many in what looked like their original gilt frames, lay stacked on their sides against one wall. Lily saw a plein air landscape that might have hung in a museum. Floor-to-ceiling velvet drapes of flaming burnt orange covered a large window. The room was clearly used for storage, with only a narrow path leading to an iron bedstead, made up neatly with tightly pulled blankets, muslin sheets, and a flattened pillow.

Pico moved past her to the curtains, pulled them open, and slid up the casement window. Fresh night air poured in, soft light from the courtyard. From far away, she heard laughter and languid *canciones* in Spanish.

"It really is a museum," she said, looking around.

The fireplace mantel was crammed with nutcrackers and cigar clippers, old menus written in sepia ink, hand-drawn maps, flasks, a carved-wood hunting rifle with ivory inlays — mementos and knickknacks of all sorts. She ran her finger along the mantel and it came away clean. Someone cared about this place.

"This is only a sample of what's been lost."

She nodded at the oil portrait glowering down at her, an imperious look in the haughty eyes. "Is that . . ."

"It is indeed. Lily Kessler, meet Pío Pico."

"How do you do, sir?" Lily curtsied and extended her hand for the portrait to kiss. "It's a great honor."

Pico took a step toward her, hesitated, then turned on his heel and pulled down two stacked chairs. He brought them to the window, then cleared a space so they could sit down. Crossing the room once more, he got two glasses from a built-in cupboard. He produced a bottle of brandy, poured them each a snort, and handed hers over. Etched onto the glasses in a handsome script were the words *Pico House Hotel.*

"Salud."

They clinked glasses and drank.

"What a strange night." He shook his head. "But then, this case has been strange from the beginning. The more I learn, the more bedeviling it gets."

"I don't understand."

"I don't either. But I've been thinking

369

about it, and you've got to be careful. The last thing I'd want is for you to get hurt."

"Why is that?" Lily held up her glass, turning it around. She tried to empty her eyes of all emotion. A pulse beat strongly in her neck. She breathed in, then out. The room seemed to shimmer at the edges.

"Because we don't need anyone else getting killed," Pico said with barely suppressed annoyance.

"Of course not," Lily said, disappointed.

"We should go." He stood up, collected their glasses. "C'mon. It's late. I need to get you home."

Reluctantly, she rose.

Pico moved toward the door, stopped. "It's no good," he said, his back to her.

"What's no good?"

"This case. It's making me insane. I can't think straight. I can't concentrate."

"Maybe you'll feel better after a good night's sleep."

He groaned and pressed his hand to his forehead. "No. And it's not that."

He turned. "Isn't it obvious? I can't stop thinking about you, and how much I want you. I'm sick with it. You're all I think about, night and day."

Lily felt a tremor somewhere near her heart. A current moved between them. She hadn't felt this way since Joseph. She'd been young then, and the war had been on. Every moment was dangerous, every sensation heightened, and she'd assumed that was the way of it and things would always feel like that. It was only after he was gone that she realized how rare it was, and that she might never feel it again. That she'd been given one shot, and that was already more than some people got.

She was shocked to see how miserable he looked. Shoulders hunched and twitchy, lines creasing either side of his mouth.

"Ah, to hell with it," he said, slamming the crystal glasses down on a shelf. They spun, then slid across the wood. "I'm sick and tired of trying to stay away from you, Lily. I can't do it anymore."

Then his arm was around her, tugging her toward him, pulling her close. His lips met hers, and he was kissing her, drinking her in. She clasped her hands around his neck, pressing against the yielding warmth of his mouth, tasting him.

Heat spread from somewhere inside her lower belly. She felt a familiar tingling, the terrifying and delirious plunge of a roller coaster at the amusement park. Shivering, she closed her eyes and felt the sinews of his arms wrap tighter around her, enveloping her. They stayed that way, suspended in space, and she had no idea if twenty seconds had passed or twenty minutes. She didn't care, so long as it never ended. Somehow, she managed to breathe.

They broke apart finally, his eyes wide and dilated, then he pulled her to him again, breathing in the essence of her, caressing her hair, cradling her head, whispering her name and something more as she leaned against him, her limbs heavy and languorous, until suddenly she made out that he was saying he was sorry.

"What?" she said, giddy and confused. "Why are you apologizing?"

His lips went to her ear; his fingers tucked back her hair. "You probably think I brought you up here with this in mind. And I didn't. I swear."

"I know," she said. "I'm the one who suggested it, remember?"

"Yes, but —"

"Sshhh. It's only ghosts watching."

She pulled him down onto the iron-frame bed, modest and narrow, little more than a camp cot, really, but perfectly adequate for their purpose.

They fell onto the mattress, already intertwined, making the springs creak, the frame slam against the wall, and she would have stripped her clothes off in a fever, but he pinned her wrists against the sheets and whispered that there was no hurry, he wanted to take his time, relish every bit of her, every valley and swell, that this was what he'd thought about since the first time he'd laid eyes on her.

She sank back against the pillow and gave in to his tongue, his fingers, his mouth. The ceiling spun and the cracks in the plaster danced and shimmied and she gasped, her legs spasming uncontrollably. Then, still trembling, she pushed herself up. Kneeling on the bed, she explored him in turn, the constellations of muscles, the fine whorls of hair, making her way across the tawny landscape of his skin to the pearly wetness at its tip, sliding against his slickness, and when he was inside of her at last, she knew finally that she had come home.

Afterward they lay there a long time, feeling the night breeze dry their sticky flesh.

He caressed her hair and said, "This isn't how I'd imagined —"

She put a finger to his lips to silence him, then her mouth, then pressed her entire body against him, and they began all over again.

The moon shone through the window-pane, the stars wheeled across the sky, same as they ever had, and it seemed that nothing at all had changed. And yet everything had.

They left the old hotel like ghosts out of time, tiptoeing past the receptionist snoring on his army cot behind the counter. The moon was down, the streets spectral and empty. They rode in silence, flanks and shoulders pressed together, not needing to speak.

When he pulled up in front of the boardinghouse they said good-bye, limbs tangled, lips swollen and bruised, then she got out, moving like an automaton, the slam of the car door reverberating in the silence. She ran up the steps, then turned to wave as she slipped inside.

"Good-bye, Lily," came Pico's voice, already so far away it might have been underwater.

At the sight of the car pulling up, a shadow hidden in the shrubbery stirred. He'd expected her on foot. Plans would have to be adjusted. The figure watched patiently as Lily got out. Soon the car would leave and she'd be alone. But the car lingered until the girl was inside. He waited, ears cocked to see if she'd lock the door. They probably didn't do that where she came from. But the lock slid home. He watched the upstairs intently to see where the light went on. When it did, he smiled, memorizing the location of the room. Bunch of girls. Thought they were so smart. He waited another half hour until he was sure nothing was stirring. Then, clad in black, with noiseless, crepe-soled shoes, he crept around to the back door and tried it. Locked. Slowly, he made his way to the windows. It was October, but the nights were still pleasant. He was patient. He'd try every one.

Lily turned off the lamp but tossed restlessly in bed, touching the tender parts of herself, drinking in the smell of him that wafted off her skin when she moved, replaying everything they'd done, the brawny feel of him, the sheer vastness of what they'd unleashed. *What's the use of sleep?* she thought. In a few hours it would be dawn. She felt like a particle hurtling through space, gyrating madly, moving toward eternity. She longed for the ordered symmetry of the atom, electrons and protons orbiting the nucleic core in perfect harmony. Then how it would split. She imagined surrendering to such a cataclysm, the totality of the destruction.

She was drifting off at last when a creak

jolted her awake. She felt a presence just outside her door. Then, just as it had the other night, the knob began to turn. But this time, Lily felt brave. Her evening with Pico had left her thrumming with strange energies.

Snapping on the lamp, she jumped out of bed and hunted for a weapon. She grabbed the bottle of Arpège off the vanity and she crept to the door.

"Who's there?" she whispered.

Silence. She heard a creak, footsteps moving away.

Lily turned the lock and flung open the door. In the shadowed hallway, a spectral figure clad in white receded.

"Who's that?" Lily whispered more loudly, recalling Mrs. Potter's offhanded talk of ghosts.

The figure turned. In the dimness, Lily made out a face.

"Oh," she said, lowering the bottle as Red hastened toward her.

"Sorry if I scared you," she whispered. "I wanted to borrow an aspirin."

"Why didn't you knock?" Lily asked, suspicious.

"I didn't want to wake the others."

Lily sighed. "Come in."

Red glided in, self-conscious, looking around.

Slowly, Lily's hackles settled. She went to her makeup bag and pulled out a bottle of aspirin, poured a glass of water from the pitcher.

It was only later, after Red had returned to her room, that Lily wondered if she'd come creeping around because she'd thought Lily was still out or sound asleep and figured it was a good time to snoop through her things.

CHAPTER 23

October 16, 1949

Pico was driving, Magruder slumped in the front seat, morose and silent. It was a blustery day in the valley, clouds drifting across the blue sky, aimless as Pico's sleep-deprived thoughts. He wanted to sneak away to call Lily, see how she was doing, but they were chasing a new lead. A tipster claimed to have seen Kitty eating lasagna with two men at an Italian restaurant in Sherman Oaks the night of October 7. But the staff didn't recognize the photos the detectives shuffled like a deck of cards. And the tipster, who lived around the corner, had suddenly become less sure. The dead girl had become a phantom hovering at the edge of things, a projection of the city's fears and desires, its flickering whims, a celluloid will-o'-the-wisp. The Regal Theater on Beverly was even running a Scarlet Sandal marathon featuring all the movies she'd been in. Patrons were urged to come dressed in red. A particularly notorious female evangelical preacher would perform a funeral service afterward while the organist played "Amazing Grace" and theatergoers lit candles, acolytes to a morbid shrine. There'd been a lively debate this morning on KNX about whether the spectacle was appropriate.

Pico glanced over at Magruder. He smelled like a distillery, even after his garlicky chicken cacciatore. His hair was lank, his suit rumpled, his jowls grizzled. His eyes were bloodshot, the skin underneath like twin eggplants. He wasn't even up to his usual jibes.

"Are you okay?" Pico asked finally.

Magruder muttered something unintelligible. They were almost to the Cahuenga Pass when Magruder said, "Turn left here."

"Where're we . . . ?"

Magruder lurched upright and gave an evil belch. "Shut up and do as I say."

Pico shrugged and made a left onto Vineland. The area was all orchards and fields, with ranch houses hidden behind the trees.

"Make a right," Magruder said as they neared an unmarked road.

They bounced along the rutted surface.

"This have something to do with the Hayden case?" Pico asked finally.

Magruder turned baleful eyes on him. "Everything."

"This where she was killed?" Pico asked, his nerves trilling. Some isolated hideaway shack used for an awful purpose, with only the owls and bats and coyotes as witnesses. How did Magruder know, anyway?

"Diseased whores, all of them," the older cop announced. His voice fell to a hoarse whisper, then slowly rose in volume. "Blood begets blood. Bodies stacked everywhere. The tribes of the night advance, and we cower in shadow, paralyzed and helpless before the apocalypse."

With that he shrieked and slumped against the passenger door.

He's mad as a hatter, Pico thought. *And now he's had some kind of fit.*

"Magruder," Pico said tersely. "Sir. Snap out of it. Look at me. You okay?" He slapped his partner's beefy arm. Had he swallowed his tongue? Should they drive to a hospital?

Magruder gave Pico a ghastly grin. "A-OK," he said.

"Jesus, you scared me."

With effort, the older cop roused himself. "Pull in here," he said, pointing.

Pico turned up a driveway and stopped in front of a ranch house. Magruder threw the door open and lurched out.

"I'll only be a minute," he called.

Pico slammed the car into park and ran after his partner, tripping over a tree root. By the time he picked himself up, Magruder had disappeared around the back. Pico found him handing a farmer a bill and receiving a burlap sack. At their feet, chickens scratched in the dirt.

"Much obliged," Magruder said.

Then he saw Pico. "C'mon. Told you I'd be right back."

Whatever Magruder had in the bag was thrashing and making panicky sounds.

"What the hell is going on?" Pico said.

"None of your business," Magruder mumbled.

"What's in there?"

"See for yourself. Then maybe you'll shut the fuck up."

He opened the bag and Pico peered in with caution, half expecting something to jump out and fasten sharp teeth onto the end of his nose. A trussed-up chicken looked back, eyes darting nervously.

Pico was angry that Magruder had taken them so far out of their way for a stupid bird.

"You can buy those at Ralph's, you know," he said as he drove back to the main road.

"All plucked and cut and wrapped in plastic. Save you some work, you got a hankering for soup."

"That's not the kind of hankering I've got," Magruder said unpleasantly.

"We going back to headquarters?"

"No. We're going to Angelino Heights. I've got some business there."

Pico was irritable. "You've got business everywhere. It's just that none of it is *police* business."

In the back, the chicken squawked futilely, then subsided.

"What would you know about it, snot-nose? I've been a cop longer than you've been alive."

Pico's cheeks burned. He wanted to punch Magruder, could already hear the satisfying crack of fist against cartilage as the older man's nose broke. He gripped the wheel tighter.

The address was a dilapidated Queen Anne Victorian home on Carroll Avenue that had been prime real estate about sixty years earlier. Now the paint peeled off its lacy, ornamental spindles and the wrap-around porch sagged. With a strange impatience, Magruder grabbed his bag and told Pico to follow. They walked up a pink granite path and past stone pillars onto the front porch. Magruder gave an elaborate series of knocks and an iron grate in the door slid open.

"Hattie," Magruder said. "I've come for a visit."

The grate swung shut. A moment later, the heavy oak door opened and they entered a house that smelled of hamburger grease, wax candles, and cloying perfume. The woman Hattie, huge and slovenly, led them into a living room filled with cheap plaster figurines. Crocheted lace covered every surface. From upstairs came the sound of laughter. It was a whorehouse, but worlds removed from the one on Vine.

Magruder exhaled heavily and huddled in a chair, his sack squirming on his lap. "I'm in a bad way, Hattie," he mumbled.

She gave him a practiced look. "Okay, hon, we'll take care of you. Your room's all set up."

She led the old cop out and the last thing Pico saw was the bloodshot whites of his eyes.

Pico seethed with impatience. He wanted to be working on the case. His mind inflamed by Lily, he found the entire idea of whores repulsive.

Hattie bustled back into the room. "Your partner said I was to take good care of you.

So what's your pleasure, mister?"

Pico felt a warmth stain his cheeks. "I'll wait." Like he was declining canapés at a dinner party.

Hattie put a hand on her hip. "You like boys, maybe?"

"I'm not in the mood today."

"I'll send the girls down, maybe you see something you like."

"No, thank you," Pico said.

Throwing up her hands, Hattie left.

Pico walked to the fireplace. The ashes were covered in cobwebs. Dust bunnies slept in the corners. There were crumbs, dog hair, and some kind of stain on the carpet.

Outside, bees buzzed. Far away, a car honked. All at once, Pico heard Magruder's voice rising in a crescendo, then veering into an unearthly howl. It was followed by the higher-pitched screams of a hysterical girl, then the pounding of feet. Pulling out his service revolver, Pico ran out of the parlor. In the hallway, a naked girl, sobbing and covered with blood, was fleeing toward him.

"Help me!" she cried.

Behind her, also naked and smeared with blood, lumbered Magruder, cursing and shrieking as he pursued her.

Pico's eyes went from the girl to Magruder

to the girl, desperate to figure out what had happened, how badly they were wounded and who was to blame. After what seemed like an eternity, his gun settled on Magruder.

"Freeze."

Just then the girl reached Pico and plucked at his arm. Hyperventilating, he flung her off, hitting her in the face with his elbow. She began to wail anew.

The sight of Pico training a gun on him seemed to snap Magruder out of his madness. He looked around, as if baffled to find himself naked and drenched with blood.

"You sick fuck," Pico screamed. "What did you do to her?"

Just then Hattie burst in. She took one look around and said "It's okay, everybody. Calm down. You, put that gun away. No one's hurt."

She bustled over to the naked girl. "May, honey, why'd you have to go off like that? I told you it was just pretend."

She led the crying girl out, apologizing over her shoulder. "Sorry, Mr. Magruder, she's new. It won't happen again. Why don't you go shower, big boy."

Magruder's shoulders sagged. He looked spent, but the glazed far-off look had left his eyes.

"Son of a bitch," he said, walking back.

Pico put his gun away and let himself out of the house. As he sat in the car, smoking and waiting for his partner, he tried to calm down. What had happened in that room? What did Hattie mean about "pretend"? What the fuck were they pretending? One thing Pico now realized — Magruder was far more disturbed than he'd imagined.

Fifteen minutes later the older cop strolled out, tucking his wallet back into his slacks and smoking pensively. His hair was damp, the metallic smell of blood still clinging to him. But he moved easily, as if some great tension had been released.

They drove to headquarters and Pico said, "You want to tell me what happened back there?"

"No," Magruder said truculently.

"Goddamn it. I'm your partner. Tell me now, or I swear, I'll go up the ladder, I'll file a complaint. Visiting whorehouses is one thing. Beating a girl bloody is altogether another."

The face that Magruder turned on him was eerie in its serenity. "You heard Hattie. Nobody got hurt."

"Then why was that girl covered in blood?"

Magruder looked straight ahead and said

nothing.

"You think I don't remember what Olga said, at that house on Vine? About rough stuff?"

"It was chicken blood, Stephen."

Pico imagined all sorts of depraved scenarios.

"Why else would I bring a chicken in there?" Magruder said in a perfectly reasonable tone. "So Hattie could put it in a pot and make soup?"

"I have no idea why you'd bring a live chicken into a whorehouse," Pico yelled. "Whatever you did, you scared that girl half to death."

Magruder gave a rueful laugh. "But that's the whole point. She's alive. The bird dies so she can live."

Pico snorted, shook his head. "Is it black magic?"

"Hardly." He puffed his cigarette, exhaled thoughtfully. "It's a fucking exorcism."

"What's that supposed to mean?"

But Magruder would say no more.

Pico wondered how long it would be before the urge came upon Magruder again. He felt he was swimming in dark waters, with peril all around, but that he was part of the peril. He couldn't kid himself. He wasn't worthy of Lily. He should stay away from her. He'd only taint her too, in the end.

CHAPTER 24

"Hey, Lily," Beverly called, knocking on her bedroom door. "Want to go to a real Hollywood premiere? Fumiko has an extra ticket. Jinx was supposed to come, but she had a date last night, the dirty dog, and she must be asleep, she's not answering her door."

Why not? Lily thought. She ate a packet of saltines, brushed her teeth diligently, and gargled with Lavoris ("It tastes good, it's good taste").

The front yard had already sunk into shadow when they set out. The bungalow across the street glowed with the day's last light, the stucco shining like cake frosted in broad, undulant strokes. The cactus was majestic in silhouette, all prongs and ornamental spikes, its nocturnal blooms white and sepulchral. If landscape shaped mythology, then Southern California's was solitary heroes moving against an empty horizon, Spanish missions rising from sun-baked land, fasting and fleshly mortifications, Indian animism under the desert moon. L.A. was the anti-paradise, its dreams written on parchment-thin bougainvillea that crumpled with the first breeze of fall.

Strange desires stirred inside Lily. She yearned to slip inside these houses, assume a new identity. She'd be an actress or a pit musician, a high-priced call girl, a secretary preparing a solitary meal, a dowager awaiting death. So many lives behind those iron-studded oak doors. She wanted to flit in and out of them like a diffident angel.

On the Boulevard, they stopped at the window of an appliance store where a television tuned to KTLA was broadcasting Korla Pandit's *Adventures in Music.* An impeccably dressed Indian man wearing a jeweled turban, Pandit played the organ with a serene smile while dancers pranced among fountains and pillars. Fumiko said Mrs. Potter wanted to install a TV in the rooming house with a coin box that would provide a half hour of viewing time for each quarter. The others agreed this was a good idea.

A flickering neon sign across the street caught Lily's eye. THE CROW'S NEST.

"What's that place?" she asked Beverly, recognizing the nightclub Harry Jack had mentioned.

"I've never been inside. It's supposed to have a strange clientele."

"Extra, extra," the newsboys called from far away, but Lily barely heard them.

"I've changed my mind about the premiere," she said. "Meet you back home."

Before they could stop her, Lily ran across the street. From inside the bar came the sound of piano music. The neon tubes hissed in a sinister fashion. Lily pulled on the door. Locked. She peered through glass bricks that formed a ship's porthole, but saw only her own distorted reflection. She decided to try the rear entrance.

The alley was dark, but there were plenty of people about, and it was early. Lily counted the storefronts as she walked. The Crow's Nest was twelve buildings in. She'd reached six when she heard someone behind her. A man's tread, not a woman's light, tapping heels. She walked faster. The footsteps sped up. The businesses weren't marked from the back and she'd lost count. Lily stood before a black door with a brass handle. Was this it?

An unearthly howl split the air, making Lily flinch, and she turned and saw a figure in a long coat approach. Across the alley, two shadows raced atop the wall. Cats, she thought with relief. The figure drew nearer. Lily grabbed the brass handle and pulled. Locked. He was almost upon her. The piano music grew louder. She pounded.

Fingers tapped her shoulder and she turned, ready to scream.

A pale, clean-shaven man stood there, an unlit cigarette dangling from red lips. Under the hat, she saw cropped black hair, parted severely on the side and slicked back.

"Might you have a light?" he said, his English accented and musical. His eyes were warm and amused, above high cheekbones. "Ah," he said in a rich contralto. "You are new to the game. Do not be afraid."

She watched, mesmerized, as his hands dipped gracefully into his pocket, past an antique watch on a chain. He pulled out an engraved silver case, opened it, and offered her a cigarette. They were like none she'd ever seen before, short and wrapped in black paper embossed with gold lettering.

"Please," he said. "They're handmade for me in Turkey."

"I'm sorry, I don't smoke."

"Suit yourself." The corners of his mouth turned down and he lit his own, inhaled, and blew out the smoke. He was slender under the coat, wearing an old-fashioned jacket with buttons and epaulets that tapered at the waist, then flared into tails.

"Very well," he said. "Shall we make our entrance?"

"You're going in too?"

"But of course."

It dawned on her. The fey, flirtatious banter. The exaggerated, theatrical movements. He was homosexual. That was probably what Beverly had heard.

"I'm afraid it's not open," Lily said.

He cocked his head. "Oh, but it is. To the right customer."

He knocked twice, waited, then gave three more short raps.

A porthole opened.

"We're closed," came a voice.

Lily's new friend put his face to the porthole and whispered. Lily saw that his eyes were made up like a woman's.

The door creaked open.

"After you, mademoiselle." Her new friend flourished his arm.

Lily swallowed and stepped through the door.

Despite the bar's penumbra, Lily could see it was crowded. A man was playing standards on the piano while couples slow-danced.

"Over here Alex," came a gruff voice from a table against the wall.

"Patience, good people," Alex said, shrugging off his coat. He slung it over his arm, took her elbow, and led her to the bar, where he ordered them both champagne.

"Is it selfish," he said, "to keep you all to myself for a while?"

His eyes wandered over her body and Lily wondered if she'd misjudged the situation. Maybe this wasn't a homosexual club. There was something illicit here, she felt the underground currents lapping all around. Drugs, perhaps? Or some more refined decadence?

The bar was so tightly packed their thighs almost touched. It was hot, loud. She felt claustrophobia descend like a clammy blanket. She wondered if anyone at the rooming house would notice her missing if she didn't come home.

Lily shifted away as Alex's thigh pressed against hers, even as her brain flooded with sense-memories of Pico. After almost a year alone, she'd forgotten how it felt. At first she'd moved awkwardly, like rusty machinery. But he'd awoken something dormant that had roared back to life. She felt Alex's thigh again and wished he could be Pico.

And yet. The contrast between the swagger and pale delicate features, the rouge over pale skin, the eyeliner, the sureness of his touch as he'd maneuvered her through the club. It was oddly titillating.

"My, you're a pretty little thing," he said, cupping her chin.

He leaned in with those full red lips, and feeling dizzy, she closed her eyes and whispered, "No," but somehow his lips were on hers now, billowy and soft. For a moment she gave in, then pulled back, bracing her hand against his chest to push him off.

And felt . . .

Breasts.

"You're a woman!" Lily whispered.

"So are you."

"You kissed me."

"You liked it."

"That's when I thought you were a man."

"What does it matter? I should have been a man."

"It's not the same."

"I'll be a man for you."

Alex moved toward her again. Lily turned away and stared at her drink. Alex's face hovered, then withdrew. "The ice princess," she said. "You want to be seduced." There was a pause. "Or maybe I'm not your type?"

"It's not that. It's . . ."

"It's a game for you. Why else would you come?"

Lily decided to be blunt.

"Remember Kitty Hayden, the actress found below the Hollywood sign?"

Alex's eyes flickered with distrust. She didn't answer.

"I'm a friend of the family. Kitty's shoe and purse were found less than a block away from here. This place stays open late, so I was wondering . . . I came here to ask . . . to find out . . . if any of the patrons saw or heard anything unusual after eleven p.m. on October seventh."

Now it was Alex's turn to shrink away. "Nobody here had anything to do with that."

"I'm not saying they did."

"We don't want trouble with the police. We pay money, each month, to be left alone."

"I'm sorry you have to do that."

"I wasn't even here that night."

"But others were. If you could introduce me to some of your friends, I'll ask them."

Alex shuddered. "And where would it end? With us testifying in court? Such a thing could ruin careers. Lives."

"Not in court. Just to me."

"You're naïve to think it would stop there."

"Two girls are dead. They didn't deserve to die. I'm betting somebody here saw something."

"And I can't afford to lose my job," Alex said. "There's already talk about a loyalty oath, to weed out Reds. And because of my accent, I'm . . ." Alex's mouth twisted. She tapped the ash off her Turkish cigarette. "This is exactly why I left Europe. I care nothing for ideology. Only to be free."

"Kitty Hayden didn't get freedom. Her killer's still out there."

Just then another pretty young man in slacks and an open-neck shirt came up. "Really, Alex," he said. "You and your friend must join us."

"So that's why I need your help," Lily concluded, after she'd bought drinks for the table. She didn't understand Harry's complaint about the piano player, he really wasn't bad. When she mentioned it, everyone burst into laughter.

"I bet he started playing 'God Save the Queen,' " Alex said.

Lily nodded.

"It's code, darling. To warn the men to start dancing with women and vice versa. Charles must have suspected your friend was an undercover detective."

Then it was Lily's turn to laugh. Wait till she told Harry. It felt good to laugh. She'd done so little of it lately.

Alex's friends assured her that they hadn't been at the Crow's Nest the night Kitty disappeared. Just then another mannish girl walked into the bar and joined their table. She carried an evening newspaper that smelled of fresh ink.

"There's been another girl strangled and dumped below the Hollywood sign with only one shoe," the newcomer said.

Lily's skin burned prickly hot as she crowded around the paper with the others.

The photo of the dead girl's face was indistinct this time, and most of her body was concealed by a . . . Lily's brain exploded as she recognized her coat. It stood out immediately because the lapels and buttons were of a classic prewar European style, a cut rarely seen on L.A.'s streets.

"Oh my God." She grabbed the table and tried to read, but in the dim light the letters blurred across the page.

"Here, darling." Alex flicked her lighter. Lily read:

" 'The body of a third strangled young woman was discovered below the Hollywood sign this afternoon wearing only one shoe, leading police to wonder whether a demonic Hollywood Strangler is preying on the city's young, beautiful female population. Police are trying to establish the identity of the unknown woman in her twenties, who was found fully clothed and wearing a wool coat with fur trim. Anyone with information as to . . .' "

The thought struck Lily like a punch in the gut.

"It's Jinx," she said with sick certainty. "One of Kitty's roommates. She borrowed my coat last night."

Beverly's voice echoed in her head: *Fumiko has an extra ticket. Jinx was supposed to come, but she had a date last night, the dirty dog, and she must be asleep, she's not answering her door.*

The table erupted as everyone sought to speak.

A clanging echo filled Lily's ears, drowning out all other sound. Three girls dead now, all of them strangled. Lily felt a chill creep up her own neck, imagined bare fingers tightening around her throat. The last embrace.

"I've got to get back," she said, standing unsteadily.

Had Fumiko and Beverly already heard the news? Did they realize it was Jinx? Were they at the house right now, being interviewed by detectives?

"Before you go, let's see if the bartender

recalls anything unusual that night," Alex said.

But the bartender told them the place had pretty much cleared out by midnight. Then a gleam came into his eye.

"Oh, I almost forgot. One of our Hollywood friends showed up right before closing. He didn't stay long."

"Ah," Alex said.

"Who was it?" Lily asked.

"Here at the Crow," the bartender said, "we believe discretion is the better part of valor."

"But what if this man saw something on his way out?" Lily pressed.

The bartender laughed. "He was too busy making cow eyes at his new friend. They didn't see anything but each other."

Lily couldn't force the bartender to reveal the man's name, and it might come to nothing anyway. Alex said she'd hail a cab.

"I'm only a few blocks away," Lily protested. "The walk will clear my head."

"Are you crazy?" Alex exploded. "There's a killer out there, looking for girls to attack. He's found three already. Do you want to make it four?"

Her words made Lily wonder. Why would a killer randomly pick off two girls from the same rooming house? What if Jinx had been *targeted?* Either because she knew Kitty or . . . because the killer thought she was someone else? Jinx had been wearing Lily's coat. What if Lily was the real target? What if the Hollywood Strangler thought she was getting too close to unmasking him?

"We'll take the cab together, and I'll drop you off," Alex said. "Don't worry, darling, I don't bite."

"Where to, fella?" the cabbie asked Alex as they climbed in.

Lily rattled off the rooming house address and Alex said the cabbie could take her to Silver Lake after that.

"Do you know who the bartender was talking about?" Lily whispered after they set off.

Alex looked out the window and said nothing.

"I thought you were going to help me. If this man knows something, he's got to come forward before more lives are lost."

Shrouded in the big coat, hands shoved down pockets, Alex murmured something.

"You'll have to speak up," Lily said.

"God forgive me."

"For what?" said Lily.

"For what I'm about to do. You'll have to

lean in, darling. I'm not going to broadcast it."

Lily did and Alex whispered a name, breathing minty bourbon breath her way.

With a sound of disbelief, Lily pulled away. "That's who was in the bar?"

Alex nodded solemnly.

"But Rhett Taylor's a heartthrob. The girls are crazy for him."

How could it be? Rhett of the sculpted face, the sexy, sleepy blue eyes. The inarticulate mumble, the blond hair, the aw-shucks poses for the camera.

Alex gave a sad smile. "Metro's sent him away for 'rest cures' several times already."

She stared out the window. "I feel like a traitor."

CHAPTER 25

It was late to be shopping at the Hollywood Ranch Market, but Harry Jack had been busy all day. He'd pocketed a clean hundred bucks from the *Mirror* for his exclusive photos of Kitty's purse and shoe, then given an interview about how he and Gadge had found the evidence. They'd barely returned home when Pico and Magruder arrived. In a black rage, the cops had searched the apartment, then taken him and Gadge downtown for questioning. Four hours, including fingerprints. Then a lady from Children's Services had shown up. Harry said a prayer of thanks as he recognized a gal he'd gone to school with at Brooklyn Avenue Elementary. The gal had taken Gadge with her, assuring Harry she'd place him with her cousin's family while they sorted out where he belonged. Gadge had cried, perking up only after he learned that his new foster father was a fireman and he'd get to tour the station. Harry promised to visit in a few days and agreed, after much grumbling, that Trouble could stay with him temporarily.

Harry had a loaf of rye, a pound of bologna, and six cans of tuna fish in his basket when Florabel Muir walked in with her husband, Denny Morrison. The queen bee of Hollywood correspondents scooped up all the evening papers, bantering with the clerk as she paid. Then she spied Harry.

"Well done on the Scarlet Sandal photos. Looks like this fellow's going to keep us all busy for a while. Say, how'd you like to go with us to Sherry's tonight?"

Harry considered. Stars often dropped by Sherry's after dancing and clubbing on the Strip and you never knew who'd deck a rival or smooch someone else's wife. He might get a pic he could sell.

"I need to stop at home first," Harry said, thinking he'd dump the groceries and grab a camera. He flashed on Lily. She might get a kick out of it. "Can I bring a date?"

"So long as she won't embarrass anyone."

Harry thought of Lily's cool poise. "She won't."

Despite the late hour, Lily was the first one home. She waved good-bye to Alex in the taxi, locked the front door, then ran upstairs to Jinx's room. It was empty.

She called Pico, but neither he nor Magruder was in, so Lily left an urgent message saying she feared the murdered girl in the paper might be Jinx.

"Lady," said the LAPD operator, stifling a yawn, "we got everybody and their brother calling tonight, saying she was their daughter, wife, sister, and neighbor. We even got two callers confessed to killing her."

"But I was her roommate, and she hasn't come home, and I think that's my coat in the picture. Do you want me to come down and look at the body?"

"Don't waste your time, hon, they wouldn't let you in. I'll ask the detectives to call."

Uneasy, Lily hung up. Despite their night together, she had no idea where Detective Pico lived or how to reach him outside work.

She jumped when the phone rang. Finally! God she wanted to talk to him. When Harry Jack's voice came on instead, she felt a crash of disappointment. She told him she couldn't go to Sherry's and had to keep the line free in case Pico called.

"The third girl they've just found, I have an awful feeling it might be Jinx Malloy, one of the girls here. She's not home.

Nobody's home except me, and —"

"You're all alone?" Harry erupted. "Jesus Christ, do you have a brain in your head? I'm coming over right now and get you."

"But what if the detectives need me?"

"When's the last time you saw Jinx?"

"Yesterday. She drove off with a man in a convertible. She said they were going to La Jolla."

"Did you get a license plate? Could you identify him?"

"No."

"Do you know anything about her life, her friends, her dates?"

"Not really. You know I just moved in."

"Then you're not going to be much help to the detectives."

"What if they need someone to identify the body?"

"Whoa, whoa, whoa. It might not even be her. I don't know how you can tell anything from that awful grainy picture they ran. I would've taken a better photo than —"

"I still think I need to wait here."

"If Kitty's killer has struck again, you shouldn't be alone there like a sitting duck. I'll be over in twenty minutes."

"But I feel so helpless, Harry, I —"

"Look at it this way. Kitty mighta known some of the people who will be at Sherry's.

They get a Hollywood crowd. We'll keep our ears open for talk about Kirk. We find out who killed Kitty, we may nail the other two as well."

Or maybe Rhett Taylor would be there, Lily thought, and she'd find a way to talk to him. Anything was better than sitting here stewing.

"All right," she said morosely.

Lily changed into her one cocktail dress, an off-the-shoulder black crepe number by Dorothy O'Hara, and went downstairs to wait for Harry Jack. When she heard a key turn in the front lock, she jumped and ran to the hallway.

"What took you gals so long?" she called. "Have you heard the wretched news?"

The door opened and in walked Jinx, carrying a small bag. "What news?" she asked.

"Jinx? Oh my god, Jinx, you're alive." Lily grabbed the bewildered girl and hugged her tight.

"Lily, what's wrong?"

Still stunned by Jinx's miraculous return from the dead, Lily said, "You gave me such a scare. No one's seen you since yesterday."

"Well," said Jinx, a deep blush rising along her throat, "we motored down to La Jolla and ended up staying overnight. And Lily, he's wonderful, I have to tell you all about him, he's a professional golfer and —"

"I thought you had an agreement to tell the other girls if you were going to be gone overnight."

"I did. I called yesterday afternoon," Jinx said.

"Then maybe everyone knew but me. I was so afraid the girl they found was you."

"What girl?" Jinx said.

"Haven't you heard? There's been a third strangled girl dumped in the Hollywood Hills with just one shoe on. Like Kitty and that Florence Kwitney. I guess I got a little hysterical and . . . well, I thought it was you because of the —"

"I'm sorry. I figured Louise would tell everyone."

"Never mind. You're safe. It was silly of me to think the worst, but when I saw the photo and the girl was wearing a coat that . . ."

The doorbell rang, drowning out her last words.

They raced to answer it and found Harry Jack.

Jinx put a hand on her hip. "Who are you and why are you ringing our doorbell so late? I'm Jinx Malloy, by the way."

Harry Jack squinted at her. "You look plenty alive to me."

Lily noticed he'd left the car idling.

"Are you ready," he asked Lily, "now that she's turned up safe and sound?"

Lily glanced at Jinx. "I don't think I want to leave her after —"

"Bring her along. Feel like hitting Sherry's tonight, Miss Malloy? It's a great spot for stargazing."

"I'm bushed," Jinx said, stretching languorously. "All I want to do is crawl into bed."

"Aren't you afraid to stay here by yourself?" Lily asked.

Jinx waved aside her protests. "The others will be home any minute."

"What could be taking them so long?" Lily asked.

Jinx yawned. "Maybe they tagged along to the dinner afterwards, and then there's usually a party. Go, Lily, have fun. I'll be fine. Anyone tries to break in, they'll be sorry when I land a few kicks below the waist."

Seeing the startled look on Harry's face, Jinx giggled. "Sorry, but a gal in this town has to defend herself."

"I still don't think I should have left her alone," Lily said in the car.

Harry glanced at his watch. "She'll be fine. It's late and the others are probably on their way back."

"Do you think it's the same killer?" Lily asked after a moment.

"Because of the shoe, you mean? Could be. Or else a couple of other killers have decided it's a good MO to pin on Kitty's murderer. Copycat killings."

Lily shook her head. "I don't know about Florence Kwitney, but I could have sworn the dead girl in that photo was wearing my coat."

"You're just a little jumpy."

"That poor murdered girl."

Lily thought of Jinx walking into the foyer. She'd been wearing a wrap, Lily realized now, not the borrowed coat. But her relief at finding Jinx alive, then Harry's arrival, had pushed the coat from her mind. Lily hoped Jinx hadn't left it behind in La Jolla. It was chilly tonight, she could have used it. Oh well, she'd get it back tomorrow.

Lily saw Sherry's up ahead, the marquee lit up in lights, Louis Prima and Keely Smith headlining. Her thoughts skittered in a different direction.

"Wouldn't it be wild if Kirk Armstrong was there and I could ask him about Kitty?"

"You wouldn't have the nerve," Harry said.

"I most certainly would. Not that he'd say

anything different than what he told the cops."

Harry shook his head. "I'd be surprised if he's involved in this. I've worked in Hollywood enough to know the stars are leery of blackmail and paternity suits. Why would Kirk Armstrong risk sleeping with a fifty-dollar-a-week contract actress?"

"Maybe he was thinking with the wrong organ."

Harry snorted. "This is what comes of consorting with soldiers for five years. Jesus, what a mouth you've got."

"I'm just saying."

"And what I'm saying is, these stars got an itch, they can take it to a high-class call girl. One screenwriter I know, he won't even date a woman unless she pulls down a thousand dollars a week."

The idea of so many zeros made Lily dizzy. "He must not get many dates."

"In this town? He does okay." Harry stopped. "Ya know, what girls don't understand is that the bed is not gonna make a girl a star unless she's got some objective talent."

"Kitty had talent."

"But even that's subjective, if you know what I mean. And these guys are diabolical. One picture I shot stills on, the director was

411

sleeping with his actress. And one day, he's telling her how to play a scene, and she says, 'But John . . .'

"And right in front of the crew and everyone, he says, 'You may call me John in bed. On the set, it's *Mr. Ashford.*' "

They pulled into Sherry's parking lot and saw Sergeant Darryl Murray of the L.A. police Gangster Squad standing outside with Harry Cooper, an investigator for the state attorney general's office.

"Whaddaya doing out here, fellas, trying to get shot?" Harry called out.

"How ya doing, Harry?" Murray responded.

Once they got inside, Harry understood why the badge boys were outside. Florabel was sitting with Mickey Cohen, some henchmen, and two starlets who looked underage, a pair of San Quentin quail. *That Florabel's got the instincts of a cobra,* Harry thought.

The press had been following Mickey around for weeks because of rumors that the dapper little gangster was marked for death. He made colorful copy, with his 'youse' and 'dems,' his retinue of sharky derby-clad men that trailed him everywhere, his romancing of strippers like Miss Beverly Hills while his wife sat home in Brentwood, where his neighbors had once gotten up a petition asking him to move out.

Then, last week, grandstanding California Attorney General Fred Howser had ordered his people to follow Mickey around, announcing that gangsters had the same right to protection as any other citizens. Not to be outdone, the LAPD Gangster Squad had joined the entourage, so that it now looked like a parade anytime Mickey left the house. Harry figured the real story was that neither Murray nor Howser wanted to end the lucrative tribute and favors that flowed from the mobster.

"You want to meet the 'King of the Sunset Strip'?" Harry asked Lily.

Lily looked and saw a small, homely man with heavy black eyebrows and a round face. He was built like a fireplug and had a humble, almost abject look about him. Then he turned and his small black eyes drilled into hers.

"The big handsome feller is Johnny Stompanato."

"Both real gentlemen, I'm sure," Lily sniffed.

"Mickey's always trying to improve himself, on account of he didn't get any formal schooling. Florabel's husband gives him vocabulary lessons. C'mon."

413

Florabel spotted them. "Think you're too good to sit with the likes of us?" she called out gaily.

Mickey looked away. Despite his money and immaculately tailored suits, the gangster was sensitive about social snubs. Two more champagne glasses appeared, along with bottles on ice. Mickey was drinking coffee. He almost never touched alcohol, and the cigar clenched between his teeth was rarely lit. He passed Lily a champagne glass, then wiped his hands with a napkin before excusing himself to go to the men's room.

Harry nudged her. "Washes his hands dozens a times a day," he whispered. "It's like he's washing off the stain of blood and vice."

Mickey returned, wafting clouds of cologne. Florabel was recounting her surprise at finding leather-bound classics in the gangster's home library.

"Takes good care of them too," Stompanato said with pride. "Remember when that little actress asked to borrow *War and Peace* and you told her be sure and bring it back?"

Mickey stirred his coffee and his eyes flickered unpleasantly.

"Aw, c'mon, Mickey, don't tell me you planned to read Tolstoy," Florabel needled.

Mickey cleared his throat. "Not in a thousand years. I got a war and peace of my own to deal with. But I don't like to see a gap in the volumes, it don't look so good."

The table erupted in titters.

"But you won't read about my library in the press," Mickey said. "The editors just use my name as a red flag to sell papers. Except for the Hearst papers. William Randolph ordered them to start calling me a gambler instead of a hoodlum." He shook his head. "But the pols? Notice how they're always vowing to run me out on a rail at election time?"

Florabel put a hand on his arm. "I hope you don't take it personally."

"It's just politics. I know it don't mean nothing. We're all friends. The last time I was in the pokey the head of detectives brought me up a steak sandwich."

"I think gangsters are sexy," the peroxide blonde announced, thrusting her ample bosom in Mickey's direction. Lily felt the room heat up.

"How's that?" Stompanato grinned.

"Well, they take what they want, don't they?" the blonde said.

"That's attractive in a man," the brunette piped up, not to be outdone by her friend.

A glow suffused the table. The blonde

poured herself more coffee. Mickey picked up the creamer.

"Some milk with that?" he inquired, pinkie outstretched.

"Ain't he a gentleman?" the blonde said. "The other night he let me win at cards."

"Why'd you do that, Mr. Cohen?" her friend inquired.

"Noblesse oblige," Mickey said, his tongue tripping over the French words.

"What's that?" a gangster named Neddie asked.

"Something a peasant like you wouldn't understand," Mickey said.

The table laughed uproariously.

"But seriously, folks, Mickey's very o-bleejing," Florabel said. "He gets stacks of mail from all over the world, people asking for money and favors."

"They're always putting the touch on him," Stompanato said, "on account of he's so generous. Word gets around."

Lily watched the girls, wondering how generous he'd been with them. Was this what Kitty's nights had been like?

Mickey turned to Lily and Harry. "The place where you live, is it nice?" he asked.

Did Cohen know she'd moved into Kitty's rooming house? Was this some kind of obscure threat? She pushed her silverware around on the tablecloth and glanced at Harry, who said, "Lily's at a boardinghouse here in Hollywood and I've got an apartment in Larchmont. They're okay."

"The girls here" — Mickey nodded at the starlets — "have to get out of their dump and into something classy. I'm helping them look."

"My building doesn't have any vacancies right now," Harry said.

"Mine either," Lily murmured. The conversation was skating perilously close to Kitty.

"Vacancies can be arranged," Mickey said.

Around five a.m., they packed it in. The gangster and his entourage stood up first, handing out hundred-dollar bills that had the waiters hitting the ground in supplication.

When they reached the lobby, they saw that Cooper and Murray were still outside.

"You paying the shield boys to guard you?" Florabel teased.

"Those guys?" Mickey said incredulously. "They're so on the up and up, you couldn't give 'em a nickel. But they wouldn't frame a guy either. They're real square policemen."

They strolled outside and Mickey waited

for his car to be brought up. Harry and Lily were standing behind the gangsters, Harry handing the parking attendant his ticket, when it started.

Pop, pop, pop, like champagne corks going off into a microphone. Cooper staggered backward. Lily screamed. Sparks of light came from the vacant lot directly across Sunset Boulevard. Something grazed Harry's thigh and a flattened deer slug the size of a fifty-cent piece clattered to the ground. Another shot whizzed through a glass door inside the nightclub. Hoisting his camera, Harry went instinctively to work. Neddie was on the ground. Mickey had disappeared. For a few moments, it was mayhem. Then Mickey, his right arm hanging limp and bleeding, screeched up in a blue Cadillac, jumped out, and ran to Cooper. The lawman was clutching his stomach with one hand and waving his pistol with the other.

"Coop, get in the car," Mickey screamed.

The cop took a step forward and sagged, about to collapse. Then little Mickey, who'd once been a welterweight boxer, grabbed the six-foot-six cop, dragged him to the car, and threw him inside, blood spurting everywhere.

"Johnny," he yelled, "get Neddie to the

hospital. Let's move it."

Harry snapped away, feeling like he was back in the war. *Holy crap,* he thought. *The whole city's been holding its breath, waiting for this to happen, and I land right in the middle of it. There's going to be a bidding war for these pics.*

Florabel scampered off to find a phone, yelling "Get me the city desk."

The gangster named Neddie lay facedown on the sidewalk, screaming with pain, hollering that he couldn't use his legs. There was a big hole in his lower back where a deer slug had penetrated, and his legs were riddled with shotgun pellets.

"Neddie, Neddie," the brunette screamed.

Lily ran back inside and gathered tablecloths. She came back with a waitress and they bandaged up Neddie, trying to stanch the flow of blood. Then an ambulance arrived. Deputies from the Hollywood Sheriff's Station were piecing the story together and every witness agreed that it had been Mickey's finest hour.

A tablecloth draped across her shoulders against the night air, Lily hiked with Harry and Barney Ruditsky, the burly New York ex-cop who ran Sherry's, across Sunset Boulevard, where they fanned out across the vacant lot with flashlights to look for

419

evidence. The gunmen had piled brush in front of them before they laid in ambush. Halfway up an old concrete staircase, Harry and Ruditsky found empty shells and the remnants of sardine sandwiches the shooters had dined on while they waited for Cohen to come out.

"What a punk operation," Harry said in disgust.

"These guys don't have the decency of rattlesnakes," agreed Ruditsky.

As daylight broke, the police announced they'd found abandoned shotguns on Harratt Street, a short block away. Nearby residents reported a car backing up and almost colliding with another vehicle as it raced down the hill.

"What a bunch of cowardly rats," one of Mickey's men said. "Wouldn't even come out into the open, give a guy a fighting chance."

Reporters were rolling in now, sniffing around one another like strange dogs at a fight.

"Yeah, but who were they?" Harry said, his voice low.

"Same ones that got Frankie and Li'l Dave, maybe. And the Scarlet Sandal."

Lily pricked her ears up.

"If Dragna's people are behind this," the gangster said. "This means war."

CHAPTER 26

October 17, 1949

"Who are Frankie and Li'l Dave?" Lily asked Harry as he drove her home. Dawn was streaking across the sky, all persimmon orange and cotton-candy pink.

"Two of Mickey's guys who have disappeared."

"Were they killed?"

Harry explained what Shorty had told him, dropping Lily off at the rooming house as the sun rose. She climbed upstairs and fell into bed like a dead thing.

A loud pounding woke her up four hours later.

"That Detective Pico said he's on his way," Mrs. Potter announced through the door.

Lily threw on clothes, swiped on lipstick, and powdered her face. Heading out, she stopped at the tarnished silver mirror by the door for one last look, her heart trilling with anticipation at seeing him again. Something caught her eye on the bookshelf. Next to the Bible. Something fancy, bound in red leather. Lily could see the mirror image of the title in the reflection. She let her brain disentangle the letters. *War and Peace.*

The gangsters last night had mentioned a "little actress" who'd borrowed a book from Mickey. Was this it? Lily wondered if Kitty had been sleeping with the kingpin himself, not just partying with his underlings. With a last look at Tolstoy, she locked the door and saw Jinx emerge from the bathroom, wrapped in a bathrobe. That reminded her.

"Did my coat come in handy down on the beach?" Lily asked.

Jinx looked puzzled.

She remembered again how Jinx hadn't been wearing the coat when she walked in. And it wouldn't have fit in her overnight bag.

"You didn't leave it in La Jolla or in your friend's car, did you?"

Jinx's face was still blank.

"That's why I was afraid something had happened to you."

"What do you mean?"

"The third girl they found strangled hasn't been identified yet, but in the newspaper photo she was wearing a coat with fur trim that looked awfully like mine . . . Jinx, why are you staring at me like that?"

"I didn't end up taking your coat. We stopped at the corner market to get sodas and Louise was there buying cigarettes. She asked if she could borrow it for a photo shoot. I didn't think you'd mind."

They stared at each other. "Louise," they said together, and rushed for her door, throwing it open. The room was empty, the bed hadn't been slept in.

Pico blinked at the sight of Jinx in her bathrobe.

"Alive and well," he said. "I should have known."

The two girls started talking at once.

"Hold on," Pico said. "One at a time. You first." He pointed to Lily.

"I loaned my coat to Jinx, but she loaned it to our roommate Louise, who went on a photo shoot two days ago and hasn't come back. And the dead girl in the photo is wearing a coat that looks just like mine." Lily took a deep, shuddering breath.

"Would one of you girls be willing to come downtown to look at the body?" Pico said, looking grave.

"Certainly," they said together.

"Do you know the photographer's name

or where she was meeting him?" Pico asked.

Lily and Jinx shook their heads.

"Get dressed," Pico told Jinx. "You knew her longer. I'll drive you down."

Jinx trudged up the stairs. Suddenly Pico's arms were around her, his face nuzzling her hair.

"Lily." His breath caught, warm and sweet against her cheek. "Lily. You're all right."

I'm alive, thought Lily. *I'm here with you. That's what I am.*

Ear pressed to his chest, she heard the thud of his heart. She stood very still, listening to him repeat her name. It had never sounded so beautiful to her. And yet she felt such anguish. Out of all the roommates, Louise was the most self-assured, practical one. She'd been the one who'd cabled Mrs. Croggan when Kitty disappeared. She'd been the one who first called the police. Louise was the last girl Lily imagined falling prey to a slick stranger. If she was dead, then it could happen to any of them. She kept flashing to a scenario . . . Louise walking home at night, or sitting at a bus stop, wrapped in Lily's coat. She'd be wearing a hat, which would obscure her face. She had the same proportions as Lily, the same color and style of hair. The night would have blurred their identities. The killer would have been in a hurry.

"Stephen," said Lily. "I'm afraid it's my fault Louise Dobbs was murdered. No, listen. I think the killer thought she was me. Someone who knew I owned a coat like that. Someone who thought I was getting too close to figuring out who killed Kitty."

He examined her face, reading every tremor of emotion.

"We don't know that the dead girl is Louise," Pico said. "Let's take it one step at a time."

Pico went to call Magruder and request a tech team to go over Louise's room.

When he returned, he cleared his throat. "I called you back last night, but the girls said you were out. Where did you go at midnight?"

"I was at Sherry's." Lily launched into a description of the shoot-out.

Pico's face grew stormy. "I thought I told you to be careful."

"I had no idea what would happen. No one did. But based on what I heard, I think Kitty was more involved with Mickey Cohen's people than anyone knew."

She told him about the book, then ran upstairs to get it. Pico flipped through it and a scrap of paper fell out. He unfolded it. In Kitty's handwriting, it read: *Frankie,*

10/7 @ 9 pm.

"Frankie Niccoli," Pico said wonderingly. "He's one of the gangsters who partied with Kitty in Palm Springs and has disappeared. The other is Davey Ogul. Mickey's people told me they're just lying low, but we've got bulletins out at police departments across the country to pick them up on sight."

"What if these two guys killed Kitty, then took off for Mexico to avoid getting caught?" Lily said. "Or it was a love triangle, and one guy killed the other, then Kitty, and went on the lam?"

"What's also possible is that Jack Dragna's mob killed all three. But then why haven't Niccoli's and Ogul's bodies turned up?"

Lily's eyes glittered and she explained the theory about the forfeited bail that Harry Jack had recounted on their way home. "Do you think Dragna would go to such elaborate lengths to ruin Mickey?" she asked Pico.

"I don't know. And damn it, Lily, I want you to stop hanging around with gangsters. Kitty may have been murdered because she got too close to Cohen's people. I don't want the same thing to happen to you."

Lily pointed out that Cohen should have been well protected, what with so many cops standing guard outside. "I thought I might even see Magruder," she joked.

Pico's mouth twitched. "There's something I should have told you earlier, and it's been eating away at me. Magruder and I were at Keck's apartment the morning he jumped, asking him about Kitty."

Lily had a sudden, awful fear that the very thing that had brought them together — finding Kitty's killer — might tear them apart once the full truth became known.

"How did you know about Keck?" she forced herself to say.

"One of Magruder's pals had heard that Keck was calling around the station, asking questions about Kitty."

"What exactly was he asking?"

"That's what we went there to find out."

"Couldn't the DA's office help you? If there was an investigation, there should be a file."

"They didn't know anything about it. If there was a file it's disappeared."

Lily walked to the window. The Santa Anas had kicked up again. Wind devils moaned and shutters creaked.

"How could a file just disappear?"

"Beats me," Pico said. "The DA said Keck had been out sick since October twelfth so we thought maybe he'd taken the file home. But when we get there, he didn't want to let us in at first. Didn't know about any file. Seemed scared for his life."

"Why?"

"I don't know. But if Keck really was investigating, why didn't he contact us when she turned up dead?"

"Because the file was opened under the name Doreen Croggan, not Kitty Hayden," Lily said. "She must have wanted to do this under the radar."

Pico was across the room in a flash. "So there is a file! How do you know?"

Lily sat down heavily. "I intercepted a letter Keck sent Kitty. It was misaddressed and only arrived a couple mornings ago."

"Christ on a crutch," Pico said. "What'd it say?"

"No details. Just that he had to talk to her again."

Pico exploded. "You should have told me. That's enough to get you killed. And you can't get killed. Not now. Not after . . ."

Lily wanted to focus on the concern in his voice. But something nagged at her. Something he hadn't explained yet.

"Stephen, what else happened at Keck's apartment?"

"Nothing," Pico said in disgust. "We warned him we'd be back with a search warrant and a subpoena to compel him to talk."

"And that freaked him out so much that after you left, he jumped? Or someone came by immediately after and killed him?" Lily watched him carefully.

"I'm not sure how it happened."

"That's convenient," Lily mused. "Kitty's dead and the only other person who knew anything took a swan dive off a seventh-floor window ledge."

"That coincidence has been worrying me. In the middle of our interview with Keck, Magruder asked me to go down to the car and get his wallet. Said he'd forgotten it."

"Why did he need his wallet?"

Pico shot her a look. "He's my senior partner. I didn't ask."

"But Keck was still alive when you got back?"

"He was a sniveling wreck, but he was alive."

"You think Magruder threatened him?"

"I couldn't find his wallet."

They looked at each other.

"When we got back to the car," Pico continued, "Magruder discovered his wallet in his jacket and apologized. Said he'd stuffed a few hundred in it and gotten nervous. Then he dropped me off at the Farmers Market. A greengrocer had seen a girl who looked like Kitty lingering by the fruit tables on October seventh and Magruder wanted me to interview him."

"Why didn't you do it together?"

Pico looked away. "Magruder said he had an errand to run. I figured he wanted to place a bet."

"What did the greengrocer say?"

"That the girl seemed to be waiting for a rendezvous. She didn't look scared or unhappy. He heard her greet someone whose name might have started with an *M* but just then a car honked and he missed the rest of it. The next time he looked up she was gone."

"*M?* Could it have been Max? Max Vranizan?" Lily said.

"The guy's just not sure."

Lily turned it around in her head. "Vranizan said he hadn't seen Kitty since Labor Day. Is the greengrocer sure it was Kitty?"

"Not a hundred percent. He thought he recognized her from the newspaper photos."

"Why didn't he call earlier?"

"He did. It's taken us a while to work through all the leads. We showed him Vranizan's photo, but it didn't ring any bells."

Pico shrugged. "Anyway, Magruder was in a foul mood when he got back from his errand. We were picking up the search warrant when the news came on the radio."

"You think Magruder went back while you were at the Farmers Market and killed him?"

Pico stared at his hands. "It's a possibility I can no longer ignore."

"Why would he kill Keck?"

"Because he was about to blow the lid on something."

"Something Magruder wanted covered up?"

Pico's eyes flickered. "And one more thing. He's got this briefcase he always carries. He dropped it on the way to the judge's chambers and a manila envelope slid out. It was sealed, but Magruder acted like he couldn't wait to get it back in his briefcase."

Lily exhaled. "You think Keck had the file at home and Magruder took it when he killed him."

"I don't want to think that," Pico said. "It troubles me. But he's a loose cannon. He tried to strangle a bouncer the other day and I had to pull him off the guy."

"Strangle?" Lily whispered, her hand going to her throat.

They were silent.

"You should report him," Lily said at last.

"I can't."

"Why the hell not?"

"Because it's . . . personal."

"You have to. It's wrong not to."

"Let's put it this way. It would be like turning in my own father." Pico stared steadily at Lily. "Besides, who should I tell? The chief of police has just been indicted; so has his deputy. Half the force is crooked. There's even rumors about Simpson, the district attorney."

Lily watched Pico drive off with Jinx to the coroner's office, feeling sick to her stomach. Pico had searched Louise's room and found a calendar with the photography appointment and an address. Magruder was already headed to the studio. Lily considered the three murders. All were young, pretty women. All had been strangled and left clothed with only one shoe. All had been dumped in the Hollywood Hills near the symbolic sign. Could the killer be a disgruntled person on the fringes of show business, extracting symbolic revenge against Hollywood? But then how did Florence Kwitney fit into that equation? And what did the one-shoe business mean? If Louise really was dead and Lily's theory of mistaken identity was correct, then she was in grave danger. But she had to stay alive long enough to unmask the killer.

There was another reason to live. And that

was Pico.

She was completely smitten with him, even though she suspected he knew things about Kitty's murder he hadn't yet told her. He might even be covering up for someone. But he wasn't a killer himself. She couldn't explain how she knew, it didn't spring from reason or logic. But she felt she could trust him.

Lily was still lost in thought when a woman emerged from alongside the rooming house. She wore a scarf over her blond hair and oversized sunglasses, but Lily recognized Violet McCree. Clutching a satchel and gloating, she hurried to her car and drove off.

"Someone named Alex is on the phone and says it's important," Jinx called to Lily.

It was midafternoon and the news was official. Louise Dobbs was dead, strangled like Kitty Hayden and Florence Kwitney before her. The photographer she'd met the day she disappeared had been released from custody after witnesses corroborated his story of dropping Louise off at a trolley stop after the shoot. There were no other immediate leads.

"I thought you'd want to know," Alex's musical voice said when Lily picked up the phone. "Rhett Taylor just walked into the Crow's Nest."

Lily said she would be there in ten minutes.

"Come around the back. The password's 'violet.' And remember the knock. Two big raps, then three small ones."

CHAPTER 27

Rhett Taylor was at the bar. There was no mistaking the tousled blond hair, the smoldering sky-blue eyes, the slouch that translated into such sexy rebellion on the screen. Lily sat down one stool over. Rhett Taylor glanced at her, then went back to his drink, his eyes registering no interest.

She smiled and cleared her throat.

"I understand you were here the night of October seventh," Lily said.

"I think you must have me confused with someone else."

"An actress named Kitty Hayden was murdered that night. The Scarlet Sandal? I'm sure you've seen her picture in the paper."

Rhett Taylor yawned elaborately. "I was on location that week."

He hiked up one cheek, got out his wallet, and placed a $5 bill on the bar. Then he slid off, leaving a barely touched beer.

"See you later." He grabbed his hat and slouched out the front door.

Lily followed and saw him cross the street, wearing his hat and shades.

"Mr. Taylor sir," she said, catching up, "I'm not some loony fan who wants your autograph. I was a friend of Kitty's and I'm trying to find out if anyone at the Crow's Nest saw anything the night she disappeared."

"Sorry, can't help you." He walked faster.

She thought about the sudden exit when he could easily have gotten the bartender to throw her out.

"Rhett Taylor," she called loudly.

Several pedestrians turned around. "Look, Mama," said a girl. "That's Rhett Taylor."

The actor froze. Quickly, he walked back to Lily.

"Sure, sweetheart, I'll give you my autograph," he said loudly.

Putting his arm around her, he pulled her into a restaurant, down a hallway, and out the back door, checking to make sure they hadn't been followed.

"Don't you ever pull a stunt like that again," he said, breathing heavily. "The last thing I want's a goddamn scene."

"Then talk to me."

Rhett Taylor ran a hand through his hair.

"If you won't talk to me, I'll shout your name again. People will come running."

"And I'll call the police and tell them you're a nut job."

"Then I'll tell them where you were just now," she said, knowing full well she wouldn't have the stomach for it.

Rhett Taylor gave her an easy smile. "What is that place, anyway? Never been there before."

"You didn't know it was a homosexual bar?"

He drew back in shock. "You're kidding me."

"What did you see the night of October seventh?"

"Let's get this straight," he said. "I didn't see anything and I've never been there before."

"I think you're a great actor, Mr. Taylor," Lily persisted. "And I'm not trying to cause you any trouble. But please help me. For the sake of the dead girl."

"Don't you understand? Police and press nosing around in my private life could really make things difficult for me."

He fixed her with those sad, soulful eyes, the famous anti-charisma that confessed every sin in the book but only made the sinner more desirable.

"So would knowing you didn't do everything in your power to catch a murderer."

"You think I don't have nightmares every time I close my eyes and see that girl . . ."

"What did you see?" Lily asked softly.

"Those newspaper photos. Like the rest of Los Angeles."

"That's not what you were going to say."

"Are you one of those Freudian doctors my friends go to? Look, that poor girl is dead. But we're still alive, and I, for one, intend to make the most of it."

He adjusted his shades and walked away.

As Lily walked the two blocks home, she couldn't quite believe she'd just had a conversation with Rhett Taylor. Every woman she knew would envy her, but it was all a glorious façade: Rhett Taylor was as remote and unattainable to her as any movie star filling the screen in a darkened theater in Kansas. For him, enchantment lay elsewhere.

But she was certain that he was holding something back. More than ever, she felt on the verge of a breakthrough, if she could only put all the fragments together.

Ignoring the reporters in front of the house, she quickly walked inside and ran upstairs. After locking the bedroom door, Lily pulled down Kitty's Bible and reread

Keck's letter, wondering what new clues it might reveal now that he was dead.

Studying it, she noticed something she'd passed over before. The initials at the bottom read *BK/ph.*

Lily knew what that meant: BK stood for Keck's initials. And he had dictated this letter to someone with the initials *ph.* Or else *ph* had transcribed it from a machine. *Ph* was probably Keck's secretary. Which meant she might know about the case.

Lily ran down to the hallway nook where the phone sat. Mrs. Potter was in the parlor, dusting her collection of ceramic shepherdesses. The landlady cast an inquisitive eye on Lily. She'd hear every word, which wouldn't do at all.

"Off to the drugstore," Lily said, flying out the door. "That time of month."

At the cashier, she got a dollar's worth of nickels and settled into the phone booth that was fast becoming her private office. She called the DA's office and asked for Keck's secretary. A wavery female voice answered and Lily heard snuffling in the background.

"Is this Bernard Keck's secretary?"

"She's being interviewed by the police," the woman said.

"What's her name again? I know it starts

with a *P . . .*"

"*P?*" the woman said. "I don't think so. It's Agnes Ferny. She's been with him forever and she's mighty broken up about this."

"I thought his secretary's initials were *PH.*"

"Someone's misinformed you."

Lily tried to picture the setup. It would be a big office. Not enough stenographers to go around, so there'd be a secretarial pool.

"Has Agnes been ill this month? Flu, maybe?"

"We had a virus sweep through the office last week. I was flat on my back for three days, couldn't keep anything down. Are you with the insurance company?"

"Not exactly. So, the secretarial pool. Do any of those gals have the initials *PH?* Penny, Polly, Patty," Lily spoke fast. Any second now the woman would grow suspicious.

"We've got a Pearl," the woman said reluctantly. She covered the receiver, but Lily heard her whisper. "Madge, someone on the phone wants to know Pearl's last name."

"It's Hegland," came a far-off voice. "Why? Who are you talking to?"

The woman came back on the line. "Excuse me, but who's speaking?"

"It's a personal matter. Could you put Pearl on the line, please?"

"Why, I declare. No, I cannot."

Lily bit the inside of her mouth, drawing blood. "It's urgent."

The woman hesitated. "Pearl isn't here. May I take a message?"

"Where did she go?" Lily knew she was pushing her luck.

"Home, I presume. She left in a hurry yesterday, saying she didn't feel well. Now good day, miss," the woman said, hanging up.

Lily chewed her cheek and pondered a message carved into the wood that said: *Johnny loves Rosie 4Ever.*

Then she got the phone book and looked for a listing for Pearl Hegland. Not finding one, she tried different spellings: Helgand, Haglund, Helgund. There was a Pearl Heglund in the Fairfax District, but no one answered. She wrote down the address, then she took a trolley down Hollywood Boulevard and changed at Fairfax Avenue. She surveyed her fellow passengers. People talked to one another, read the paper, filled out crossword puzzles, held transistor radios to their ear. Where did he come from, this murderer? How did he hide his true nature?

Or was he asleep now, emerging at night to prowl while the city slept?

Soon Lily was ringing the buzzer of a duplex with drawn venetian blinds. The sky was dark blue, puffy clouds like cotton balls overhead. There was no answer. Lily thought about going to the DA's office to inquire, but she'd already aroused their suspicions. She tried next door, ringing a long time before a woman in a muumuu answered.

"Pearl ain't home," the woman said when Lily inquired.

"When did you last see her?"

"Yesterday afternoon. She came flying in like a bat out of hell, then back out with an overnight bag."

"Alone?"

"Yeah."

"Did she say how long she'd be gone?"

"Never does. She's a young thing. Bit of a flibbertigibbit."

"She have a car?"

"Not any more'n I do."

In her mind's eye, Lily saw Pearl racing out the door. Was she leaving town? But then wouldn't she have taken a suitcase? Why was she so afraid?

The sky darkened and the day grew cool as a cloud scudded across the lowering sun.

"You have a message for her?"

Lily jotted down Mrs. Potter's number. "Please have her call me. It's about a mutual friend of ours . . . Doreen."

The woman nodded, then closed the door. Lily walked to the sidewalk, thinking. Pearl was in a hurry. She carried a bag, probably wouldn't walk too far. What would she have done?

The sun came out from behind the clouds. Lily raised her face to soak up the warmth and saw a retirement home a half block away called Firestone Arms. It looked regal, with Tudor architecture and a fountain out front and a red brick driveway where cars pulled up and disgorged spry old ladies. A taxi was parked out front.

Would Pearl have sprung for a taxi? She would have stuck out in the crowd of old gals. The driver might remember . . .

The cabbie was writing something on a clipboard.

"Excuse me," Lily said.

"Where to, miss?"

"I'd like to know if you gave a young woman a ride yesterday afternoon, about this time. She was carrying a small overnight bag and . . ."

Lily realized she had no idea what Pearl Heglund looked like.

"Not me." The man settled back into his

seat and opened a newspaper. "Might have been my colleague as took her around, miss."

"How could we find out?"

"I'll raise him on the radio. There's a couple of us stationed here pretty regular to ferry the ladies to their club lunches."

The cabbie detached a two-way radio from the dash and gave his location and the number of his cab. It crackled, then a female dispatcher came on.

"Yeah, hi, Sandy. Can you ask Higgins if he picked up a fare in front of the Firestone Arms yesterday afternoon? Young gal with an overnight bag."

"And if so, where he took her?" Lily interjected.

Soon the dispatcher was back. "Affirmative. Says he took a gal to, ah, Echo Park."

"Where in Echo Park?" Lily asked.

There was another lag and more static. Soon the answer came back: Barlow Respiratory Hospital.

Maybe Pearl Heglund really was sick.

"They treat TB there," the driver said. "Want me to take you?"

"Yes," Lily said, and slid into the cab.

They drove east along Sunset, making for the hills northwest of downtown, where shacks and small terraced houses dotted the open land.

"It's like the countryside," Lily said.

The cabbie waved an arm. "That's why they built it here. Fresh air cures the lungs. Been around since the 1920s. Very popular with out-of-towners. That'll be three-twenty," he added when they pulled up. "Want me to wait?"

"That's okay. I don't know how long I'll be."

"Don't let 'em cough on you."

Barlow Respiratory Hospital was a cluster of three dozen buildings on twenty-five rolling green acres. It looked like the Three Little Pigs and their extended families had set up housekeeping. There were Craftsman cottages, Spanish bungalows, and barnlike buildings that looked slapped together overnight. Lily saw elderly people in wheelchairs with blankets over their knees, sickly young men playing dominoes, and matrons knitting. The largest building, two-story and built of red brick, was Birge Hall.

"Hello," she said to the woman in the white uniform at the reception desk. "Did a patient named Heglund check in yesterday around this time?"

The woman looked through a large book. "I'm afraid not."

"Hmm," Lily tapped a forefinger to her

cheek. "Her full name was Pearl Heglund. Youngish. Taxi dropped her off yesterday afternoon."

The woman shook her head.

"So you don't have anyone here by that name?" Lily repeated. Rephrase the question and you may get a new answer.

"Not any patients, no."

Lily paused. "How about an employee? A visitor?"

"Visitors I wouldn't know. But we have a groundskeeper named Norm Heglund."

"Could I talk to him?"

"I'll see if I can locate him."

Lily sat down. Twenty minutes later, a bearded man in his seventies clomped up. He wore overalls and an old straw hat and his face was weathered, the tip of his nose peeling.

"Got a message someone wanted to see me."

"This young lady, Miss . . . ?" The receptionist looked at her.

"Lily Kessler. I'm looking for Pearl Heglund. Could she be your daughter or granddaughter?" Lily smiled.

The man did not smile back. His eyes narrowed and he tugged at his hat. "I haven't seen her."

"A taxi driver told me he dropped her off

yesterday."

"I was out mending a fence in the back forty. Maybe she left when she couldn't find me."

"Is she your daughter?"

He hesitated. "I do have a daughter named Pearl."

"When's the last time you saw her?"

He scratched his head. "Couple weeks ago. She's a working girl. Not likely to give me grandkids anytime soon."

"Has she mentioned a case at work involving a Doreen Croggan?"

"I don't believe I've heard that name before."

"Has she seemed afraid recently?"

"Why would she? She hasn't done anything wrong."

"Of course not. So you haven't seen her?"

"Already told you that."

"When you do, could you please ask her to call me?" Lily scribbled her number.

"I'll give it to her." The man stuffed it in his pockets. "You with the police too?"

"The police have been here?" Lily asked quickly.

"No. You just sound so official, that's all. Why you looking for my Pearl?"

His gruffness seemed put on now, his questions a beat too late. Wouldn't he have

448

asked immediately? Or did he already know?

"We have a friend in common."

The man nodded. "I'll tell her," he said. "Next time I see her. I'd do anything for her. You understand, miss? She's my blood. I've got a shotgun and I know how to use it. No one's going to hurt my daughter."

Lily could almost hear the shotgun loading as he spoke. Something told her that despite her father's denial, Pearl Heglund was right here. There were plenty of places to hide on this rolling property, and who'd know better than the groundskeeper? She resolved to wait until he left, then have a look around.

Lily strolled the property, looking for places where a girl might hide. She began hiking up a hill and was startled to see a man in a suit step out from a copse of trees at the ridge. She flinched. Was he looking for Pearl Heglund too?

He said, "Those people down there don't have proper sanitation or paved roads, but they're happy. They live close to nature. Sometimes I wonder, who are we to take it away in the name of progress?"

Curious, Lily hiked to the top and joined him. A dusty shantytown clung to the hillside, peaceful and remote as Shangri-la. Lily saw fruit trees and grape arbors, discarded tires, woodpiles, and old trucks on cinder blocks. Chickens scratching on the ground, goats hoofing it up a rocky hillside pasture. A woman with a brown braid down her back, filling a kettle at an outdoor tap. A man in a black cassock carrying a white cross, his robes whipping in the breeze, trailed by smaller black-clad figures, the entire swaying line disappearing into a whitewashed chapel.

Beyond lay the flats of Atwater and Glendale, then the swell of Glassell and Cypress Park. And to the north, the San Gabriel Mountains rising majestic and bare in the autumn sun.

"It's like some pueblo in Mexico," Lily said, as the wind carried up a snatch of guitar music.

"Chavez Ravine," the man said. "We're going to tear down those shanties and build them new homes that will be a model for public housing across America. Richard Neutra's already done the designs."

"Who's 'we'?"

"Frank Wilkinson," the man said, extending his hand. "With the city Housing Authority."

"Lily Kessler," she said, shaking his hand. "Good luck to you, sir. I'll remember your name."

■ ■ ■ ■

Lily hiked down to a windbreak of eucalyptus trees. Her shoes sank into the mulch and she smelled the invigorating, medicinal tang of eucalyptus. The wind soughed through the slender leaves and she heard singing. She drew closer. Beyond the trees, a girl was hanging overalls and chenille shirts on a clothesline.

"Are you Miss Heglund?" Lily asked.

The singing stopped. The girl whirled around, poised to flee. "How do you know my name?"

Lily smiled. "Your dad told me."

"Are you a patient here?"

"I'm nobody to be afraid of."

Pearl Heglund took out another shirt. With smooth easy motions, she flapped the wet fabric and fastened it to the line with a wooden clothespin. Lily picked up a shirt and reached for a pin.

"Leave it."

Lily shrugged. "If I can't help you, maybe you can help me. A family friend —"

"I don't think so. I'd better go." The girl took a step down a gravel path to the cottage.

"You can't hide here indefinitely, Pearl."

451

The girl turned. She looked queasy, her skin the silvery green of the fallen eucalyptus leaves. "Who are you?" she said hoarsely.

"I'm Lily Kessler. A friend of Kitty Hayden's family. Or should I say Doreen Croggan?"

A look of instant recognition came into the girl's eyes. "You knew her?"

"I knew her brother. We were engaged, over in Europe, but he got killed."

"In the war?" The girl's voice wavered.

Lily heard something she recognized. "Did you lose a loved one too?"

"My brother Edward."

Lily smiled. "You and Kitty had something in common."

Pearl's voice hardened. "Except I'm not going to get killed."

"Then you should talk to me. I want to bring her killer to justice."

"Are you with the police?"

Lily smiled. "Have they started letting women on the force?"

Pearl Heglund shook her head. "I guess not."

"Tell me about the complaint Kitty filed with the DA's office."

"How do you know about that?"

"I saw the letter Bernard Keck wrote to Kitty."

Pearl was silent.

"Keck's secretary was out that day. You typed it for him."

"I never did."

"It had your initials on it."

"That's a load of bunk." Her voice rose.

"I saw the letter, Pearl. And I need to know why Kitty went to the DA."

"If you read it, you know it didn't say," Pearl whispered.

"But Keck told you, didn't he?"

The girl hesitated. "No."

"Then why are you in hiding? You found out somehow, and it scared you."

Slowly, Pearl nodded.

"If Keck didn't tell you, who did?"

"I have a key to the file cabinet. I looked it up after he went home."

"What made you do that?"

"I heard him talking to the district attorney about a hot potato. I guess I got curious."

"What was in the file?"

Pearl covered her face. "I can't say."

"Yes, you can. It's okay."

Pearl exhaled. She kept her face covered, peeking out from between her fingers like a child. "Keck took notes when he met with her."

She stopped. Lily waited, encouraging the

girl with her eyes.

"The notes alleged, they indicated . . . that she'd been raped."

Lily's head reeled. She'd been expecting some revelation about Kirk Armstrong. Was it possible that the actor had . . . ?

"By whom?"

The girl gave a wail. "Kitty told Mr. Keck she was afraid of her attacker."

"What was his name?"

"Keck's notes only referred to him as Mr. X."

"Was there any mention of Kirk Armstrong? The actor?"

Pearl's mouth hung agape. She swallowed. "Not a one. Kirk Armstrong? Is that what this . . . ? I don't believe it. Why would he, when he could get any girl he —"

"What about an initial, then? Like 'the Big K'?"

"No." The girl sounded bewildered. "Just Mr. X. Do you really think . . . ?"

"I don't know what to think."

"Is that why she and Mr. Keck were killed? Oh, I wish I'd called in sick that day."

"Let's backtrack a little. Did Kitty go to the police about the rape?"

"Mr. Keck's notes indicated that she did."

"Did they investigate?"

"They took a report, but she felt the officer didn't believe her. She called back twice, but the policeman claimed he was still investigating."

"Did Keck get the name of the man she talked to?"

Pearl Heglund thought for a moment. "The guy who took the complaint was LAPD. His name was Pico."

For a moment there was silence. When she finally spoke, Lily thought her voice sounded strange and distant. "What was his first name?"

"Let me think. I believe it was Samuel."

"Are you sure?"

Relief coursed through her, followed by disbelief. She remembered Pico's words.

It would be like turning in my own father, he had said.

"When did this happen?"

"Last month."

"What else did the notes say? Take yourself back to where you were standing, what went through your mind as you read it."

Pearl shivered. "Mostly I was terrified I'd get caught."

"Think hard."

"There was a news clipping in the file with a bunch of things underlined. She must have given it to Keck. It was stuff politicians say when they're running for office, like, 'The public must know that all men and women are created equal when they come before our courts and that no one can violate the law and escape punishment just because they're wealthy or powerful.' "

Pearl broke off. "I guess she believed we'd help her."

"I think Keck wanted to. And he got killed for his troubles. Does your name appear anywhere on those notes?"

"No. He took them himself, in longhand, but —"

"And the file was locked in the cabinet?"

"Yes, but there's a master key. That's what I used."

"Then no one will suspect you've read it. The letter he sent out was very vague. I think you should go back home. The police may want to talk to you, but just play dumb. It's safest. If they ask where you've been, tell them you've been out with that flu."

"You think I trust the police, after the way I see them fiddle with cases?"

"They're not all on the take," Lily said, flashing to Stephen and hoping she was right.

Behind her, Lily heard a shotgun load. "Put your hands up," a voice said.

Lily obeyed. Next to her, Pearl Heglund exhaled loudly.

"It's okay, Daddy," she said. "She's not going to hurt me."

"Goddamn it, Pearly, I told you to stay inside. How do you expect me to protect you if you don't do as I say?" he asked in a querulous voice.

"Maybe I overreacted," Pearl said. "I think I'm going to go back home."

"What about those criminals that are after you?"

"They would have come looking for me by now, I think."

"Can I put my hands down?" Lily asked.

"You keep quiet, young lady, until we sort this out."

Lily's back was getting itchy, imagining the old groundskeeper's loaded gun.

"You can put down the gun, Daddy. Really."

"All right." He seemed disappointed. "If you say so."

Lily waited a moment, then lowered her arms and turned around. The old gardener stood there, ready to avenge his daughter. Behind him, in the distance, a turkey buzzard flew across the sky, its black shape ancient and foreboding.

"You," said Mr. Heglund, recognizing her.

"It's okay, Daddy. This is Lily Kessler, and she's been explaining a few things to me."

"Pearly, this job of yours is working my nerves. Even if you are meeting eligible men."

Pearl cast a sheepish glance at Lily. "I keep telling you, Daddy, that's *not* why I'm working. I like being a career girl. It allows me to be independent."

"Yeah," the old man said. "But you come running back here at the first sign of trouble, ain't you?"

"That's because you're my daddy."

CHAPTER 28

"Who is Samuel Pico?" Lily demanded, reaching Pico from a phone booth on Sunset Boulevard.

There was a strained silence on the other end.

"Detective Pico?" Lily said. "Are you there?"

"He's my father. Why?"

"Is he still a policeman?"

"He retired last month."

"From what station?"

"Hollywood. Why?"

Lily explained that she'd tracked down a woman in Keck's office — she left the identity vague — who'd recounted an astounding story.

"Rape, good lord. But how does she know this?"

Lily didn't say anything.

"What? Now you don't trust me?"

Lily bit her lip. She didn't want her feelings for him to cloud her instincts. Everything was shrouded in shadow, vague and unclear. She didn't want to put Pearl Heglund in danger.

"If I tell you, you have to promise not to tell Magruder," Lily said.

"I told you this morning, I don't fully trust him myself. And my father and Magruder go way back together."

Lily recounted how Pearl had snooped in Keck's files and read his notes.

"And Kitty claimed a policeman named Samuel Pico sat on her story," she concluded.

"No wonder she's scared," said Pico. "I've got to talk to her and get her statement."

"Why on earth should she trust you when your own father —"

"Lily, I swear on my life this is the first I've heard of this," he said. "But I am going to find out."

"Please be careful."

"He's my father, I'm not afraid of him."

"Maybe you should be."

His stomach churning, Pico left headquarters and drove to the Hollywood Station, where he spent an hour talking to people and looking through files. He left empty-handed.

Soon, he was pulling up to a bungalow on Citrus Avenue near Melrose.

He found his father in the garage, oiling a revolver and listening to a horse race on the radio. Pico saw a notepad jotted with names and dollar amounts and realized his dad was betting again.

Samuel Pico smiled and put down his gun.

"Lemonade?" he asked. "Your mother just made a pitcher. That tree's a workhorse, never stops producing."

"No, thanks, Pops," Pico said. "I wanted to talk to you for a minute, if I could."

"Pull up a chair, son," his father said in a hearty voice.

"How're the ponies?" Pico asked, wondering how to begin.

His father's eyes grew evasive. "Not so well today. But I got a good tip for tomorrow. A sure thing."

He'd had sure things as long as Pico could remember. Just one more and he'd quit. But somehow it never happened. Then last month Sam Pico had been suddenly awash with money. A windfall at the track, he'd said.

Pico stirred uneasily, not sure how to begin. "Pop, you were with the force so long. You hear things. Tell me about Magruder."

A canny look came into the old man's eyes. "Your new partner?" Sam Pico's chin went up. "We go way back. He's stand-up."

Pico knew that in any family, there were things you didn't talk about. Questions you didn't ask. You pushed them to the back of your head and forgot about them, but sometimes, instead of lying there quietly, they grew into monsters and when they finally burst free, it was with the compressed force of a hurricane.

"He's dirty, Pops," Pico said, his voice quavering at the taboo subject. "He doesn't even try to hide it when we're out together."

Sam Pico picked up his gun again.

"People do what they have to do, son," he said. "What they feel they're *entitled* to. It doesn't make him a bad cop."

Pico wouldn't meet his father's eyes.

"He's not hurting anybody," the elder Pico said. "That's where you draw the line."

Is that where you drew it?

"I don't know about that, Pops," he said.

Once, his dad had been his hero. Pico had dreamed of following him into the force. When his dad made detective, he'd made that his goal. He'd been a rookie when the war took him. Since his return he'd risen steadily, making his dad proud.

Pico stared at the concrete floor.

462

"What?" Sam Pico said harshly. "The way I put bread on the table wasn't good enough for you? How do you think I paid your fancy tuition at Black Fox Academy? Your sisters' music and dance and elocution lessons? New bikes at Christmas each year during the Depression, trips to San Francisco, summers in Coronado at the Hotel Del? You think I did it on a policeman's salary?"

"I didn't ask for any of that."

"Kids are always asking for things. Wait till you have your own, you'll see."

"I don't want to bring kids into this world just to see them die in some atomic war."

His father laughed. "You just haven't found the right piece of ass to do it with."

When had they become so different? Pico wondered.

". . . instead of thanking me," Sam Pico continued. "We all need a leg up and I'm glad I was able to catch the chief's ear and his pocket last month, when I was flush. I put your name in for Central Homicide."

Pico sensed the malice that glittered at the edge of his father's words, payback for his impertinent questions. Then the world caved in and he realized it was the truth, a truth neither of them wanted to acknowledge, which Sam Pico would never have revealed if his son had played by the rules.

He lowered his head into his hands. "They must all be laughing behind my back."

He felt his father's gnarled fingers, prying at his hands. "No, son. They're not laughing. They respect and fear the power that put you there."

Pico groaned. "That's even worse."

"Fear is a useful emotion," Sam Pico said. "Cultivate it. But the time may come when something is asked of you in return."

There it came again, that odd phrase of Magruder's.

"Who'll ask? What will they want?"

"When it comes, you will know it."

For a long moment, Stephen Pico sat, head bowed. Then a flicker of resolve caught fire inside him.

"They got me working a big case first time out, Pops," he said. "That starlet who was found strangled in the hills. The Scarlet Sandal."

"Oh yeah?" A guarded caution in his father's voice.

"There's all sorts of rumors swirling around."

"I thought you had a good lead," Sam Pico said sharply. "The special effects guy."

"How do you know about that, Pops?"

"Pshaw. Still got my contacts, don't I? Like to keep my hand in." -

"We've got lots of leads."

"You be sure Magruder looks at everything too. Don't go off half-cocked. The man's got twenty years of experience on you."

Twenty years of graft is more like it.

"Any other rumors?" his dad asked, fiddling with the gun.

Pico got up, walked to the worktable, picked up a card the squaddies had sent for his dad's sixtieth birthday.

"There's a rumor she went to the cops last month and made a serious allegation," Pico said.

"What kind of allegation?"

"Claimed she'd been raped."

His father sucked his teeth. "All those starlets gotta put out, they want to get roles."

"This wasn't putting out."

"Who was it?"

"I don't know."

His father ran a finger along his gun. "That's too bad. And you say she filed a complaint?"

"That's what she claimed. She lived in Hollywood, so my guess is she went there. You hear anything about that, Pops?"

"Hell, no. Never talked to her. Pretty little

thing." His father paused. "From the pictures."

"Eventually she took it to the DA. They opened an investigation. But that file's disappeared and the investigator committed suicide or was pushed out a seventh-story window."

"That's a crying shame." His dad thrust out his head like a turtle. "Do they have a date when that gal supposedly came to the Hollywood station? They could trace back the records, see who she talked to."

"There's no paper trail. I was just there."

Sam Pico considered. "Makes it pretty difficult." There was another long pause. "Son?" he said at last.

"Yes?"

"Who told you about this DA investigation, if there's no files anywhere?"

Pico hesitated. He felt like he was tiptoeing through a minefield wearing a blindfold. "One of my sources."

"Who's your source?" His father coaxed out a smile.

"I'd rather not say."

" 'Course you wouldn't." His dad's eyes were hard again. "Because the whole story's a crock. Can't you see that?"

"I don't think so," Pico said.

"What's that supposed to mean?"

"You want to tell me, Pops?" Pico said softly.

"I don't know what you're talking about, son."

Pico stood up. He stared at his father for a long moment. Then he walked to his car without looking back.

Samuel Pico watched his son drive off. Then he walked over to the phone and made a call.

"It's starting to leak," he said.

Samuel listened as the voice on the other end exploded.

"Relax," Samuel said. "Nobody knows about the ten thousand dollars. And I can't give it back, it's gone."

There was a bigger explosion.

"I *did* destroy the police complaint," Samuel said. "Who knew she'd go to the DA?"

The voice on the other end of the line rumbled.

"Why didn't Simpson put the kibosh on the investigation?" Samuel asked.

The man on the other phone spoke softly.

"Okay," Samuel responded, "so things were moving too fast. You did what you had to do. And I'm going to need your boys to do it again as soon as I find where it's coming from."

The man said something, but Samuel interrupted. "I don't know why you didn't deal with this last month. She didn't want to get rid of it; you could have offered her a nice vacation and some dough, she goes away for a few months, comes back tanned and rested, the baby's adopted by a nice barren family, and no one's the wiser. But no, you have to get carried away. Teach her a lesson. Looks like you found the one dame who could fight back. From beyond the grave."

CHAPTER 29

Stephen Pico pounded the steering wheel as he drove, crying tears of impotent rage. He hadn't wanted to believe it, but Lily was right. His own father had some connection to Kitty Hayden's murder and maybe the others too. Solving the case would mean exposing, perhaps even destroying, his old man. How could he pursue it? How could he not?

When he arrived at headquarters, there was a message from the Crime Lab — they had an ID on the trace fur found on Kitty Hayden's clothes.

In the lab, technician Franklin Abbott, fifty, balding, and baby-faced, bent over a microscope.

"You led us on a merry chase with this one," he said.

"Thanks for hurrying it up."

"I like a challenge." Abbott straightened.

He walked to his desk and picked up a report.

"Damnedest thing. We had to send out to a dairy in Artesia for samples. Then I called a pal of mine out in Animal Sciences at Cal Poly to make sure. It's fur of an unborn calf."

Pico's face wrinkled, trying to make sense of it.

Abbott pushed his glasses up the bridge of his nose. "But it gets even better. There's a sediment coating one end of the hairs. Near as we can determine, it's glue or latex. Something artificial."

Pico had a flash of insight. "Like a doll or stuffed animal?"

"Don't know who'd give a kid a toy like that," Abbott said.

"I do." Relief surged through him. Maybe his dad was off the hook after all.

"Where'd it come from?"

"My guess'd be it's the model ape they used in *Mighty Joe Young*," Pico said. "But I've still got a lot of work ahead of me."

Abbott grinned. "I loved that picture. How'd they do that, anyway?"

Pico looked away. "Haven't the foggiest."

Abbott leaned against the porcelain sink. "If you find out, let me know. I'm nuts for that stuff."

■ ■ ■ ■

"Looks like one more nail in the coffin," said Magruder, feet propped on the desk, chomping on a bag of pretzels.

"Circumstantial," said Pico. "She had one of those apes in her room, remember? Maybe she handled it that night and some hairs came off. It doesn't mean he killed her."

Magruder slurped salt off his fingers. "He was obsessed with her. He showed up delusional at the rooming house pawing at one of the other girls. His colleagues say he goes into rages."

"You're not exactly Mr. Even Keel. Does that make you a murderer?"

Magruder's jowls quivered with outrage. "Bring him in. It's time we have another chat."

CHAPTER 30

Wearing dark clothes and comfortable flats, Lily made her way up Canyon Drive to Rhett Taylor's house in Beachwood Canyon. She'd gotten the address from Jinx, who'd gotten it from a friend who answered mail for a Rhett Taylor fan club.

"I thought you weren't interested in movie stars," Beverly said.

"I promised Kitty's niece in Illinois that I'd get his autograph," Lily lied. Ever since the *Confidential* story, she'd been careful about what she said around the rooming house.

Rhett Taylor lived in a Mediterranean-style villa behind a high stone wall a mile up the canyon. The gate was locked. Lily gripped the ornamental iron bars and peered in. The property was overgrown, ancient carts and plows rusting in the tall grasses. Rows of citrus trees, fruit rotting on the ground. Old pines, their trunks green with lichen. Lily walked the length of the property, halting at an old oak whose branches overhung the wall. It was tall and gnarled, with a saddle four feet up where the trunk split. Finding a toehold, she climbed into the cleft, then inched her way along a branch and lowered herself onto the wall. From here, she could see Rhett Taylor's house. Two people stood silhouetted behind a curtain in a ground-floor window. Feeling like a cat burglar, she leaped down.

At once a bloodcurdling shriek split the air. Then another. Lily expected Taylor to charge out. She'd be caught. The moon came out from behind a cloud and she beheld a peacock, moving like a majestic ship through the underbrush. Its iridescent feathers rustled. Another followed, bobbing its tiny crested head. The bird opened its beak and gave another unearthly cry.

Lily practically fell against the bushes in relief.

Rhett Taylor kept peacocks. Their plumage was gorgeous, which made her think of Rhett himself. Of course he'd admire these haughty, glittering birds.

Lily crept toward French doors that opened onto a flagstone patio, the susurrus of falling water from a fountain camouflaging her steps. She heard a man speaking softly, in pleading tones. Then a woman's voice, cool and hard. A lover's tiff? Maybe Alex was wrong about Rhett Taylor. And then she heard, ". . . would kill my career. I beg of you."

Lily shrank into the shrubbery.

"You should have considered that before making a pass at your driver, Mr. Taylor," the woman said. Her voice sounded familiar.

There was a gasp, then silence. Finally, Taylor said in a dull, defeated voice, "You can't run a photo like that."

"So you know which one I mean?" The woman laughed.

And then Lily knew her, saw bottle-blond ringlets piled atop her head, the lascivious red mouth like a gash, the bleached white teeth. Violet McCree.

"You're right," Violet said amiably. "We can't run a photo with your hand on his crotch, but —"

"Don't," Taylor pleaded.

"But we can crop it at the waist."

"I'll deny it," Taylor said wildly. "I'll say I did it on a drunken dare."

"The driver will say otherwise. I paid a little visit to the studio today, and they told me he can be persuaded." Lily could almost see Violet's lip curl. "That's right. And they gave me the photo too. We did a little switcheroo with some other sensitive photos I've recently acquired. So this is just a courtesy call, really. I'd like to get your side of the story before we go to press."

There was a muttered oath.

"Yes, I know you'd like to wring my neck, but that would only add a murder charge to everything else. The photo's locked safely away, the story's ready to go. So come on, Mr. Taylor, won't you talk to me?"

A crystal decanter flew through the air, hit the French doors, and shattered, brown viscous liquid dripping down the glass. Lily could see their shadows, backlit by dozens of candles, the flames shivering in the night breeze.

"How dare you?" Violet McCree screamed in outrage. "It's no wonder Warner's sacrificed you to save him. Why, Kirk Armstrong . . ." Violet's voice faltered, then continued, "Or any of those guys, Burt Lancaster, Jimmy Stewart, Henry Fonda, they've got more class in their little fingers than you've got in your entire body. I'll ruin you, you cheap thug."

Lily crept closer.

"I'm already ruined," Rhett Taylor said, and lunged unsteadily at her. She dodged and ran out of the room. Lily heard heels clattering on tiles. Then the front door slammed and Lily saw a small figure in a pastel suit running down the walk. Soon a car started up and zoomed down Beachwood Canyon.

The noise had riled the peacocks. They returned, circling and screeching, as if she were to blame for disturbing their rest. She tried to push them away, but they jostled one another, milling stupidly, blocking her.

She heard the crunch of dead leaves.

"Why are you molesting my birds?" asked Rhett Taylor.

She turned. He wore a monogrammed silk bathrobe and slippers, and his wavy hair stuck out in an unruly fashion. He also had a gun.

"This isn't a studio prop in my hand, pardner," he said, his words ever so slurred. "Answer me."

Lily realized he couldn't see her in the dark, probably mistook her for Violet Mc-Cree. Or maybe a prowler.

"Don't shoot," she said, stepping into the courtyard light. "It's just me, Lily Kessler."

He blinked.

"You again! Not the other one? Gone, is she?" He jerked his head from side to side like one of his infernal peacocks.

"She drove off."

"What did you hear just now?" His jaw

twitched.

Lily put on her most innocent face. "Nothing. Were you doing an interview?"

He drew himself up and said, with all the dignity he could muster, "Absolutely not. I refused to grant her one."

"Glad to hear it. You tell her what you had for breakfast, she'd find a way to use it against you."

Rhett Taylor's eyebrows beetled suspiciously. "What are you doing on my property? Are you two in league?"

"We never finished our conversation this afternoon," Lily said.

"And we're not going to." Rhett Taylor's gun sagged at his side and he mopped his brow. "Allow me to escort you out, Miss Snoopy."

"Do you think I might have a glass of water first? I hiked up from Franklin and my throat is parched."

Rhett Taylor inspected her suspiciously. "Make it quick, then."

The gravel crunched under their shoes as they walked to the house. Candles cast a pale light onto adobe walls in the living room, where an Indian-weave rug lay over the tiles. Behind an iron grate, a mesquite fire crackled.

He bade her sit and went to fetch water.

Lily felt a stab of pity for this man. "Mr. Taylor," she said gently when he returned, "I heard part of your conversation with that reporter."

His head jerked up. He poured himself a neat drink and belted it back with trembling hands. When he sat down, his body crumpled. And just like that, it was over.

"I'm ruined," he said, burying his face in his hands. He stayed like that a long time. When he finally raised his head, his eyes had a haunted look.

"Isn't there anything you can do?" Lily asked.

Rhett Taylor shook his head. "They've got photos of me in a . . . compromising position. There's a man . . . he tried to blackmail me once before and the studio paid him off."

"Won't the studio help you again?"

"I just tried to get through to Warner, but he wouldn't take my call. The head of publicity says he's sorry. The studio thinks I'm too much of a liability. They've decided to cut their losses."

"Do you think she was lying about how she got the photo? I wouldn't put it past her."

"I don't know," Rhett said, mystified. "I even called a producer I know, but he said there was nothing he could do. He seemed to take pleasure in it, because of the time he tried . . . and I wouldn't . . . Oh God, my life is over. I might as well kill myself."

He looked around wildly and Lily was afraid he'd grab for the gun.

She walked over, sat down by him.

"You can't. Imagine the headlines that awful reporter would write. You have to hold your head up and go on living. It's time to plan your strategy."

"My strategy?"

"Look, Mr. Taylor. Here's your opportunity to salvage your pride. To redeem your soul. If *Confidential's* going to make good on this threat, you might as well step forward and tell the cops what you saw October seventh."

"I can't," Rhett whispered hoarsely.

"Sure you can. *Confidential* doesn't come out until Monday. Right now this is Violet's monster scoop and she's not going to breathe a word because she's terrified someone will beat her to it. So if you tell the police what you know tonight, then hold a press conference tomorrow to announce that you came forward in good conscience, for the safety of the city blah-blah-blah, you'll beat her at her own game."

"Except that after I do, I won't have a

479

career to go back to," he said glumly. "I'll be box office poison. Denounced from every pulpit in the country. Do you know the studio wanted me to marry a starlet? We'd share a house but lead separate lives. They said it wasn't unusual. But it would kill me to live that way."

Lily wondered if it was the booze talking, pumping him full of liquid courage.

"Then talk to the cops. Will you do it, Mr. Taylor?"

Rhett stood up. "There's nothing to lose anymore."

An hour later, Lily, Rhett Taylor, and the detectives sat in an interview room at LAPD headquarters. Magruder had protested Lily's presence, but Rhett said he wanted a witness and wouldn't talk unless she was allowed to stay. Pico depressed the start button on the tape recorder and they began.

"Mr. Taylor, where were you the evening of October seventh?"

"I was at a nightclub called the Crow's Nest on Hollywood Boulevard," the actor said.

When Magruder asked whether Taylor knew the Crow's Nest was a hangout for homosexuals, the actor looked him in the eye and said that he did.

Magruder leaned forward intently.

"What time did you arrive?"

Taylor said he'd gone there alone around midnight and left around one-thirty a.m. with another man as the bar closed.

"What's his name?" Magruder asked.

Taylor stared into the middle distance. "I don't know."

Lily thought Magruder would blow a gasket.

"You leave a bar with a man you've never met before, and you don't even know his name?"

Slowly, Taylor met the older cop's eyes. "We would have had plenty of time to get acquainted that night."

Magruder looked like he'd sucked on a lime.

"And did you see or hear anything unusual that night, either in the bar or as you walked out?" Pico said, taking up the questioning.

The actor shook his head. "That's just it. I was looking, but I wasn't seeing. There was a disheveled girl running down the Boulevard. A man was chasing her. Claimed she was his wife. His mentally ill wife."

"And you think the girl was Kitty?" Pico said.

Taylor nodded. His face was tragic and scared and very beautiful.

"We need you to say it aloud, sir, for the record," Pico said.

"Yes, I believe it was Kitty."

"And someone was chasing her?" Lily said.

Magruder gave her a look that said, *Butt out.*

"Yes," said Taylor. "But at the time, I had no reason to doubt the man. The girl did look crazy. Her eyes were wild. Her dress was torn. She'd lost a shoe."

"So what did you do?" Magruder asked in a voice filled with scorn.

"You have to understand," the actor pleaded, "the studio had warned me about indiscretions. It would have been the last straw, after the photos they'd already had to . . . I couldn't afford to get involved."

"Aren't you the Good Samaritan." Magruder's voice dripped loathing. "What did you do then?"

"I ducked down a side street and disappeared like a good fruit," he said angrily. "They'd seen me come out of the Crow's Nest." Rhett Taylor's face scrunched up. "I didn't want to draw any more attention to myself." His voice took on a beseeching tone. "I swear, it wasn't until I saw her picture in the paper that I realized . . ."

Rhett Taylor blinked rapidly. "And now I

can't get her out of my mind. I see her terrified face. Her pleas for help. She haunts
my dreams."

"What about your friend?" Magruder
asked.

"He disappeared at the first sign of
trouble. I never saw him again."

Pico leaned forward. "Describe the man
chasing Lily."

"Tall guy, maybe six-foot, broad-
shouldered, big and beefy, clean-shaven,
brown hair. Between thirty-five and fifty.
Dark suit."

"Would you be able to identify him?"

There was a long pause.

"Yes," Taylor said.

Magruder went to a desk and returned
with a photo, which he laid on the table.
With shock, she saw it was Max.

"Is this the man who was chasing Kitty?"

Taylor examined the photo.

"No," he said with certainty. "This guy's
face is different. And he's skinny. And
there's something else."

"Yes?" Magruder was like a bird dog,
ready to pounce.

"She got in a car."

"How did you see that?" Magruder
erupted. He took out a handkerchief and
dabbed at his forehead. "Hold it," he said.

"Let's take a break. Miss Kessler shouldn't be here. This is privileged police information."

"She's the one who brought him in," Pico said. "And Mr. Taylor wants her here. Let her stay."

"We're not continuing while she's in the room," Magruder said. "She already blabbed to *Confidential* once."

"No, I didn't," said Lily. "I told you."

"I refuse to be a party to this miscarriage of justice if regular department rules aren't followed," Magruder said, rising.

"Fine," said Pico. "Then we'll do it informally." He turned off the tape recorder. "Did you get a license plate, Mr. Taylor?"

"As your senior partner, I command you to stop this instant or you're going to read it in every newspaper in town tomorrow morning," Magruder yelled.

Taylor looked at Pico.

"Please, go on, Mr. Taylor," the younger cop said quietly.

Taylor nodded. "It was a California plate, but I only caught part of it. The numbers 724."

Slowly, Magruder crept closer, a look of malice on his face. "I thought you said you ran away. Are you perjuring yourself, Mr. Taylor? Because they'll put you on the stand. They'll tear your statement apart. They'll hound you about your personal life, your proclivities, they'll hammer you and say your testimony is unreliable because you're a faggot."

"I don't see things any differently than you do, sir, just because I like to sleep with men," Taylor said, his face ashen.

"Aw, do we have to go into that?" Magruder screwed up his face.

"You brought it up, sir," Taylor said.

"Tell us exactly where you were and what you saw," Pico said in a softer voice.

"When the girl ran past, with the man chasing her, I slunk into the nearest side street," Taylor continued. "I didn't want to be around if the cops came. But my motorbike was on the Boulevard, so I made my way back up. As I reached my bike, a car passed me. I couldn't see the driver, but there was a woman in the backseat. Her face was pressed against the glass. It was the same woman. She didn't look scared. I would have remembered that. More like she was trying to figure something out."

"What kind of car was it?"

"A black Studebaker. About a year old. I wish I could remember the entire license plate. I only remembered the first part because it's my birthday."

"What do you mean, your birthday?" Magruder said.

"I was born on July 24, 1925. 7/24."

"You could have sent an anonymous letter to the police, describing what you saw," Pico said, an edge in his voice. "Especially after you read the paper."

"I know." Taylor hung his head. "But I was too scared. I couldn't admit it to myself, because of where I'd been."

"Cuz you're a fucking homo perv coward, that's why," Magruder said.

"There's no cause for that kind of language," Pico said. "What made you change your mind, Mr. Taylor?"

"*Confidential* magazine's found out about me. They're preparing a story. Lily convinced me I have nothing to lose."

"We appreciate you coming forward. It took courage," Pico said. He pulled out a piece of blank paper. "One last question, sir. I've got a fifteen-year-old niece who's got a terrific crush on you. Could I please have your autograph?"

Taylor gave a weak smile. "She's not going to want it after tomorrow."

"Are you kidding? She'll be the envy of all her classmates."

Taylor took the pen, asked for the girl's name, and scrawled, *Follow your heart and never let anyone tell you what to do. Take it from someone who knows. Your friend, Rhett Taylor. October 17, 1949.*

Lily and Pico dropped Rhett off at the run-down Hollywood Hotel, where he'd decided to hole up under a false name until the uproar over his revelations to the police died down. Then Pico drove her home.

In the dark of the car, his hand groped for hers.

"Will you sit closer?"

She scooted over, studying his profile in the dark, the classic nose that started high in his face and came down straight and long, the curve of his lips. They didn't speak.

"That was a tricky piece of work back there, the way you coaxed him in from the cold," Pico said at last. "I'm impressed."

Lily gave a wry smile. "It was my specialty back in Europe, with the Reds. Everyone's got a trigger, you just have to find it. Money. Power. Sex. Fame. Revenge. Occasionally you even get one to turn because it's the right thing. But in my experience, right and wrong aren't always so obvious."

"If it helps us catch Kitty's killer, it's the right thing," Pico said through clenched lips.

"So what's your next step?"

"Finding the car. It shouldn't be too hard,

with Rhett's description. No one saw Kitty Hayden alive after she got in that car. So when we get an ID on the owner and learn who was driving it that night, we'll be closing in on the killer."

"You're assuming Kitty stayed in that car. Maybe she jumped out, or the man dropped her off, and then the real killer found her."

"Whoever drove that car the night of October seventh has information we need. We're going to find him. It's the best lead we've had yet."

Lily gazed at the sleeping city just outside the window, trying to puzzle it out. She gathered the night about herself, the people she knew, felt them moving across a huge stage in all directions — Pearl Heglund sleeping in her apartment. Alex kissing another mannish girl in a bar. Magruder tossing back a nightcap, counting his ill-gotten gains. Harry Jack in his kitchen, reheating a midnight snack of Campbell's tomato soup. Gadge asleep in his new bed, a fireman's hat clutched in his arms. Max hunched over his studio workbench, tinkering with his werewolf. Mrs. Potter and the girls in the old creaking house. Rhett Taylor slumped on the hotel sofa over a drink. She gathered them all, trying to weave them into a pattern that made sense, but she only felt a strong foreboding. The old children's prayer went around and around in her head: *If I should die before I wake, I pray the Lord my soul to take.* Sitting next to Pico, their thighs and shoulders warm and touching, Lily shivered.

CHAPTER 31

October 18, 1949

Pico was back at work by eight a.m. For once Magruder had beaten him in. Or maybe he'd never been home. There was a rumor he kept a cot in the warrens of the LAPD building. Now he swaggered over.

"You believe that load of crap from last night?"

Pico looked up. "Best tip we've gotten all week."

"I want to read the report before you send it over."

"Why?"

"Because I'm your senior partner, that's why. You let me take the lead on this, Pico."

"Why do I get the feeling you won't?" Pico said, glad he hadn't told Magruder what Pearl Heglund had learned from Keck's file.

Magruder's voice grew soft.

"You're really beginning to bother me," he said. "You take yourself too seriously, when the truth is, you're green as a Victory cabbage. Don't forget about Vranizan."

"Taylor said Vranizan wasn't the one behind the wheel. But whoever owns that Studebaker has got to know something about what happened."

Magruder grew contemplative, not an emotion Pico usually associated with the older cop. "It may not be so simple, old son."

"We need to run those plates this morning," Pico said stubbornly.

"Relax, amigo. I put in the trace first thing this morning."

Pico was on the phone when Magruder walked in.

"The car the homo told us about? We got an ID," he said.

"That was fast work."

"It's hot. Reported stolen off the RKO lot October seventh."

Pico smashed his fist into the steel desk and cursed.

Magruder looked almost cocky. "Told you not to get your hopes up."

"So who's it belong to?"

Magruder scanned his sheet, and Pico got the feeling he already knew exactly and was just doing it for show.

"Fella by the name of Roy DiCicco." Magruder clicked his teeth.

"He work at RKO?"

"Stuntman."

"Let's bring him in."

"What's this all about, fellas?" Roy DiCicco said, sitting in a room in police headquarters. "Seems like a lot of fuss over a stolen car."

A tall muscular fellow, DiCicco was thirty-two and single. He told them he lived in a guesthouse in Santa Monica and didn't know Kitty Hayden personally, though he remembered her from the lot, you didn't forget a face like that. His name had come up clean, except for a narcotics charge in '46 that had been dismissed.

While Magruder interviewed him, Pico studied the stuntman's calm demeanor, contrasting it to the twitchiness Vranizan had displayed when they'd asked him about the fur. They'd been over it several times now, the stuntman recounting how he'd walked out of work on October 7 and found his car missing from the RKO lot. DiCicco had gone back inside and called the police, who'd taken a report. Then a friend had picked him up from the lot and they'd spent the evening in San Pedro, barbequing white croakers and playing poker. Around two a.m., DiCicco had gone to sleep on the friend's couch, rising early to take the streetcar to work. Pico asked for the name and number of his friend.

"You're not going to call him, are you?" DiCicco asked.

"Any reason we shouldn't?" Magruder asked.

"What's this all got to do with my car?"

The cops watched suspicion dawn on DiCicco's face. They'd asked about Kitty. They wanted his friend's name to check his alibi.

"Hey, now," he said nervously. "I didn't do anything wrong. I'm a law-abiding guy."

Magruder smiled, all teeth and lips.

Something moved behind DiCicco's eyes. "If you find any dope in the car, it's a plant," he said.

"We'll keep that in mind," Magruder said. "Awfully nice wheels you've got, by the way. The union must be doing well by you fellas these days."

"I'm a car buff," DiCicco said. "That's where all my money goes."

Magruder nodded. "We'll check on that too, but it looks bad, son. Girl you work with disappears. And the same night, you claim your car is stolen out of the RKO lot."

He leaned forward with lightning speed, lifting DiCicco out of his seat by his collar.

"Did you kill Kitty Hayden?"

DiCicco made a series of unintelligible noises. "No," he finally choked out.

"Do you know who did?"

"No."

"What *do* you know?" Magruder shook him like a rat.

"Nothing," DiCicco squeaked.

Magruder let go and the man slumped.

"Check my alibi," he said. "Why would I report my own car missing to the police if I killed her?"

"To throw off suspicion, in case a witness spotted the girl in your car that night," Pico said.

"Shut up," Magruder said to Pico. He shoved Roy DiCicco hard. "Get out of here, punk. But stick close to home. If we're not convinced by what your friends say, we'll haul you back in."

Roy DiCicco got his hat and adjusted his jacket. His cheeks were red and blotchy.

"I think you're forgetting that I'm the victim here. I just want my car back."

"Well?" Magruder said when he was gone.

"He's scared about the reefer business," Pico said. "He knows there's a connection between his car and Kitty's murder."

"That's it?"

"He got more nervous as time went on. Vranizan was nervous from the get-go."

"Guilty conscience?"

"This is Hollywood," Pico said. "Even the criminals are actors. And the Academy Award for most convincing pack of lies goes to . . ."

Magruder turned his meaty face on Pico. "You think Vranizan stole DiCicco's car and used it to abduct and kill the Scarlet Sandal? And that set him off on a murder spree?"

"Or DiCicco killed her, then covered his tracks by reporting his car stolen."

"I've got an APB out. Soon as the car turns up, the crime lab boys will be crawling all over it. Pray for prints."

"Should I go verify DiCicco's alibi?"

"I'll go," Magruder said. "They got a shack down in Pedro, sells smoked albacore by the pound. Want me to pick you up some?"

"Why, thanks. That's mighty white of you."

"White?" said Magruder. "What would you know about that, *amigo?*"

Pico finished writing up the Rhett Taylor interview, then wrote up Roy DiCicco's. Then he grabbed a pastrami sandwich.

495

Magruder returned, dumping a package wrapped in butcher paper on his desk. It had a gamey, smoky smell that wasn't unpleasant.

"Nobody home," Magruder said. "I'm gonna send you back there at the end of the day."

Twenty minutes later, they got the word: a prowl car had found DiCicco's car parked at the Compton train station. It looked like it had been there a few days.

They left headquarters and drove south down Normandie, past the bean fields and farms, dairies and orchards. Compton was a tough white town of blue-collar workers who labored in the factories of Southeast Los Angeles. But with all those pumping oil derricks, it felt more like Tulsa. Many of the lots went back a quarter mile, deep and hidden, little fiefdoms where sunburned Okies gathering for cockfights on Saturday nights and housing covenants kept Negroes out. Even colored servants had to be gone by sundown.

The police tow truck was there when they arrived, preparing to impound the car. Pico searched the inside and the trunk, finding old newspapers, tools, a girlie magazine, and a dirty flannel shirt. The techs would go over it with a fine-tooth comb, dust for prints, but Pico's heart fell a little. For a moment there, they'd seemed on the verge of something, but things were fizzling like yesterday's champagne.

"They took my prints," Max gulped over the phone to Lily.

He sounded more hysterical and unhinged than the day he'd grabbed Fumiko in front of the rooming house.

"Twice now they've come to RKO and hauled me away in front of everybody. It's so humiliating. They take me downtown and grill me. Today they asked if I stole a car off the RKO lot and used it to abduct Kitty. What am I supposed to say to that?"

"You're supposed to say no," Lily paused. "Unless you did."

"How can you even say that?"

"Whose car got stolen?"

"Some guy named Roy DiCicco. A stunt-man."

"Did Kitty know him?"

"She never mentioned him. I never saw them together."

Max described his police grilling. He seemed especially upset that they'd found fur from the Mighty Joe Young model on Kitty's suit.

"How do you think that got there?" Lily asked.

"Maybe she was playing with it, or dusting it or something, the night she was killed. But remember I told you one of the models disappeared? Maybe the killer took it."

"Don't worry," Lily said. "They'll clear you. They won't find your prints on the car." She paused. "Will they?"

"Of course not. But I'm afraid for my job. You should see the way the bosses look at me. And I have to work, Lily. If I can't build my creatures, I might as well die."

"Stop talking about dying."

"Something doesn't smell right," Harry Jack said, after Lily finished recounting her conversation with Max.

They were sitting at a soda fountain on Sunset, Harry treating them to banana splits. He figured he'd be treating for months, after hitting the jackpot with his Mickey Cohen shoot-out photos. Every paper in the world was screaming for them, the *Mirror*'s Rights Department working overtime. And every licensing deal was a fifty-fifty split.

"So this guy reported the car stolen October seventh?" Harry said after a while.

"That's right."

"Did he talk to RKO security before he called the cops?"

"He says he went back inside and called the police."

"Wouldn't he have talked to the guard at the gate?"

"Guess not. Culver City cops came right out."

"Culver City?" Harry said excitedly. "That's right, it's not LAPD territory."

Lily suddenly remembered her brush with Officer Tranow outside Dr. Lafferty's office. "They're crooked, those cops. And they're in bed with the studios."

"It's a company town," Harry agreed. "If Roy DiCicco called them from RKO, the studio operators must have put through the call."

"So?"

"You want to know what's going on," Harry said, "ask a studio operator. They know everything. Which stars are having affairs, how many child extras they need on any given day, whether a picture has made money."

"But they must route hundreds of calls," Lily said, recalling her stint with David O. Selznick.

"Not hundreds to the police."

"Can you find out?"

Harry slid off his stool and went to the pay phone to call his friend, RKO operator Edith Blyton. Soon he was jotting notes on a napkin. Lily joined him in the phone box to listen in.

Harry put his hand over the receiver. "This gal at RKO remembers the call."

"Ask her what time Roy DiCicco called the cops," Lily said.

"Eight-oh-five," the answer came back. "They took a report and stayed forty-five minutes."

Lily thought hard. "Ask her what day."

"We already know that."

"Just verify it."

Harry repeated the question, then listened and nodded. "She just checked the calendar and she's sure. Her sister had a baby October ninth and she'd been counting down the days."

Harry thanked Edith and hung up and they filed glumly back to their booth.

"I still think it's odd he didn't talk to RKO security," Lily said.

"Maybe the car was never stolen. Maybe Roy DiCicco reported it missing and the Culver cops came out and took a report and played along."

"Why would they do that?"

"Because DiCicco needed an alibi for

500

October seventh."

"That's quite a long shot. Do we know anything else about this stuntman?" Lily asked.

"I can call back and ask." Harry pulled a fistful of coins from his pocket.

When he returned five minutes later, his eyes glowed with excitement. "Edith says there's a rumor his brother works for Jack Dragna."

Lily's mind whirled like a spinning top. Maybe Dragna had used the brothers to get to Kitty. "Jeez, why didn't she tell us that in the first place?"

"She didn't know it was important."

"I think I'm beginning to see."

"Don't jump to conclusions. Edith says the brothers are estranged. It's Cain and Abel and Roy's the good one. Wants nothing to do with his brother's rackets."

"We've got to tell Pico right away."

Pico was on the phone trying to reach the DiCicco alibi when a pencil hit him.

It was Magruder on *his* phone, motioning frantically.

Pico hung up — the line had rung about twenty times already to no avail — and walked over. The older cop's eyebrows drew together as he scribbled. "We'll be there in twenty minutes." He replaced the receiver.

"I knew it," he said triumphantly. "That was a waiter at Panza's Lazy Susan in Hollywood. Claims he served dinner and drinks to Kitty Hayden and a guy named Max the night of October seventh and overheard them fighting."

Pico crossed his arms. "Why didn't he call earlier?"

"He finished his shift October seventh and left on a camping trip to the Sierras. He just got back, opened his first newspaper in a week, and calls us. C'mon. We'll talk on the way."

As they drove to the waiter's apartment, the detectives debated it further.

"But if Vranizan killed her, why would he leave such a public trail?" Pico said.

"Crimes of passion are rarely logical. But he lied about when he saw her last. He's hiding something, and I bet it's Kitty Hayden's murder."

Magruder enumerated the evidence. "We've got a greengrocer at the Farmers Market who heard her meet someone whose name started with *M*. A stolen car from the RKO lot where he worked. Known volatility and rages. Obsession with the first victim and loitering around a house where two of the dead girls lived. The fight at the restaurant, then Kitty spotted inside the stolen car around midnight. Fibers from the ape on her body. She was killed between eleven p.m. and five-thirty a.m. and we haven't found anyone who can confirm Vranizan's alibi that he was home asleep."

Pico shook his head. "It's all circumstantial. And we haven't cleared DiCicco yet. There's something squirrelly about him too."

Magruder nodded. "When we get back, I want you to drive out to San Pedro and recheck his alibi. Everything has to be nice and tidy. Last thing we want is the media braying that we got it wrong on such a high-profile case. But I'd lay money on Vranizan."

"What about Florence Kwitney and Louise Dobbs? He kill them too?"

"Who knows what shop of horrors we'll find when we search that home studio of his?"

"What about the note to Kirk?" Pico persisted. "What about her being pregnant?"

What about the criminal investigation by the DA? What about my father? he thought.

"Let me put it this way," Magruder said. "If the girl you loved told you she was pregnant by another man, wouldn't you want to kill her?"

CHAPTER 32

Lily called Pico from the drugstore, eager to tell him about Roy DiCicco's gangster ties, but he and Magruder were out on an interview. She left an urgent message, then walked home in time to take a call from Louise's parents, who sounded shell-shocked and said they were en route to Los Angeles to escort their daughter's coffin home. Lily tried to comfort them but burst into tears herself. An hour later Pico phoned back.

"Roy DiCicco at RKO has a brother who works for Jack Dragna," Lily said.

There was a sharp intake of breath, then Pico said, "How do you even know about Roy DiCicco?"

"Max called and told me you brought him in and accused him of stealing a car off the RKO lot the night Kitty disappeared."

"He's supposed to keep those interviews to himself," Pico snapped.

"Well, just this once, I'm glad he didn't."

Lily recounted what the RKO operator had told them and the speculation that DiCicco's car hadn't really been stolen.

"Maybe Roy DiCicco only wants people to *think* he's estranged from his gangster brother," Lily said. "He could have stolen that gorilla armature out of Max's studio, it's not like they keep them locked up, then sprinkled some fur on her corpse to make it look like Max did it. Everyone at RKO knew Max was mooning over her."

"I'm going to check DiCicco's alibi right now." Pico paused. "And we'll see if Rhett Taylor can ID him as the driver that night. But there's another development."

He explained what they'd learned from the waiter at Panza's Lazy Susan.

"Good God." Lily's voice caught. "Max told everyone he hadn't seen her since Labor Day."

"It's a lie. They fought, and from what the waiter heard, it was vicious. After forty minutes, Kitty stormed off. Max Vranizan proceeded to get smashingly drunk and left around midnight. Don't forget he lives close to the Crow's Nest and where the kid found the sandal. His RKO colleagues say he came in the next morning looking like he hadn't slept."

"He probably looks like that a lot when he's got a movie in production," Lily said. In the distance, she heard Magruder calling.

"I've got to go," Pico said.

"Be careful when you talk to those Dragna people," Lily said.

"And you sit tight until you hear from me this evening."

Lily hung up, wondering whether Max Vranizan had really strangled Kitty — and perhaps the other two girls as well — or whether there could be another explanation for his deceit.

There was no doubt he was a brilliant artist. He was also eccentric, obsessive, and a liar. The more Lily thought about how he'd manipulated her, the angrier she got. She itched to confront him and hear for herself what he had to say. Rhett Taylor had eliminated Max as the driver of the Studebaker, so the more she thought about it, the more her gut told her that he was probably innocent of Kitty's murder. But what if Max erupted into one of his black rages with the police and somehow incriminated himself? What if he was convicted of murder while the real killer went free? Lily picked up the phone and called RKO.

But Max was gone for the day. Lily sat, lost in thought, then it came to her. It was Thursday evening. He was at Clifton's Cafeteria, with his science club cronies. Grabbing her purse, she ran to the Boulevard to catch the trolley downtown. As she waited impatiently, she heard newsboys yelling, "Extra," and thought she heard the name Rhett Taylor. She bought a paper just as the trolley pulled up. At least three women on board were reading the same story, sniffling into tissues. Taylor had been found dead in his room at the Hollywood Hotel of an overdose of sleeping pills, an empty whiskey bottle by the bed. The papers were saying he was despondent because *Confidential* was about to run a story about his homosexuality. There was a quote from Violet McCree.

As she read, Lily felt numb, like she was slowly disassociating from her body. He'd asked her and Pico to stay until dawn, but they'd made excuses and left. Why hadn't she realized his desperation?

But what if it wasn't suicide, but homicide? Rhett Taylor was the only one who could identify Lily's pursuer and the driver of the car that had picked her up. Without him, the killer might go free.

When the trolley reached downtown, Lily

hopped off and walked the few blocks to Clifton's, where a busboy directed her upstairs to a brown room where a dozen men sat talking over plastic food trays. A cloud of silvery blue smoke hovered above them.

"It'll be a space elevator, mark my words, all the way to the moon," a young man wearing a green cardigan and brown pants said.

"Violates the laws of physics," said another, dressed in a suit and ascot. "I just had this discussion with my class at Caltech, and . . ."

The man stopped midsentence. "Well," he said, standing up, and Lily got the feeling that women were rarer here than dragons' teeth.

"Lily, what a surprise!" Max said, hastily putting down an octopus armature. His hand slid into his pocket, fingering something. "What brings you here?"

"Lily?" a young man with wavy hair said, waggling his great bushy eyebrows inquisitively at Max.

"Forrie, this is Lily Kessler," said Max. "She's a friend of Kitty Hayden's family. Lily, meet Forrest Ackerman, a movie collector extraordinaire and the biggest science and fantasy buff around. He's got Dr.

Frankenstein's electrodes, Bela Lugosi's fangs, part of Fritz Lang's *Metropolis* set."

The man named Forrie grinned.

Lily said, "Max, I've got to talk to you."

"Okay," said Max, motioning her over.

"In private," she said crisply.

The room erupted in guffaws and good-natured ribbing.

"You're in for it now, Max," said a studious-looking young man with a goatee.

"Did he leave a gorilla in your bed, miss?" said a young man with a thick shock of hair, spectacles, and a fiendish twinkle in his eyes.

The room erupted in hoots of laughter.

"Ray, you be quiet," Max said.

"Watch out for Bradbury," called a voice from the back, "or he'll turn you into a gold-skinned Martian girl."

"They could very well have golden skin, Nathan," the man named Ray said mildly, puffing on a meerschaum pipe with a hammered silver unicorn winding around the bowl. "We won't know until we meet them."

Max led her into the hallway, the raucous shouts of the science club following them.

"Are you all right? You look all out of breath."

"I'm okay. But Max, I . . ."

"Let's go for a stroll," he said brusquely. "These fellows are getting on my nerves."

"Here is fine."

"I need some air. Damn eggheads smoke too much."

It was dark outside. The October days were whittling down to winter, leaves rusting on the trees. The wind kicked up.

"Just a little stroll," Max said, moving along the sidewalk.

"Why?" A jolt of suspicion went through her. What if she was wrong, and he had killed Kitty and the others? Would he now abduct her? But that was crazy. The streets were full of cars and people.

"Max, stop."

"Okay." He turned. His hand went to his pocket. "What is it?"

"You lied to me, Max. You saw Kitty the night she disappeared and I want to know why."

"Why?" he echoed.

"The police know. I'm afraid they're going to arrest you for Kitty's murder."

"But I loved Kitty." His brow furrowed.

"I know. But people have been known to kill the ones they love. Especially when they can't have them." She paused. "What happened between you and Kitty on October seventh? Tell me the truth this time."

"It was our anniversary," he said glumly. "I took her to dinner."

"What anniversary?"

"Of our meeting at the Pig 'n Whistle."

She shook her head. "Let me get this straight. You took her to dinner to celebrate the one-year anniversary of your *friendship?*"

"That's right. And then she had to ruin it." A peevish tone crept into his voice and he stroked something in his pocket. Lily wondered if he had a gun. She began to back away.

"How did she ruin it?"

"She told me she didn't have all night because she was meeting a guy named Frankie at nine for a drink."

Lily grew very still. "And that got you mad?" She forced a casual tone into her voice.

"It wasn't so much that. It was . . . she told me . . ." Max's voice dropped to a whisper. "She told me . . ."

"What?"

"That I had to stop pining for her. That we were never going to be together." He looked at her miserably and his hand slid out of its pocket, large and pale and . . . empty, she saw with relief.

"And you couldn't live with that?" she said softly.

Max hung his head. "No," he said

hoarsely.

"Max," Lily said. "What did you do?"

"I told her I'd kill myself." His eyes were shrouded suddenly, something tricky in them.

"What else did you tell her?"

"I told her I'd kill her, and then myself."

Could Pico be right? Lily scooted down the sidewalk. "You obviously didn't kill yourself," she said.

"And I couldn't kill her. Especially after she told me she was going to have a baby."

"That must have upset you. Did she tell you who the father was?"

"No."

"Did you kill her, Max? Maybe it was an accident. You were angry and things got out of hand."

"No." He looked panicky, his eyes rolling and darting.

"The bartender overheard you fighting. He told the cops. What happened after that?"

He gave her a bleak look. "She ran out and I got drunk. Eventually I just went home."

"What time was that?"

"Around eleven forty-five."

Rhett Taylor had seen a man chasing Kitty at one-thirty. It wasn't Max Vranizan.

512

"And you went right to bed, and never saw her again?"

"No." He made a choking noise. "I . . . I went for a drive."

"Where?"

"I drove up the Coast Highway. It was foggy, I could barely see. And I was drunk as a lord. But I didn't care. I thought, *If I die, what does it matter? My heart already died tonight.*"

"How far did you go?"

"Up to the 'Bu and back."

"What time did you get home from Malibu?"

"Around three-thirty."

"So you didn't see Kitty again?" Lily pressed, suspicious.

"No. But there was something by my doorstep."

"What?"

"This." He reached into his pocket and Lily flinched, until she saw the carved bone button. A red thread looped through the hole.

Lily's breath caught in her throat. She'd seen one just like it.

"It's a button from the outfit Kitty was wearing that night. She must have come by while I was out. Maybe she wanted to apologize. Maybe she was on the run and needed help. And I wasn't there. I let her down."

"It wasn't your fault."

"It was. If I had been home that night, she'd still be alive."

"Why didn't you tell the cops?"

"Because they would have suspected me. I was the last one to see her alive."

"But don't you see you've made it much worse?"

"I was scared they'd think I'd done it. And I was right."

At that moment, a black coupe with tinted windows cruised past slowly. A window came down and they both saw the muzzle of a pistol. Before she could scream, she heard the *rat-tat-tat* and ducked, but a crimson stain was already seeping down the front of Max's shirt. She saw his eyes, confused and beseeching, as he slumped against the wall, one hand trailing down her side. Inside the car, a man lowered the gun again and took careful aim. Lily jumped back and ran, people already screaming and scattering in the street. The sound of more shots rang in her ears.

CHAPTER 33

Lily wanted to grab one of the smartly dressed people and scream, *Help me,* but feared the shooters would just mow them both down. *Max,* she thought as her legs pumped, her mind refusing to believe it.

Who could want Max dead? Any last vestiges of suspicion she had that the animator had murdered Kitty Hayden now evaporated. Max was innocent. But he knew something. He'd told her Kitty was meeting someone named Frankie at nine p.m. *Frankie Niccoli?* Was Dragna behind it after all? Had his men killed Bernard Keck and Rhett Taylor too?

Ahead of her was a coffee shop, lit up like a beacon. If she could reach it, she'd be safe.

A flamboyantly dressed man fell into step beside her. Then another. Lily stiffened and slowed. The men slowed too. Was she imagining it? The coffee shop was only a half block away now.

515

She quickened her pace, decided to scream after all, and felt something hard push against her ribs. She took a step forward, and the gun moved with her. "Easy," one said. "Keep walking."

Lily pretended to stumble, then jumped back and ran helter-skelter the way she'd just come. She heard an oath, the men turning around. They wouldn't risk a shoot-out with people on the street, would they? But they were breaking into a trot. They intended to kill her.

At that moment, a bus pulled up and its doors opened, disgorging a flow of people. They poured onto the sidewalk, blocking her escape. She thought about jumping on the bus, but she'd be swimming upstream. On the other side of her was Barker Brothers Department Store. Hoping the disembarking passengers would shield her from view, she ducked inside and found herself in a furniture showroom. There had to be an exit in the back. The place was a maze of heavy wooden furniture as she threaded her way. The front door opened with a blast of air and her pursuers burst in. She ran into the back office.

A young man looked up from his typewriter and adjusted his glasses at the sight of her. He looked seventeen and wore a name tag that said BOB.

"Is there a rear exit? Quick! There are two men after me."

"Excuse me?"

Lily ran up and seized his lapels. "For the love of Christ, help me. They've got a gun."

Her terror seemed to galvanize him. He vaulted over his desk. "Follow me." Bob led her down a hallway.

"Gee whiz, this is pretty exciting," he said.

"Too exciting. We'd better hurry, unless you want brains and blood splattered all over Barker Brothers' fine furnishings."

"Golly," said Bob. "Are you a spy?"

She didn't answer. They ran downstairs and Bob looked around, as if thinking of where he could hide her amid the china sets and dining tables, beds, and draperies. Then his eyes lit up. "C'mon, I've got just the place."

He crossed the basement to another flight of stairs. Lily scurried after him. Above, they heard the pounding of feet and breaking glass.

"Where are you taking me? They're going to find us like cornered rats," Lily panted.

They were in the subbasement now, a dusty place stacked high with broken chairs, tables, and lamps with torn shades. Lily looked around in dismay.

"There's nowhere to hide."

"Yes, there is." Bob picked up a flashlight atop a stack of boxes. He walked to the wood-paneled wall, stuck two fingers inside a knothole, and tugged. A hidden door swung open. Bob turned on the flashlight and played its light along a narrow, low-ceilinged passageway filled with cobwebs and crumbling plaster. "In there."

Lily shrank back. What if Bob meant to keep her captive in some secret room off the subbasement of Barker Brothers?

"Aw," said Bob, "you don't trust me. I'll go first. Come on."

"What's in there?"

Bob's eyes danced. "It's a secret passageway to the Paramount Theater next door."

He entered, beckoned her to follow. With little choice, she did. He pulled the door shut and gave her a huge wink. "Follow me."

She crept behind Bob the bookkeeper, down a cold passage that smelled of mice and musty air, the flashlight picking out bumps on the plaster wall, bits of straw poking out.

"Where do we end up?" she whispered.

"Just outside the theater bathroom." He gave her an impish look. "Our custodian discovered this passage years ago. There used to be a speakeasy next door and they stored liquor here and used it as a getaway during raids. I use it to sneak into the pictures."

Lily saw a wooden crate marked with a skull and crossbones that said DANGER.

"What's that?"

"Dynamite," Bob said. "Custodian uses it for fishing. The wife won't let him store it at home."

Lily was already reaching inside, comforted by the familiar heft of it, the smell.

"Hey!" said Bob. "Don'tcha know that stuff's dangerous?"

"Not without a match, it's not." Lily shoved a stick in her purse and looked around. "Does he have any grenades?"

"Are you crazy?"

"Fishermen use them all the time." Lily grinned. "Relax, big guy, it's just a precaution."

She gave him a push. "Go on."

Bob hurried, eager to put distance between himself and Lily.

They reached a door, opened it, and found themselves in a hallway.

"We'll slip into the theater and go out through the fire exit into the alley. Then you're on your own. What exactly are you running from, if you don't mind me asking?"

"It's a long story. You wouldn't believe it anyway."

"I bet you really are a spy. You've got that look."

Lily pursed her lips, as if deciding something. "I can't lie to you," she said. "I am a secret agent. You figured it out."

"Jeepers." Bob's eyes widened.

She squeezed his hand. "But I'm on our side. Those guys chasing me are Soviet agents. You'd never guess it, but they speak perfect Russian."

"Why are they after you?" he asked hoarsely.

Lily patted her purse. "I've got some documents they want. Top secret. I'd rather blow myself up than give it to them."

"Well, please don't do it here."

They hurried down the darkened aisles, Lily seeing Technicolor as a giant blue arm, red dress, and yellow car flashed across the screen. Then they were in the alley.

"Should I call the police?" Bob said.

"I would," Lily said. "One last thing. I'll need your lighter."

Bob looked terrified. "Just in case," she said.

He gulped and handed over a Zippo.

"Congratulations, Bob. You've helped your country."

They shook hands and Lily ran to the next street. Seeing no sign of her pursuers, she hopped on the first trolley she saw, which was heading west. She felt as if her legs might give way. She'd escaped once, but she wasn't really safe. She wished she had a gun, instead of a lousy stick of dynamite and a lighter. When the trolley reached Holly-wood, she jumped off and ran all the way to the rooming house. She didn't see any strange cars out front. Nobody lurking. She let herself in, locking the door with a spasm of relief.

"Running away, are we?" a voice asked.

Mrs. Potter stood in the dim light of the hallway, arms crossed before her.

"Running away from what?" Lily asked.

The landlady gave a thin-lipped smile. "Your fate. It's catching up, isn't it, dearie?"

Lily wanted to shriek. Instead, she forced a smile. "Stop trying to spook me," she said.

"You think you're so high and mighty," the landlady said. "Putting on airs, just like that other one. I see the fear in you. It's growing, taking over. Soon you'll —"

"Stop," said Lily, running up the stairs to escape.

Then she turned and crept back down.

She had to call Pico. Mrs. Potter was gone. Lily heard crying from the old servants' quarters behind the kitchen. Beverly had said this was Mrs. Potter's domain and off-limits to the girls. Lily hesitated, then pushed through the swinging door.

The hardwood floor in this hallway was scuffed, the wallpaper yellow with age. Lily came to a bedroom with plush curtains. Beverly lay on the canopied bed, sobbing next to a pile of suitcases while Mrs. Potter patted her back. There was an intimacy to their posture.

"It's time," Mrs. Potter said.

"But I don't want to," the girl answered.

Lily remembered Mrs. Potter gliding out of the girl's room the other day.

"Leave her alone," Lily said.

Mrs. Potter looked up in surprise, then laughed. "Isn't that adorable, Beverly? She's come to rescue you."

"You're not allowed here," the girl said sullenly. "I told you so the first night."

"Neither are you," Lily said.

"My daughter has full run of the house," said Mrs. Potter.

Lily looked from the landlady to Beverly and then back again. And she saw what had eluded her before: Mrs. Potter's face was a poorly cast die of her pretty daughter's. But in the landlady, meanness and resentment had burned away all fairness, leaving a crudely knit collection of angles, a flintiness outside and in.

"Beverly should have gotten that RKO contract, not Kitty," Mrs. Potter said. "They both had screen tests that day, but Kitty's was the one they chose. That shack trash from Illinois stole my daughter's contract. And they'd promised it to you, hadn't they, pet?"

Beverly sniffed in agreement.

"We're not unhappy that she's gone," Mrs. Potter said. "We let nature take its course."

Lily recalled Mrs. Potter on the back porch, watching her cat torture a mouse.

"You wanted her out of the way," Lily said. "What did the two of you do?"

"We didn't *do* anything. She was very useful to us, wasn't she, Bevvy?"

"I was Kitty's best friend," the girl said. "She told me *everything.* She never trusted Red or Fumiko like she did me. A girl needs a confidante. I've got Mama, and Kitty had me."

"I told you, Lily, that information was valuable," Mrs. Potter nodded. "Maybe you'll realize that when we're gone."

"Where are you going?"

"Beverly and I thought we'd go abroad

until things cool down. Now that we've got the means." She patted her handbag. "I hear the dollar goes far in Paris these days."

"Who killed Kitty Hayden and the others?" Lily said.

"What do you have to trade? That reporter gal had cash. That's why we did business."

"What did you sell her?"

"A couple of —" Beverly began.

"Let's keep the details to ourselves, shall we?" Mrs. Potter broke in sharply.

The girl bridled. "Why should you get all the credit?"

"Because a deal's a deal and we agreed. I've got to call for the cab," Mrs. Potter said.

After she left, Lily moved closer to Beverly, gave her a sympathetic look. "She bosses you around a lot, doesn't she?"

Beverly looked resigned. "It's always been that way, from when I was little and she'd take me to *Little Rascals* auditions. Mama wants me to make it big." She scowled. "Just because *she* didn't. And I don't even like acting. I throw up before every audition."

"Must be tough, her living through you."

"Especially when I do all the hard work."

Lily ran her hand along the quilted bedspread. "Like what?"

"Getting chatty with all the boarders. Convincing Kitty to confide in me, always pretending she's my friend. Sneaking into her room to steal things."

"I thought a phony RKO employee stole her journal."

Beverly smiled. "Maybe so, but only another gal's going to look inside a sanitary napkin. That's where she'd hidden her photos of her and Kirk on the yacht."

"Kirk Armstrong? So they *were* having an affair?"

"Kitty met him two months ago. On that movie. She fell head over heels in love."

Lily remembered what Kitty had told the RKO makeup artist: *No, it's not serious, Marion, but it sure is a lot of fun.*

"Was he the father of her child?"

"Kitty hoped he'd marry her when he learned about the baby. She didn't always live in the real world."

"I thought he was already married."

Beverly rolled her eyes. "Don't believe everything you read. He's separated and headed for divorce. The last thing he wants is to get hitched again, so when he found out Kitty was pregnant, he told her to get rid of it. My, how the tears flowed that night. Mama and I explained that he's a star so she should blackmail him. Mama's good at that. But Kitty wouldn't go for it. The poor dope loved him."

"Did Kirk Armstrong kill her?"

Beverly walked to the bureau and pulled out a reel-to-reel recorder. Lily remembered the girl's mechanical aptitude with the radio the night she arrived.

"This is our insurance, for when we come back," Beverly said, depressing a button.

The machine hissed and popped. They heard quiet weeping. Then a girl's ragged voice. Kitty. Speaking from beyond the grave:

"He told me to meet him at a motel in Duarte. He said it was safer if we went far away from RKO, where no one knew us."

"I guess you had no choice." Beverly's voice oozed sympathy.

"He knew all about Kirk and the baby." There was muffled crying.

"Good heavens, how did he find out?" Beverly said.

"I h-h-have no idea," Kitty hiccupped. "But I explained that Kirk's marriage was on the rocks and he loved me and we were planning a future together. Then he told me not to be a stupid little twit. He said, 'You are going to break off with him immediately, and you are going to get rid of it.' "

"Was Kirk there too?" Beverly asked.

"God, no." Kitty's voice choked and dissolved again. "If he had been there" — Lily

heard her struggle to get hold of herself —
"it never would have happened."

"What happened, hon?" Beverly's voice
rose with urgency.

Lily heard sniffling, then a stuttering
intake of breath.

"He forced himself on me." Kitty's voice
was flat and without emotion. "He'd made
passes before and I'd always managed to
avoid him. Until that day."

"But hon, you agreed to meet him at a
motel . . ."

"I didn't realize . . . When he grabbed me,
I pulled away and he got mad. 'You only
want the stars, you think you're too good
for me?' The look on his face was terrifying.
'But you haven't paid your dues, Kitty.
Every starlet has to pay dues.' I shoved him.
But that just excited him. I fought, but it
was no use . . . Afterward, he said I had to
do whatever he told me, that I was a slut,
and if I didn't, the hotel manager would
testify I'd gone there willingly, and that I'd
cooked up these lies to blackmail Kirk and
attract publicity for myself. Then he pulled
out some photos."

"What photos?"

"Oh, Beverly. I did a stupid thing some
time back. I let Freddy take pictures of me."

"What kind of pictures?" Beverly's voice

quavered.

"Not nice ones. Of me tied up. With my clothes torn. And fake blood."

"Kitty! How could you?"

"I had no idea he would show them to anyone. He said they were for research."

"He must have sold them."

"Yes." Kitty's voice was tiny. "I don't know where to turn anymore. Dear, dear Beverly, you're my best friend in the whole world. If I couldn't tell you, I'd just die."

The machine whirred, then Beverly's voice continued.

"Now, hon, we've got to get some things straight. Does Kirk know what happened?"

"I can't imagine he did. Kirk is a good soul. And he loves me. I know he does. That's why I couldn't tell him. I was so ashamed. What if he thought I'd brought it upon myself? It's not like I see him every day, with his schedule, his family . . . we have to make elaborate plans. And now he won't return my calls. Just when I need to talk to him so badly."

Lily turned the machine off.

"Who raped Kitty in that motel room?"

"I don't know," Beverly's eyes glittered. "She said it would come out with his arrest. Mama and I told her not to go to the police. We warned her it might be dangerous. But

Kitty was determined to get justice against the man who wronged her."

"Wouldn't her gangster friends have taken care of this guy if she asked them?"

"She wanted him led off in handcuffs in front of everyone," Beverly said. "Not dead."

Lily thought about the note in Kitty's purse. "But eventually she changed her mind about keeping the baby? How did she even know it was Kirk's?"

"Kitty wasn't sleeping with anyone else. Mickey Cohen and his men, that was just a good time. She was pretty old-fashioned, really. And she wanted to show Kirk how much she loved him. She wrote that note in my room: *Dear Kirk, I'm going to see the doctor next week. I think it's for the best.*"

"And just when she decided to take care of the problem, she gets killed?"

"She shouldn't have gone to the DA. The police were bad enough."

Lily wrinkled her brow, trying to put the pieces together. "How did Kitty's rapist find out about the affair and the pregnancy?"

Beverly didn't answer. She carried the tape recorder to the suitcase, wrapped it in a towel, and laid it inside. She covered it with clothes, lowered the lid and locked the suitcase.

"Mama might have had something to do

with that," she said at last.

Just then, Mrs. Potter came back into the room.

"All ready, pet?" she asked. Seeing Lily's stricken look, she added, "Kitty was stubborn. She insisted on heading down the path of destruction. We just gave her a helping hand and helped ourselves in the process. Information," she said cheerily. "The best currency."

"Who killed Kitty?" Lily said.

"You'll find out," Mrs. Potter said. "I made a call. They should be here soon."

And then Lily knew she had to get the hell out of that spider's lair.

"Go ahead and run, coward. It won't be long now. Why don't you try the Hollywood PD? I hear Kitty had a lot of luck there."

Mrs. Potter's caustic laughter trailed after her as she fled.

CHAPTER 34

Harry's police radio was squawking like a cageful of parrots. There had been a shooting in front of Clifton's Cafeteria and a man was down, the ambulance on its way. A young woman who'd fled the scene after dodging bullets herself was wanted for questioning. The mystery gal had auburn hair, was about five foot six, midtwenties, and was wearing a white blouse, black skirt, and black high-heeled sandals. Harry's first thought was he had to get over there with his camera. His second, especially after hearing more details, was a queasy fear that he knew who the gal was.

He remembered Shorty's questions about Max the other night, feared he'd given too much away. Trusting his instincts, he sped to Mickey's haberdashery, where a nattily dressed clerk, a tape measure around his neck, asked if he could help him.

"I'm looking for Shorty Lagonzola."

"If you'd like to wait a moment, I'll see if —"

"To hell with that," Harry growled, already stalking into the back, where he was confronted by a gun muzzle in a twitchy hand.

"Jesus Christ, Harry, I almost blew your head off," Shorty said. "What the fuck you doing here?"

The bonhomie of earlier was gone. Shorty's eyes were flat and reptilian.

"Some men in a car just —"

"Harry, Harry," Shorty said. "You look like you could use some fresh air. Let's take a stroll around the block."

As soon as they were halfway down the alley, he said, "Don't you ever talk like that inside. There could be bugs. We never discuss —"

"Your boys just killed an innocent man. Mickey's behind this, isn't he?"

"What if he is?"

"Max Vranizan is innocent of Kitty Hayden's murder. You got the wrong guy."

Shorty's eyes flickered. "That's not what the LAPD says. They were getting ready to arrest him, according to our source there. Got some new evidence that looks pretty bad. When I told Mickey, he gave me the green light."

"Oh Christ. Oh no. It's too late for Vranizan, the poor bastard, but you've got to call off your thugs before they kill Lily."

"Who?"

"There was a girl with him. They shot at her too, but she got away. They'll turn the city upside down looking for her."

"What girl?"

"Shorty, look at me. By all that's holy. You can't let them kill her."

"Stupid jackasses were supposed to get him alone," Shorty muttered.

"Well, they didn't."

"If she got a good look at them, she'll be able to ID them. The rule is, no witnesses."

"She'll forget what they looked like." Harry proceeded to invoke Boyle Heights, their shared history. "On my father's grave. I promise. Call them off."

Still, the gangster said nothing.

"Don't you see the cops are setting up this guy to take the fall for someone? And you fell for their little plan. It's perfect, they announce they know who killed Kitty Hayden and right before they arrest him, he gets popped. You've done their dirty work for them. Dead men tell no tales. Call off your boys before they kill another innocent person."

Shorty shifted uneasily. "I can't. No way to reach them."

Harry stared grimly at the ground. *Lily,* he thought, picturing her running for her life. *I've got to save you.*

Shorty cleared his throat. "But we fixed it so they'd call at eight with an update."

Hope filled Harry once more. "When they call, you hafta tell them. Please, Shorty. You saved my pa's life years ago. Then I helped you the other day. Now it's your turn again, and then it'll be mine. As long as we live. Cuz we're brothers, right, Shorty? And brothers have each others' back. This gal is dear to me."

Shorty Lagonzola gritted his teeth. The boss would be furious. But if Harry was right and they'd killed the wrong man, there'd be hell to pay.

Lily ran all the way to the drugstore, and made for the phone box in back.

Stephen, she prayed. *Please be there.* If Magruder answered, she'd hang up. But when the older cop's raspy voice came on the line, she changed her mind.

"Could I please speak to Detective Pico?" Lily said, trying to keep her voice normal.

"Miss Kessler? It's Magruder. Pico's not here, can I help you?"

"Where is he?"

"Interviewing a witness."

With a sinking heart, Lily remembered. Pico was at the harbor, checking DiCicco's alibi. "I need to speak to him. It's an emergency."

"Please calm down, Miss Kessler. Tell me what's wrong."

"No." She felt the room spin. She hadn't escaped the carnage downtown, and then Mrs. Potter, only to waltz into this dirty cop's arms. What if he had orchestrated Max's murder? Pico was the only one she could trust. Pico loved her. Pico wouldn't hurt her. She had to get through to him. He'd protect her. That was the only thing she knew beyond a doubt, and she clung to it.

"Are you at home?" Magruder asked.

"I'm at a pay phone."

"Where?"

Lily knew he mustn't find out.

"What's the number at the San Pedro Station? I'll call him there."

"Whatever you have to say to Detective Pico, you can share with me. We're partners on —"

"No." Lily crouched over the phone, panting. "I'll only speak to Pico."

There was a short, deadly pause in which she wondered if she'd gone too far.

"Very well," Magruder said, giving her the

number. "But bear in mind that he's an hour away. If you're in immediate danger, he can't help. Tell me where you are. I'll send some men. I'll come myself —"

But Lily had already replaced the receiver.

When she got through to the San Pedro Station she asked for Detective Pico.

"He's doing an interview," a gruff voice said.

She gripped the walls of the phone booth, trying to catch her breath.

"It's an emergency. Tell him Lily Kessler's on the phone."

"Hold on."

She waited, glancing over her shoulder. Mrs. Potter knew she often ate here. Would she send Kitty's killers after her? Two men entered the drugstore and looked around and she felt sure they were after her. *Please,* she thought, pressing her forehead against the cool glass. When they headed for the lunch counter, she was sure it was to keep an eye on her, grab her as she came out. She trembled. She had to get hold of herself.

After what seemed like hours, Pico came on the line.

"Lily? What's wrong?"

Hearing his voice, she almost started sobbing.

"Two men just shot Max Vranizan. Downtown. They opened fire in front of Clifton's. I was with him, they shot at me too, then chased me into a department store. I managed to ditch them and ran home, but Mrs. Potter —"

"Where are you?"

"In a phone booth on Hollywood Boulevard. What should I do? Stephen, I'm afraid."

She heard him breathing heavily. "Go right home. Lock yourself in your room. I'll be there as soon as I can."

"It's not safe. Mrs. Potter and Beverly are tied up in this somehow."

"Then stay put. What's the address? I'm on my way."

"I don't know if it's safe here either. They shot Max, Stephen," she cried into the phone.

"Okay, okay. Try to stay calm. Who knows you're there?"

"I had to call Magruder to get your number. He knows I'm at a phone booth. And this is the one closest to the house."

"Oh no."

Lily ran her nails along the glass, relishing the screech. "Tell me what to do."

"You've got to put some distance between yourself and that house. Let me think . . ."

"Should I go to a police station?"

"No! I don't know who we can trust. I'll take the coast back, it's fastest. That'll bring me in to Ocean Park. Yes. That's where I want you to —"

"Oh, Stephen, I don't —"

"I've got a friend who runs the oyster bar at Ocean Park Pier," he interrupted. "He's a retired cop. Next to the carousel. You know where that is, right? You grew up around there."

"Yes, but —"

"He'll hide you until I arrive. Can you get a cab?"

Lily's hands were slick with moisture as she held the receiver to her ear.

"I suppose. But are you sure? That's so far."

"Far's what we want right now. My friend's name is Ernie Carlson. Tell him I sent you. Everything will be okay. I'll be there before you know it."

"Hurry. Oh God, please hurry."

"Lily, I love you. I'm on my way."

Lily hung up and looked around. The men she'd found suspicious earlier were laughing as the waitress took their order. But there could be others. On their way. Looking for her. She realized she didn't have enough money to get a cab all the way to Ocean Park. That left the trolley.

■ ■ ■ ■

At the San Pedro Police Station, Pico hung up the phone, his heart pounding.

A uniform popped his head in. "Call for you on the captain's line."

"Where is she?" Magruder bellowed when Pico picked up.

"Who?" Pico said, playing dumb.

"The Kessler broad. She called here, sounding scared to death, and demanded your number."

"It's nothing," Pico said. "She gets overly dramatic sometimes. I'm going to meet her and then I'll call you —"

"Don't bullshit me. Someone just gunned down Max Vranizan downtown and I know she was there. They'll come for her next. She's scared shitless and whatever's about to go down, you're not going to get there in time. Where is she?"

"I'd like to handle it, sir."

"All you're going to handle is a dead body if you don't let me get some men out to protect her. You can't be the knight in shining armor this time, Pico. There isn't time."

Pico wondered if his partner wanted to get there first to silence her.

"Sir, I have reason to believe that whoever

killed Kitty Hayden and Max Vranizan has ties to the LAPD. And with all due respect, she may not be safe with your men."

There, he thought, *it was out in the open.*

"So that's how it is," Magruder said, his voice cold as steel.

"Let me bring her in," Pico said, "with enough media hoopla and some high-ranking official from the DA's office along to take her statement, so that she's protected. I don't want any more blood shed today."

"Where is she?"

"Sir! I respectfully decline to say."

"Why?"

"Because the truth of the matter, sir, is that I don't trust you either."

Instead of exploding, Magruder's voice grew soft.

"Stephen, Stephen. We both know my hands aren't exactly clean. And my son's care doesn't come cheap. But if you think for one second that I'd kill an innocent girl, you're out of your mind. I'm not an animal, Stephen."

Pico stared into the phone. He remembered Magruder staggering into the hallway at the whorehouse, naked and covered in blood, the girl screaming. But it had been chicken blood, the girl scared but unhurt.

"I don't know, sir. I'm only trying to do the right thing."

"As am I, Stephen. And I give you my word. Tell me where she is and I'll be there with two men in twenty minutes."

Pico looked at the clock. It would take him more than an hour to get to Ocean Park. And whoever was chasing her might find her first.

"Where is she, son?" Magruder asked again. "For god's sake, if you care about this girl, if you ever want to see her again, except stretched out on a coroner's slab, tell me now."

Pico doubled over in a soundless cry. He thought of Lily in his arms last night, her smooth flesh and scent, the way she'd cried out, the hunger he felt bubbling up for her even now. He had to protect her. Again, he heard the terror in her voice, recounting how the men had shot at her and chased her. Two men. Thuggish men. Not cops. Not Magruder.

"I sent her to Carlson," he whispered. "At Ocean Park Pier."

Magruder gave an enormous sigh of relief. "We'll be waiting for you there, Stephen. I'll see to it that she doesn't come to any harm."

■ ■ ■ ■

As soon as he hung up the phone, Magruder collapsed against the wall, then crossed himself, ending with a reverent kiss on his thumb.

Picking up the phone again, he dialed a number.

"Boys," he said, "Lily Kessler is on her way to Ocean Park Pier. Pico's sent her to the oyster bar next to the carousel. Yeah, Ernie's place. We'll need to get out there on the double. And you're not to move in until I give the word."

The trolley dropped Lily at the foot of the pier. As she stepped onto the boardwalk, her eye was drawn to the marquee of the Moroccan-themed Dome Theater, where a Kirk Armstrong movie was playing. A bad omen. She thought of Kitty running through Hollywood on the last night of her life, seeking safety and shelter, much as she was doing now.

Would the oyster bar even be open? She hurried toward the illuminated attractions, unwilling to linger in the dark. She heard the muffled roar of the surf, smelled the briny sea air shot through with the sweet-

542

ness of caramel corn and cotton candy.

When she'd left in '44, there had been blackouts, the beaches closed and battened down for fear of Japanese invasion. Now electric lights glinted wetly off the rides. She heard the rackety clack of the wooden roller coaster, the screams of the riders, the asthmatic wheeze of the diving bell plunging people to the sea bottom, the carnival barkers and touts.

The damp wood splintered under her black heels. *Please, Lord, don't let me become the Black Sandal,* she prayed. There were people fishing off the pier, raggedy hobo men and tiny Asians, bent as commas. A sailor with his arm around a girl lurched out of an arcade, their laughter emerging in puffy white clouds on the sea air. She saw crabs and lobsters scrabbling desperately against the glass walls of their tanks, knew exactly how they felt. But she was confused. There were two stands advertising oysters, one close by, another past the carousel.

Lily looked at her watch. In her clandestine days she'd never waited more than five minutes for a rendezvous. After that, you became a target for anyone watching. She hurried toward the first oyster bar. She felt vulnerable out here in public, where anyone could see her.

Someone called her name. Lily froze.

She turned, cringing as she recognized the voice.

It was Magruder. With two more cops behind him, blocking the mouth of the pier and any possible exit back onto the streets.

"Lily," Magruder called. "Over here."

Lily's eyes widened. She shook her head and took a step back. "No," she said.

"It's all right, Lily," Magruder said. "I spoke to Pico. How do you think we knew where to find you?"

He spread his arms, palms up, to show he had nothing to hide. His voice was patient, encouraging, the way you'd coax a stray dog to shelter.

Her thoughts went around and around. It was a trap. Pico didn't trust Magruder. This wasn't in the plan. He wouldn't have told Magruder where to find her. But then how had he learned? How else could he have gotten here so fast? Around and around her thoughts went, like the carousel on the pier. She couldn't think straight. She had to. She struggled to reach a decision. She'd do what Pico told her. She trusted him. He wouldn't betray her.

"You must be chilled, this damp night air," Magruder said, taking off his coat, holding it out to her. "Come in out of the cold, Lily. Put this on. It'll keep you warm."

His solicitous attitude chilled her even more than the clammy night.

"No," she screamed, running toward the nearest oyster bar a mere ten feet away. That way lay safety. Not toward Magruder and into the arms of a corrupt cop. "Dear God," she cried. "Will no one help me?"

Just then another figure stepped out from behind the oyster stand. He was tall, wearing a suit and a black overcoat. He looked vaguely familiar, but she couldn't place him.

"Lily," he said, extending a hand.

She froze, hoping beyond hope.

"Who are you? Are you Car—" She stopped, realizing she had to let him identify himself. For all she knew, Magruder had men all over the pier.

The man gave a reassuring smile. "It's okay, Lily. You're safe now. You'd better come with me quickly."

She looked from him back to Magruder forty feet away, whose men had bunched around him now, the three of them pushing through the crowd toward her.

The man in the coat was holding something up. It was a badge. She couldn't read it properly, but she made out an embossed shield.

Magruder and his men drew nearer.

Thirty feet. Twenty-five.

"Lily, get away from him," Magruder called.

"Are you Carlson?" Lily asked, desperate now.

"He's not a cop, Lily," Magruder screamed. "It's a trick. Run."

The black-coated man looked steadily at the beefy cop. "You're making a big mistake, Magruder. The debt must be paid. It's time. Now back off."

"I don't care. I'm not going to stand by and let you kill this innocent girl. Run, Lily, I've never seen him before in my life."

"Lily," the other man said. "I'm Carlson. You need to trust me, not that pathetic excuse of a cop over there. He's dirty, Lily, and more than that, he's a murderer. He killed Kitty Hayden. You're lucky I found you before he killed you too."

Magruder's mouth was moving, foam gathering at the corners as he fought to speak.

"Whatever he says, don't believe him, Lily," the man who called himself Carlson said. "Your only chance is to come with me."

Magruder was fifteen feet away now. He reached for his gun. The men behind him did too. The older cop looked at the revelers thronging all around. He wouldn't get a clean shot.

"Let's go," the man with the badge said urgently. "Before they shoot."

Lily saw the homicidal rage on Magruder's face as he strode forward, the crowd parting at the guns. Ten feet. Who could she trust? If she chose wrong, she'd die.

Lily turned and ran with the man across the pier. They ducked behind a ring-toss booth, hurrying along the backs of tents. The man steered her toward a set of stairs that materialized out of the fog and led down the side of the pier.

Lily balked. "This isn't what Pico said to do."

"Change of plans," the man who called himself Carlson said. "We didn't expect Magruder to show up either."

Magruder's shouts rang in her ears. He was coming closer. With a last look behind her, she started down the stairs, seeing the parking lot below where a car waited, idling.

"Where are we going?" she asked.

"Hurry," the man said, bundling her roughly toward the car. He wore a signet ring and it pressed unpleasantly against her bare arm.

From inside the car, Lily heard a strange sound.

It was the sound of laughter.

And then she knew she'd made a horrible mistake.

As the car door opened, she turned and kicked the man between the legs as hard as she could. His grip loosened and she broke free.

"Help," she screamed.

And then she ran.

Pico kept his foot on the gas pedal the whole way up Highway 1, running stop signs, passing the occasional car, veering into oncoming traffic, cursing and crying. The fog was so thick in places that he couldn't see. The world had narrowed down to one overriding goal and one person, and as the car raced toward Ocean Park Pier, Pico's thoughts raced as well, arguing and making deals with God.

Let her be alive, and I promise I'll never take another free meal or drink again. I'll be righteous and set an example and do anything you want.

But as he flew toward his rendezvous with Lily, Stephen Pico knew the real bargain God wanted. What he'd only danced around until now. There was only one sacrifice God would accept and he'd always known it. Saving Lily meant destroying his father. His father, who had used blood money linked to Kitty Hayden's murder to buy his son's promotion into Homicide, where his very first assignment had been to find the girl's murderer. With the tacit understanding that maybe he and his partner wouldn't look too far or ask too many questions. So he cursed as he drove, at the impossible circularity of it, and how inevitable it all seemed. And he vowed to break the chain.

Lily wove through parked cars, trying to escape her pursuers. She screamed, but her cries were muffled by the thickening fog and obscured by the shrieks of roller coaster riders, the general cacophony from the pier. Soon the parking lot ended and she was running on the sand. *Damn these shoes,* she thought. She'd never wear heels again. She wanted to stop and bend down, shuck them off, but her pursuers were gaining on her, they were right behind her. With each step she sank in sand to her ankles. She was going to die, just like Kitty, just like Louise Dobbs and Florence Kwitney. But these weren't the same men who had chased her downtown. She still believed in Pico. But something had gone wrong, just when she'd been so close to safety. More than anything, she wanted to feel Pico's arms around her right now, to escape this nightmare and crawl into his warm embrace forever. But five years in Europe should have taught her that she couldn't depend on anyone else to save her. She was on her own.

She heard shouts now. Footsteps pounding nearby.

"My wife," the man yelled. "Please, sir, help me. She's not well."

"He's not my husband," Lily screamed. "I'm being attacked. Help."

But her words were muffled in the cotton-batting fog, lost on the wind.

"Come back, dearest," the man's voice called. "You know you've had too much to drink."

Lily's heels sunk too deep and she fell. She scrabbled to stand up, and found herself jerked roughly to her feet. The man with the badge, and another one, larger, with a bandage on his nose, and eyes that reflected back emptiness. She smelled black rubber.

"Gotcha," the bandaged man said, holding her in a vise-like grip.

Lily let herself go limp as they hustled her back to the parking lot, where a car pulled up, the driver shrouded in shadow, his face hidden behind a hat. Above them the pier was alive with echoing cries, police sirens, lights. Why hadn't it been that way fifteen minutes ago? She wanted to weep.

They shoved her into the backseat and got in, one on either side, a gun pressed against her ribs. The driver took off. She studied the men from the corners of her eyes, memorizing their features in the flicker of the streetlights so she'd be able to pick them out of a lineup. If she lived. The big one on the left with the bashed-in nose, a black eye that was healing purple and yellow. The one on the right fleshy and rugged, almost handsome, like a bit actor. No wonder she'd fallen for his cop impersonation. Again it nagged at her. Impersonators. Actors. Movies. Studios. She remembered the artist she'd glimpsed painting a landscape in the RKO special effects hangar the night she'd met Max. His curious interest. She was almost sure it was the same guy. Was this Roy DiCicco? But Harry had said he was a stuntman, not a prop guy. Could he be both? Were these Dragna's men?

"Where are you taking me?" she asked.

"Stupid bitch," the prop painter muttered, hand at his crotch. "I oughta kill you right now."

Lily sat very still. What did they have in store, then?

"Are you Roy DiCicco?" she asked.

"We're God's avenging angels," said the

551

painter. "Putting the world to rights."

Again, she thought of the men who'd killed Max. They must be connected with these thugs, somehow. Which meant . . . mobsters?

"Why did you kill Max Vranizan?" she asked.

There was a low chuckle from the front. The driver spoke for the first time. She still couldn't see his face. His voice was familiar, but in the utter blankness of her terror, she couldn't place it.

"There's animation, and there's puppetry," the voice said. "We prefer invisible strings. And actors like Rhett Taylor with great tragic timing."

CHAPTER 35

Ocean Park Pier was a melee of police and lights and people running madly when Pico screeched to a halt. Magruder was briefing two uniforms.

"He got her," the older cop said as Pico raced up. "Some guy flashing a badge, pretending he was Carlson. I pleaded with her, but she wouldn't come with me. They had a getaway car down below in the parking lot, and one of my men got a description of the car and a partial plate. We've radioed —"

"You scumbag piece of shit," screamed Pico. "I should have listened to my instincts. I swear to God, Magruder, if anything's happened to her, I'm going to kill you with my bare hands."

"Get a grip, Stephen. Didn't you hear what I just said? We're on the same side. I want her found safe and alive as much as you do and I've got an APB out and all prowlers in the area on red alert. She didn't trust me. I'm sorry, Stephen."

The older cop placed a hand on Pico's arm, but he threw it off.

"What have you ever done in your entire sorry life that should make anyone trust you?"

Even now, Pico wasn't sure whether Magruder was telling him the truth. But the other policeman nodded in solemn agreement. And the prowlers would be on the lookout . . .

"Which way did they go?" Pico asked.

"They peeled out of the lot and one of our guys chased the car but lost it six blocks inland. Far as we know, though, she was alive."

Pico stood still, forcing his brain to work. They hadn't killed her yet. Where were they taking her? He put himself in the killers' mind-set. And then it hit him.

"Get in the car, Magruder, and pray we're on time. I know where they'll be."

When the car carrying Lily reached Hollywood, it turned north toward the hills.

"Where are you taking me?" Lily repeated, beginning to fear that she knew.

"Up to the Hollywood sign," the RKO

prop painter said. "It's a popular place these days."

An evil chorus of laughter ricocheted around the car.

"You're going to kill me and dump my body. To make it look like it's connected to the other murders."

"It *is* connected. We should have stopped you a long time ago. We thought we had, but Taunton steered us wrong about the coat."

"Louise," Lily cried. "You thought she was me."

"That's right. And the Kwitney gal, she was just to throw everyone off the track. Now the Hollywood Strangler claims his fourth victim."

"I've got sand in my hair. In my shoes. They'll know you abducted me from the beach."

"Thank you, Miss Kessler. Louie, take off one of her shoes." He gave a sadistic smile as the thug with the smashed face bent down to unstrap it. "Bye-bye, Black Sandal."

Lily noticed a scabrous model of Mighty Joe Young shoved halfway under the seat. It looked like someone had yanked off a patch of fur.

"It'll never work," Lily said. "Magruder was there. He saw what happened."

"Magruder will be taken care of," the man up front said. "He and his men will recall nothing. Magruder loves his son, and has hefty medical bills."

Lily fell silent, wondering when she might have a chance to escape. The odds weren't good. An idea came to her. But she'd have to plan carefully. Timing was crucial.

She turned to the prop painter. "You raped Kitty Hayden," she said.

"I didn't rape anybody," he said angrily. "I get all the girls I want, giving it away."

"You stole Roy DiCicco's car off the lot and used it to abduct Kitty. But Rhett Taylor saw you. He gave police a detailed description of you and your pal" — she glanced at the man with the bandaged nose — "who chased her through Hollywood."

The RKO painter smirked. "She almost got away too. But not quite. My stepfather was very relieved."

"Who's your stepfather?"

The gun jabbed her ribs painfully. "None of your business."

They wound through the Hollywood Hills, the lights of the city sparkling like jewels on black velvet. The car pulled over. The driver turned around. He wore a gloating smile. Lily saw the face of RKO Security Chief Frank Rhodes.

And then she understood.

"It was you . . . behind everything. You're the one who raped her."

The expression on Rhodes's face grew pinched and mean. "Why should the stars and the moguls be the only ones to enjoy the spoils of Hollywood?"

"How did you learn about her and Kirk?"

"Mrs. Potter told us. So I called up my old friend Bernie Jones at Warner's and warned him that his golden boy was about to get hit by a major scandal. I owed him a favor, so I promised him I'd take care of it. So what if things got a little out of hand? She should have just shut up about it and done as I told her."

Joseph's words echoed in Lily's head: *She's absolutely fearless, and she hates like hell to see people get pushed around.*

"But Kitty defied you," Lily said. "She fought back and took her complaint to the police. And when they sat on it she went to Bernard Keck. So you killed her. And you sent your stepson to steal her diary. It might have ended there, but Bernard Keck was an honest man and he'd started asking questions. So you had to kill him too. Then you killed two more girls to make it look like there was a Hollywood Strangler killing girls at random."

"I didn't kill anyone," Frank Rhodes said. "Did I, Stanley?" His eyes went to the fleshy, handsome prop painter who held a gun to Lily's side.

"You're disgusting," Lily said. "Forcing your stepson to do your dirty work."

"He's well paid for his troubles."

"I hope everything's ready in TJ," Stanley said.

"Five hours from now you'll be in the penthouse suite of the Tijuana Palace Hotel with a bottle of tequila, two hookers, and a twenty-thousand-dollar stake at the casino," Rhodes said.

"No, he won't, because Detective Pico knows all about you," Lily lied in desperation. "He'll be here any moment."

Rhodes laughed. "Your Detective Pico was born in thrall to us. He's second-generation. His father was one of the best bagmen in the business."

"Stephen is different."

"Don't delude yourself."

Rhodes handed his stepson a pen and a cocktail napkin with the word *Largo* inscribed in fancy script.

"Write *HELP* on the napkin," Rhodes ordered Lily.

"Why?"

"You want to die now or later?"

Lily wrote, the letters coming out shaky, the napkin tearing.

"Perfect," Frank Rhodes said. "Stuff it in her purse, Stanley. A little mash note for the detectives."

"What's Largo?" Lily asked.

"Jack Dragna's nightclub," Frank Rhodes said.

"You're trying to set them up for my murder," Lily said. "To make it look like one of their guys is the Hollywood Strangler. But it won't work."

"Shut up," said Stanley.

Frank Rhodes reached into his pocket and pulled out a length of wire.

"It's time for you to join your gal pals on the sacrificial altar of Hollywood," he said. "Get her out of the car," he told Stanley, "and keep that gun on her."

Lily prayed a car would drive by, but the hillside was deserted, no one around for miles. It would be useless to scream.

They hustled her out so fast that her purse tumbled into the dirt.

Rhodes approached, smiling and pulling the wire taut. It made a little metallic *ping* that jangled her bones.

"We gonna do it right here?" Stanley asked.

"I don't see any reason to wait," his

stepfather snapped.

"And we dump her by the side of the road?"

"It should be like the others. Below the Hollywood sign."

Stanley shuffled, then squinted at the giant white letters rising high above them.

"How are we gonna get her up there?"

Rhodes sighed in exasperation. "You and Louie are going to carry her."

"Dead bodies are dead weight," Louie said.

"Couldn't we kill her when we get up there?" Stanley whined.

Rhodes drew closer, still holding his wire. Lily stood between the thugs, unable to move, a gun jammed into her ribs. The security chief's eyes flickered over her, as if assessing her weight versus the likelihood of her somehow making a break for it and running away.

"Give me the gun," he told his stepson.

When Stanley handed it over, he belted her in the jaw with it. Lily staggered and fell to her knees.

"All right, we'll walk," he said, hiking off. "But no funny stuff."

And then she was stumbling uphill in the dark, the men surrounding her. At least she'd been able to grab her purse. The sign loomed above them, the letters huge and white and monstrous in the moonlight. She heard the scuttling of small nocturnal animals, the faraway screech of a hunting owl. Stanley Rhodes lobbed her high-heeled sandal far into the canyon. It cartwheeled and disappeared, landing in a ravine and startling some unseen animal that crashed through the undergrowth and was gone.

Then they were below the letter *D,* in a spot darker and colder, where even the moonlight didn't reach. It felt like she was already in the grave. Lily stopped.

"How about a smoke, Stanley?" she said. "Even condemned prisoners get one final request."

Without thinking, Stanley reached into his pocket, pulled out a pack. A cold breeze whipped at their clothes. Above them, where Frank Rhodes waited impatiently, the scaffolding swayed and creaked. Lily took the cigarette Stanley offered, stuck it between her lips, and waved away the match he offered. "My father gave me a lighter years ago," she said. "I'd like to use it, for old times' sake."

"What's she doing?" Frank Rhodes asked above her, his voice full of suspicion, the gun still covering her. He started down.

Lily rummaged in her purse, pulled out

Bob's lighter.

"Here it is. Oops, I dropped it."

Pretending to hunt in her purse, she found the stick of dynamite.

"Dang," she said, flicking the lighter several times inside her purse. "Must be low on fuel. Wait a minute, here we go." The fuse caught, began to sizzle. Frank Rhodes had almost reached them. The men's faces narrowed with puzzlement at the sound, then with suspicion. *One, two, three . . .*

Screaming, "Catch!" she flung her purse at the security chief. Just then the dynamite exploded.

Rhodes shrieked and fell down.

Running helter-skelter down the hill, Lily didn't dare turn around to see if he was dead. She heard them crashing behind her. She ran at an awkward gait, with one shoe on. Her remaining heel caught on the root of a bush and she went flying head over heels, her arms plowing a furrow in the earth. Skidding to a stop, she jumped back onto her feet, only to feel a large hand clamp down on her shoulder.

"Got you," Stanley gloated.

"Bring her up here," screamed Frank Rhodes, staggering to his feet. By the light of the moon, Lily saw that the side of his face was bleeding, the skin and hair singed black. But he was still alive. And he was enraged.

When she refused to stand, Stanley and Louie dragged her back uphill to the sign.

"Stand her on that promontory. Good. Step away from the edge now, boys, I don't want to shoot you by mistake," the RKO security chief said

"I thought we were going to strangle her," Stanley said.

"Change of plans."

There were three of them and only one of her. If she ran, she'd be dead before she took two steps. If only she could create a distraction.

Just then they heard the whine of a car moving uphill. Headlights raked the hillside and they heard shouts. From her vantage point, Lily saw that the car was still a good distance below, but on that silent, dark hill, it sounded a lot closer.

"Someone's coming, boss," said Louie, moving closer to the precipice to look down.

Lily edged toward him. Then, looking past Frank Rhodes and up the hillside, she waved her arms ecstatically and cried, "Pico, Magruder, over here. Watch out, he's got a gun."

Startled, Rhodes turned to look behind him.

At that moment, Lily body-slammed Louie. For a moment, he teetered, trying vainly to right himself. Lily planted her foot on his bottom and pushed hard. The man tilted and fell. Gravity did the rest. With a banshee wail, he plummeted down.

Rhodes turned, firing blindly. Lily ducked, zigging and zagging as she made for the opposite end of the sign, hoping the metal letters would offer some protection.

"Get her!" Rhodes cried. Stanley advanced, but Rhodes kept firing. Two bullets whizzed past Lily's head. The third hit Stanley Rhodes just as he reached her. The prop painter dropped to his knees, clutching his stomach. In the confusion, Lily retreated behind the scaffolding and tried to shrink into the shadows. Rhodes still had the gun, and she was trapped here with him.

"Stanley! No!" Rhodes shouted, reaching his stepson. He probed the wound with one hand, holding his gun with the other, scanning for her, screaming that he would kill her.

From below came shouts, and words she couldn't make out as uniformed men crashed through the underbrush. Lights played over the hillside, the beams illuminating Rhodes and his injured stepson. The security chief had no way of knowing how far away his pursuers were.

"Stop right there or we'll shoot the girl," Rhodes shouted into the night. "There are three of us and we're all armed. And after we kill her, we'll pick you sorry bastards off one by one as you come over the hill."

Lily wanted to yell down that it wasn't true, but knew her voice would tell Rhodes exactly where to aim. The RKO security chief waited, gun at the ready. Stanley pressed his hands against his belly, trying to stanch the flow of blood, his hands sticky with it.

There were more shouted commands from below. The cops continued their ascent. "I'll give you till the count of three," Rhodes shouted. "One . . . two . . ."

The crashing sounds stopped. Lily heard Pico's voice, his breath coming in ragged gasps. "Don't hurt her," he shouted up. "We're doing what you asked. But I want to hear her voice. Lily, are you all right?"

Just then they heard movement to the right and a lumbering shape appeared. Lily recognized Magruder, creeping along, trying to get close enough for a shot. Rhodes saw him too. He aimed and fired.

From the shadows came a scream, then something crashing down.

"Magruder," came Pico's anguished cry,

then a string of curses.

"I warned you that we're armed," Rhodes screamed. "Try that again and the girl dies."

Pico's voice, heavy with desperation, floated up. "You'll never get away with it. Every prowl car for miles is on its way up here."

"Call them off," Rhodes said. "Go back to your car and radio them that the suspect has fled up Pacific Coast Highway. Do it, or I swear to you, I'll kill the girl."

No, Stephen, don't do it! thought Lily. *You're my only hope. If you retreat now, I'm finished. He'll run me to ground like a fox. But if I call out, he'll know where I'm hiding and I'll die all the faster.*

Breathing shallowly, Lily looked around for a weapon. Spotting a rock the size of a grapefruit, she picked it up. Then, knowing she'd only get one chance, she aimed and heaved it at Rhodes's head. It flew through the air and hit his temple. Rhodes fell backward. Lily saw the glint of metal as the gun fell from his hand. She sprinted for it, scooping it up, finding the trigger, and spinning around, hands clasped and extended like she'd been taught, aiming right for the security chief's chest.

"Freeze," she screamed. But Rhodes wasn't moving. Next to him, Stanley moaned as blood soaked through his shirt and seeped into the ground.

Lily swallowed.

From below she heard a shout.

"What's going on?" came Pico's voice, bouncing up the canyon. "I swear to God, if she's . . ."

"I'm fine, Pico," Lily called, keeping her eyes on the fallen men. "You can come rescue me now."

"Hold on," Pico bellowed. "Everything's going to be all right."

One side of Lily's mouth twitched. Just then Frank Rhodes braced his arms against the ground and she thought he might try to rise.

"Stay down," she ordered. "Or I shoot you in the thigh. And maybe I miss by a couple inches, know what I mean? Everyone knows girls can't shoot straight."

Rhodes's mouth twisted. "I should have killed you when I had the chance," he slurred.

"But you were too vain and sure of yourself. Playing God. You're about to get the justice you deserve, Rhodes. I'm just sorry it comes too late for Kitty Hayden and those other girls."

"What was she to you, anyway?"

"You might say she was the only family I

567

had left."

Lily heard a commotion just below the sign. Pico's head popped up, then the rest of him, gun drawn. He gaped.

"Well, I'll be damned, Lily. I guess you didn't need me after all."

"That's where you're wrong, Stephen," Lily said. "I need you very much. Now will you get over here so I can put down this gun? My wrist's starting to ache."

Chapter 36

October 19, 1949

It was dawn by the time she finished re-counting everything that had happened. Frank Rhodes and his stepson were in the medical ward of the county jail, under arrest for murder. Their cohort, Louie, was dead of a broken neck from his fall.

After a long series of interviews, the last remaining pieces of the puzzle had fallen into place.

"So Magruder wasn't in league with Rhodes after all?" Lily asked Pico, feeling numb as they sipped coffee in the hallway of the LAPD headquarters.

Pico looked solemn. "He was dirty, and that's going to come out, but he wasn't a murderer. He proved it last night. He died trying to rescue you."

"Then he didn't kill Bernard Keck?"

"No. Rhodes's thugs did. That stepson of his is a real piece of work. Turns out he has a rap sheet as long as your arm and five aliases. Narcotics, petty theft. Assault with a deadly weapon."

"I thought Magruder dropped you off at the Farmers Market so he could go back and kill Keck."

"He wanted me out of the way so he could go to Paramount and get more autographed photos for his kid. That's what was in the manila envelope in his briefcase."

"Then why'd he hide it?"

Pico shrugged. "Maybe he was embarrassed. A grown man . . . But he loved that kid. Left quite a nest egg for his nursing care."

"So how *did* Rhodes find out about Keck?" Lily persisted.

Pico wouldn't meet her eyes. "My father," he said at last. "Kitty had threatened to go to the DA if the LAPD kept stalling. Then one day Hollywood Division gets a call from Bernard Keck asking all sorts of questions. My father went right to Rhodes. Apparently dear old Dad's been on the payroll at various studios for years. I knew some of it but had no idea how deep it went."

She touched his cheek. "What will happen to him?"

"His pension's suspended and they've launched an investigation. I don't think they'll be able to sweep it under the rug this time."

"What about you?"

"I'm on leave until they sort everything out."

"I'm very sorry, Stephen. But you're not like your father. You have nothing to fear."

Lily's brain moved backward, unwinding the tape of memory. Suddenly she clutched Pico's hand, hoping beyond hope.

"Max?" she said.

Pico's jaw twitched. He shook his head. "Gone."

A series of images came to her — Max, his face aglow as he described the werewolf movie he wanted to make. Leaning against a wall in his studio, explaining the magic of stop-motion animation. The purity of his convictions and the ferocity of his rage as he brought the terrarium down on the producer's head. His howling-mad unrequited love for Kitty.

"Did Rhodes kill him too?"

"We're looking into it. He denies it."

"And what about Mrs. Potter and Beverly?"

"They're gone. Cleared out, left your roommates high and dry. Turns out they were only leasing that place. They owe the owner six months' back rent."

"They're blackmailers. They sold information about Kitty to Frank Rhodes."

"They ever come back, the police will want to bring them in for a long talk. And there's a reporter who keeps showing up saying you two are old friends from Berlin and she wants to see you. Violet McCree. My buddies have been chasing her away."

"Keep doing it, please."

Lily looked out the window. She was grateful to have survived, when so many others hadn't. And to be here with this man, who stood awkwardly before her. Outside, another flawless California day was under way. It still felt strange to see the blue sky, the red tile roofs, and the tropical foliage. And yet this landscape was imprinted on her psyche. It was the New World. The land of limitless possibility and expansion. Of shucking off the past like last year's frock, of reinvention and second chances. And then something clicked and Lily realized that it was where she belonged. It was home.

She turned to Pico and her smile grew more somber. "What about Kirk Armstrong?"

"He issued a statement through the studio saying he's very sorry about everything that happened, but he wants to make it clear he had nothing to do with any of it and reiterated that he only knew Kitty Hayden casually from the studio."

"Beverly played me a tape of Kitty admitting the affair and naming Kirk as the father."

Pico looked at her. "But where's the proof?" he said. "And it's bizarre, but I heard the editor of *Confidential* talking on the radio this morning and he didn't even mention Kirk Armstrong. I guess Violet's too busy with the Rhett Taylor scandal."

Lily thought about how both Armstrong and Taylor were signed to Warner Brothers. Again, she saw Violet McCree hurrying alongside the rooming house. With the photo of Kitty and Kirk that Mrs. Potter had sold her? She recalled Vile Violet taunting Rhett about how the studio had hung him out to dry.

"I think Jack Warner cut a deal with that *Confidential* reporter to hand over Rhett Taylor if she killed the Kirk story. Oh God, I wish none of it had ever happened."

"Then I never would have met you." Pico leaned in, and his face loomed closer. She saw those lips, the tawny skin, the long, straight nose that had so captivated her, it seemed like ages ago. She lifted her chin toward him and felt her jaw throb where Rhodes had hit her with the pistol butt.

"Be still," he said, his mouth inches from hers.

And then they heard a voice.

"Whaddaya mean, we can't come in? I'm a staff photographer with the *Mirror* and Gadge here has known her for ages. Why, we're practically family."

And then Harry Jack stomped into the police station, awkwardly holding a bunch of flowers.

"Lily," he said, the delighted look on his face fading as he saw Pico. "I'm so glad to see you."

He paused, wiped something from his eye. "I'm so glad you're alive."

EPILOGUE

October 29, 1949

Lily and Pico were walking out the door with her belongings, moving them to her new apartment, when a pretty girl with a fresh, scrubbed face walked up to the Wilcox Boardinghouse for Young Ladies.

She carried a battered brown suitcase in one hand and a *Daily Variety* with an advertisement circled in red in the other.

"Howdy and good day to you," she said. "My name is Ruby Ann Packard and I have just arrived from Montgomery, Alabama. I understand that there is a room to let at your fine establishment."

Lily pushed her hair out of her face. "Pardon me?" she said.

"I've come out here to be an actress. I've had major parts in seven theatrical productions back home and I was voted 'most likely to succeed' in our high school yearbook. So I sure hope that room is still available."

She handed the newspaper ad to Lily, who took it and read:

CASTING NOW UNDER WAY

Be a STAR at Wilcox Boardinghouse for Young Actresses
Room to Let Starting Nov. 1, Reasonable Monthly Rate
Safe, Clean & Respectable
Run by Experienced Matron
Call SR-7 5903 and ask for Mrs. Potter
References provided upon request
"Let Our Home Become Yours"

"Might you be Mrs. Potter?" the girl asked politely.

"Why, no," Lily said, startled. "She's gone away."

"But this is the place where they're letting the room, isn't it?"

Lily examined Ruby Ann Packard's hopeful face.

For the briefest second, she hesitated.

Then she smiled.

"Come in, Ruby. There's a room that's just become available."

ACKNOWLEDGMENTS

Thanks to Cecilia Rasmussen, who writes the delightful *L.A. Times* "Then and Now" column, where I first learned about Jean Spangler's short and tragic life.

Ray Harryhausen, the master, generously shared his recollections about working in Hollywood and the techniques he pioneered in stop-motion animation.

Several books shed light on the era: *From the Land Beyond Time: The Films of Willis O'Brien and Ray Harryhausen* by Jeff Rovin and *Ray Harryhausen: An Animated Life* by Ray Harryhausen and Tony Dalton. Also helpful was the DVD of the 1949 movie *Mighty Joe Young,* especially the audio commentary and the interview "featurette."

Stephen Chiodo kindly showed my boys and I exactly how stop motion works, patiently answered my endless questions, and vetted a key scene. Any mistakes that remain are solely mine.

Librarian Carolyn Cisneros at the American Film Institute Library got me started researching behind-the-scenes Hollywood.

Laura June Kenny's memoir *Fleeing the Fates of the Little Rascals* gave me insight into early Hollywood. Steve Stevens and Craig Lockwood's book *King of the Sunset Strip* provided firsthand accounts of life inside Mickey Cohen's circle. Autobiographies by Cohen and Hollywood journalist Florabel Muir brought the era to life, though I diverged from history as needed to suit my creative purposes.

Writer gals Kerry Madden, Lienna Silver, Heather Dundas, Ellen Slezak, Diane Arieff, and Diana Wagman offered coffee and comments, and Donna Rifkind read the novel in manuscript and made it better.

Marissa Roth provided friendship and walks. Co-*madre* Julia Spencer-Fleming inspired me on the road and off.

Thanks to Anne Borchardt and to everyone at Scribner and Pocket, especially Maggie Crawford, Susan Moldow, Louise Burke, Katherine Monaghan, Kathleen Rizzo, and Dave Cole.

Hurray for librarians everywhere, those wonderfully sly, subversive supporters of literacy who are the unsung heroes of American letters today.

And last, thanks to my family, David, Adrian, and Alexander, who had to live with me while I wrote this book. Watching *Joe* through the fresh eyes of my children brought home the timeless magic and wizardry of this art, which gave me a new respect for what Harryhausen and his mentor, Willis O'Brien, created so many years ago.

MY INSPIRATION FOR *THE LAST EMBRACE*

As an L.A. native who grew up in the shadow of Hollywood, I've long been fascinated by classic noir literature. Authors like Raymond Chandler and James Cain were my touchstones, and I dreamed of escaping into their dark and alluring worlds. But if you really want to know why I wrote this book, well, it started with a dress.

I was eighteen when I bought it for five dollars at a vintage clothing store, a glamorous frock of black crepe that clung and draped with such panache that the girl who looked back in the mirror might have stepped out of the Cocoanut Grove Nightclub, circa 1949.

Back then, I had no idea that the designer of my dress had worked as a costumer for the studios, leaving in the late 1940s to launch her own line. All I knew was that the elegant label in cursive writing — *Dorothy*

O'Hara, California — had a tantalizing, noiry magic all its own.

But those were the punk years, and the nightclubs I frequented were a far cry from Hollywood's Golden Age. Eventually spilled beer, perspiration, and fraying seams took their toll on my lovely frock.

By then, the dress and the world it evoked had become part of my inner landscape. Driving around L.A., I saw ghosts on every street corner, heard snatches of big band music on the wind, sipped bourbon in oak-paneled bars on foggy, neon-lit nights.

Eventually I became a reporter, then a novelist. My books filtered Chandler's Los Angeles through a twenty-first-century lens.

But somewhere in my head, a 1940s soundtrack kept playing. I pictured a girl in her twenties, bantering with gangsters and crooked cops and Hollywood special effects whizzes, living in a rooming house with aspiring starlets, crisscrossing the city by trolley, and slipping into a Dorothy O'Hara cocktail frock for a night of dancing at the Mocambo.

In my imagination that girl already existed, I just didn't know her story yet. Then one day while researching Hollywood's Golden Age, I ran across an *L.A. Times* story by Cecilia Rasmussen about Jean Spangler, a

Hollywood starlet who vanished without a trace in October 1949.

Jean disappeared two years following the Black Dahlia murder after telling her mother that she was going out on a night shoot. When I examined the characters that swirled around her, I knew I had found the inspiration for my next novel.

Jean had a violent ex-husband and was fighting a custody battle for their only child. She'd partied in Palm Springs with two associates of L.A. gangster Mickey Cohen, men who also disappeared mysteriously that fall. Her purse eventually turned up in L.A.'s Griffith Park, bearing a cryptic note to a mysterious "Kirk" that suggested she might have been pregnant and was seeking an abortion.

It soon emerged that Jean had just filmed a movie with Kirk Douglas. The handsome star said he only knew the actress casually, they hadn't been having an affair, and he knew nothing about her disappearance. After interviewing him, the police agreed.

As I read, I realized that Jean Spangler's very desires and dreams had made her vulnerable. She symbolized every modern girl who yearned for independence at a time when society was lurching back toward more traditional roles. And she disappeared into thin air, creating the perfect mystery template.

Jean's body was never found and the puzzle was never solved, but almost sixty years later, I had no interest in recounting the real story. I wanted to write a novel with new characters that would bring the world of 1949 Hollywood to life in all its brawling, contradictory glory.

It was a fascinating and transitional time — just after World War II, at the beginning of the Atomic Age and the Cold War, just before the conservative 1950s. Los Angeles was teeming with intrigue and crime: a mob war raged between Mickey Cohen and Jack Dragna for control of L.A.'s turf and there were shoot-outs on the Sunset Strip. The police were notoriously corrupt. (Both the LAPD chief and his deputy were indicted that summer.) It was the waning days of the studio star system, the dawn of television. We had the Hollywood blacklist, the rise of lurid tabloids like *Confidential,* closeted gay actors, and the explosion of suburbia.

It was also the golden era of movie special effects.

I've always been intrigued by the inner workings of the Dream Factory, the technician magicians who create the illusion of reality up on the big screen. I also realized I needed to infuse my 1940s world with fresh, ahem, blood and find a new window into a Hollywood world that people already knew so well.

So I decided to create a character who was a special effects wizard. Through him, I could explore the world of movie animation long before Steven Spielberg and George Lucas made CGI geeks hip and trendy.

I had the great good fortune around this time to meet the legendary Ray Harryhausen. With his mentor, Willis O'Brien, Harryhausen pioneered stop-motion animation. Harryhausen was eighty-six and hale and hearty when I interviewed him at Dark Delicacies Bookstore in Burbank and learned what the special effects world was like in 1949, the year *Mighty Joe Young* came out. (Harryhausen did most of the animation on *Joe;* O'Brien had animated *King Kong.*)

Thanks to the generosity of Chiodo Brothers Productions, especially Stephen Chiodo, I also toured an animation studio and watched stop motion in progress and was greatly impressed by the painstaking detail, dedication, and artistry involved. In addition, I read several books and watched documentaries and the DVD of the original *Mighty Joe Young,* in which Harryhausen describes how he filmed each scene.

In reading oral histories, I was also struck by what a small town Hollywood was, even fifty years ago, and how movie stars were just part of the landscape. You'd see Marlon Brando shopping with his wife at the Hollywood Ranch Market or Montgomery Clift studying his lines at the local coffee shop. You could sit in on Steve Allen's midnight radio shows, watch Frank Sinatra record at Capitol Records. The access was amazing.

Emerging from the dreamworld of my writing, I'd grow melancholy at how much of historic Los Angeles was gone. We all yearn for authenticity, we're nostalgic for the past, yet we systematically destroy what made us unique throughout the world.

On most days, it's difficult to envision how the city must have looked in 1949. But cock your head and squint and it falls into focus, in the bas-relief façade of a downtown hotel, the deco tile of an old bar, the scattered oil derricks that still pump in L.A.'s forgotten quadrants, and in thrift stores where forlorn frocks drape on hangers like bashful starlets, waiting to be discovered once more. And hopefully, in the pages of this book.

— Denise Hamilton
January 2008

READING GROUP GUIDE

When Lily Kessler, a spy for the OSS, returns from Europe to the United States she learns that her late fiancé's younger sister, Kitty, has gone missing from her Hollywood boardinghouse. Lily heads to L.A. to put her investigative skills to good use. When Kitty's corpse turns up under the Hollywood sign, Lily sets out to unravel the mystery of the young starlet's disappearance and brutal murder.

Along the way Lily will meet Kitty's former friends and housemates, her admirers and coworkers, along with gangsters and members of L.A.'s seedy underbelly. Teaming up with a well-meaning news photographer and a handsome detective, Lily slowly uncovers the details of Kitty's life leading up to her tragic, untimely death in her adopted city of angels.

Discussion Questions for *The Last Embrace*

1. Throughout the course of the book Lily, Harry, and Pico each take a serious interest in finding Kitty's killer and bringing him to justice. What motivates each character in his or her quest? What do each of these characters have riding on the investigation? Who is depending on them?

2. Though Kitty is the character whose life and death propels the action in the story, she is only actually a character in the first few moments of the narrative. By what means do we, along with Lily, fill in the blanks of Kitty's life in Hollywood? How did you, as a reader, decide which sources were trustworthy, and which warranted closer inspection?

3. How did actual, historical events and figures referred to in the novel help you relate to the characters and contextualize the story?

4. For many women, World War II opened doors professionally and personally that had only been open to men before the war; for many the barriers went back up when the war ended. Of this Lily says, "We're not helpless simpering creatures that have to be protected. We've held down jobs, traveled the world. Seen people

die. Nobody's innocent anymore". In what ways has Lily's gender role been affected by the time she spent in Europe? Do any of the other female characters in the book strike you as feminist? How do you think they were affected by the war experience?

5. The narrator often refers to smells to help describe scenes and characters in the novel. The killer smells of black rubber; Kitty's room smelled like "newsprint, cigarettes, talc, and stale perfume". Why do you think Denise Hamilton took pains to include such vivid descriptions of scent? How is scent tied to memory?

6. Though the narrator throughout the book remains third person, the point of view shifts among many of the characters, and the narrator is never completely omniscient. How did this affect your reading of the story? Did you think this lent the narrative further mystery? Was it helpful to see the story from several viewpoints?

7. Like every good mystery writer, Hamilton sets up circumstances that would support the reader being suspicious of just about anyone. Which leads did you find most compelling? Who did you think had the most motivation to kill Kitty? How did your suspicions change when more

girls turned up dead under the Hollywood sign?

8. Pico thinks of Lily as, "Feminine. And yet so hard. Like a steel blade wrapped in crushed velvet." How is this metaphor suited to Lily? How does she use her OSS skills to help solve Kitty's murder? Can you think of an apt metaphor for any other characters in the story?

9. When Pico and Lily are first getting to know one another he says, "Maybe home's not a physical place, but something we make in our heart and carry around with us". Do you think that this applies to Lily? What becomes "home" for others in the novel? In what ways do Pico and Lily come to represent home for each other?

10. Hamilton takes us behind the scenes of Hollywood's Golden Age, exploring the secretive world of stop-motion animation and its technical whizzes. How did Max Vranizan's obsessions and eccentricities make him both a genius and a legitimate suspect in Kitty Hayden's murder? What did you learn about Hollywood special effects and its practitioners?

AUTHOR Q & A

1. This is your first novel outside of the Eve Diamond series. What made you want to branch out and try your hand at Lily Kessler?

I loved the idea of taking a female OSS spy and setting her down in postwar Hollywood. After surviving World War II, Lily Kessler thinks finding a missing starlet in L.A. is going to be a cakewalk. She quickly finds out that the city and its denizens are every bit as treacherous as the world she left behind. But the sun is shining and the birds-of-paradise and bougainvillea are blooming and everyone's well-dressed so it doesn't *look* dangerous. So that's one thing. Second, as an L.A. native, I've always been fascinated by the huge shadow cast by Hollywood and I'm also an absolute sucker for the 1940s — music, fashion, art, design, political crosscurrents, and the criminal underworld that thrived hand in hand with the police. Sometimes I think I was born in the wrong era. When I learned about the real-life 1949 disappearance of a young starlet that was never solved, I knew I had the creative inspiration for my fictional tale.

In many ways, 1940s Hollywood wasn't so different than today — the same desperate longing for success existed, the cravings for power, sex, riches, and influence. There was corruption and moral decay. People were not who they seemed. There was artifice and scheming. There were just fewer people and buildings, and more natural landscapes. I also think, oddly enough it was a hopeful time, this era of transition between World War II and the 1950s. That flies in the face of traditional noir, but then so does my book.

2. There is an underlying feminist message in _The Last Embrace_. What do you hope some female readers will gain from "meeting" Lily Kessler?

I think Lily was emblematic of her time, as are many of the other female characters in this book. They've tasted freedom and independence during the war, it's given them self-confidence, and now they're trying to navigate through an increasingly conservative postwar era that would like them to give up much of the freedoms they've learned to enjoy. I wanted to dramatize that conflict. I also love the dramatic possibilities inherent in a group of young women all living under one roof and trying to make it as Hollywood actresses. They're vying for stardom, for boyfriends, they're silky and competitive as cats yet they also take the time to help one another. It's a very conflicted kind of friendship, but it seems very real to me, not sugar-coated.

Noir has traditionally been an overwhelmingly male genre where female characters are portrayed as sexpots and femme fatales. In *The Last Embrace,* I've tried to reimagine that macho male noir territory with a variety of female characters — starting with Lily Kessler — who are every bit as capable as the men, but without the swagger. Even though they're plunged into a very dark swirl of intrigue, there's a basic life-affirming optimism that prevails, a ray of light that pierces the cynicism and fatality that would triumph in traditional noir.

3. In *The Last Embrace* the narrative point of view shifts among many of the characters. Why did you choose to tell the story this way?

My Eve Diamond series is narrated in first person and I wanted to try something new after five books. I also felt that multiple points of view suited this story better as this type of narration is more cinematic, which is how I envisioned the action in my head as I was writing the book. The story unfolds kaleidoscopically, and everyone perceives a different reality. It's only at the end that all the characters and strands come together.

4. How did your years as a journalist help you prepare to write mystery fiction? Is Vile Violet based on anyone you really came into contact with while you were a reporter?

Journalism taught me how to write in a fluid, narrative style, meet deadlines, and sidestep writer's block (you acknowledge you have no idea what happens next, then put one word in front of another until you have a sentence, then another, and somehow it all catches fire again after a few pages). Journalism honed my sense of wonder about stories and people, it helped me listen for accents and marvel at the way people speak.

It brought me into contact with criminals and cops and victims and survivors and con men and saints and everybody in between. Violet McCree is entirely fictional, and yet her personality weaves bits and pieces of many people I have known, not all of them journalists.

5. As a Los Angeles native you are in a unique position to imagine your hometown sixty years ago. What parts of the backdrop of the novel come from your own experiences in California, and what is the product of research?

So much of old Los Angeles is gone now, razed to build high-rises and shopping malls, but you can still catch glimpses of an older, more genteel city in certain streets and alleys, in some residential neighborhoods, in hotels and watering holes where old ghosts still hide out. As a journalist I interviewed a lot of people on the fringes of old Hollywood. They're still around, but they dwindle with each passing year. To research the era, I read lots of oral histories of people who grew up in Hollywood, plus biographies, memoirs, and histories. When I'd meet someone who remembered that era firsthand, I'd badger them for details and recollections. My own mother came to

Hollywood (from France) in 1949 and told me stories about riding the Red Car home at night and studying English at Hollywood High. It was a smaller, more friendly place, and you'd run into movie stars doing their grocery shopping or walking down the street. People talked about hearing Steve Allen perform his radio monologues, watching Sinatra record, helping Montgomery Clift learn his lines at a coffee shop. I tried to convey that small-town feel, the serendipity, but the book is really a mélange of all my experiences and research; it's hard to separate it out.

6. You dedicate your book to Ray Harryhausen. Did he act as inspiration for the Max Vranizan character in any way other than his career choices? What was your reasoning behind the dedication to him?

I knew from early on that I wanted to have a character who could epitomize the Hollywood "back lot," the magic that goes on behind the scenes to create the illusions that we all love about the movies. The more I learned about Harryhausen and his mentor Willis O'Brien, the more I realized that it was basically these two guys and their brilliant obsession that created the entire industry. So they were towering giants to me. I hadn't seen this part of Hollywood examined in fiction, but I thought it was perfect for this novel. A very different twist on the tortured eccentric artist.

7. What can your devoted readers expect from you next? Are you working on anything currently?

I hope to revisit Eve Diamond soon, and I'm also working on another stand-alone, a thriller set in contemporary Los Angeles.

Enhance Your Book Club Experience

1. Research some of the historical figures that Denise Hamilton refers to in *The Last Embrace:*

Pío Pico: http://en.wikipedia.org/wiki/ Pío_Pico

The Black Dahlia: http://en.wikipedia.org/ wiki/Elizabeth_Short and http:// 1947project.com/

Ray Bradbury: http://en.wikipedia.org/ wiki/Ray_Bradbury

Benny Siegel and Mickey Cohen: http:// www.crimelibrary.com/ gangsters_outlaws/mob_bosses/siegel/ index_1.html

Ray Harryhausen: http://www.rayharry

hausen.com/

2. *The Last Embrace* recalls noir films popular in the 1930s and '40s. If you enjoyed this novel, why not watch a DVD of a noir classic?

Some noir favorites include:

The Postman Always Rings Twice
The Big Sleep
Double Indemnity
L.A. Confidential
In a Lonely Place
Out of the Past

A site where you can explore film noir is www.filmnoirfoundation.org.

3. Listen to some of the music that was popular during 1949, the year when *The Last Embrace* is set.

"Again" sung by Vic Damone
* "Baby It's Cold Outside" sung by Esther Williams and Ricardo Montalbán
"Autumn in New York" sung by Frank Sinatra
"It All Depends on You" sung by Frank Sinatra

*indicates a song mentioned in the novel

"Some Enchanted Evening" sung by Frank Sinatra

"Careless Hands" performed by Sammy Kaye and His Orchestra

* "Diamonds Are a Girl's Best Friend" sung by Carol Channing

"Far Away Places" performed by Bing Crosby with the Ken Darby Choir

"Forever and Ever" sung by Perry Como

"I Can Dream, Can't I?" performed by Patty Andrews with Gordon Jenkins and His Orchestra

* "I've Got My Love to Keep Me Warm" performed by Les Brown & His Orchestra

ABOUT THE AUTHOR

Denise Hamilton, a Los Angeles–based writer-journalist whose work has appeared in the *Los Angeles Times, Cosmopolitan,* and *The New York Times,* is the critically acclaimed author of the Eve Diamond mystery series. She lives in Los Angeles with her husband and two young children. Hamilton is also the editor of and a contributor to the short story anthology *Los Angeles Noir.*